Gold Baron

A. Dru Kristenev

Gold Baron

First Printing: October 2008
E-edition, ChangingWind.Org: 2008
Second Edition: 2012

Cover Photo: A. Dru Kristenev

ISBN: 0615647553
ISBN-13: 978-0615647555

Reason is the heart of freedom...
B. Johnson

Author's Note...

This endeavor came about in a matter of three short months from concept to print in order to address the unique conditions of this election season. Past national elections have been fraught with partisan shenanigans, voter misdirection and even fraud. This year is appearing to be no different. In our view, things have gone not just one, but many steps further in the scams that are being perpetrated on unsuspecting voters.

The worst offenders in my opinion, however, are the media. As a refugee from the press corps, I have been appalled at the lack of objective coverage of the campaigns, primary and post-convention, that has been purposefully initiated by major networks. What is most offensive and incredible is the ingenuousness with which these supposedly seasoned and savvy correspondents and anchors are promoting a candidate that is unrepentant in his socialist agenda that would destroy the very fabric of their trade. Were they to actually follow the creed of true objective reporting, both sides would be covered in a manner that would supply real news, issues and character profiles. Instead, the public in inundated with skewed polls – oh yes, I know how those are crafted as well, just finish a post graduate degree to be well steeped in the process of research methods and survey development.

In writing this book, I had the assistance of an unbelievably gifted researcher who constantly supplied me with so much information that I couldn't incorporate even a fraction of it, and may have misunderstood the essence of what I did use. You can read the investigative links yourself by visiting the website www.changingwind.org.

To the few friends who had the constitution to read through this, I offer my abiding love and gratitude. I will also admit to probably offending every known minority, including my own – journalists. I must apologize for the mistakes herein for all of them are mine. I cannot even blame the editor. Since the timeline was so short, that job came to me as well. In all, solid research was the basis for the story, but remember, this is a story.

This is a fictional account that does not apologize for using real personalities upon which to craft some characters, nor does it attempt to make the reader believe that the characters in the book are completely factual representations of the characters walking the media stage. It does, however, encourage the reader to reach critical mass and do their homework on what really is happening in front of our very eyes… the loss of this country and the freedom to work and seek a fulfilling life through productivity, a charitable heart and an unsullied desire to pursue the dreams our forefathers envisioned with the grace of God.

Complacency has brought us to this brink of intellectual incarceration. The true idea of an open society is best found through the institution of capitalism. It is not perfect, but then no endeavor of man is. It is the best system we have by which we can truly attempt to better ourselves and our society.

Remember who you are, what you truly want to achieve in this world, most importantly your beliefs and faith and VOTE!

A. Dru Kristenev
October 9, 2008

Pretty lies lead down a false path to ruin...
A.D.K.

Addendum…

Even now in the Spring of 2012 amid a new campaign season, all of this story and the author's note are still applicable.
Little has changed...
Complacency is our demise.

Additional Addendum...

Ten years after the first edition of "Gold Baron," what has come to be called the 'Deep State' has finally bared its teeth. This book is a cautionary tale revolving around facts that have been woven into an infonovel, as one reviewer has dubbed my efforts. If nothing else, I pray that American voters have learned their lesson that mainstream and social media are not to be trusted. The one bit of advice I leave for my readers is this: Always return to the primary source to uncover the truth.

A. Dru Kristenev
May, 2018

Gold Baron

... 21 And he said, I will go out, and be a lying spirit in the mouth of these prophets. And the Lord said, Thou shalt entice him, and thou shalt also prevail: go out and do even so...

2 Chronicles 18

Gold Baron

Prologue

1882

In the north of England, near the Scottish border, a towering manor whose façade more closely resembles a castle than a house, sits astride a lofty, rugged bluff overlooking the North Sea. Waves crashing against the granite cliff face, the sea foams around the tumbled troll-sized boulders at its base creating swirling eddies and tidal pools along the narrow wedges of rocky shingle.

The owner is not walking along the wide, grassy plain that stretches from the wings of the hall to the edge of the precipice, acres of windblown seedheads sloping toward the steep drop, though it is his habit to take his daily constitutional along the rim. Today he is settled in a favorite armchair, tucked in his private library where no one is allowed to enter except by special invitation.

This is where he keeps his treasures. Priceless art objects and invaluable relics of bygone eras, obtained by means legitimate and illicit, are displayed around the expansive room, the walls lined with tomes and scrolls representing every age of civilized man. Religious and philosophical writings stand next to works describing the romantic and chivalric escapades of characters real and imagined. Few private collections of this magnitude and diversity exist outside of libraries maintained by states or the Church.

None of those books or artifacts captures his notice today. Only one object has his attention riveted. He rises to walk closer to it and admire the flawless workmanship of an ancient craftsman. Holding a crystal glass, a quarter filled with liquid amber, he strokes a fine line of inlaid gold that travels across the surface of the indigo lapis of the plaque with a crooked and arthritic finger.

Shifting his attention to the glass in his other hand, he lifts it to the light cascading from the high window in the east wall. Shafts of sunlight play on the cut surface, creating rainbows that shimmer and flash, arcing onto the polished hardwood floor of the room, creating a lesser copy of the rainbow God supposedly created as a promise for Noah and his heirs.

This is my inheritance, he gloats. *The promise of power, not just a feeble hope of fair weather. Too many are duped by faith in something that does not exist. Power is not given but must be taken, just as I have done.*

His aged face wrinkles as he smiles in recollection of his recent coup in the House of Lords. Already he had purchased his will among the other half of Parliament. That was uncomplicated. They are businessmen. The aristocracy, however, are smug, obstinate and arrogant. They are also apt to outspend their fortunes, leaving them exposed to the pirates of the world, otherwise known as entrepreneurs. Men like him. Men who have clawed their way to the top. For him, it was with enterprise, begun with this fluid gold he holds aloft. One distillery that he parlayed into a business empire that now straddles continents.

And now, his power base in Empire is secured.

He settles himself back into his chair, contemplating the significance of the artifact that has captivated his eye as well as his imagination. It is the depiction of a changing universe – symbolic and real at once. Symbolic of the real power he now wields to press even the Queen to his bidding. He has indeed inherited the legacy of the enlightened ones.

He lifts his glass in salute to the exquisite gem encrusted and gold curried tablet that is displayed on an extravagant tripod also wrought of gold. Bringing the crystal to his lips he takes a long drink, savoring the fruits of his long labor.

It's not long before he feels pain branching from behind his sternum down his arms and throughout his body. He loses his grip on the glass and it tumbles to the ground, rolling and spilling its contents on the plush pile of the Persian carpet that covers part of the glossy hardwood. His smirk of self-satisfaction is replaced with a grimace of anguish as the pain intensifies, burning through his limbs and up his throat. His head drops to his chest as he attempts to bring his hands up to clutch at his chest, the agony engulfing his body. *No! Not now when I have finally reached the apex of my life! Noooo....*

He slumps forward, falling almost in slow motion to the floor. Sprawled at the foot of the golden stand that supports his precious treasure, he is gone.

After many minutes, a figure steps from the shadows into the room. He stoops by the old man checking to ascertain that death has taken him.

Leaving the body collapsed in a heap, the figure carefully wraps the artifact in a silk cloth and slips through the French doors and into the rays of a sun setting over the bluff, trailing miles-long shafts of blazing light across the eastern sea.

Present Day

A suite of rooms in an exclusive hotel on the outskirts of London is playing host to a privileged few. The building is converted from what was once a summer residence of a duke with close royal ties whose fortunes had deserted him, mainly through the profligate waste of a fruitless life as a gambler and libertine.

The property now is often leased to private parties for activities of a confidential nature. No one knows what business or pleasure is conducted within those walls and no one asked. The fee always changes hands without question. Better for the proprietor to be uninformed than to find himself caught in a sticky web of possible intrigue.

This day, the purpose for the estate's hire is not so conspiratorial. It is simply for conducting an auction of undisclosed objets d'art. The potential bidders were carefully selected, quietly informed of the event and are not privy to the identity of the other participants. Extra care has been taken to keep the individuals divided, directing them to separate entrances that lead to discreet apartments adjoining the main drawing room where the event would take place at the appointed time. While they wait for the time to arrive, each guest is provided with an elaborate array of canapés, beverages, or if they prefer, cocktails.

Finally the last guest enters the building not ten minutes before the auction is set to commence. Never one to waste time, he asks to be seated in the chamber where he can view the items to be sold. As all of the apartments connect to the main room via concealed entrances, each of the bidders is led inside to a carefully guarded area, keeping their identities unknown from any of the other participants. The areas are basically three sided cubicles that open to the front of the room where the items are displayed. The bidders cannot see one another but have an unobstructed view of the items and the auctioneer is able to observe each of them.

Anonymity is essential since the items being sold have not necessarily come to this pass with unimpeachable provenance. The shady circumstances don't concern those in the audience. Their interest is solely in augmenting their personal collections, not in public exhibition. And they are willing to pay heavily for the privilege of owning these articles, even if no one other than themselves will ever lay eyes on the trophy.

Climbing the single step to the podium, a striking blonde, svelte, clad in a suit from an exclusive Parisian designer, gavels the surface once to begin the bidding.

There are four items on the auction block for this evening, only one of which holds any interest to the latecomer and it is the last to be sold. The object is a two by three foot plaque of midnight lapis lazuli, an unusually dark shade of blue bordering on violet that has subtle striations of azure coursing across the surface in circling patterns that is flecked with gold. The one-half inch thick panel is inlaid with shimmering filaments of gold creating coronas that radiate from magnificently sized gemstones. The jewels are either cabochons or faceted in a precursor to what has become known as a 'brilliant' cut. Each stone surpasses forty carats and some are so large as to be the size of a small child's fist. They are arrayed within the panel in a representation of the solar system or what was known of the solar system in Ptolemy's time, which means the planets furthest from the Sun were Saturn, an inlaid ring of variegated tourmaline encircling the oversized topaz, and Uranus, the embodiment of which is a nearly black emerald, the green practically unfathomable in its luxuriant depth.

The Sun appears as a dying star, a ruby cabochon of the deepest purplish red, the color of blood running through veins back to the heart to be oxygenated once again, whereas the fifth planet, Jupiter, is the largest and brightest jewel among the planets. The brilliant canary diamond eclipses all the surrounding astral bodies in size and far outshines the others. It is obviously the emerging star shown as replacing the light source that was once the Sun, which is fading toward collapse.

This is the item for which the last bidder has come and is determined to acquire. Only three of the original five attendees have any interest in the final offering, two of whom eventually drop out of the contest when the price reaches a point far beyond the appraised value recommended by their expert consultants.

The last remaining participant fully realizes that the worth of the artifact is not to be calculated in coin alone but in its significance to the enlightened power brokers that have been subtly directing western culture for centuries.

Its value far outstrips that of the gilt and antiquity of its design, he muses as he contemplates the prize he has just won with a pittance of his billions, a mere 40.6 million euros.

A bargain.

Chapter 1

Anthea Keller's frustration level was rapidly ascending to a threshold beyond which she was certain she would simply explode, bits of her brain scattering through the universe, never to reconvene as functioning synapses again. Not that it was functioning now. Since slamming down her laptop would only damage a valuable tool that held half of her life's secrets, she flipped the textbook closed with a vehemence that satisfied her need for violent action. Math was never her strong point and Quantitative Research was driving her rapidly toward seriously contemplating a holiday in a mental institution.

After finishing her master's degree a year ago, she and her new husband decided that if she was going to do it, now would be the time to tackle a Ph.D. Slapping the side of her head, she derided herself as an idiot for thinking she would have any use for a "piled higher and deeper" in education. *Hell, it's all mind control and class management anyway.* She genuinely wondered if she was only wasting her time and money. *Yeah, well the alphabet after your name makes everyone else think you're intelligent, whether or not there's any truth to the assump - tion.*

Gary, her husband, had embarked on his second career as a foreign language professor at a local college, specializing in French, Arabic and Russian. He had retired from a big city police force where he'd worked a special unit, and now was far happier dealing with students rather than terrorists. Though he was fond of saying that there really wasn't much difference between the two.

She, on the other hand, left the field of newspaper publishing to settle in a fairly rural area and ply her trade as a public relations agent and freelance journalist. She still speculated as to why she decided to advance her academic achievement after reaching forty, hmm, something. No, she knew part of it was just to prove to herself that she could accomplish the feat at her age. It certainly wasn't about to up her pay grade since she was self-employed.

Slowly inhaling through her nose, she made an effort to calm herself and, standing, stretched then walked away from the paper that was due the next day, knowing that she'd just have to come back to finish it later.

She hadn't taken two steps before the phone rang, which, in her way of thinking, was a respite even if it was a solicitor. Which actually might be a good thing – then she'd have someone to yell at.

Looking at the caller ID, she noted that it said 'private.'

Must be Toddy. Everyone else hardly bothered with privacy issues these days, though it was more necessary now, probably, than ever before.

She picked up the handset and almost before she finished saying hello, he blurted out the question most pertinent to him at the moment, "Have you heard about the newest purchase by some 'anonymous' billionaire at private auction?"

"Can't say I have," she replied casually, knowing full well that she would get not only a thorough description of the article but also a history and maybe even a philosophy lesson to boot. "I haven't *always* been absorbed by how the ridiculously wealthy spend their money. Should I be interested?" Stupid question.

"Oh yeah. This is an artifact that is legendary among the 'elite,'" and he stated that with exaggerated emphasis, "or 'enlightened,' as they'd prefer us to think of them. So far as I know, and all I know is fable mysteriously shrouded in the mists of time, this development could be telling." Toddy had a tendency toward hyperbole and fanciful language despite the fact that he'd never bothered to obtain a college degree. Frankly, he hadn't needed one. His brilliance was evident to every professional, entrepreneur or theoretician he'd encountered over the years.

"Go on…"

"From what I've gleaned from my readings, this object has been surreptitiously passed from one of the noble class to another throughout the ages, always to signify a transition of the brandishing of power to the next successor. It's said to be thousands of years old though it's hard to find an actual description of it. Kind of like the Umim and Thurim that was a part of Aaron's priestly vestments that was lost from the Tower of Antonia during the Roman administration of Judea before the fall of Jerusalem. Anyway, when the successor takes possession of it, those within a supposed 'inner circle' consider it be a sign of an upcoming coronation of sorts."

"You lost me. This artifact is passed down from generation to generation and is a symbol of someone having some sort of power? Is that right?"

"Yup," he agreed, "that's about the size of it."

Slightly exasperated since she still didn't know any more than when they started the conversation, "So, what is it?"

"To the best of my knowledge, which in this case is rather limited, it is basically a map of our solar system devised of outrageously fabulous gems and gold."

"And?"

"Its antiquity is supposedly tied to Solomon's Temple. Anything to do with Masonry and the illuminati are always somehow traced back to that one glorious point in time, according to the people who believe all this is of import."

"So, you're saying that this is part of some long lost treasure from Solomon's Temple that is apparently revered by the conspiratorial Masons, or has an illuminati connection," Anthea flatly stated.

"Well, that's the theory. But I don't believe that this buyer purchased it because he's part of any so-called Masonic or illuminati scheme. He's interested in the symbolism of *owning* it. Rather like, by taking possession of this revered object by whatever means, it infers his place as virtual monarch… the one who is inexorably destined to rule."

"So, who is this guy?"

"Well, I'm not certain yet, though I have my suspicions. The whole thing is just rumor after all, though it seems verified that the item *was* sold at private auction outside London just a couple of days ago."

"Do they know the price tag on this little bauble?" she asked.

"Above 40 million euros."

"Well now you *know* the world is coming to an end when immense purchases are measured in euros and not dollars anymore," she chuckled.

Generally serious, Toddy continued, "It's not so far from the truth. The dollar *is* losing ground to the euro and the yen. Gold is climbing at a fantastic rate. It's my contention that the two are related.

Someone and/or some entities are pushing gold values through the roof expressly to devalue the dollar and weaken the U.S. economy. *And*, I think the purchaser of the solar plat and King Midas are the same."

"Why would anyone want to weaken our economy? What's the point?"

"Power, pure and simple. By bringing the economy into a slump in an election year of this magnitude, the one backing the gold surge is looking to back a puppet as well. There is no one in line for the presidency and the state is sliding rapidly toward a socialist bent. Capitalism is on the outs with the Congress that's currently seated and it's highly possible to move even further to the left if this broker gets what he wants. And what he wants is *more power*. That's it. When you have more power than you need all you can do is covet more. Hence, the purchase of the symbol of passing the scepter to the next king. And, oh yes, he believes in a king and that he is the heir apparent. He has been working diligently to reinstate the feudal code. Face it, we've been reinventing serfdom over the past half century or more without anyone taking any particular notice." Toddy finally paused to take a breath.

"Whoa," was all Anthea could say. "Maybe it's time we did some research on the gold market and who you think is backing the demise of the dollar…"

"Oh, it's far more than that. It has to do with hedge funds and using gold and gold production as leverage against the falling dollar, manipulating the collapse of some currencies in favor of the real value of the commodity and making governments vulnerable to outside influences that will drive their markets into the dust, thus leaving them susceptible to economic raiders and vultures. *And* the people unable to create enough wealth to even feed and clothe themselves properly."

"Wait, wait, wait," she stopped him. "Too much information. You know I can't keep up with you, particularly since I have a limited – no, make that totally inadequate – grasp of all things monetary. Well, I can count change."

He laughed at the usual self-deprecating humor that was Anthea's hallmark.

"Look, I have to finish some bookwork for a research methods class tonight. Let me mull over what you've been talking about and see if I can get the gist of it. Maybe you can e-mail a thumbnail sketch of your major points so I have a better understanding. Then we can move on to the next step."

"Sure," he said. "I think you'll find this whole thing fascinating. But I also think that once we delve further, you're going to see what I do."

"And, what's that?" she asked with some trepidation.

"That we are truly on the precipice here. This isn't conspiracy theory. This is someone with a real ability to wield an unholy power that can bring this country to a grinding halt," he stated with grim meaning. "I think it's up to us to *do* something."

Trying to get back into the study at hand was difficult for Anthea. She didn't have much passion for the subject to begin with and having Toddy Littman call sent her mind skittering in another direction. Could he be overreacting? There was always some element of reality in his peculiar estimation of events and somehow, he could always see connections that slipped past the rest.

A predilection for gold by some billionaire that has the capacity to influence national markets by manipulating the currencies through outside pressure – *using* gold. How can that be done? He must employ other stratagems, too. Shaking the cobwebs from her brain, she realized she simply didn't have enough data or understanding of how stocks, commodities, precious metals and foreign currency trading worked, and she wasn't about to be miraculously enlightened in the next half-hour.

Toddy always had some new insight on the mechanics of government as it related to legal structure, markets and theory that someone (other than the typical citizen) was applying to affect the whole. It *was* about control and how some crave it to the point of developing a sense of guardianship over everyone else. The concept has always been around and it wasn't about to 'go away.' There would always be someone who believed they are ordained to decide how others should live their lives, for reasons acceptable or not so palatable to the Average Joe.

Tomorrow. I'll get his e-mail and catch on to what he's talking about. I hope.

Chapter 2

Anthea was parked behind her makeshift desk she had set-up on the patio – a portable pine TV table just large enough to hold her laptop, an iced beverage at her elbows as she cradled her chin while reading over the e-mail Toddy shot off to her the night before. The morning was turning warm for a late June day and she had her unruly curls clipped at the back of her head in an effort to keep her neck cool as the sun climbed higher in the sky. Lifting her eyes from the mass of data he had managed to cram into a couple of pages, she followed the wake of a small steel-hulled boat with a single fisherman piloting up the river, his hand on the tiller of a merc outboard.

Before she could readjust her focus to the screen in front of her, she was interrupted by the arrival of two imposing figures, a man and his pregnant wife, climbing the steps onto her deck. The couple were tenants of Anthea's, occupying the small cottage that lay just to the south of the main house.

"Shouldn't you two be working or doing something worthwhile like, oh, I don't know, painting the baby's room?" she inquired as Lainie, the mother-to-be, settled into a chair next to Anthea.

"We've got months yet to do that and we haven't decided what theme to use." Lainie wriggled her behind as she tried to find a comfortable position. She was a tall girl, who had tied her long sable locks into a twist that was skewered by a refashioned chopstick decorated with bead work in the Nez Perce colors of sky blue and an old rose-red that her paternal grandmother had made for her.

"Two and a half months go faster than you think. Particularly when you start feeling more awkward as the baby grows. Not to mention the heat index rising during the summer," Anthea pointed out. "Who wants to be climbing ladders and painting walls when it gets more difficult to move around?"

Lainie's eyes narrowed a little, then laughed. "I'm not having twins!"

"Maybe not but you're 5'10" if you're an inch and that giant of a husband of yours is, what," she eyed Cisco Rafael good-naturedly, "6'5"?"

He just looked at her and shrugged.

"Your point?" she asked.

"Tall parents, big baby," Anthea smiled.

"I guess. But that's not a worry."

"No, it's more like Lainie hasn't made up her mind on décor," Cisco tossed in.

"No joint decision on this?"

He just gave her a sideways look, as if to say *'right.'*

"So," said Anthea, deciding it was time to change the subject, "to what do I owe this pleasure?"

"Auntie Sol is getting a baby shower organized for next week and I wanted to make sure that you had an invitation." She sat with her hands clasped across her growing stomach. Like most social events in Lainie's family, there wasn't the formality of a printed invitation. Information was shared by word of mouth and everyone just passed the message down the line. There would be a full house when the time came and plenty of helping hands.

"I'd love to come. When and where? Is there anything I can do?"

"Just bring yourself. She's taking over the back room at that little bakery café downtown, Olyve Oyl's, next Saturday afternoon. A lot of family is coming in for the weekend. P'lahka and Grandma Aline will even be coming back from one of their road trips." Lainie smiled at the thought of her husband's grandparents who'd been off on their Harley touring bike most of the spring since he'd retired. This year they'd been through the Dakotas and down across the plains to Texas, then back up by way of New Mexico, Colorado and Utah.

"How about your mom?" asked Anthea. "Will she be able to come in from Montana?"

"I just talked to her this morning and she said she would be bringing Mama Ciel into town for the shower." She sighed. "It'll be good to see them."

Anthea had already heard the tale of how Lainie's mother, Neta, had to return home to the family ranch near Livingston, Montana, to help her mom who was having some problems with her blood pressure. The problem had been a byproduct of onset diabetes, which has become a growing problem among the Indian population. Although Mama Ciel was just part Crow, she had been diagnosed only after suffering a mild heart attack the year before. Getting her blood pressure under control had entailed regular trips to a cardiologist and endocrinologist in Bozeman, both of who prohibited her driving until her precarious condition was stabilized. Neta would be spelled by Grandpa Allen (who was actually their uncle, but tradition is that all the elder siblings in the family are respectfully referred to as 'grand-mother' and 'grandfather') by the time her first grandchild was ready to make his or her debut. The couple wanted to be surprised. In the meantime, Solana Greyfisher, who was now living near her niece after assuming the role of managing editor for the Nez Perce tribe's week-ly newspaper, was playing the overprotective auntie.

Generally speaking, even though the situation and family con-nections had been explained to Anthea numerous times by Cisco and Lainie, she found it confusing nonetheless. One of these days she was just going to ask for a genealogical diagram so she could keep it straight unlike her own family which was small and easily followed.

"I'll bet Sol will be happy to see everyone as well. I think it's been a little lonely trying to get her footing here after so many years away. Seeing family always helps." Anthea had gotten to know Sol through her niece, who sat complacently caressing her belly. Since the two of them had a strong history in journalism, Anthea as a former newspaper publisher and Solana, a correspondent for large dailies in New York and Denver, they had bonded in a way that only new-shounds can. She looked back out across the water and contemplated her own return to Idaho after a few years of sojourning in Southern California. Although it was good to feel at home it had also been a rough adjustment leaving family and friends in another state.

Lainie hefted herself out of the chair and catching her hus-band's eye, motioned she was ready to go. "So we'll see you for sure next Saturday, right?"

"I wouldn't miss it," smiled Anthea. "Is this a co-ed event?"

Lainie shook her head. "Oh no. This is just us girls. The men are going fishing."

"Had to ask. These days everyone seems to get caught up in a party atmosphere and some guys seem to feel left out," Her smile grew larger as she directed her gaze to Cisco who gave Anthea a look that indicated he had no need to fuss with baby gear. "I'll see you before then," she said as the two left. Following their progress back to their quarters on the other side of the lawn, Anthea thought about how protective Cisco had become after a brief episode early in the pregnancy that had scared them both. Lainie seemed to be doing fine and a smoldering fire burned behind her eyes on occasion when she couldn't shoo him off to do something else. It being the first baby, Anthea assumed it was only natural that he would impersonate a hovercraft but thought it might be time to lighten up a little.

Drawing her eyes back to the computer, she started a second scanning of the articles that Toddy had sent. A name kept popping up throughout the varied information that skirted international currency trading, gold speculation and, of all things, land conservation by environmental activism.

"How does that tie together?" she asked the empty air around her. Ignoring her tendency to talk to herself, she continued re-reading the news clips and Toddy's notations on relevancy. She came across that same name being mentioned in a few of the stories gleaned from national news sources and internet sites, *Grigor Scirras*.

Why was that familiar? Oh right, he'd been on the board of directors of that land conservancy outfit that she and her now husband, Gary Mathers, had cornered in a land grab scheme not quite two years ago. Scirras had been a peripheral player and wasn't implicated in the federal charges that had been leveled against the conservancy that was gobbling up private land all across the western states after financially destroying, and in some cases, killing the owners. A very nasty business that was still pending in the courts. *Probably forever, if the mon - eyed perps get their way,* she thought bitterly. *The cogs of justice. What was it her friend, the attorney had said? Oh yeah… there is no justice in the justice system.* She was beginning to believe him, God rest his soul.

She let her thoughts drift along the lines of where the money had come from to finance the acquisition of millions of acres in the Nature's Wilds racket they had been instrumental in busting. A lot of it had been diverted from a digital entertainment giant but whatever cash this enigmatic character Scirras might have supplied had yet to be discovered – part of the reason why the whole case hadn't come to trial yet… the government was still tracing the dough. Why was this guy's name coming up again?

She dug a little deeper through the files in the e-mail and saw that Toddy had dropped in a link to something called rosaliamonteyn.org. What was that? May as well take a gander, she wasn't getting her work done anyway. At least she had e-mailed her assignment earlier and was free to play a little bit. *Like this is fun. Finding even more skullduggery among the nouveau riche.* She wagged her head in exasperation at herself… *of course this is fun.*

She watched the website materialize on the screen and read the lead lines. Weird. This was someplace in Romania, oooh, Trahnsylvahnia (she pronounced it in her head the way she imagined Bela Lugosi would). Vampire heaven. She smiled briefly until she started reading the content.

This was a small town in a rural region of Transylvania that had one industry, an industry that was being shut down by the environmentalists from everywhere but Romania. *Can no one mind their own business?* So what had this to do with one of the land barons? Reading further she began to see the connection to what Toddy had been talking about… gold. The world environmental movement had been bringing pressure to bear on the Romanian government to close down the only income producing business that everyone who lived in Rosalia Monteyn depended on. The gold mine. But this gold mine had been the recipient of millions of dollars worth of environmentally friendly upgrades, making it one of the cleanest as well as most productive gold mines in the world. *Who'd have thought, gold mining in Transylvania.*

There was a two-minute video that she accessed through the website. Clicking on the 'play' button, she settled in to watch the blurb. As the short story unfolded, she went from surprised to shocked and finally outraged at what she saw. The fact that the region's populace was dependent on the mine for their modest income was one thing, but for foreign 'do-gooder's' to climb on their high horse, ride into town and force it's closing was unconscionable. Anthea was dumbfounded at the comment by one of the organization's benefactor's when he said, "Just go pick mushrooms and sell those," referring to one of the few food sources left to the villagers. As if that would take the place of a twenty percent ownership in a successful gold mining operation. Was he nuts? And who was he anyway? She scanned further into the information until she hit upon the answer. Scirras.

But Scirras, she remembered now that she had the connection of Romania in her mind, was a name that she had stumbled across years ago while writing a column on the coup that occurred there in 1989. A brief and bloody coup d'etat that brought down the longtime communist leader, Nikolai Ceausescu. She had been doing some basic research on the uprising when Grigor Scirras was mentioned as a known arms dealer. She knew that she had neither seen nor heard anything of the sort in years. Now he was only known as a philanthropist who had come by his billions through foreign currency trading. Maybe he'd really made his money as a successful gunrunner, parlaying that into the foreign currency market.

She must be slow. All of this was beginning to come together in her mind as to what Toddy had been alluding. He'd mentioned currencies, gold and governmental instability. Well, here was one instance that dated back almost twenty years in, lo and behold, Scirras' old stomping grounds. Could he have been instrumental in the demise of a regime? Was he tied to arms dealing in the past and could he still be involved? It made her wonder. And how could this be tied into philanthropy? Wasn't he renowned and revered for giving to the poor and downtrodden these days? *Right, and then telling them to 'pick mush-rooms.' Is that anything like Marie Antoinette and the 'let them eat cake' nonsense? Elitism at it's finest.*

Disgusted, she closed down the site, flipped down the monitor, propped her chin in her hands, and started watching a couple of powerboats motor by on the Snake River. There's something going on and she needed time to dig deeper into all of this. Try to figure out where Toddy was steering her. She realized that this was going to take some real time to research because even with what he'd forwarded, her brain started clicking onto a thousand different possibilities as to where this financial trend could really be leading. What really worried her was whether or not she was stepping into another minefield.

Sometime later, Anthea was dredged out of her reverie by the arrival of Gary. She heard his footsteps advance onto the deck and the hiss of an effervescent beverage as he removed the cap from a beer. It must have been later than she thought, she realized as he handed her a bottle and deposited his long body into the chair that Lainie had occupied hours earlier.

"Thanks, babe. I hadn't noticed how fast the day had disappeared," she said as she took a sip and he popped the cap off his own beer. "How was the drive?"

"Not bad at all. Little traffic and perfect weather." He had been in Portland for a seminar at Clackamas College, where he taught a couple of workshops for peace officers dealing with the growing multilingual community. While there, he'd had the opportunity to spend a few days with his daughter's family, playing with the grandkids.

He shot a questioning look at her as he drank from his bottle. "You were really preoccupied when I came out here. Didn't even hear me get into the fridge, did you?"

"Nope." She sat back and sighed. "I've been digging through some information Toddy sent me on a new conspiracy he's uncovered." She smirked just a little.

"Conspiracy? You don't mean that."

"Not really. He's just working overtime on a subject that's gotten wedged in his craw about international currency and gold market maneuvering. Piqued my interest to see if he's got a point or just an overactive imagination," she chuckled a little.

"That boy needs a life. All he does is find how someone is managing to get a stranglehold on the rest of us poor peons." He shook his head, but winked.

"That 'boy' is over forty, made more than one fortune in his short lifetime and, unfortunately, his conjectures are usually right on the money, if you'll pardon the pun."

He laughed then sobered slightly. "I know. That's what so disconcerting about his *finds*. We've yet to prove him wrong, damn it."

Anthea allowed another chuckle to escape. "Got my work done for the week. How about you?" She swept his form with the clear blue glint of her eyes, smiling.

"I'm all caught up. School's out for me," he took a drink. "You're the one with a summer class to contend with. Got something in mind?" A corner of his mouth curled up.

"Yes. I need a break." She rose, tucked her laptop under her arm and grabbed her drink. "Let's pack and go to the house in Marcasite for the weekend."

Standing up, he fairly towered over Anthea's petite stature. Bending down, he bussed a kiss across her forehead and said, "You're on, girl. Let's go."

Chapter 3

Solana Greyfisher was ensconced behind a solid old pine desk that was lodged into a small cubicle, pushed up against the wall with a cockeyed view out the window that overlooked the parking lot. The building was an antiquated frame house on Main Street situated next to another older home that had been converted into an artsy Indian trading post. No expense spared, she had thought sardonically when she first arrived back in town after debating whether or not to accept the lower salary to publish the tribal weekly paper. All caution aside, she conceded that it had been a good decision to dump Denver and reinvent herself as a small town newspaper publisher after taking all she could handle of years at the Post. Big city reporting had gone from having a journalistic calling to being little more than a media hack, and she had finally tired of turning out stories that met an agenda rather than reporting news.

Back here on the reservation there were agendas as well, but they weren't to benefit some old money publishers with bottom lines that catered to advertisers. Not that that was necessarily a bad thing. Papers had to pay their bills too. The trouble was that so much of the conglomerate-owned press was more interested in politics than objectivity. Well, that was her perspective, so she was content to cover small town news, sports and family activities. There was an important place for this kind of reporting and it couldn't be found in the metro sections anymore.

She was going over the stories that were set for this week's issue and dummying the paper on the computer. Now in her middle thirties, Sol hadn't had to deal much with the old style of physically measuring inches of copy with a ruler and figuring where to place the stories on a dummy sheet. Life was much simpler in some ways with the new programs that made it less complicated to just drop a story in place and run the tail onto an inside page. Positioning photos was a breeze in comparison too. Every once in a while she'd have lunch or drinks with Anthea Keller, who was a decade older and had worked in the business before everything had been computerized. It was interesting to hear about *her* dad and how he'd taken the kids to have their mirror-image names stamped out in hot lead for the old letterpresses before offset printing became the industry norm. That always made her think of the old Hollywood flicks like "The Front Page" romanticizing the newsrooms filled with copyboys, reporters and a cigar puffing city editor. That was the kind of newsroom she had envisioned when she went off to college to study journalism – a time when hard-drinking, smoke-trailing reporters vied for story placement above the fold. Like hard copy cowboys, they rode the back of breaking news, bleeding ink when they were thrown and dusting themselves off to catch another ride on their way to penning a career-making story, sliding it in just before deadline.

Definitely not reality, which is where she was now, placing ads and getting ready to e-mail the whole schmeer to the printer. Somehow the professors neglected to mention what drudgery was really involved in putting a paper to bed. She sighed as she hit the 'save' button and completed the layout of another page in the modern world of publishing.

The paper was a small one, a tab running about sixteen pages each week. During the tribal elections, advertising would pick-up and they'd get twenty-four pages on the stands. Maybe even boost the profit margin for the week. She operated with a minimal staff of one part-time reporter, a couple volunteer stringers and a production/IT manager who doubled as an editor. Since the Nez Perce Reservation was the largest Indian reservation in the state of Idaho, she also wore another hat as a contributor to the Boise paper, the Boise Statesman. They didn't find it worthwhile to keep a full-time reporter in the area, so she would clear a few extra dollars when one of her stories was picked-up for the state capital's daily.

Just as she was compiling the last of the pages and preparing them to send to the printer, her screen went belly-up blank and she let out a yip of consternation. Pulling her fingers through her shoulder-length hair until she had two black wings extending straight out from her temples, she yelled for Drury to come to her rescue.

The young man, who wasn't much taller than a tree stump, and built solidly across the middle to match the description, stuck his head around the corner of the partition, brown eyes cocked with slight aggravation and subtle amusement at being called to save Sol… again. She caught his knowing look and laughed at her own distress and comical ability to hit a wrong key, sending something off into the ether only to be rediscovered in some strange and unexpected corner of the computer hard-drive. Some ridiculous niche that, unfortunately, *she* could never find but Drury could.

"Where did it go now?" he asked calmly, replacing her in the chair she had just vacated.

"Who knows," exasperation and resignation seeping through her voice. "I have an incredible skill for misplacing files in some deep, dark trench of computer hell. I hope you can find it. I was ready to upload the paper for the printer."

"No sweat." Confidently gliding his fingers across the keyboard, he had this week's paper displayed on the oversized screen in no time. "You want me to send this off for you?" he gazed up half-mockingly.

"You'd better. I'm apt to send it to Kansas and have it disappear in a twister with dear, old Dorothy," she said, shaking her head with disgust. "I keep wondering if I'm *ever* going to get the hang of this new program."

Drury punched a few more buttons and the screen changed to show that the file had been sent on it's merry way to press. He stood and, hitching up his trousers, said with finality, "Done."

"Thank you for saving the day, yet again."

He dipped his head, bringing his hand up as if to tip his non-existent hat. "All in a day's work, ma'am. Will there be anything else today?"

"Nope, that ought to do it. We're done for the day and I owe you a latté."

"Just chalk it up to the 4,312 other ones already on your IOU," he grinned and did his best imitation of a John Wayne gait returning to his cubicle. The sight was incongruent considering Drury, when he pulled himself up to his full height was only 5'5", a full five inches shorter than Solana. She just smiled and pulled out the bottom drawer to grab her purse before leaving the office. She had a list as long as her arm of things she needed to prepare before her niece Lainie's baby shower tomorrow. Throwing the strap of her bag over her shoulder, she swept out the door, just managing to wiggle her fingers in farewell at Drury while reminding him to lock-up.

Saturday afternoon at Olyve Oyl's was usually pretty tame. The bakery would get busy with morning coffee hounds and then the lunch crowd would come in for a salad or deli sandwich made with their fresh whole-grain bread. They even offered a nice selection of espressos and gourmet panini as the owners had been expanding the menu to garner more patrons from the college. Saturdays, though, were slow. Business people didn't come downtown and students slept in, saving their energy for whatever trouble they could drum up on a weekend in a relative backwater like Lewiston, which made the bakery a perfect choice for a little party.

Well, not so little. Lainie's and her husband's family were what some might refer to as 'extended,' in that it extended to virtually everyone who lived in a fifty mile radius from town. And, of course, that didn't count anyone from out-of-state.

The back room was packed with ladies and quite a few children climbing over the seats and slipping under a few of the tables. It was an informal gathering mostly to share news and good food without the rigid schedule of games, contests and prizes that some showers emphasize. No one was really interested in anything other than getting together for the afternoon to see the mother-to-be and visit with family they hadn't seen in a while.

As a local friend, Anthea joined Sol in helping out with the abundant food and few organized activities. By the time the crowd started to thin, the two of them were exhausted. Lainie was ready to collapse so she was bundled off home under the care of her mother, Neta, and grandmother, who'd made it down from Montana, leaving Sol and Anthea to close up shop.

"How is everything going at the paper?"

"Not bad," replied Sol as she loaded packages into the back of her rig. "Though if I could get a handle on the new programs, I wouldn't have to call Drury in to bail me out every ten minutes."

"That, I don't envy you. There's something to be said for the old fashioned way of cut and paste. Nothing's going to disappear into a black hole." She looked up from the boxes in her arms with a grin. "'Course, that doesn't discount butchering a halftone with an x-acto and having to re-shoot a photo." She shrugged her shoulders. "Every method has its drawbacks."

"You can say that again." Sol pushed the tailgate down and dusted off her hands. "I think that's about it."

"Where are they going to put all this stuff?" Anthea dropped her hands to her hips and studied the pile of goods stacked in the back of the truck.

"They'll figure it out. It'll get spread around between grandparents and family so everyone has necessities on hand where it's needed."

"Good idea," Anthea concurred. She looked up at Sol and changed the subject. "Are you interested in hearing about a little research project my friend and I have started?"

Solana cocked an eyebrow. "What kind of *project*," suspicion floating cheerfully in her voice.

"Well, it's hard to explain in a brief minute but he's stumbled across some information that may have bearing on the election."

"The *presidential* election?" Sol said incredulously.

"Yeah, could be." Anthea's expression became clouded. She brightened quickly. "You want to have lunch Monday?"

"Sounds intriguing," she stopped to mentally peruse her calendar. "Yes, I can meet you for lunch. Where? I can get free around one p.m."

"Let's go to the marina. We can sit on the deck and it'll be fairly private since it will be thinning out by then." They agreed to meet and, while Sol was contemplating what her friend could possibly think was pertinent to a presidential race, Anthea climbed into her truck and wheeled away from the curb.

Solana walked into the restaurant, pausing by the hostess station to scan the deck that lined the whole west side of the establishment. She spotted Anthea, perched under an oversized red umbrella, hunched forward with her chin in her hands, watching a houseboat pull into its slip. She looked pensive, the muscles in her back taut under the teal tank top she wore tucked into the waist of a patterned broomstick skirt that fanned over the sides of her chair.

Sol straightened the viridian silk tunic that fell just past her hips over trim black capris. Pushing through the glass door with one hand, she held it open for a tiny female server to slide through who held aloft a tray stacked impossibly high with dirty dishes. The girl smiled her thanks as she steered toward the kitchen.

Setting her purse on one of the extra chairs, Sol parked herself next to Anthea who hadn't moved an inch during the process.

"What could possibly have you so absorbed in concentration?"

Anthea blinked away the invisible cobwebs she had been spinning in her mind and focused on the poised woman who was absently fingering an old style squash blossom necklace, the heavy silver framing impressive turquoise stones laced with variegated colors of sea-green and sky blue.

"What a beautiful piece. Must weigh enough to cause you chronic neck pain," she winked with humor.

Sol looked down and holding out the central stone, studied the vividly mottled strata. "A gift from an ex-boyfriend. Guess he wanted to be sure no one overlooked the fact of my heritage." She raised her slightly tilted eyes to meet Anthea's. "Took me long enough to realize I was a novelty he liked to drape over his arm, kind of like a platinum Rolex." She added almost under her breath, "of course, he already had one of those. "You know, the token Indian in a crowd of country club snobs. The type who wear elephant-skin cowboy boots and a two-inch cab Burmese ruby on their bolo tie to the opera, but couldn't climb astride a horse to save their lives." Her lips turned up in a mordant smile. "The West is full of displaced money folks who like the look of ranch life but haven't a clue what it means to live on one, let alone work it. Some of them are even fervent vegans," she was slightly irked at the memory. "Save a cow but cap the ends of that fancy bolo with poached African ivory." She didn't have to voice the word that came to mind, *hypocrites*.

Anthea's eyes widened in disbelief. "How did you end up with a cowpie like that?"

Solana dropped her hand to the table and clasped the stem of a water glass. "I was having a little vision problem. Temporary blindness."

"We've all been there. Sometimes it takes years to see straight again." She sat back and smiled at Sol. "You shoulda used them shit-kickers to stomp on the cockroach. Isn't that what those pointy toes are for? Catchin' the vermin and smashin' them in a corner? I know I saw it done plenty of times in Mexico," Anthea grinned attempting to lighten the mood.

"Yeah, well, it was time to get the hell out of town anyway." She changed the subject. "So what's good here?" She lifted the menu to examine the offerings.

The waitress came by and took their orders, returning a few minutes later with a couple of iced teas.

"Okay, so tell me. What's up? Is this something every reporter dreams about? Pulitzer winning material?" Sol stirred her tea and looked sidelong at Anthea.

"Don't know about that." She dropped into her pensive mode again. "What do you know about environmental action groups that might have been low-key in the Denver area."

"What do you mean?"

"Background supporters of politicians, groups that didn't look for headlines but gave money to the ones who made them," Anthea elaborated.

"Not the Sierra Clubs, then."

"Definitely not. It kind of sounds like you might even have been hanging with some of the types of people who'd be the funders behind the scenes. Cowboy wannabes with the soul of earth muffins." She raised her blue eyes to connect with Sol's tawny brown gaze. Sol had eyes that hovered between the color of rich coffee and ochre, shot through with golden highlights.

Sol let her head fall back and laughed. "That's the first I've heard that one."

"I stole it from a friend," Anthea confessed.

"Okay, yes," said Sol, sobering. "These people would fit the bill. A lot of money, Western art dripping from their skyscraper walls and turquoise and malachite concho belts circling the ladies' fashionably trim waists. It's all about the look and feel of the West, not about what built it." She took a breath. "What is it you think they might be up to?" She arched a brow.

"Did you hear much about that conservancy group that was

gobbling up land around here and all over mostly the western states?"

"I know a little bit about what you and Gary got wrapped up in around here. Even the local rag couldn't avoid writing something about that. What were they called? Nature's Wilds?"

"Well, it wasn't for lack of information that the papers didn't run with the story. I supplied plenty of facts and releases to everyone," Anthea bristled a little. "The truth is, money buys a lot of silence as well as publicity.

"Nature's Wilds had its hands on millions of acres all over the west and was even acquiring pristine lands in states like Mississippi and Minnesota. Not that you'd know by reading any newspaper." She let her disgruntlement show. "Hardly anyone knows that the investigation is ongoing and acreage is being swapped back and forth between government and private concerns constantly, in this case and others. I'm not holding my breath that the ringleaders will be brought down. Actually, I rather doubt it."

Sol turned to look more squarely at her lunch partner. "So, what's this to do with anything? You've confused me."

"Oh, this is just the beginning of confusion," Anthea closed her eyes for a second. "Nature's Wilds had some major benefactors that appear to be inserting themselves into other areas of diversionary activities."

"Diversionary?" Sol shook her head in puzzlement and opened her hands, palms upward as if in supplication for enlightenment.

"Maybe not the right word. Hmmm. Okay the front man for Nature's Wilds is under indictment, though he may yet skate."

"You mean Chamberlain, that digital media and entertainment mogul with Solis Industries."

"Yes. However, there was one other name that came up in our rooting around. A billionaire who has kept a pretty low profile most of his investing career. He was forced out of the closet in the 90s when he managed to bring the Bank of Britain to its knees, crippling the pound by speculating that its value would fall. The bank was forced to keep buying their own pound by the billions to offset the precipitous drop in value against the German mark. All of this had to do with the ERM, the Exchange Rate Mechanism that was set-up in Europe in 1979 to bring the currencies into alignment foreseeing the development of the European Union. The only currency that kept its value through this whole mess was the mark because the Bundesbank wouldn't rescue anyone by lowering their interest rates.

"Frankly, I have a really limited understanding of the machinations of the international currency market. What I *do* know… is that this hedge fund operator bet against most of the European currencies and, particularly, the British pound bringing the economy to a standstill and raking in billions of dollars for his private investors. He so impressed the world that there are now groups that just *watch* his market manipulations. He also crashed the Thai *bat*, and monkeyed with the Malaysian currency. Of course, that was chump change in comparison."

Sol was quiet for a few moments. "I've got that this billionaire basically crushed the bank in a billion dollar gamble. So what has he to do with environmental organizations? I don't get the tie-in."

"This guy was the other mover on the land-acquisition scheme, as I said, but it looks like he's dipping into much bigger pies here, in the U.S., and around the world. He seems to be taking a stance that suppresses entrepreneurism. I don't even know if that's a real word, but you get the gist. The policies of Nature's Wilds and other organizations like it is to take the land out of the hands of people who work it in order to *preserve* it," she enunciated the word with derision. Anthea sat back trying to think how this all really coalesced, because even though Toddy and she had gone over it, the concept was far too broad to accept and absorb.

While they were ruminating over the basic information Anthea had just detailed, their meal was delivered and they raised their forks to spear leaves of romaine, arugula and radicchio that lay artfully intermingled with morsels of halibut, shrimp and scallops.

Picking up where she left off, Anthea asked once more if Sol had come across any environmental busybodies while she was in Denver. Maybe she knew of some other connections besides this one.

Sol sat back and gave the question some consideration. "There are plenty of front organizations that have become more vocal in meddling in private ranch and farm land use. Not to mention development. And yes, it was people like my friend's friends who were inferring their opinion through gifts of money to different organizations. Mostly, they backed the obvious groups like the Sierra Club. A few liked the more militant World Wildlife Fund and Greenpeace." She placed her fork on the table and lifted her glass distractedly. "You know, there was a time when I believed Greenpeace had a point. Now look at them. Even one of the founders has distanced himself from their wild accusations about the inevitable destruction of eco-systems left and right; that Man has done nothing but wreak havoc on the earth since time immemorial." She looked up ruefully. "Well, I may be over-stating it a bit, but some think its fashionable to give aboriginal people a pass. It's finally become cool to be an Indian or wishing you were one. Trouble is, they think they understand our cultures and make assumptions about Native peoples and their relationship to the earth, but the philosophies aren't the same among all of them... us. You know what I mean. Nothing is simple and no one group can, or should, make decisions for others about how to live." She sighed. "Been there, done that." Sol tugged up a corner of her mouth in an apologetic smile.

Anthea sat back, deciding that she'd finished with her salad. "So you're saying that the country club buds of your *friend* might have been a tad elitist in their attitude? Sticking their nose in the business of local landowners who were just trying to do their best for their families and communities?" The flippancy was evident.

"That's the way it looked to me and it was part of the reason they fawned on me. I represented the *real* people who they thought they were trying to emulate. They wanted so badly to believe that if they associated with an Indian, what they perceived to be Native American wisdom would rub off on them, or some such nonsense." She gazed out over the river's current. "Yep, just a novelty, an orna-ment. People have such skewed views of the world. Makes you remember Martin Luther King, Jr. and his message that one day we would be able to judge one another by the content of our character and not the color of our skin."

"I do know what you mean. It's what you're made of, not what you look like or even who your ancestors are. My father was in the pressbox when Dr. King gave his "I Have a Dream" speech the last time he spoke in Southern California. Stayed with Dad for life. Now, if only that true wisdom of Dr. King had lodged with the general pub-lic rather than the twisted interpretation that displaced it."

"We've gone wa-ay off track, haven't we," Solana turned her gaze back to Anthea. "What has all this to do with the presidential pol-itics and promise of a Pulitzer Prize winning story you lured me here with." Her eyes flashed with mischievous fire. "I feel like I've been led astray and all my breadcrumbs have been eaten by birds. We'll never find the trail again."

Anthea chuckled under her breath. "Oh yes we will. The billionaire was, *is*," she added a question mark in her tone, "funding land acquisition for preservation and he has taken a more public role in American politics, particularly backing the most liberal candidate via the backdoor of 527s. Toddy and I think there is much more than meets the eye. That there's some connection between environmental agendas, politics and maybe even currency manipulation."

"I don't get the correlation," Sol's skepticism was seeping through.

"I'm not positive that I do either. Maybe I can have my friend Toddy contact you. He comprehends these things better than I do, but he's hard to follow, I'll warn you. He makes leaps of logic that leave me in the dust more often than not. However, he's rarely wrong and, right now, that scares the hell out of me."

Anthea gave her a look of trepidation that made Sol wonder if she was going to have to step lively around more cowpies than she'd ever seen in her life.

Gold Baron

Chapter 4

The gleaming Gulfstream G-5 taxied to a stop on the nearly empty airstrip. The private airfield curried to test flights and a few tycoons who kept hangars where they housed their personal aircraft. Coming to a complete stop, a mobile stairway was quickly rolled out to dock with the plane's fuselage. A whoosh sounded as the airtight seal around the cabin door was broken to reveal the co-pilot as he breached the exit, securing the door open to give the sole passenger a solid path to the tarmac. Thirty seconds later the man, dressed impeccably in an understated Saville Row suit, disappeared within the interior of a customized, black limousine – an elongated Range Rover fitted with armored skin and bullet-proof glass. Luggage and a sturdy wooden crate were loaded into the rear cargo compartment. Doors slammed shut and the vehicle pulled away from the corporate jet not five minutes after landing.

The sky was practically cloudless, sporting a brilliant blue canopy that wasn't an everyday weather pattern in Seattle. Half the time he was here, precipitation drizzled from the sky in a steady patter. But then, even his tropical getaway suffered from similar spates of rain, the difference being the mean temperature. Western Washington was temperate this time of year, ranging mostly in the upper 70s to low 80s. Comfortable. The island, well, you could be drenched in the sodden air just by walking through the air-conditioned barriers of ceiling-high glass. For that reason, he preferred to make that address a winter waystation.

Today was a special day, however. Not only was the weather complying, but he was bringing his little prize home, completing his collection for the time being. He was always searching for similar objects of historical significance such as the one bundled safely in the cargo hold. The drive to his suites, which were perched atop a highrise in the city, would take some time. Seattle traffic was no better than L.A. anymore. He sat back viewing the empty sky through the moon roof and occasionally letting his eyes drift to the right to capture the looming presence of Mt. Rainier on the horizon, and silently congratulated himself on another successful mission.

He had left his wife behind in London who, always dissatisfied with some aspect of their Belgravia residence, had decided to redecorate for what seemed the thousandth time. That didn't bother him in the least. It gave him the luxury of spending some quality time admiring the gems of antiquity that surrounded him in his little retreat buried among the many rooms of his penthouse, a full three floors he occupied overlooking Elliot Bay. Although he appeared motionless in his contemplation, his thoughts were flashing at lightning speed. His business and charitable endeavors kept him perpetually busy, a natural state for him. He wasn't happy unless he was in constant motion even if the activity wasn't evident to observers. Mulling over financial plans, market data or organization details, where he appeared to be immobile, his mind was never still. His eyes would seem glazed over while his brain whirred in myriad directions, constructing new strategies and designs that not one of his associates could truly follow. The thought made him smile. He was always a step ahead of his partners and office assistants – Ivy League pedigrees notwithstanding, let alone his competitors… and he thrived on competition. It was perhaps the one pleasure he most enjoyed. Nothing was as gratifying as winning and he always won big. When he lost – a rare occurrence – he generally did that with inordinate panache as well. There was no point in doing anything if not with verve and magnitude.

For the moment he was engrossed by the newest addition to his gallery of ancient and precious wonders, most of which the public believed to be mythic or long-since vanished from existence, destroyed by time and corruption. Each of the articles, displayed for advantageous viewing, had long since faded from the knowledge of man and were now arrayed for his scrutiny alone. Aged beyond memory, they carried a significant history to men of power, past and present. Power inferred but not conferred. The kind of power these bejeweled and golden artifacts of antiquity inspired was that of complete control, plied from the recesses of veiled thrones. Influence could be wielded from a public platform or as a hidden presence, and he preferred the latter choice of traveling through life unnoticed except by the supremacy he exercised from the shadows.

His eyes lighting on the newest panel estimated to be some 2500 years old, he recalled his own humble beginnings, so disparate from the men who began the quest for dominance and had commissioned its crafting. He'd always had an inclination that he was bound for greatness. Yet subtlety had also always been his brand of manipulation. Others felt his sway but never knew him as the puppeteer. God had gifted him with a special ability to surpass his so-called equals, bringing them under his command whether or not they realized it. That is, of course, if you believed in a God, which he had long ago decided was an absurdity. *There is no right hand of God, as those others had perceived themselves to be – sanctified to dominate others.* He shook his head in denial. *God is here. This flesh.* And he stretched out his arms to examine his aging but still strong hands. Even as a child he had heard the words flit through his mind. *I am God.* Immortality is at my disposal, he reasoned. It's all a matter of how you use that immortality to bring others to view you in the light of divinity, the price of which is wealth, the untold power to follow.

Cluj, Romania – 1942

The Vienna Diktat has been in place since 1940 and the Horthyst Hungarian government, colluding with the Nazis, have become entrenched in Northern Transylvania. For centuries this region of Romania has been pulled to and fro between the two nations, pressur - ing the Jewish population to assimilate with the surrounding culture. Hostility between the neighboring countries has ebbed and flowed over time, the Jews finding themselves in the role of pawns in the tug-of-war. Since 1867, Transylvanian Jews have enjoyed rights that a Hungarian regime had bestowed. Romania, which until the Diktat had reasserted jurisdiction in Transylvania, is engaged in an ongoing estrangement of the Jews, referring to them as hated 'Hungarians.' They are wallowing in a no-win situation of rising anti-Semitism under the Antonescu government, the successor to King Carol II who abdicated the same year of the German and Italian forced decree that ceded the land back to Hungary. It wasn't long before the Conducator, *'Leader' as General Ion Antonescu is known, became complicit in the fascist alliance, handing the Nazis control of the Ploiesti oil fields near the shores of the Black Sea. Caught between two Nazi collabora - tors, the Transylvanian Jews are ensnared by a tightening noose of Romanian* Judenhein *(the code for annihilation) and the Hungarian disenfranchisement.*

It is in this atmosphere of abject fear and mounting hate that Alec, a successful real estate investor, is able to play both ends against the middle. He has long since cultivated his ability to beguile poten - tial clients with an inborn charm that inspires trust. Everyone assumes they know him because he has a talent for listening while offering up very little real personal information. He is accepted in both the Jewish community and among the Gentiles and no one knows for certain where he belongs. His wife, a beautiful blonde, perhaps a shicksa, and he had lived in Budapest before moving here. The couple has three children, two boys and girl. All curly towheads with big brown eyes. Beyond this, he never imparts more of his history, but it doesn't mat - ter, he is established as having dual citizenship within the oft-split community – an up and coming businessman who always seems to have the right answer about property transactions.

Today, Alec is acting on behalf of a prominent accountant who has appeared at Alec's office, an official government notice clutched in his trembling fist. Alec ushers the man to a guest chair facing his sturdy oak desk and offers him a cup of ersatz coffee, the genuine item having become almost extinct after years of war. The accountant bare - ly nods his head, his shock and dread evident in his usually composed features. Accepting the china cup with a shaky grip, he lays the notice on the blotter facing Alec and runs that hand through his already rum - pled hair, making his appearance even more disheveled.

Alec places his own cup on the desk and reaches over to pick up the legal-looking paper, large print announcing the accountant and his family's order to 'relocate.'

A sympathetic expression on his face, Alec looks across at the distraught man, offering a safe platitude or two and asks what he can do for him.

The accountant lowers his eyes and says what is obvious on the notice, he has only one week to settle his affairs before being deported to Transnistria, where there were purportedly new communi -ties being constructed for Jewish émigrés.

Alec has acquired a reputation for assisting families who were being targeted for repatriation. At least, that's what the deportation is being called by bureaucrats whose offices had Nazi officers ensconced at desks situated at their elbows.

Cluj is a fair-sized town practically sitting astride the demar -cation line drawn by the Vienna Diktat. It is physically located on the Hungarian side, but Alec frequents both sides of the artificial border in his business, and his business these days is mostly to deliver these relocation notices as an agent of the government. Yet he also tries to warn members of the Jewish community when orders are about to be released. Although he possesses papers indicating he and his family are of Aryan descent, he is widely accepted as being an undercover Jew among that population, a notion that he has encouraged. His true ancestry he keeps as a closely held secret, allowing him to come and go on either side of the fence, playing the part of confidante to the Jews in dire straights and as a mediator representing the fascist aligned governments that hold sway in both Romania and Hungary.

The accountant's property is actually on the Romanian side of the boundary although his workplace is in Cluj and it is the Antonescu administration that has ordered his family's reassignment. Alec sits back with a somber frown and offers the accountant his best advice for liquidating his property and setting up an account that he will be able to access upon his arrival in Transnistria. Gradually, the ruffled accountant breathes a little easier as he nods his head in agreement with the plans Alec helps him formulate. It isn't long before they com -plete the arrangements and fill out some paperwork that will suitably settle the accountant's affairs.

Throughout all of these proceedings, a young teen, the eldest of Alec's offspring, is watching his father's machinations from the anteroom. Masterfully bringing the client from a quivering mass of panicked flesh to a more composed man who has been given a little hope, the elder Alec is earning the awe of his son. This is not the first time that he has observed his father at work. No, even he has been used as the instrument of fear by the bureaucrats, sending him to the homes and businesses of Jews to deliver the notices. The youth appears less alarming than a uniformed official as he hands the legal document to the nervous householder or merchant, during which exchange he surreptitiously informs them that his father can help them with their circumstances.

It's something of a racket. Alec manages to ease the minds of his fellow Jews (or so it's believed he shares their heritage) while mak-ing a percentage from the liquidation of their property, which is either handily turned over to the authorities, or, if Alec actually manages to legitimately sell the property, is deposited in the client's account. Either way, the families rarely have the opportunity to access those funds, since most are never heard from again.

These are lessons that his son is storing away for his future… the importance of relying on his intellect and, when necessary, sub-terfuge to survive.

Drawing himself out of his reverie, he deposited his past in a compartment deeply recessed in his mind, and refocused his vision on the newest addition to his clandestine collection. Resplendently displayed before his eyes, he is reminded of the tenets by which he conducts his life – the superior intellect with which he was endowed by nature, not by a benevolent or even a ferocious God. Oh no. It is advanced intelligence that gives him the advantage over the average, and especially the quick-witted, entrepreneur, philosopher or financier. He never believed in divine right, or any right to rule, for that matter, except by brilliant attention to the habits of man. The herd instinct is obvious among common humanity, which means there is a literal need for a shepherd, or more properly, a cattle driver. The concept makes him smile, particularly as his eye wanders across the planets as they are depicted on the lapis plaque and he recalls how this object has been considered like a staff of power to be transferred to the next in line. Well, he took the staff, the symbolic scepter, to himself using the means available – wealth. There is no heir apparent that the so-called illuminati, a conspiracy of over-heated minds run amuck, can name. The concept is anathema to him. No, there are only usurpers of power; self-made kings; men such as he. He knows too, that there is only one man of his caliber ready to seize the throne. Himself.

Having indulged himself with time spent among his treasures, he turned his attention to affairs of business before planning to return to the residential suites where his chef will have laid a simple but elegant late supper.

His office was designed more like a comfortable study, with sumptuous leather wing chairs and sofa to complement the more characteristic desk with credenza and recessed file cabinets. Sitting behind a sweeping semi-circular surface that supported two computer monitors with separate keyboards as well as the usual arrangement of a writing blotter and sundry office items including telephones, he pulled open a keyboard drawer to his left. Logging into his private database, he spent time glancing through incoming financial records and statistics regarding a few particular market trades he had been following closely, preparing for his next move. Absorbing the facts in record time, he closed out the program and logged out of his computer.

Swiveling to his right he pulled out the keyboard of the computer that he utilized to check online news and other open communication channels. He pulled up website after website touting, in the almost yellow journalistic style of the previous century, a breaking story on the untimely demise of one of the most respected journalists in the country. Olin Girard, the moderator of the most watched television network news magazine, had suffered a sudden collapse, dying instantly of what appeared to be a massive heart attack at the television studio where he was preparing to tape that week's episode.

He quickly scanned the rest of the articles and screaming headlines. Allowing himself a small smile of satisfaction, he logged off, closed down the computer, and slid the keyboard back under the lip of the polished ebony desktop.

Gold Baron

Chapter 5

Busily shuffling her attention between redesigning a promotional packet and glancing up at Fox News, Anthea was finding her concentration lagging as she updated a biography with her client's recent television appearances and trying to catch the latest stories. *Not like they don't recycle the whole thing after thirty minutes anyway,* disgusted with herself for not being better at multi-tasking. *Guess I wasn't raised right with computer games, blaring television and an i-Pod stuck in my ear all at once.* As a matter of fact, she remembered having a book tugged out of her hands by a teacher in eighth grade. Come to find out, class had been in session for ten minutes and she hadn't had a clue. *One track mind...always did get me in trouble.*

Her rambling thoughts were stripped away in an instant when she heard the breaking news that Olin Girard, Newsline's anchor and the network news bureau chief in New York, had died.

"What was that?" she caught herself speaking aloud to an empty room. Picking up the remote control, she raised the volume and listened more closely to the report.

"Girard, a hale and hearty journalist in his late forties has succumbed to what appears to be a heart attack not long after arriving at work earlier today..." the sleek brunette stated with a properly furrowed brow, showing concern while reading the teleprompter, her expressive brown eyes conveying sympathy without appearing to lose her objectivity.

A heart attack? Anthea thought about what she knows, er knew, of Olin Girard. Though she'd only met him once at a press dinner in L.A. when he was out on the West Coast covering some national story – she didn't even remember what it was – she did remember him as being the picture of health and that wasn't but a few years ago. Does your health deteriorate that quickly that you're struck down by a massive coronary in the middle of a normal workday? *It could happen.* People die every day without any hint of a previous problem, it seemed. But Girard had been one of those guys who was stable and seemed truly happy in his marriage with a couple of teenagers. He'd even published a recent book about family values, which is unusual enough for a media leader particularly when the news world is all over supporting anything and everything that undermines the traditional family. And this, of course, was the premise for his book. It wasn't bad either, she noted in her head as she skimmed across the book spines that lined her wall until her vision came to rest on the title.

Still trying to wrap her head around the fact that someone close to her own age, whom she'd met, however briefly, and who worked in a related occupation... news is news, though she'd been in print media... was dead. The inevitable ring of the phone broke through her maundering thoughts.

Lifting the receiver, she hears, "It's Toddy..."

"Who else?" she asked, half mockingly. "Wherever a conspiracy can be ferreted out, expect the call of Toddy, master of reference, research and all things arcane."

He barked out a laugh. "Yep, that's me. And I've got one now."

"Olin Girard," she cut him off.

"Of course! Men like him don't just drop dead from, what? Stress-induced heart failure when he's just back from a cruise with his wife? Relaxation must be hell on the arteries," he sniffed in disdain at the barrage of reports and conjectures pouring out of the three televisions she could hear in the background. Not to forget the two computers he had on at all times of the day or night. Anthea wasn't sure if Toddy *ever* slept.

"So you knew Girard, didn't you?"

"That's blowing it way out of proportion," she sighed at his exaggeration. "I met him once and we had a very nice chat in a social atmosphere, but that hardly certifies me as a family friend or a confidante."

"Still enough to get an idea as to whether or not he had a florid complexion or displayed any signs of high blood pressure or heart trouble," he prodded.

"I'm obviously not a doctor, but no, he didn't have broken blood vessels in his skin or appear overly ruddy faced, and his hands were elegant. No stubby ends that can be an indicator of heart irregularities."

"See, I knew you were observant," he crowed.

"Yes, well, he was something of a celebrity and I was paying attention how he held his glass of zinfandel."

"He even drank red wine. Probably health conscious," his voice softened as he absorbed the little facts. "Good physical condition?"

"From what I could tell," she shrugged into the phone. "He looked like he took care of himself and had a reputation for keeping fit. Baseball with his kids. That sort of thing.

"Okay, so bottom line. What's going through that massive head of yours?"

He was immediately more subdued. "I just think it's rather odd that the most visible news anchor, and the most respected for his unwillingness to suffer the political shuck and jive, vanishes, poof, right before the real debates begin between the candidates. We're still in the primary season and the democratic contenders have yet to deal with a single hard question from the press. Though it's my contention that you can't even call them 'press' any longer because they have abandoned the principle of objectivity, thus forsaking their calling and their profession. They are now 'editorialists.' A different animal altogether." He was fairly incensed by the whole concept of disavowing one's credo, something that Anthea knew Toddy would never do. She admitted to herself that he adjusted his conclusions according to reliable, factual and vetted data that he was perpetually seeking and assimilating, but he'd never sell out.

"I will admit that of the mainstream press corps (we will not argue the validity of the label), Girard was by far the one with clout that would be most apt to pose tough questions to buildingbridges.org's new savior, the Holy Kasili. There isn't a network news maven that has given him a run for his money yet. The democrats have shunned Fox for fear of being put to the test. Easy enough to bypass a sticky situation that way, but they wouldn't be able to sidestep Girard in the debate format." She paused briefly. "He's, ah, was, an institution. So who would, or could, drop him, if that's what you're suggesting?" Now she was intrigued by what kind of scenario he would paint for her.

"Who's backing buildingbridges.org? And who is building-bridges.org backing in the race?" As usual he waited a beat and then answered the question himself. "Scirras, of course. It's been common knowledge now for the last year. The *philanthropist*, and I use the term with derision, crawled out of his hole last year when someone finally connected the website to his money. He has been vocal about his disdain for the current administration for some time. You know he has a number of books published on his philosophy, not that anyone bothers to read the propaganda," he sneered. "For a self-proclaimed philosophy drop-out, he certainly has tried to shove his thinking down everyone else's throat."

"Even if this guy's funding is behind the 'dot org,' don't you think this idea is really crossing the line?"

"Depends on how much one believes they have the divine right to intercede on behalf of frail humanity and its inability to function on its own. This man has an unmatched ego, in my opinion. The fact that he has managed to wreak havoc in the financial markets when he feels called to do so, following his inclination for understanding the 'herd mentality' of the stock market." Toddy was getting incensed. "That's how he refers to the rest of his own kind, you know, as a 'herd' that cannot think for itself. I'm not saying that the stock market doesn't bear out some of that concept when you follow the general trends, but the fact that he has relegated everyone else to the level of cattle in relation to his own superiority… it's unacceptable," he spluttered with energy.

"Let's say, you're right. You think it's possible that Girard met his demise because he was the one who would corner Kasili, tarnishing the armor of the knight of 'change' and leaving a chink that his opponent might exploit," Anthea reasoned.

"Why not? Kasili is Prince Grigor's puppet and you can't have the royally designated successor run into a brick wall and be embarrassed by a couple of simple questions. Better to have sycophants kowtowing and licking boots, and you and I know that the so-called press fit that description with ease."

"I'm not going to deny that the mainstream media is acting as if they have the power to bestow the presidency on whoever they deem worthy, but I'm a little skeptical that Scirras, or anyone else would take out a major newsman."

"Uh-huh," he smirked into the phone. Not that she could see it, but she could hear the tenor of his voice. "What exactly happened with that brouhaha you and Gary got sucked into not long ago." It wasn't a question. "How many people died for the appropriation of land titles? We're talking the highest office in the nation here, not just some rolling hills and majestic waterfalls for someone's personal hide-away."

"I get your point."

"Also, look who they're immediately calling to pull his one foot out of the grave and replace Girard? It took them no time at all to announce that the old retiree, who has been doing nothing but slavering over Kasili in his thankfully infrequent op-eds, will be taking over the helm of Newsline. Eddinger, the republicans' tried and true warhorse won't be able to get a word in edgewise with the mainstream bunch. He's up against one of his hardest fought battles as it is, just to be heard. The only ones to give him a fair shake will be the one cable channel and talk radio. The *press* has jumped ship."

"They are indeed more fickle than a randy sailor in a whore-house on payday," Anthea gibed. "But you've got a point in that they're definitely falling all over themselves to make the candidacy of an African American into the Second Coming. No one's been immune to reading the agenda here and I believe that Kasili's background merits some scrutiny. I have a friend who has only recently left the big city newsroom and I'll bet she'd be interested in a challenge, which this seems to be. We've talked once but this puts a whole new spin on things, far-fetched as it seems," she chewed her lip.

"I'll lay money on my theory of *scirracide,*" Toddy said in all earnestness.

"An interesting twist of the tongue, but you infer this is a method rather than a single incident," Anthea said.

"Could be...could be..."

Gold Baron

Chapter 6

The two remaining democratic candidates had been running neck and neck for months. What seemed to be a runaway lead for the initial favorite had become a close race, and finally, it came down to the wire. After three days of applied pressure from the party, the initial frontrunner agreed to step aside for the Boy Wonder, but not before making her dissatisfaction felt by anyone and everyone within reach.

Governor Corinne Castor, of the Commonwealth of Pennsylvania, was just stepping down from the podium, having delivered her rather backhanded support to Yakub Hamid Kasili moments before.

The whole of the speech had been televised nationally and Kasili, along with his advisors, watched it from his campaign headquarters in Washington, D.C. where he was currently beginning his second term as congressman from Michigan. Before being elected to the House seat representing a sector of Detroit, he had served a single term as lieutenant governor of the state, an undistinguished office.

After listening to the content of Castor's remarks, Kasili frowned with displeasure. "She couldn't have been more insincere if she tried."

"What did you expect? Glowing adulation?" The campaign manager wrinkled his forehead. "Come on. Much as we want her out of this so you can work unimpeded, she has a strong base of support that about rivals yours. Forcing her out is a good step but it's gonna be a haul to get her people to just drop their druthers and back you with everything they've got. This is gonna take real work."

Kasili rubbed his neck as he paced the room. He was a tall trim man whose father had been a world-class marathon runner from Ethiopia, a man who had trained with Adebe Bikila, the barefoot Olympic gold medalist from the 1960's. Although his father had never won the gold himself, he had managed to land a scholarship at a major American university before returning to Africa to work for the government. That was where he met Kasili's mother, the daughter of a U.S. envoy to Addis Ababa who served as an observer to the Organisation of African Unity formed in 1963.

The phone rang and an assistant answered the call, tucking the handset between her ear and shoulder while she typed away on her keyboard. After a few peremptory noises of assent issued from her otherwise clamped lips, she held out the phone to the campaign manager, who, lifting his ruddy eyebrows in question, was rewarded with a brief, "DNC chair," as a reply.

The manager took the phone and after abbreviated acknowledgements remained quiet while the committee chairman gave instructions. No parting words were exchanged before he punched the 'off' button and hung up. Looking up from his seat on one of the two sofas that faced two televisions in what they called the conference room, the CM said, "We've got our marching orders."

"And they are?"

"You get to make nice with Castor tomorrow at a meeting to discuss her combining forces with yours for the campaign. You're going to have to kiss some major butt," he grinned.

"No joke," the assistant added under her breath. "We're talkin' one big ass there."

The CM shot her a look that said, "Can it," but didn't actually open his mouth.

Kasili gave a short laugh, then sobered. "What do we concede?"

"You? You don't concede anything, that's her job, but you're going to have to act like you really want her as part of the team. Maybe even make it look like the ticket is open, since that's what her banshees are already screaming for, according to the chairman."

"So, when do we have this confab and where."

"It's got to be on neutral ground. If we go to the governor's mansion in Harrisburg, it'll look like you're groveling and if she comes to you, she'll lose face. Considering that the primaries were so close, we have to coax her to ante up her supporters," said the CM.

"She's in a very powerful position," threw in an advisor, a senior senator from a midwest state who until now had been keeping his thoughts to himself. "She has almost half the committed delegates and, as I'm sure you noticed, she did not release them to you. This is a suspended campaign and she could rise up in revolt at any time." He ran a hand through a thick graying mane, and aimed his piercing blue gaze on Kasili. "She is a caged lioness."

"And that cage door hasn't been locked," continued the CM.

"Yet…" added Kasili narrowing his eyes with determination. "Just point me in the right direction and we're good."

The CM raised his eyes from his PDA where he had been entering the information on the upcoming conference, which was to happen the next day. "Don't get overconfident. She has decades of experience in pitted battle. The Castors have been a driving force in national politics for a long time. Their favor has to be curried. You are hardly safe, but we're getting there."

The meeting broke up almost immediately with the CM wandering off to follow-up on plans and the senator shaking Kasili's hand and heading home. Kasili, alone with his personal assistant, muttered almost to himself, "Oh, I think I'm safe. More than you'll know." He then nodded at his assistant, giving her the high sign to make a call.

❈ ❈ ❈

Solana had been watching the concession speech that Governor Castor delivered to a packed audience of devotees, most of who filled the room with noises more suited to a disgruntled crowd than loyal democrats. Her curiosity had been revived in the seesaw between the two players. An odd battlefield between two firsts in terms of candidacy: a woman and a black man. *The perfect PC skir - mish. No one can say anything about the other for fear of being labeled a racist or a chauvinist. No wonder I'd lost interest. Boring...* She decided she'd call Anthea for her take on the speech.

"So what's your assessment of the Castor concession," Sol asked once she had Anthea on the line.

"If that's what you want to call it," Anthea stopped to turn down the television. The fireworks were over for the time being anyway. "I find it hard to believe that she'd roll over after showing that she still carries a lot of clout with her delegate numbers. Someone must have had a really big gun."

"Or one of her skeletons was ready to escape the closet," said Sol.

Anthea was quiet for a second. "I wonder if Girard's death had any bearing on the situation."

"Now that's a new one," Sol fell back in her office chair with surprise. "How'd you arrive at that incredibly strange conclusion?"

"Oh, you just have to have a wild imagination and be able to picture subterfuge behind every door," She didn't quite chuckle, thinking it was funny but all things considered, not really amusing.

Sol let it pass but made a note on her pad, *Girard?* "Well, Castor's not going to fade into the woodwork. That's not going to happen with this woman. She's all steel."

"Yeah, just like the steel mills that are disappearing from her home state maybe she's been targeted for obsolescence too."

"You're too clever by half, girl." Sol wagged her head side to side. "But you may not be far off the mark. A lot of people seem to think that this country has had enough of the Castors over the years." The governor's husband, Dean, had served three terms as senator from Missouri before being drafted to fill the vice president's slot on the democratic ticket. That administration held office for eight years but Castor wasn't able to capture the White House one more time for the democrats as the heir apparent. There were a few too many scandals emanating from the vice presidential residence, and his reputation as having a wandering eye and a randy disposition pretty much put the kibosh on his aspirations to the highest office in the land.

After the fiasco of a close but decisive loss to the republican contender, the missus made a run for the office of governor in her home state of Pennsylvania, winning handily against a relative unknown. The republican incumbent had decided not to run again after his own run-in with scandal and gossip.

Anthea switched gears. "Has my friend Toddy called you yet?"

"As a matter of fact, we had a conversation just the other day. A fascinating take on the world, or so it seemed, considering he was way ahead of me in some places. I don't consider myself slow, but it's a trial to keep abreast of his concepts. He would have run circles around me if I hadn't made him stop and reiterate what he was explaining in layman's terms."

A laugh emanated from the receiver into Sol's ear. "That's Toddy. It takes a lot to stick with him, but if you do and you make him repeat it until you get it, the time is well spent." She chuckled again.

"He drives Gary to distraction with his rapid fire speech pattern, though he has less trouble than I do assimilating the information. Must be a personality thing."

"Gary doesn't like him?" Solana was interested in Anthea's husband's opinion.

"Oh, he likes him well enough considering the fact that they've never met face-to-face. It's just a difference in style because both of them are linguists after their own fashion. Gary with foreign languages and Toddy with semantics, word origins and computer languages." She laughed again, "I'm surrounded by geniuses. Would be nice if I could just keep up."

"But you do. Man, if you can follow Toddy's train of thought, you are hovering in the realm of brilliance yourself, by my thinking. Anyway, he has so captivated me with his off-the-wall theories that I'm contemplating cashing in some vacation time and heading to the Southwest for a little sightseeing and maybe to check out a few things. Visit some old and new friends."

"You must have been talking quite a bit in order to decide to travel all the way down there," said Anthea, a note of surprise in her voice.

"Well, I've actually been planning on a trip to New Mexico to visit some college buddies. I'll stop along the way to see Mom and Neta in Montana and drop by Denver for a day or so. The 'down home tour,' you might say. So, it's not such a stretch to meet your pal in Ruidoso. Besides, it's a great place to visit. Artsy, lots of charm, even a campus of Eastern New Mexico University."

"Oh yes, I remember. Toddy teaches there sometimes," filled in Anthea. "I'd say it sounds like a plan worth implementing… travel and fact finding all rolled into one."

"You two have reeled me in and I want to learn some more, maybe dig around a little in this politico-environmentalist-currency agenda. Determine if there even is such an animal," said Sol.

Anthea cocked her brow as if to impart some prudence, even though she was on the telephone and Sol couldn't see her features. "A word of caution. Watch your step and definitely watch your back. Unfortunately, I know whereof I speak. What may appear to be an innocuous treasure hunt could lead down some dangerous roads." She sighed a little.

"You read about all the nefarious activities of the group that Gary and I ended up confronting. You should know that it was mostly accidental that we stumbled across the scheme. And I *mean* stumbled." Anthea tried to be reassuring but wanted to make sure Sol understood how devious these folks could be. When Gary had literally tripped over thugs employed by the Nature's Wilds Conservancy two years before, he had let his hunches get himself and his then new acquaintance, Anthea, drawn into an investigation of what turned out to be a highly organized land acquisition scheme. It had turned out that a few very powerful individuals were gobbling up ranches, farms and undeveloped acreage – millions of acres – under the guise of a preservation group. They were going so far as to displace families by means fair, but mostly foul. Including murder. "Curiosity damn near did get us killed and I want you to promise that you'll be careful when you go rooting around for information. Journalism is not supposed to be a life-threatening occupation."

Sol filed the admonition away as being somewhat overly dramatic since she'd never read about anything quite so sinister as Anthea was implying. But then, she also knew that the case was still in process and a good deal of information would be withheld during the ongoing investigation.

"I shall heed your words," Sol replied, "but I don't plan on doing much more than flushing out some information. My idea of investigative journalism does not include going behind enemy lines or getting in the line of fire," she tried to lighten the mood after Anthea's solemn warning.

"I'll keep you informed of all my inquiries and what they yield, though I suspect that you'll hear everything from Toddy as soon as anything pops up. Can you e-mail me all of the information and theories you've developed so far? I want to go over it and see if I can't make sense of everything you two wiz kids have been attempting to teach me. Hopefully, I will prove to be an apt pupil."

"No problem," agreed Anthea. "I'll correlate what I have and send it out. It'll take a couple of hours to compile. By the way," she added with a tinge of mischief, "you'd better make sure you contact Lainie regularly too. She'll have a fit if she finds out you're off chasing shadows. She is *very* pregnant and not that far removed from delivering your great-niece. And, if you'll pardon the expression, you know she'll be on the warpath at the drop of a hat, or should I say 'feather'?"

Sol laughed hard enough that she had to wipe tears from her eyes. "You *do* know Lainie well. Stoic as a post until you tick her off. But she told me they didn't know what sex the baby is. How do *you* know?

"I don't. Just a feeling. Strong women in the family…"

Two hours later, Solana was at home, parked in front of her own computer busily opening all of the attachments that Anthea forwarded. There was so much that it didn't take long to realize it would take half the night just to skim through the data.

Figuring it was a toss-up on where to start reading, she decided that personalities make the play. Develop the character and the dots should connect as the story unfolds, or so she hoped.

Having made her decision, she opened the file with a bio of Scirras. *Well, he is the main character, I think.* Right away, she saw how sketchy it was.

As she scrolled down one page after another it was evident that he'd done an impressive job of keeping his past something of a mystery because the pages were riddled with conflicting information.

He's Hungarian. He's Romanian.

He's Jewish. His father was a Nazi sympathizer.

He helped the Jews settle their estates. He benefited from the Jews' misfortunes.

He was a poor refugee from a war-torn nation. He managed to underwrite an education at the Britain School of Economics.

He is an unknown entity. He heads up of one of the richest hedge funds in the world.

He has no real assets. He leverages billions in a coup that nearly crashes the Bank of Britain.

He was a philosophy student who couldn't grasp his renowned philosophy professor and mentor's concepts. He is exporting the very same concepts to politically rocky nations in his philanthropic work. Solana wondered, so how can that happen if he didn't 'get it'?

He's all about making billions of dollars.

He's all about giving away billions of dollars.

Who *is* this guy? We really don't know where he came from or where he got his start. Look at this… he worked as a drudge at Claridge's and at some fancy restaurant, Cesarés, that catered to movie stars and the criminal underworld, yet he managed to pay for a first class education after coming to England as an impoverished teenage refugee? The confusing jumble of contradictory information was making her crazy. The man was a failed philosophy student but a dazzling money manager that could play currencies and political principles against each other. And, on top of that, Anthea was certain that he was somehow involved in arms dealing, and Solana knows that Anthea's memory was crisp and assured, not to be easily doubted.

Solana decided it was time to put in a call to Toddy. Okay, so it was one a.m. According to Anthea he never slept anyway.

That wasn't much help, she told herself an hour later. Consuming a pot of coffee and taking notes while trying to absorb everything he was espousing left her with little more than a pounding headache. She was worse off after the conversation than when she started because, *now*, she was trying to factor in gold markets and worldwide gold production, and, and, how did that relate to gunrunning and politics?! Oh, and let's not forget, environmentalism run rampant. Ay, ay, ay…

Enough is enough. She closed down the computer and went to bed.

Later in the morning, her head cleared some after a few hours of only intermittent sleep, Sol got up and padded to the kitchen. She gulped down a huge glass of water and made another pot of coffee. Looking up at the clock, it said '7:30,' she figured she had a couple hours before she needed to show up at the office. Then she'd give Drury his instructions for running the paper while she was gone. He'd have no trouble.

Hoping it wasn't too early, even though it felt like the crack of dawn to her, Sol picked up the receiver and dialed Anthea's number.

The phone rang a few times and a husky voice answered with the ever popular, "Hello?"

"Oh. I'm sorry if I dragged you out of bed. This is Sol. Are you awake enough to try to straighten out all the kinks Toddy put in my thought processes?"

"Sure. I'm awake. I just don't sound it. Generally takes half the morning before I appear human. Ask Gary." Sol heard a grunt of agreement that seemed to come from somewhere in the background. Smiling, she pressed onward.

"Good, because after talking to him in an effort to understand the cross-currents of information that lurked within all those files you sent, I came away without much more than a confusion induced headache, for which I took two aspirin and called *you* in the morning."

Anthea laughed and said she'd try to help but couldn't guarantee anything.

"Good enough. I'll take what I can get and I know that you and I, at the very least, speak the same language." She mulled over what question to ask first. "Okay, let's start with the Jewish/maybe not Jewish angle on Scirras. What is he and why sell yourself as something you're not? It can't be that hip to be Jewish."

"Think about it," answered Anthea. "You're the one who was telling me that it's almost a fad to be Indian. Well, that's exaggerating, but you know, the wannabe thing and if you are a minority it gives you bragging rights... kind of. Well, the Jewish thing isn't much different. If you claim to be Jewish then you can get away with anti-Semitic remarks."

"Why would Scirras be anti-Semitic?" *Oh, Lord, this was going to be worse than I thought.*

"Let's start with his rationale for asserting that he has Jewish heritage which principles, by the way, he eschews according to his own writing and biography. By claiming he's Jewish he creates the aura of being both someone who is persecuted *and* becoming a target for the anti-Semite charge that Jews are the financial evildoers and economic lords. He's playing both ends against the middle. A valuable lesson he learned from his father during the Nazi occupation when the elder Scirras both worked for the Fascists delivering notice of deportation to his Jewish neighbors and, *then*, playing the sympathetic helper who settled their estates. All for profit, of course."

"How could anyone be so calculating," Sol was having trouble grasping the concept.

"Hey, look back on your own people's history," Anthea reminded. "There were some similar occurrences, all instigated by supposedly well-meaning non-Natives. Unfortunately, humanity can be ruthless and callous far too often.

"Back to Scirras. He's made public statements that the Jews create anti-Semitism through pursuing the Zionist ideal of creating an independent state for self-protection. It demonstrates a complete lack of understanding or appreciation of Jewish history, i.e. centuries of discrimination and persecution. And let's not forget ghettoes, which most people don't know were first developed during the dark ages in what is now Italy to separate the Jewish population from the Christians.

"He's also ignorant of the basis of anti-Semitism. It grew out of a misunderstanding of their religious beliefs and cultural distinctions by invading forces (and here I'm talking about in the Holy Land before the destruction of Jerusalem in 70 A.D.) and, later, the surrounding larger populations after Jews had been dispersed through Europe by the Roman Empire, mostly as slaves." She stopped for a moment and then said. "Bet that sounds analogous too."

"Do people never learn from history?" Sol asked to the air, but Anthea answered.

"No, because we forget to be good students of history. I just happen to be fascinated by it. Sort of makes me a boring character."

"Hardly. I didn't expect that this would end up being such a worthy lesson."

"Thanks for the vote of confidence, because there's more," warned Anthea. "He's also ignorant of the scapegoat mentality, which proliferated in the Gentile populace despite its Judaic basis. By this I mean that the idea of a scapegoat arose from the Temple rites of sacrificing an unblemished lamb or goat after the priest symbolically placed the sins of the people on the head of the animal. This you'll recognize as the foreshadow of Christian tradition that Jesus Christ is the Lamb of God, the perfect, unblemished One who, by taking the sins of believers unto Himself and then sacrificing all, was the fulfillment of the blood sacrifice that had been performed ceremonially for centuries."

"I didn't expect to have a little theology thrown in, too," said Sol, lightheartedly.

"Unfortunately, all of this longwindedness is related to the reason the modern state of Israel was formed. I apologize."

"Don't. I'm enjoying the schooling. Go on," Sol prompted. "I just wish I'd thought to tape it. I'm getting writer's cramp."

"So, it comes down to the fact that if you are a Jew (or, in his case, claim to be), you can pretty much get away with saying what you want regarding your own heritage. I don't believe that he *is* Jewish, but by claiming to be so, he can take a stand against Israel without suffering the consequences of his words. He holds Zionism to be a thorn in the side of the Arabic world, which is where most of the investors in his Herculaenea Fund come from, there and Europe. When he started the fund, hedge funds were not sanctioned in the United States and he based it in Aruba with foreign investors. American citizens were barred from investing in them, which is another quandary because he was a naturalized citizen and yet he managed to own a percentage of Herculaenea.

"Herculaenea has been deeply involved in the gold market, leveraging it against the dollar. The U.S. is the major supporter of Israel and our dollar is deflating against the euro, the yen, the pound and gold. Gold is where Islamic republics are hedging their bets. Iran, not long ago, traded 17.5 billion worth of assets for gold and they're not alone. By sponsoring the rise of gold, he is supporting the power drive of oil-rich nations that do not have the best interests of the United States or Israel at heart.

"Now, if Scirras claims to be a Jewish refugee from Nazi-run central Europe who has managed to make good in the financial world, and is now known and lauded for his philanthropy, he places himself above condemnation. And, maybe suspicion." She paused for a beat.

"Not sure I get the suspicion part," said Sol.

"Well, if you were Jewish but were managing billions of dollars of assets for oil-rich Arabs – and, you should know that the investor list of Herculaenea is confidential – it would be hard for the rest of the world to accept that you just *might* not be pro-American, in the economic sense, anyway. I think that Scirras has used what is basically a false identity to create a sympathetic response to his philanthropy (which, personally, I don't think it is at all). He paints himself as a Hungarian Elie Wiesel, even though he never spent any time near a Nazi death camp and never lost a loved one to the depredation of the Nazis. Wiesel, on the other hand, a Romanian Jew, escaped the hands of the Germans and became a well-respected journalist, a hero of the Holocaust and an advocate of Israel. Scirras is using the image to *undermine* Israel and boost the power of terrorist and terrorist leaning nations."

"Good Lord, *why?*" Solana was incredulous and shocked by the possibility.

"Power. Could be that it all comes down to an attempt to keep the American public from wielding any control over energy resources. Devaluing the dollar keeps oil at an astronomically high price, which adds to the coffers of prospective enemies, and, although we have resources that could be developed here in our own backyard, Congress and environmentalists are tying the hands of oil companies to do so. It keeps America under the thumb of foreign interests and underwrites an economic slide."

"But why?" Sol was trying to digest the concept. "I still don't get a motive. This is all far too convoluted for me to grasp."

"All of it comes down to attempting to shift the balance of power outside of the U.S., I think, though I don't get it either. Just the lure of power seems to be the answer. But then, I'm not pathological in my thinking, are you? The one must surely be related to the other."

"I wouldn't consider myself pathological, but then my 'ex' might disagree." She attempted to inject a little levity then took a deep breath.

"I'm planning on leaving for Montana tomorrow," added Sol. "It's a nice long drive. Plenty of time for some of this to sink in... I hope."

Chapter 7

The week's paper long since gone to press and Drury installed as the acting editor-in-chief, his choice of title for his temporary position, which she felt was no skin off her nose to bestow, Solana was busy packing her belongings into the back of her Chevy Tahoe. Sol had made a fair living while working at the Denver Post, not that being a star reporter is all that well-paid a position. However, not being one to blow her money on fashion items such as Jimmy Chu shoes or Coach handbags, she had spent her hard-earned dollars on a 4x4 with all the options – satellite radio, MP3 player, heated seats (a real luxury during cold Colorado winters) and the like. Her ex-boyfriend had supplied the necessary fashion accessories to be certain she looked the part of a gentleman rancher's companion (though she would hardly call his actions chivalrous).

Although the rig had all the electronic amenities, it was also outfitted for hauling a horse trailer and even sported a gun rack in the rear. Sol had grown up in the high country of southern Montana and could dress out a deer as well as any of her uncles who'd trained her early on during hunting trips in the Absaroka Mountains. She did love to travel and was apt to jump in the truck for a trip whenever an opportunity offered itself.

Before she headed out to her family's ranch near Livingston, Montana, she'd dropped by to see Lainie the night before. Sol shook her head as she recalled the encounter. Boy, if that girl wasn't as stubborn as her mother, *well, and me too, I guess.* Cisco had just sat back on the sofa, coolly observing his wife's pique, though she'd tried to conceal it. His barely visible smirk wafting fleetingly across his lips when Sol caught his eye.

Lainie wasn't happy with her aunt's decision to go on a wild goose chase.

"And who said anything about chasing wild geese?" Sol had asked. "I'm just on a vacation to visit Mom, *your* mom and some friends back in New Mexico."

Lainie had given her a narrowed look. "I haven't heard you talk about anyone in New Mexico in years. What's so special down there now?" She was a little peeved that the one family member she could rely on was 'abandoning' her as she was about to enter her seventh month of pregnancy and seemed to be expanding across the middle daily.

Looking back on it, Sol thought that no one had a command of the guilt factor to the extent that Lainie had mastered it. She'd asked her outright about 'some man' that Sol was going to visit in Ruidoso.

Sol was stunned and amused at the insinuation and just asked her how she knew she was going to visit 'some man'? Trying to back off and play coy, Lainie had just lifted her shoulders, momentarily closed her eyes in mock innocence and said nothing.

"Well, if you already know so much, why the third degree? What are you so peeved about?"

"I'm worried about you. We had enough excitement around here the last time someone," and she slid her eyes sideways to indicate the big house next door, Anthea's house, "went traipsing off to just 'check out a little information.'"

Sol dropped her head back briefly and raised her gaze to the ceiling. "Oy vey," she'd breathed, an expression she'd acquired while interning in New York. Looking her niece in the eye again, "Don't get so upset. I'm just off for a little rest and relaxation and seeing how excitable you're becoming, I'm sure you can agree that I could use it. Store up a little calm before we get any closer to your due date." She had inhaled. "Don't worry. All I'm doing is enjoying a well-deserved road trip."

With that, she had hugged her niece, given Cisco a look that said "keep an eye on her" and slipped out the door.

Since she'd been in the neighborhood, so to speak, she also dropped by to check in with Anthea and Gary before hitting the road. Letting them know that Lainie was going to require a bit of attention, Sol asked if they wouldn't mind calling on her occasionally to make sure she was doing all right. They'd said there wouldn't be a problem. Gary was getting used to dealing with expectant mothers again, having been on call during his daughter's pregnancies.

Finally feeling that circumstances were handled, if not actually under control, Sol steered her Tahoe toward home and caught a good night's rest.

Being somewhat obsessive about work, Solana decided to make one last stop at the office. On her way in, she pulled into a drive-through espresso stand and ordered two drinks to take with her.

After parking on the street, she climbed out of the driver's seat, grabbed her handbag and the two coffees, crossed the overgrown grass bank that doubled as a curb, and shouldered her way through the front door at the paper. Drury was hidden behind the partition that created her office cubicle, no part of him visible around the oversized monitor as she leaned her head in the opening that should have had a door but didn't.

She placed a latté on the desk next to him, "This is number one. I still owe you 4,311, but don't get your hopes up that you'll see them in this lifetime."

"What, no pastry?" He poked his head around the side of the computer screen, a big smile splitting his gnome-like face.

"You're on a diet, remember? And don't get too comfortable in that chair. I'll be back in two weeks."

"I have no hope of supplanting an ace journalist of your stature," he quipped looking up at her.

"Hm-hmmm. Is that a tall joke?"

"Nope, just a tall tale." He took a sip of the coffee. "Oooh, cinnamon. You didn't forget. I thought you might, considering how long it's been since you bought." He raised his thick brown eyebrows in a respectable impression of a leprechaun. He wasn't much bigger than one, in Sol's estimation, but his abilities and intellect far outstripped the requirements of his job. There were times when she wondered what a kid with his abilities was doing out here in the boonies. He could definitely make it in the city at a major daily if he wanted. But then, maybe he wondered what she was doing here, too.

"Just consider yourself fortunate that I remember your name." She cocked her head and asked, "Drury is an interesting name, come to think of it. Know where it came from?"

"Mom mentioned once that it was a favorite name of her mother's. Some actor I think. Having an odd name helps with the ladies," he waggled his brows in an attempt to look flirtatious.

She laughed. "Right." She considered. "Bet your grandmother liked TV westerns."

"Yeah, she did, actually. How'd you know?" His face looked all of his twenty-four years.

"The Virginian. My parents loved the old shows from the sixties."

"The Virginian?" he looked querulous. "What's that?"

"A role made famous by James Drury. A very slick, understated character. Man of mystery. Might give you something to aspire to," she winked. "Anyway, I'm outtahere if you're all set."

"Yup. Got it all covered, no sweat," he said with confidence.

"Well, you've got my cell number if you need me, but I'd prefer that you didn't need me for the next week or so."

"Whatever you say, boss lady. We're just gonna round up them doggies," and he elongated the 'o', "before we bed down for the night."

Sol just rolled her eyes, tossed her purse over her shoulder and headed for the door while Drury sang the theme to Bonanza with all the words sounding like "dun ta da, dun ta da, dun ta da, dun ta da, dunh daaa...."

✳ ✳ ✳

Getting a late start, Sol took her time winding her way up U.S. 12 that ran beside the Lochsa River through one of the most scenic areas in Idaho. The road twisted through the steepening walls of the canyon, tall conifers lining the mountainsides that plunged toward the swift flowing waters of the crystal river. Bluebirds flitted from tree to tree, creating bright streaks of cobalt slicing across the otherwise green panorama of pine forests. Scattered among the velvety, dark verdure of the trees, were stands of dead and dying brown shafts, skeletal fingers reaching for the sky. A testament to ravages of the pine beetle and, where the trunks were blackened, fires that had swept the area two years before. Even among the layers of ash and needles though, young saplings were beginning to sprout through the detritus, proclaiming new life.

Sol looked on the landscape as an old friend, having traveled the route year after year while growing up and, later, to reach family in between stints of work in the metropolitan areas of the West and on the Eastern Seaboard. The sectors of acreage that wore the injury of fire and pestilence were a sight she'd come to accept, however sorrowful it was to see the destruction that had raced through parts of the breathtaking landscape. Having been raised among the deep woods and craggy mountain escarpments of Montana and Idaho, she also knew that some of the harm suffered by the forest was more due to the interference of man in the normal course of nature. Decades of fire suppression instituted by government as a forest management policy had created stands of trees made vulnerable to flames and insects. The unchecked accumulation of natural debris on the forest floor provided a ready torch for spark or lightning, and the diseased trees that would have been claimed by periodic purging remained as upright lures for parasites.

Driving through the canyons was still a balm to her senses, though, taking her back to a calmer and contented time from her youth, before she became aware of the wider world and the contrasting anguish and joy that lay outside her own home.

Letting her gaze travel up the rock walls that were scored with fairylike rivulets slipping over the boulders, she caught sight of an eagle, wings outstretched, floating on an updraft.

Sighing, she quickly refocused on the curving road as it made a sweeping turn alongside the current rushing rapidly to her right.

A few hours later, Sol drove down the eastside of the mountain pass and, deciding that she wasn't in any particular hurry, pulled under the portico of a motel that flanked the banks of the Clark Fork in Missoula. She had stopped along the way for an early supper at a popular steakhouse on her route, so she wasn't hungry. Instead of entertaining the thought of any more food, she opted for unpacking her laptop and going online to do a little more research on the different subjects that both Anthea and Toddy had adamantly asserted were connected. All of which they thought led to unsavory conclusions. Well, much as she trusted Anthea's nose for a solid story, Solana didn't know Toddy – *yet. That will be remedied in less than a week.* But until then she needed to verify their sources for herself.

Googling everything about the players they'd mentioned and the topics of mining related to land use and environmental activism, among other things, she accessed website after website, news page after news page. There were tidbits of information that, if you were slyly creative, tied together by slender, if not downright undetectable, threads. The more she read, the more Sol wondered how her friends had managed to think to string these seemingly far-flung issues into an actual pattern that still eluded her for the most part. *Elusive but not unimaginable in a devious way. Whoever came up with this round - about manner of asserting influence or control… I think that's the word they used… has got to be certifiable. Or a genius.*

While she was typing away at her keyboard and scrolling through the different sites, Sol had the television on in the background. When the national evening news came on, she perked up her ears as she heard the name Olin Girard mentioned. Grabbing the remote control, she increased the volume and paid attention to the coverage that was unfolding of what was practically a state funeral.

Since when does a news bureau chief rate a memorial to prac - tically rival that of an elected official? The services had been held at the National Cathedral and looked to be attended by every loudmouth politico and TV talking head in existence. Even the president and the first lady put in an appearance. Sol was dumbfounded at the pomp that surrounded Girard's send-off. Granted the guy was well liked and had been a principal in network news for twenty years, but even Chet Huntley and David Brinkley, anchor icons for some forty years, hadn't rated anything of this magnitude. She glanced down at the notes she had scribbled when she'd talked to Anthea a couple nights before and her eyes alighted on the memo, *Girard.* Her head started whirling with even more sordid possibilities. Disgusted with the turn her thoughts were taking, she muted the television and gave her computer screen her undivided attention.

Continuing well into the wee hours of the morning, Sol found odd links that raised more questions than they answered. All she could do was wonder at herself for getting drawn into what was essentially the wild goose chase her niece accused her of following. As she closed down her computer she thought, *but, this could be just what the doc -*

tor ordered to cure my boredom… not to mention fun.

After gassing up and stopping at one of the countless espresso drive-ins that seemed to dot the Northwest with one on practically every block, Sol figured that she'd better get her shot of caffeine to go here. Missoula didn't have as many outlets as Idaho and Washington towns but once she crested the Continental Divide, coffee bars became as scarce as the general populace in Montana and she wasn't likely to find as many options down the road.

Interstate 90 ran beside the Clark Fork as it wound along the bottom of a narrow valley for quite a distance. Being in too much of a rush could be problematic if a driver tried to take some of the turns at the posted speed of 70 mph that was on some stretches. Log trucks and semis on long hauls traversed this northernmost corridor of the interstate highway system with regularity. Speeding around the bends could run you smack up against the slower moving rear end of a load of lumber with no place to go. Not that that stopped the locals, who could have driven the road blindfolded, from whipping past. Sol probably could have fit right in with the last category of drivers as well as she knew the freeway, but she held herself back, reminding herself that she was on vacation, not in a race. Years of always tackling a clock and trying to beat deadlines made it a real challenge for her to slow down, despite her upbringing in the country. She just inhaled deeply and forced herself to reduce the pace. There were still fours hours to go to get home.

Home was a small ranch south of Livingston, tucked away alongside a tributary to the Yellowstone River, a swift moving creek except at the end of summer. And cold. The water poured down from the high mountain peaks, fed by winter snows, not all of which melted during the hot months of the year. On the few scorching days of August that stream had been a crisp and cool respite from the rising temperatures when she was a teenager, riding through the meadows with her sister, Neta.

Sol smiled as she passed another vehicle heading uphill. It'll be nice to be home for a couple of days. Maybe spell Neta from her duties helping Mom around the house. Since their father had died a few years before, their mother had been having a bit of a tough time with her health. The accident had been a blow to both Mama Ciel and Neta. Their father Gaspar and Neta's husband, Frank Pearl, had been driving back from Idaho along US 12, the same route Sol was following on this trip, during a thaw in February. They'd hit a patch of black ice, spun out and off the road into the Lochsa, which was half iced-over. Neither one had made it out of the truck. Ciel's brother Allen, who was partner in the ranch that had been passed down to the two of them from their father and grandfather, had taken over general operations. Carstairs' Ranch bred Appaloosas as well as training and supplying packhorses to outfitters in Montana and northern Wyoming. Most of their clients worked out of places like Red Lodge and Gardiner, taking out hunters and recreational riders into the rugged uplands of the Absaroka Mountains on the outskirts of Yellowstone National Park. It wasn't a bad living, but over recent months, Ciel's blood pressure had spiked and it took awhile before the doctors narrowed the cause down to a complication of previously undiagnosed diabetes.

Neta had been able to take a leave of absence from her position at the hospital in Lewiston in order to come back to Montana to help their mother while her hypertension and blood sugar levels were stabilized, leaving Solana to keep an eye on Neta's daughter, Lainie, when she found out she was in the family way.

Sol watched a small herd of antelope spring away into the high grass as she sped around one of the last curves in the road before the turnoff to the ranch, their white hindquarters flashing amid the swaying black-eyed daisies and tall seedheads. Just another few miles.

Sol turned onto the lane that ran up to the house, which lay past fenced hayfields, a couple of paddocks near a barn and an open lawn that stretched easily across two acres that was freshly mowed. Grandpa Allen was still seated in the metal saddle of the Kubota that more resembled a tractor than a lawnmower. As he shut down the motor he heard Solana's Tahoe rumbling up the drive, and hitching up his slim trousers over hips that belied the ample stomach stretching the front of his Aloha shirt, ambled toward the sound.

She stopped the truck in front of the house, pulled the key out of the ignition and climbed out of the cab. By the time she was standing beside the Tahoe and pocketing her keys, Allen had come around the back of the rig and was leaning onto a straight arm supported against the side of the car, waiting patiently for her to turn around and greet him.

Allen actually stood an inch shorter than his niece, having lost a little height to age with the beginnings of a stooped stance. Both Neta and Sol took after their father, who had stood over 6'3". Allen's own father, Ollie Carstairs had been just 5'9", a rough and tumble cowboy who'd snagged himself a statuesque wife from the Crow Nation. Their wedding photo that still graced the mantelpiece in the living room, showed them side-by-side, matching eye levels. Lena had dark flawless skin stretched tight over high, elegant cheekbones, glossy black hair swept around her neck to fall across her shoulder all the way to the waist of her white lace gown, a delicate flounce brushing the top of her elaborately beaded moccasins. Ollie had been ten years older than she, hazel eyes crinkling in the sun, his face cracked by the widest smile he'd ever sported in his life, and one that appeared so rarely on his stoic countenance that anyone who knew him would swear he kept it in a jar where only Lena could access it. Both of them had been gone for nigh on twenty years.

Allen looked like his father except for dark eyes and darker hair. Neta and Sol had both attained a height closer to that of their father and grandmother, Neta having inherited the hazel eyes that twinkled just the way Ollie's had whenever he saw his children and grandkids.

"So, you gonna give the old man a hug, or what?"

"My, aren't we testy and impatient," she said as she leaned forward to squeeze him around the middle.

"Hey, girl, watch that paunch," he grinned. "I been concentratin' a lotta effort on buildin' this, so don't squeeze the stuffin' outta me. It ain't Thanksgiving."

"Baloney. It's always Thanksgiving when I come home. Bet Mom's even got a dressed turkey on the menu."

"Whole lot you know. Fresh trout from the river. Caught it this mornin'," he informed her as he pulled away and looked deep into her eyes, a glint of mischief sparkling in the depths of his own.

"Can't wait. I haven't had any time to go fishing myself this year and I really miss that quiet time sitting by the water just waiting for a nibble," she said a little wistfully as they left the side of the Tahoe and climbed the steps onto the porch. Just as they reached the top stair, Mama Ciel emerged from the doorway, pushing aside the screen door wide enough to allow herself to slip out onto the weathered decking. She was about sixty, iron gray hair forming a streak that ran from the left side of her widow's peak behind her ear, blending into a salt and mostly pepper cap of wavy hair that was cut just below her jawline. Ciel stood a few inches shorter than her daughter and almost appeared underweight, the opposite of what most people imagine to be the typical body mass of a diabetic.

A wide smile spread across Ciel's face as she exited the doorway, Sol stepping quickly forward to catch her mother in a solid embrace, patting her back. Pulling back a little, but still keeping her arms wrapped around her mother's slight frame, Sol examined her face, her notice tracing the careworn lines that bracketed Ciel's eyes and mouth.

"How're you feeling, Mom?"

"Not bad. Neta's watching my medication like a hawk and noting everything with her little pad and pencil," she frowned a little. "Darn girl carries it everywhere, and then gives a full report to the doctors like I was an invalid or somethin'." Neta was a respiratory therapist by trade and took the recording of her mother's statistical information seriously.

"Come on, Mom, you know I just want to make sure the new meds are working right," spouted Neta, sticking her head through the screen door as she held it open.

Ciel just wagged her head side to side and walked past her older daughter back inside grumbling something about leaving a woman alone to look after herself. "I'm not incapable of takin' care of myself, girl," they heard as she moved into the entryway.

Neta just smiled at her mother's back and stepped outside to welcome her little sister. "She's been doing things on her own for so long that any help is just an unwanted nuisance," she sighed.

Wrapping an arm across her sister's shoulders, Neta looked across at Uncle Allen. "Dinner'll be ready in an hour. Is there anything you need help with before then?"

"I can mind the ranch, girly," he snipped half-heartedly, a slight smirk turning up the corner of his mouth. "You just keep an eye on your mother. There's nothin' wrong with me," and he winked before moving off to put the mini-tractor in the barn.

"Let me know if you want help feeding the horses," Neta called after his retreating back. He just grunted and lifted his hand behind him to wave her off as he walked away, like he was swatting at a pesky fly.

"Those two. They really don't need me around that much," observed Neta. "Uncle's got enough help to get everything done and as soon as Mom is stabilized she'll be more than happy to see me hit the road," she chuckled.

"It must be a family trait," said Sol.

"What?" Neta quirked an eyebrow waiting for an explanation.

"Independence. Not one of us likes to be bossed around."

"True enough, true enough. Better come in, Mom will have some chore or other for us any minute now," and she ushered Sol into the house, allowing the screen to close of its own volition.

The next couple of days were filled with helping around the ranch. Weeding Ciel's garden, collecting eggs from the small flock of chickens that wandered around the barn pecking the ground for feed, separating horses and working the colts.

The second afternoon she was there, Sol saddled up one her favorite Appy mares, Seraphim, and rode out to the creek, which was still running swiftly and fairly deep with early summer run-off. The trail was narrow and rocky but the horse knew the path well and picked her way among the stones carefully. Sol was just interested in maintaining an easy gait, taking the opportunity to enjoy the relative quiet of the meadows stretching across the high valley. They unintentionally flushed a cluster of sage grouse whose noisy flight interrupted the calm of the day. A hare or two jetted from underfoot and a couple of white tail took off through the grass, streaking toward a stand of ponderosa pine. Just the usual denizens of the terrain following the natural order of life.

That evening, Sol sank into the couch next to Neta and

watched the news. Ciel was rocking in her chair, knitting a receiving blanket for Lainie's baby while Uncle Allen was fully reclined in his LazyBoy, only one eye half-open and cocked at the screen. A quick story caught her ear as the camera moved in on a file shot of the Little Big Horn Monument in southern Montana, the site of "Custer's Last Stand" near the Crow Agency. Paying attention to the correspondent's overdubbed voice, she heard that the democratic nominee-in-the-wings was due to visit and deliver an address at the monument in two days time.

Sitting forward and placing her elbows on her knees, chin cupped with her palms, she muttered half under her breath, "I think I'll go."

Neta looked at her, lashes lowered. "Go where?"

Sol nodded her head towards the TV. "There."

"Little Big Horn? Why? It's not like you haven't been there a dozen times."

"Because he's going to be there," she said, indicating the screen again as an action shot of Kasili giving a speech to some swooning audience moved across the camera's field of vision.

"Why on earth would ya want to see him?" Allen sniffed in disdain. "He hasn't said anythin' worth listenin' to besides some mealy-mouthed platitudes 'bout 'change.'"

"I'm surprised Uncle Allen. Here, I thought you were a democrat," Sol said half-mockingly.

He gave her a sideways glance that said as much as "what have you been smokin'?" It was just a few years back, just before the accident, when Gaspar and Allen had to beat back an environmental group that had attempted to condemn their property as an extension of Yellowstone's habitat. It had been a pitched battle to keep the court from allowing the conservancy to file an injunction against the Carstairs Ranch and other property owners as an impediment to the widening range of wolves and grizzlies. Fortunately, the Rutherford Foundation stepped up to protect the property rights of the ranchers in the area. Solana had made certain that the story was disseminated, playing up the angle of an environmental group trying to force a Native American family to surrender their land under pressure from a government sanctioned organization. The fact that the Carstairs' were Native American worked in favor of prompting the conservancy to back down before it was inundated by a PR nightmare. Nothing like the story of the 'government' stealing more Indian land to make a group pack up and run.

"There was a time," he intoned, "but not for awhile now. Those folks only know how to tell you what to do. Listenin' ain't their strong suit, though they sure make a good game of it." He scratched his neck. "Change, my ass."

"Allen!" Mama Ciel sputtered in outrage. "You watch your language in this house."

He just clucked his tongue and kept quiet, figuring he'd already said his piece.

Neta, however, was still interested in why Sol would want to go hear Kasili give a speech, and said so.

"Don't you think it's odd that he's coming all the way out to the Crow Agency to talk to a few Indians, particularly where a white man was surrounded and skunked? I do. Actually, I think it's staged to make it look like this man is every minority's savior just because he's black. And, as far as I can see, he has yet to say anything of substance just like Uncle Allen pointed out."

"I'll bet they're only going to let their own supporters in to watch the proceedings and, from I can see, you don't qualify," said Neta.

"No, but I am a legitimate member of the press *and* I'm Indian. I'll get in," Sol stated confidently. "I'm going to call the Statesman in the morning and have them get a hold of Kasili's campaign to put me on the list. Boise will be glad to have the extra representation on site." She paused and nodded at the TV one more time. "I've got some questions for him."

All three members of the family turned to look at Sol. Her mother just shook her head, but Neta and Allen grinned.

"Give 'em hell, girly" her uncle encouraged.

"Allen!" was all Mama Ciel could say as she drew her eyebrows together disapprovingly.

Gold Baron

Chapter 8

Sol received a call back from the paper in Boise confirming that her press credentials would be waiting for her at Little Big Horn in time for the rally, which was scheduled for the early evening hours after the majority of regular visitors had vacated the monument. It had taken about twenty-four hours for Kathy, the news editor, to set-up everything through the Kasili campaign. Apparently they were thrilled to have a Native American correspondent on-site representing one of the northwest's major metropolitan newspapers. Not that Boise was all that large, it's just that the more populous metro areas located between the Cascades and the Rockies consist of maybe three cities: Spokane, Boise and Salt Lake City. Of course, that assessment would probably tick-off anyone in Missoula. Nonetheless, Solana's way was paved to pass through Kasili's battle lines that night which meant she was packed and ready to roll.

Goodbyes were brief but heartfelt and they all knew they'd see each other soon with Mama Ciel's great-grandchild on the way, and it was no time before Sol was again eastward bound.

The trip to the Crow Reservation was just a few hours of freeway driving once she'd come out of the foothills where the Carstairs' property hugged a few hundred acres of creekside real estate, and the miles sped by at a quick clip.

When she arrived at the park entrance some two hours before the rally was scheduled to begin, she was surprised (or was she?) to see busses lined up one behind the other all across the parking area. There must have been more than twenty vehicles stacked in the lot with Montana and Colorado plates. There were even a fair number of university logos liberally displayed from University of Montana, University of Colorado and Montana State. No real Wyoming representation, Sol noticed, wondering if there wasn't that much interest in politics in the neighboring state or just not particularly supportive of Kasili. She shrugged, thought the whole thing curious and let it go.

Pulling into an area that was designated for cars and pick-ups, she parked and grabbing her notebook and pocket recorder, which she dropped into her handbag, Sol walked over to the entrance. To the one side, where the campaign had set up their staging area, a table was situated under a cabaña with 'press' prominently displayed on the overhang. Assuming that was where she would pick-up her credentials, she made her way over to the young woman seated behind the table.

The girl, for she appeared to be no older than a college sophomore, was dressed in the Kasili campaign uniform, a royal purple t-shirt emblazoned with a grand white 'K' which looked more like the logo for Kellogg cereals than a presidential candidate. The color seemed an odd choice when candidates usually opt for red or blue, or both, to demonstrate a patriotic fervor. But why a deep, visceral purple? Not the color of bright red arterial blood, but venous blood that had been drained of all its oxygen and nutrients. *What's he trying to say with that? Good grief, and why did I put it in that context?* She shook off the odd thought and focused on the girl, her blonde ponytail hanging limply down her back, a testament to how hot the day had been.

"Your name?" she asked, trying to be very businesslike though it was evident that dealing with the press corps left her a little intimidated. It made Sol remember how imperious she could appear, standing at 5'10", dark and difficult to read. Sol had perfected the inscrutable look years ago in New York as a measure of self-protection and a means to wheedle her way in the door when she would otherwise be barred from entry. There were times when being a member of a minority could be played to get you inside. Which brought Kasili to mind. How much of his campaign was based on his color and not his character? *Here we go, back to Dr. King.*

"Solana Greyfisher, Boise Statesman."

The girl swiped a lock of hair that had fallen out of her ponytail away from her eyes as she riffled through the stack of envelopes which contained laminated nametags on lanyards, fact sheets, rules for access and questions, photo and a press release. The usual tripe. The girl located her name and extricated the packet from the others, handing it across the table. "Here you go."

"Thanks." Sol shipped the nametag out of the envelope, put it around her neck and checked out the regulations for the press, fairly standard stuff. Shoving the pack into her purse, she scanned the grounds arrangement.

The first thing she noticed was the security. She expected it to be tight, but this seemed like overkill. Secret Service, reservation police, sheriff's office and even the Montana state police were all visible, many of whom were stationed around a tricked out bus that sported the big special 'K' on the side. She wondered if the bus had hydraulics to make the rear end jump like the low-rider car enthusiasts installed on their rides. The thing *was* purple, after all.

Since she had a couple of questions she hoped to ask the candidate, she went to the security gate, where they inspected everyone entering the grounds along with their belongings. There was even a portable x-ray in place to guard against smuggling in any kind of weaponry. Not so unusual after 9/11.

She handed over her personal articles for examination and allowed them to check her person then, gathering up her things, she made a direct line to the press relations' table. There they had her fill out a card with her name, news organization and the topics about which she wished to ask the candidate. A man with his shirt sleeves rolled up over his forearms and dressed in tailored pants, who appeared to be in his mid-thirties, brown hair slightly mussed from working a harried schedule, glanced up from his worksheet to catch Sol's eye as she handed him the card. Inquiry and interest ranged quickly across his features as he noted her obvious Native American heritage. He accepted the card and read from her nametag, "Solana Greyfisher. It says you represent the Boise Statesman. Are you local?"

"I'm originally from around here. Know the area and the people well." She paused and looked at him warily, "Why?"

He ignored her question and checked her card for topic content. "I think Congressman Kasili may be able to call on you during the press Q and A segment of the proceedings." He looked up again. No smile, nothing on his face to suggest what he was thinking. "Will that suit you?"

Surprised at his decree, she kept the response to herself and her features blank. "Yes, thank you very much." She nodded at him and left his station.

83

Sol decided to take some time wandering around while the rally was beginning. A couple hundred chairs had been brought in from Billings, she guessed, but the majority of the crowd was standing or sitting on blankets they'd carried in. Most of the people were milling around waiting for the main event despite the fact that a speaker was addressing the crowd. A dais had been erected with a few chairs, a microphone and a Kasili banner as backdrop for the lone orator, a short, plump woman who was probably Native, the inflections in her voice indicated as much, though she was hard to hear above the noise of the assembly. Most of those in attendance looked like college students, which was no surprise considering what she had witnessed in the parking lot. Sol wouldn't have thought they'd be able to hunt up so many students in the middle of summer break, but apparently they'd found quite a few hundred that were available and willing to travel. What she didn't see were many local people from the Crow Agency or the relatively nearby communities and she would have expected that folks from Billings would have driven down for this. Running her eyes over the host she did see pockets of older people in their thirties and up with hats and water bottles – those must be the Billingsites. So much for enticing the Native populace. Must be why the press organizer zeroed in on her to be visible.

With that thought in mind, she moved over to where the press reps were setting up their cameras and equipment. There were a few TV crews out of Billings and Denver. The major networks having sent correspondents to establish a live satellite feed. Aside from that, most of the reporters, and there weren't that many, were from comparatively local papers. The stringer from the Denver Post was someone she didn't know, so she didn't bother him, figuring it might be best to remain lowkey for the time being.

Finally, a man came out onto the dais and went through a mike level check, increasing the volume so that everyone in the audience could hear him as he thanked the previous speaker and made a general call for everyone to gather. It was evident they wanted the crowd on their feet and closed in to create the impression of larger numbers than the fifteen hundred people who were there. There were even a couple of organizers who were trying to maneuver the more visibly ethnic attendees into clear camera range. *Hey, it's all about showbiz anyway,* thought Sol. Everything was staged anymore, which she knew from past experience at political rallies and fundraisers. *Nothing more than soundbite city with a quick visual for oomph.*

The crowd congealed as directed and taped music exploded over the sound system, some popular song she didn't recognize about hope and peace while still managing to excoriate corporations and capitalism in general. The words were partially indeterminate but she did hear the refrain of "we can change the world, you and me."

The man on the stage started into a brief diatribe delivered to excite the crowd with the idea that the man they were about to see was the one and only man who had the capacity to understand all the injustice of the world and could right virtually every wrong.

It took some self-control not to allow her face to mirror the annoyance that she felt at the absurdity of his introduction.

But just before Kasili made his grand entrance, Sol was astounded to see how the campaign was going to play the race card and the fact that the Indians were complicit.

A circle of chairs had been set-up on one corner of the platform and one of the better-known family drums was seated around the circle. The head of the drum group began a song with the recognizable vocables of Northern Plains style singing, a difficult high-pitched wail that travels a range only the best Native singers can achieve. It was an honor song, not that most of the rallygoers would know that. Unfortunately, there were many people still seated as the drum rendered the song with heart not realizing that protocol called for the audience to stand in reverence of the Fathers when an honor song is played. She sighed as she made note of the fact that this would make a great soundbite for the national news gigs. As the song finished, she saw the congressman himself standing at the edge of the stage. At least someone had given him a heads up to remain at attention as the drum sang. She wondered what he would think if he knew that honor songs venerated warriors like the men serving overseas who Kasili had been known to show such little respect.

Having finished the song, the drum group stood and one by one, shook hands with the candidate as he came onto the dais. He managed to smile and look solemn at the same time.

Walking to the microphone, amid what was now chaotic yelling and whooping emanating from the crowd, Kasili raised his hands and jumped right in to his prepared speech. Sol was disinclined to listen too closely, but did so anyway in order to make certain that her questions were pertinent to what the man said. As it turned out, he didn't have much of substance to impart aside from the usual mantra about creating an equitable society and the ever-popular "change." All of which the crowd of mostly young students ate up, and yes, one of the women even swooned and was caught by a couple of her male companions standing close by. Kasili, as had happened in a few similar instances in the recent past, stepped forward with an unopened bottle of water and, squatting slightly, handed the girl what the crowd would have believed was the elixir of life, an expression of deep concern etching his strong features.

Sol almost lost it and uttered an improper 'oy vey.' Luckily she kept her mouth shut and the words in her head. Before long the girl was fine, sipping water and staring moonstruck at Kasili who, after checking one more time to be sure she was okay, rolled right back into the monologue, easily picking up the threads of where he was so rudely, or opportunely, interrupted.

Another twenty minutes of oration went by and Kasili opened the forum up to take a few questions. He took a few free (or so it seemed) questions from the audience and parlayed the answers well. Then the press coordinator appeared at his side and gave him both written and verbal directions of who to call on for questions.

A couple of other reporters from the larger news outlets were asked by name first and then, he called, "Solana Greyfisher, from the Boise Statesman."

She was on the spot now, but had been in the situation before and was prepared with a question about fuel costs.

"Representative Kasili, you've made your opinion clear that you are in favor of developing alternative energy sources to replace the United States' reliance on oil products. However, gas prices have skyrocketed in the last few months affecting millions of rural Americans, like those of us on the reservation who must travel long distances to work and obtain household goods. What is your answer to those who are dependent on their pick-up trucks for work needs and transportation? Do you have a plan to put gas in their tanks so they can put bread on their tables?"

Uh-oh. The face of the press coordinator, who was standing to the side and out of the camera angle, moved from general cool to a visible shade of red. Kasili, to his credit, didn't lose his smile. In fact, his face took on the now familiar expression of concern. It was his answer that gave him a little trouble.

"Well, as you know, I've ah-ah been advocating ah alternative fuel ah development for ah-ah-ah quite some time and we have been promoting and sponsoring ah-ah the production of ah ethanol among ah-ah other ah possibilities."

"Yes, but ethanol has been proven to be cost inefficient and, in fact, has contributed to the rise in gas prices rather than making it more affordable, and as *you* know, the reservations here in Montana and the Dakotas, in particular, are very poor," Sol interrupted.

"Well, it's ah evident that ah the program under consideration by the ah Congress to ah encourage the ah conservation of energy ah-ah will help underwrite ah a funding for new resources and ah-ah-ah alleviate the burden of the ah working poor."

Sol tried one more time, "Sir, doesn't that only add to the cost of fuel by creating a virtual tax on an already heavily taxed commodity?"

"Ah, that's all we have time for Miss Greyfisher's question," the press coordinator stepped in to reduce the hemorrhaging, directing Kasili to take another and far safer question from the press.

The question and answer period was cut short and Sol was allowed to exit without any harassment other than some dirty looks from the campaign workers. Most of the crowd had paid no attention to what the candidate said. In their eyes he could do no wrong.

As she was buckling up her seat belt before putting the Tahoe in gear, she figured that she was now on somebody's shit list. *Oh well, all in a day's work for any journalist worth her salt.*

✼ ✼ ✼

The next morning Sol fairly flew down I-90 from Sheridan, Wyoming, where she'd spent the night with some cousins, to pick up I-25 in Buffalo, which she followed all the way to Denver. She was expected in the city that evening since she'd called and made dinner plans with a couple of former co-workers who were also friends.

Frankly, Sol had been lucky to catch Allie on her cell and luckier still that she agreed to sit down at the table with her. Keeping in touch with people from her past wasn't one of Sol's strongest assets but she did e-mail Allie and Meg once in a blue moon. Being on the run all the time, they were a little more forgiving about poor correspondence (or none, as the case may be) than most. Allie had actually promised to round up a couple of other old pals for the last minute reunion, making reservations at one of Sol's favorite old haunts, Cugino's Cucina, a popular Italian spot on Broadway.

Rolling into town around four-thirty gave her plenty of time to freshen up at her hotel before meeting everyone later on at seven. Sol checked in and parked her overnight case by the door and laptop on the table before picking up the remote and flopping on the bed, spread eagle. Then she went ahead a flicked on the TV.

Man, she was exhausted and the driving wasn't the half of it. Her cousins had kept her up half the night drinking coffee and yakking about anything and everything. Anyone who ever told people that Indians are reserved and unemotional hadn't spent much time with them. Her family simply wore her out. *Bunch of partiers.*

She was beginning to think that maybe she'd have time for a nap when she noticed a blip on the early national news and she sat straight up, her mouth half open in shock at seeing a shot from yesterday's Little Big Horn fiasco, as it was becoming known in the Kasili camp, not that Sol was aware of that fact. She had expected to see some coverage on the news but she *hadn't* expected to see the networks pick-up part of her question and Kasili's bumbled answer.

She cocked her head sideways to look at the television as a camera had locked on an image of her three-quarter profile. *Okay, not too bad, girl and not overly recognizable.* Then they panned the picture back more fully on Kasili and his innumerable 'ahs'. *Oh boy, they've gotta be pissed at me, just one little Indian.* She couldn't help but smile.

She yanked her fist down hard from above her head to her shoulder, "Yes!"

❁ ❁ ❁

After watching the recap of Kasili's last stand at Little Big Horn a couple more times on different channels, all, except Fox, with an apologetic take on the incident, she felt reinvigorated and unable to lie down again.

It wasn't long before her cell phone started ringing, a tinny version of "Home on the Range" assaulting her ears. *Maybe I should change that to "Wipeout,"* she thought, considering her having laid a virtual banana peel under Kasili's feet, encouraging him to do exactly that. Some people just made it too easy.

She punched the 'talk' button and answered.

"I don't know that I've ever seen anything quite like that," came Anthea's voice without any preamble. "And I can't believe that they actually aired Kasili's snafu. Wow."

"Thanks for the applause," retorted Sol. "He did it all by himself."

"It would help if the guy had a clue but we can't ask for miracles *every* day."

"Particularly from those who believe that they *are* the miracle workers," added Sol. "At least I'm not infamous yet. I don't think anyone reported who asked the nasty questions. Did they?"

"No. Only people who know you would recognize that perfect profile," said Anthea.

"Ooooh, you flatter me. Too bad you're not an incredibly good-looking man," she laughed. "One of them with a real sense of humor would do me good right now."

"Okay, girl. I'll keep my eyes open. However, you should know by now that the pickin's are slim in these parts. You'll probably have more luck where you are, which, by the way, is where?"

"Denver. Getting ready to have dinner with some old buddies from the paper. Thanks for the call and let me know if you run across anything good in the meantime."

"Will do. Have fun."

Sol finished dressing, splashed on a very little bit of make-up – it just wasn't her thing – and left for her appointment with her recent past.

❋ ❋ ❋

As soon as she walked in the door of Cugino's she was assaulted by both Allie and Meg.

"What were you thinking?" asked a slightly outraged Allie, a dirty blonde of medium height whose corners were well-rounded with a few extra pounds. She was dressed in a khaki suit with amber accessories and comfortable but clunky sandals. High fashion wasn't in Allie's vocabulary, nor did she care. A good story that could be exploited was all she had passion for.

A little affronted by the question, Sol countered with, "I believe the question is what was *he* thinking, or rather, *not* thinking. I was just doing my job."

Allie put her hands on her hips, feet in a wide stance. "Come on, what kind of an answer could there possibly be to questions like those?"

"Truthful ones," said Sol. "If he had any idea what he was proposing, he would have an actual energy plan and be able to explain it. It's obvious that the guy has no idea what he's talking about. And," she looked her friend in the eye, "this is not a personality contest. It's the office of the President that's at stake. Look, if he wants the support of the Native population he has to address their concerns, too, and driving around on good wishes doesn't cut it." She relaxed and tried to get her friends to do the same. "Now, can we just let it go? All he has to do is a little homework."

Allie dropped her arms and put them around Sol, Meg adding herself into the hug. "Same old Sol, always fighting the battle," said Meg, who was about 5'7", a lithe brunette of around fifty years old with a runner's physique and a placid attitude. She was the classified supervisor at the Post and dealt with the public, not the newsmakers. "Come on, let's get some grub. I'm starving."

They were seated in no time and had ordered a round of drinks.

"So who else is coming? I thought you said there'd be some more people joining us?" Sol asked.

"I told Johnny from Sports and Tiff in Metro. They said they'd be here after they filed their stories," answered Allie. "Everyone misses you."

Sol cocked an eyebrow as she sipped her Campari and soda. "Right. Everyone misses a troublemaker."

"Wait a minute, I thought I was the troublemaker," a tall, rugged looking man in a cowboy hat said as he positioned himself next to Solana, placing his hand on the back of the booth behind her shoulder.

Sol looked up at the familiar voice and shivered with an unwelcome reaction. Who invited him? She just wanted to have a nice time with some friends not relive a worn-out movie.

Pasting a smile on her face that felt unnatural, Sol peered over her shoulder at her ex-boyfriend, Mac. He was the land manager for an outrageously oversized ranch owned by some Hollywood type who would find time to visit in between projects and touting environmental causes. Mac was more a realtor than a cowboy who oversaw the property, which didn't take a whole lot since there wasn't much in the way of stock – the owner was a vegan who thought riding a horse was tantamount to mistreatment. Sol still wondered how she had managed to date this guy for so long. *Brain damage, I guess.*

She wasn't going to pull any punches tonight, though. "So, what are you doing here?"

"Just here with a few buds for a couple of drinks and I look over my shoulder and who walks in? I couldn't have been more surprised if Moses had parted the Platte River," he grinned at his own joke.

"Well, it's good to see you again, Mac. Thanks for dropping by to say hello." She peered around him back toward the bar. "I'll bet your buddies are missing you. Take care, now." She held out her hand to give him a final shake off, which he took and lowered his head to brush the back of her hand with his lips before he gave her what he thought was a charming smile, winked and left.

"For lack of a better term, 'ick,'" said Allie.

"I'm glad you said that because, for a minute there, I thought you had set me up."

"No way! That guy was always bad news. You made the right choice to leave that part of your life behind." She took a drink from her glass. "Now let's get down to some gossip…"

They spent the rest of the evening enjoying good company and picking up on the latest information about one another. Johnny and Tiff arrived about eight rounding out the group for a couple of hours of swapping tall stories and reminiscing.

Just before they broke up the reunion, Tiff mentioned that Kasili was going to be in Denver the next day since she was covering the story. She added that he was then due to move on to make an appearance with the governor of New Mexico at the university in Albuquerque. Sol tilted her head with interest at the remark and thought that it might be worth a second try to catch the ubiquitous candidate in action.

Chapter 9

Solana had plenty of time to make the 350-mile drive down to Albuquerque before Kasili was due to appear that evening. According to the campaign website, Kasili was scheduled for a late morning rally in Denver at the university after which he would jet down to New Mexico. She also noted that he had been feted at a fund raising dinner the night before while she and her friends had been enjoying their mini-reunion, which made her wonder why her ex had been at the restaurant. She stared out of the windshield at the majestic line of the Rockies marching south on her right considering how Mac was a liberal to the core representing big money and yet he hadn't been rubbing elbows with his democratic buddies? She smelled a rat and suspected Johnny Sports but then blew it off as done and gone. Mac had showed up and she showed him the door. Good enough. Time to move on.

As the odometer added mile after mile she started deliberating on what questions she would pose to the savior this time, *if* she managed to get through the door. Sol realized that was a longshot after what happened in Montana, but she also knew how crazy these political gatherings could be, particularly when it was a liberal candidate at a college setting. Hopefully they'll have different people manning the press booth and she'll be able to bully her way through. There were times when having a definite ethnic look could work in her favor. Everyone was afraid of leaving themselves open to a charge of discrimination, especially a campaign that was so racially sensitive. She smiled a little. *They won't know what hit them.*

It didn't take long for her to find her way to the Pit. Solana had been a real basketball fan and often had found herself at games on weekends cheering on the Lobos during her student days at UNM. She hadn't been back in town for years and some things had changed but the university atmosphere was much the same as when she had attended more than a decade earlier.

The parking lots were jammed despite the fact that the summer break was in full swing, a good omen for her easy entry into the press area. The more chaos the better.

Sol parked and decided to wear her oversized reading glasses, not that she really needed them, and pull her hair into knot at the nape of her neck, hoping that it might change her appearance enough to let her slip through unnoticed. There wasn't anything she could do about disguising her height and if the same press coordinator were there, which she doubted after the gaffe he made in letting her past the first time, she was sunk. You can bet he'd remember her.

Entering the building she found that there were two entrances set-up, one for spectators and one for the media. Peering through the doors, she could see that the media area was roped off, so she would have to brazen her way through the sentries. She saw other members of the press walking by and noticed that the coordinators for the campaign hadn't changed the nametags for this event. Good thing for her. She just slipped the lanyard around her neck. And went through the security gate along with the rest of them. All the guards did was sort through the items in her handbag, give her a cursory check and let her through.

Sighing with relief at having bluffed her way in, she took a seat in the bleachers where she would be visible when she stood to ask a question but not easily recognized if any of the same crew from Little Big Horn was working this venue.

It wasn't long before the proceedings got underway. This time there was a warm-up speech from the local congressional representative who then handed the podium over to the governor of New Mexico. He came on stage backed by the music of a mariachi band that was set-up at the foot of the dais, hands raised hailing the audience in welcome, a huge smile plastered across his face. He used decorous language in referring to his former opponent, making sure that he didn't upstage the star despite his own popularity among the throng that filled the Pit. The governor had dropped out of the race for the nomination and had handed his few delegates to Kasili after only three primary contests. Taking just ten minutes to make his address, the governor then introduced the guest of honor and walked from behind the lectern, arms outstretched to hug Kasili and, disengaging, moved off to stand unobtrusively to the side.

As Kasili came on stage, Sol heard the same popular song blare from the speakers that had played in Montana. She found the song annoying but simply stood with the rest of the crowd at the politician's entrance. Sitting wasn't an option since everyone else popped to their feet as soon as he climbed the platform.

From there on out Kasili went through virtually the same speech she had heard in Montana with a few variations and, lo and behold, at almost precisely the same point in the talk some co-ed slumped to the ground in a faint. She was careful not to cluck aloud in exasperation as she watched the same script unfold with the benevolent candidate leaning down to offer yet another star-struck student the omnipresent bottle of water. From there it pretty much played out like the other rally. Twenty minutes of talk, comments and questions from the general audience and then questions from the press.

She kept her hand up trying to be seen but wasn't hopeful that she'd be called on. Luck hit again however, in that the campaign representative who was choosing questions had not been present in Montana and when she had handed her the card with her information, didn't recognize Sol.

Once again, the candidate was directed to call on her for a question.

"Representative Kasili, what is your opinion on coal-fired power plants?"

Kasili felt there couldn't be a problem in answering this one. "This country is duty-bound to lessen dependence on energy production that ah pollutes our air and water. My policy has been to encourage ah closure of outmoded facilities and emphasize environmentally friendly power supplies such as, ah stressing the development of solar and wind technology."

"So, it is your policy to block the Desert Mountain Power Plant, part-owned by the Navajo Nation, from coming online, thus preventing the poverty-stricken reservation a major employment opportunity, dooming them to struggle with a lack of good jobs and worsening economic outlook," she expanded on the subject.

"Ah, don't misunderstand my position. What I have said is ah that we, as a nation, must ah target the development of ah-ah clean energy resources…" he trailed off. The campaign rep promptly raised a flat hand in front of her face and then waving it in another direction, indicated Kasili should focus on another reporter whom she pointed out with her other hand.

Sol tried to continue the topic by throwing out, "Isn't that short-sighted when the Native population is reliant on the resources available on Reservation land?"

Kasili ignored the question and moved to the other woman, who was a correspondent with a local franchise of a national network. Her cameraman had picked up Solana's last follow-up before zeroing in on his charge's bland inquiry, allowing the candidate to wax eloquent without really taking a stand on anything.

Sol suddenly found herself standing between two plain clothes security guards and, with very little fanfare, she was escorted from the arena and bluntly told never to come back. They demanded the return of her press credentials and deposited her on the other side of the entrance where they continued to stand while she stopped and calmly dusted off her sleeves before turning to leave. They stood resolutely guarding the lobby doors until she had disappeared in the direction of her Tahoe.

Despite her ignominious departure from the Pit, Solana didn't feel the least bit of regret as she pulled away from the UNM campus. In fact, the one thought that kept playing in her head was how much fun it had been. Not that she really enjoyed making a national candidate look foolish so much as she had wanted to pry a solid answer out of the guy. Something he seemed to be incapable of giving. So, okay, maybe she did enjoy it… some.

In her judgment it was his *job* to answer policy questions so voters knew what they were buying when they walked into that little booth on Election Day, and as a responsible journalist Sol felt it her duty to get those answers.

She'd had enough excitement for the time being and was due to meet an old buddy from college at her house where she was going to spend the night. She'd been looking forward to catching up with her friend and meeting the new husband. She only hoped that this run-in with Kasili wouldn't make the news. She checked the clock in the dashboard. It was only 7:30. Early enough to spend some quality time over dinner before the late news.

After the rally cleanup, the campaign management team sat in the purple bus, which had been driven down to meet Kasili who had flown in for the rally. They were sprawled across the plush sofa and captain's chairs, swilling beer, which in their estimation was well-earned.

Going through his notes, the campaign manager sought out the floor rep who had allowed Solana to ask a question, skewering her with an accusatory glare.

"What happened there? That Indian gal? Isn't she the same one who was in Montana that made our man look like an ass?"

"I don't know, Rick. I wasn't in Montana," she countered with a glare of her own. "I've been here for three days coordinating this monster. The card she handed me had simple enough questions, nothing like what she asked."

He furrowed his bushy red brows in contemplation. "I don't know what her game is, but you'd damn well better make sure this broad never gets near our candidate again. Anything like this happens in the future and you're toast." With that he just dropped the subject and moved on. The damage was done and the playbacks had already made the local broadcasts. It was only a matter of time before it hit a national forum.

The next morning, Solana said her good-byes to her friend and began the last leg of her southern journey, getting onto the freeway and heading toward the resort town of Ruidoso. It had been years since she'd visited but remembered the quaint feel of the downtown area and the contradictions of a rustic, artsy atmosphere. She was looking forward to a little pure mountain air after the last couple of nights spent in the city. Denver and Albuquerque may be western cities that people had a tendency to imagine as clean and unspoiled because of their elevation and proximity to the high country, but they had all the trappings of real city living... traffic, congested population, and yes, even some smog.

Leaving I-25 to take the two-lane highway that slithered across the desert until reaching the foothills of the Capitan Mountains that rose out of the sandy flats, Sol listened to the strains of a favorite symphony penned by a contemporary southwest composer. The music matched the vast landscape with broad strokes of bows claiming the strings of violas and cellos and voices of deep-bellied brass punctuating the pulsing melody with dynamism. This piece always made her feel the texture of the wild terrain, which is why she had grown to love it when she she'd been stuck in the city, working for the big dailies. It made her appreciate where she now lived even more.

Miles later she was winding up the mountain road, watching the scenery change with the topography. Pines taking over from the junipers, which had overtaken the sage and low brush. As she reached the higher altitude, she checked her cell phone to see if she had a signal and, luckily, passing the town limits, the bars started to turn up on the digital face. Taking that as a good sign, she called Toddy to tell him she'd made it.

Toddy answered on the second ring and gave her directions to an espresso bar in town, explaining that the drive to his place was pretty convoluted so he'd meet her there. They could sit down for a bit and after coffee she could follow him home. Make it easy on her and give her a break from the drive.

She found the quaint little shop tucked between a gallery and an insurance office on the main drag, lucked out and parked right in front. The day was bright and relatively cool compared to the intense heat of the desert floor she'd left behind some thirty miles back. Slinging her handbag over her shoulder, she nudged the car door closed with her hip and went inside.

The place was an eclectic montage of local Native relics and ranching memorabilia, cattle brands burned into the wooden paneling, hand woven Indian blankets scattered across the walls and aged potsherds encased behind locked glass doors. The Mescalero Apache Indian Reservation lay directly to the south of town and a number of framed photos taken over a hundred years, depicting Indian life past and present, were interspersed among cowboy artifacts. Sol placed an order for coffee and wandered around the shop studying the images hanging in clusters between tables.

There weren't many patrons inside. Two who had laptops open and were busily at work and one individual sat at a corner table reading the local paper with an iced drink positioned at his elbow.

Not really knowing what Toddy looked like she had studied each of the customers before deciding that he hadn't yet arrived, assuming that he did have some idea as to her appearance. Besides, it wasn't easy to overlook a tall Native woman of her description in a place with limited clientele.

After exhausting fifteen minutes of perusing artifact collections on the walls, she deposited her beverage on a table by the window and picked up an abandoned copy of the local paper. Leafing through the pages she was able to glean a little bit about life in the resort town while she awaited her host's arrival.

It was a full forty-five minutes after parking her Tahoe that a tall, rangy man with a thick thatch of dark scruffy hair pulled open the door. Sol looked up from the paper to catch the dancing, dark eyes set wide in a face browned by the sun. A measured smile spread across lips that quirked at one corner, defining a look of amusement that she imagined made a perpetual imprint on his features. Although at first impression he appeared young, she noticed the crinkling around his eyes that belied an age close to ten years beyond her own. He walked over to her table and held out a hand in greeting. She grasped it with a solid grip, which he returned with vigor, simply stating her name while giving her hand one good pump.

"Good to meet you, Toddy," she said, accepting his recognition.

Seeing the beverage already situated on the small table beside the newspaper, he said, "Let me get something to drink and we can talk a little before going up the mountain," and turned away before she could respond.

Shrugging to herself, she went back to reading the broadsheet in front of her until he sat down a few minutes later, steaming coffee in hand.

Not being one for the niceties of small talk, Toddy jumped right into the meat of her trip. "Anthea said that you've developed an interest in the subjects we've been exploring of late."

"Yes, you managed to capture my attention with some of your theories." She noted the long lashes framing eyes that, upon closer examination, were more whisky colored than chocolate. "Enough to want to do a little investigating, I guess."

"Is that a hobby of yours?" He slumped back in the chair, peering over the rim of his cup with legs outstretched in a relaxed attitude that somehow didn't jibe with the excited voice she had listened to over the telephone lines.

"Used to be my job. Investigative reporting. But you knew that." She leaned forward trying to see past his leisurely appearance to dig out what he was really thinking. Maybe he didn't trust her. Wouldn't be the first time a source was wary. Odd, she hadn't thought to categorize this man as a news source until now. Made her realize how seriously she was taking this whole thing.

"Hmmm, yeah. Anthea has told me a fair bit about you."

"But you still don't trust me," she let the statement stand as a simple acknowledgment of a fact.

He cocked his head a little to the side, allowing the bright sunlight cascading through the window to define the planes of a slightly broad but long face, showing a hint of crossed ethnicities. The wide forehead was unlined, nose straight and a strong, determined chin completed the picture.

"I don't trust anyone."

"You trust Anthea."

"Yes," he admitted. "And she trusts you," he looked into her eyes as he tipped the cup for a drink, a little sparkle of mischief in his own.

"Well, it's always good to have someone vouch for my integrity." She relaxed some back into her seat.

Toddy studied her a little more and a spark of recognition flitted across his features. "You look familiar… why would that be?"

She hiked a shoulder up to her ear then let it fall back into place. "No idea. I'm just a cog in the invisible wheel of print media."

He almost sprang forward, setting the half-filled paper cup on the table so quickly the coffee splashed close to sloshing over the top. She was surprised at the catlike move toward her as he left the calm posture behind in an instant, becoming taut with energy. "Yes!" his voice rose in timbre, though not enough to draw any of the other client's attention. "You're the one who cornered Kasili in Montana."

"I would have thought that Anthea had told you already." She was slightly taken aback at his reaction to her identification until he threw his head back and laughed. A full, hearty release of tension. "Damn, that was good," he said, sincerely complementing her, humor still floating in his voice.

"Just doing my job," she wasn't about to act smug over what was essentially a lucky break. You never knew how a subject would react to a tough question, though she'd had an inclination after watching Kasili's past performances.

"I was impressed. He's a pretty slick character, but not as quick as folks would like us to think." He sat back a little and considered. "You know, even though the mainstream press dropped it about as quickly as it happened, it's all over youtube and talk radio. In fact the questions that came up at UNM last night have made it to underground dissemination despite the campaign's efforts to quash it." Toddy stopped and sipped. "That was you, too, wasn't it."

Sol settled back a bit more and sighed, "There are some things you just can't deny. There wasn't any real video of me, though, was there?"

Toddy thought she sounded just a tad apprehensive as he drained his cup. "You like to keep your anonymity. Now, *that* I understand." He shot out of his seat unexpectedly. "Ready to go?" and walked to the door, his mind already running in a new direction. Dropping the cup in the trash, he pushed the door open, barely holding it for Sol to catch as he exited the shop.

Not exactly the most gallant of individuals.

He stopped in the middle of the sidewalk almost as abruptly as he'd left the coffee bar, forcing Sol to catch herself and make a quick sidestep to avoid plowing into him.

"This must be your rig, Idaho plates," he said matter-of-factly.

"Fairly obvious in this town, I suppose," she replied.

He turned halfway around and looked down the couple of inches into her face, "Not necessarily. This is enough of a vacation spot that you'll see folks from all over the U.S." He took in her attractive features, large slightly slanted gold-brown eyes, straight narrow nose, inquisitively curved mouth all framed by thick, glossy back hair. "You'll fit right in."

Toddy pointed out an ancient Willy's Jeep she knew was a good deal older than either one of them, the body in need of cosmetic surgery but the undercarriage and wheels appearing to be well nurtured. "That's my ride, so just follow me out of town. It's about twenty minutes from here," and he just looked at her waiting for her acquiescence, which she indicated with a, "Sure," before he climbed behind the wheel.

The drive provided a relatively pleasant tour of Ruidoso, where he curiously seemed to backtrack up and down a few of the streets before leaving the city limits. The rest of the trip through the surrounding highlands to his home followed roads that were twisting, however there wasn't anything that would have made it impossible for her to find her way with good directions, a point that she brought up once they arrived on his property.

Toddy was standing beside her open car door as she reached back in to collect a few articles, "I told you that I don't trust anyone, right?"

Sol pulled her head out of the cockpit and twisting to look over her shoulder, connected her gaze with his, "And?"

"And I wanted to be certain that you hadn't picked up a tail on your way here."

She turned to face him, standing just a few inches shorter than he. "You're serious."

Nodding yes, he said, "I've expended a lot of effort to be left alone and rarely invite anyone up here, let alone strangers."

She lifted an eyebrow, realizing how little she knew about him, which was probably less than he knew about her. No, it was *definitely* less. She could be googled. There wasn't anything on the internet about him that she'd been able to find. *Great, I've got myself stuck up on the side of some mountain in the middle of nowhere with a para - noid.* But she remembered how much Anthea had to say about him and let it assuage her anxiety. *She wouldn't lead me to the door of some lunatic... I hope.*

"So, did we lose 'em?"

He chuckled. "No one to lose. Just taking precautions, particularly after your network taped lessons on how to make friends and win over admirers. Believe me, your fan club has many fewer members today than yesterday." He speared her with a grave look.

"Unfortunately, we're not playing with boy scouts. Politics has huge stakes and you managed to raise the hackles of a few very big dogs." He grabbed a bag from her cargo bay where the two had migrated during his little lecture. "It is well worth it to watch your back."

"I'll remember that," she said as she shouldered her laptop case and closed the rear hatch.

Solana trailed after Toddy as he took her around to the front entrance, leaving his rig parked in the shadow of a cavernous garage that also housed an ATV and a late model Lincoln Navigator. Before he lowered the door that was as wide as two of the bays, she had noticed skis, snowshoes and other sports gear hanging neatly on the back wall, a fancy mountain bike among the collection. Tools were lined up along the side where the ATV was parked, including a shop lift, welding gear and a number of items you'd find in a motor pool. Toddy appeared to be quite the do-it-yourselfer.

The walk to the entrance was a circuitous path of flagstone rimming an English style garden of herbs and flowers, bees buzzing among the borage and columbine. They arrived at the front door, a large solid oak affair that looked like it belonged on a fortress, which didn't quite conform to the rest of the edifice. Although it sported a stone and stucco façade, it was perforated with large windows that overlooked the mountain view. The place was huge for one person, in her assessment, and since he didn't entertain much, according to his own words, she wondered why a small castle. *At least I'll probably have my own bathroom.*

Unlocking the front door, Toddy led her into the vast entryway, leaving her for a few seconds while he disarmed the alarm system.

Returning, he said, "You can leave your luggage here for now. We'll get you situated a little later." Waving her into the depths of the house's interior, he said, "Come on in."

The tile flooring of the entrance gave way to hardwood planking that was strewn with a few large rugs of a Southwest pattern that lay adjacent to mission furniture with thick comfortable cushions. The design of the great room was such that everything angled to face both the deep hearth with a rough-hewn mantelpiece to the right and be able to see out of the wide windows that overlooked the high country vista. The furnishings weren't exactly stark but Toddy didn't seem to have too much in the way of knick-knacks or art. Just a few tasteful, and expensive, paintings depicting the old west graced the inside walls.

"Make yourself at home," he said. "I know we just had coffee, but can I get you anything? Sparkling water, soft drink?" He looked out at the setting sun, "I guess it's cocktail hour if you'd prefer an adult beverage."

"Thanks but not just yet, I'm afraid alcohol might put me to sleep. Sparkling water would work wonders at the moment."

"Coming right up," and he slipped behind an unobtrusive bar that had bypassed her notice at first glance.

Sol wondered at the switch from brusque tour guide to cordial host, then let it slide figuring that since Toddy spent most of his life in solitude, the social graces weren't something that he'd cultivated.

He came back and handed her a hand-blown glass of unique proportions filled with a fizzy liquid topped with a slice of orange for her and a bottle of beer from a regional microbrewery for himself. She was standing at the window watching the shifting colors of the clouds, moving through the spectrum from coral to scarlet, tinges of violet beginning to creep in as daylight disappeared.

He stood next to her and raising his bottle to the last of the sun's rays said, "Here's to the wonders of the earth and God's incredible palette."

Surprised by the intonation but touched, she raised her own glass and said, "L'chaim."

He burst out laughing, breaking the solemnity of the moment. "*That* I didn't expect. Are there many other Yiddish idioms in your vocabulary?"

"Nope, just picked up a little culture when I lived in New York."

He peered over at her and wagged his head, a wide smile curving his mouth, "This is going to be more fun than I thought."

She quirked her brow as she looked at him, "Odd you should say that because that was precisely what I was thinking when I left the rally last night."

He became serious for a minute. "We still have to remember what it is we're digging into here. It's not just politics as usual, though I'm not so sure there is such a thing. What has been happening in this country is a steady decline of our nation's legislators' understanding and working toward keeping the intent of our founding fathers alive.

They carefully crafted documents that would ensure that the people would be an integral part of the process, to keep the feudal system that had been basically running world realms and nations for time immemorial, at bay. They understood the difference between State and Government, two words that have become interchangeable in modern vocabulary but have opposite implications.

"The State is oligarchical in its power structure. It operates for the good of the people according to how those few in control decide that *good* can be provided. They wield supreme authority, such as one would see from a King George, from whose authority the United States divested itself, or within a despotic or communist regime construct.

"The Government is composed of the people who are able to direct the representatives toward supplying only the minimum of a nation's needs, such as necessary infrastructure and national security. The rest is left to the marketplace to provide what the people need, a truly capitalist base, which is not perfect but affords the best working solution for individuals to lead a free and unfettered life."

Solana slid her gaze sideways to watch him as he seemed to become immersed in the thought and the expression of that thought.

"Unfettered," added Toddy, "is the working term here. By concentrating power within one man, or a few individuals, i.e. the State, feudalism is still in effect. The individual is held back from truly providing for himself, herself and their families what they deem to be most important to their survival. Instead, they are fettered, or shackled, by the needs of the State and providing for its growth and self-sustenance. The Government becomes ineffectual and unable to provide for itself without the State directing its wealth to maintain the State. What has been slowly occurring to our Government is its usurpation by the State, precisely what this country's forebears so courageously fought against."

She turned her eyes back to the deepening colors streaking the sky, a beginning of the meaning of his words were starting to sink in. The vastness of this world they lived on, this earth and the constant grasping for power that is defined within the concepts Toddy was explaining. Man attempting to assert his own idea of power over his neighbors and the Creation they share, which is beyond man's understanding and ultimately his reach.

"The political whipsaw that we're observing this round of presidential elections is not being driven by the people but by another singular force, supported by media and hysteria," said Toddy. "It's happened before but no one will read history even when it's less than a hundred years in our past." Although he didn't elaborate on the repetition idea, she assumed that he was referring to the Second World War.

Toddy took a long breath, let it out slowly and came back to the present. "Look, it's been a long day so far for you. How would you feel about my taking you to dinner. You've got to be starving."

"Actually, that is an excellent suggestion. Is there anyplace to eat up here in the heavens?"

"The country club offers a terrific selection and it's not far from here," he said, looking back out across the darkening terrain.

"You belong to a country club," she stated flatly and almost disbelievingly. "I thought you were a recluse?"

He laughed again, "Not quite. Just don't be surprised when someone calls me 'Ben.'"

Again, he caught her off-guard. "Okay, then, *Ben*."

"I'll explain later. Why don't I show you your rooms and you can get freshened up or whatever it is women do when they say they're freshening up."

"Thank you, I'd appreciate a chance to do just that, 'freshen up,'" and they collected her things after which Toddy led Sol down some hallways and up a flight of stairs and down more hallways. The place seemed to be enormous and confusing. She hoped she'd be able to retrace their steps back to the living area.

� ✦ ✦

Dinner was where they had a chance to get better acquainted. As soon as the server left, a nice young man with a soul patch and a ducktail, which she didn't get – wasn't that like putting beatnik and greaser together in one? – Sol pigeonholed Toddy on the 'Ben' thing.

As he explained himself, it turned out that he does everything in Ruidoso under an assumed name, Ben Johnson.

"Okay, so I get that you're *very* private, but why 'Ben Johnson?' Any significance there?"

He sat back, "Not really, just that there was this television show I liked as a kid, "Alias Smith and Jones." Used to watch the syndicated re-runs. I guess I always imagined myself as some kind of outlaw, but one with a good cause, rather like the iffy premise of the program. However, the names Smith or Jones were a little too obvious, so I chose the name of one of the actors."

At first she nodded her head but then looked at him and said, "Wait a minute… I thought the two guys were Peter Deuel and Ben *Murphy*."

He smiled in surprise. "You must be an investigative reporter. Can't slip one past you… but how would you know the stars? It's long before your time."

"We watched re-runs too. So, 'fess up. How'd you mix up two different actors' names like that?"

"Who said I didn't know the difference between Ben Murphy and Ben Johnson? I might have my own reasons for interchanging the actors' names," and he gave her a sly wink.

At first the innuendo was lost on her, but then his obtuse reasoning dawned in her already tired brain and she opened her eyes wider in feigned shock, then laughed. From what Anthea had said, Sol had not expected a sense of humor that ran just a little toward the gutter. But that opened the floodgates to dig into his personal history.

While they ate a leisurely meal, Solana used her well-honed interview techniques to get Toddy to share about his background, not that he didn't know exactly what she was doing. He told her about his days as a wiz kid in school, when the world was being introduced to the concept of personal computers, learning the ropes about writing software for the new industry. He'd gotten himself booted out of college when he'd hacked into the school's system to help a friend who'd failed a major final that would destroy his qualification for a sports scholarship. From there he went to work on proprietary software that backtracks would-be hackers and fried their hard-drive. Figured he could use his expertise for good instead of evil. He'd ended up selling the product to the government and was inducted into the conspiratorial world of the CIA as a consultant until he realized the work was delving into areas he'd really prefer not to travel. The pressure and secrecy sent him back out on his own where he wrote another program that cracked his own anti-hacking program.

It wasn't long before another government contractor purchased the rights to that software which allowed him to retire from both clandestine work and the marketplace. So, he invested the proceeds and settled in Ruidoso to study anything and everything that interested him, mostly philosophy and law. He'd never obtained an actual degree but managed to wade through some of the most esoteric writings of the Age of Reason, applying it to understanding the workings of government and how it has metamorphosed over time. Rousseau, Payne and more recent figures such as Baudrillard and Lyotard had opened his thoughts to realizing how the process of governance, that was first mapped out by the founding fathers, had become warped. Not to forget his interest in Biblical justice and history as a core, leveling agent for all of the information he was constantly absorbing.

Sol knew that he'd glossed over much but was surprised at Toddy's opening up as much as he had. They had only talked a couple of times before today and she was still virtually an unknown entity as far as he was concerned.

Toddy lifted his drink to take a sip and asked, "So now, the tables are turned. Tell me about you." His eyes were sultry in the softened light of the dining room and she wondered about the man who really lived out here on a lonely mountain with not even a goldfish as companion.

"Don't know that there's that much to tell," she was a little shy all of a sudden, a foreign feeling for her.

He looked deep into her eyes, "I doubt that's so. Talk," he commanded in a soft but imperious tone and watched her while she launched into her history. She talked about her parents and grandparents, living on the ranch in Southern Montana. How she'd gone to a local school and had to deal with some discrimination, though not as much as others. "It's a small town. Everyone knows everyone and we didn't have quite as much problem as some areas closer to the res. I was even a rodeo princess one year. Kind of a first for an Indian up there." She talked a bit about barrel racing and going to powwows. She'd danced in the women's fancy category when she was younger.

As a coed, she'd attended Montana State for two years, competed for Miss Indian World, but didn't win the crown. However, she'd met a part-time actor at the contest who was Navajo. They got married on a whim and since he was based out of Albuquerque, she transferred to the University of New Mexico to be with him. She ended up studying journalism thinking that reporting the news objectively might help the rest of America to learn more about the Native American experience and sovereignty issues. When the marriage went sour after only a year, she finished her degree and landed an internship at the New York Times.

"That was definitely a 'brave, new world' for me." Solana characterized the experience as landing on a strange planet with a foreign atmosphere. It wasn't long before it became evident that the reason they'd hired her was due to her Indian heritage.

"Most of the management had trouble getting over the ethnic factor, which seemed odd considering that the city is overrun with people from every part of the world." She'd been fairly dumbfounded by some of the mindsets she encountered in the newsroom. It was a different kind of discrimination in the city. A patronizing attitude seemed to underlie so much of what was said.

"It was very strange. Some of those people were so certain that they needed to mentor a simple Native from the reservation, that it almost became a game to see if they'd swallow their whole foot or just nibble their own toes. I swear, the most supercilious people have got to be big city elitists who absolutely *know* what will make life better for the poor down-trodden Indian." She shivered remembering some of their foolish ideas. "Those people need to get a clue."

She continued with her story by telling Toddy that after a couple years she landed a position at the Denver Post where she stayed until about a year ago when she decided it was time to give city life a rest. The social scene in Denver was something of a wash since she was viewed as a novelty in some circles, "Not all, it just so happened that it took me a while to figure out that's what was going on with my longtime boyfriend." So she packed up and went back to her father's folks in Idaho where they'd advertised for a new manager of the tribal paper.

"It was just time to move on, you know?"

"Yes, I do know," said Toddy catching a glimpse of the strength that had grown out of the need to prove herself in a hostile world. Although his own history held some troubled times dealing with gangs in his hometown of Anaheim, ultimately it had been the pressure cooker of D.C. that had sent him running for the hills.

"Prejudice shows up in strange ways. It was more of a reverse discrimination where I came from. If you showed the least aptitude for wanting to make something of yourself and avoid the gang culture, you could find yourself in deep trouble."

"What did you do?" she was interested in his formative years.

"Got out and never went back. Wasn't much else I could do."

She was disappointed that he obviously wasn't going to give her any more than that but decided that she should let it lie for now.

"Well, are you happy with your move to the middle of nowhere?" she asked.

He just looked across the table at her, his lips turned up at one corner, "Are you?"

She laughed a little at the 'gotcha.' "Yes." She mulled it around a bit. "I'm content for the most part, just a little bored."

"Hence the road trip, eh?"

"Maybe. We'll just have to see what happens," said Sol.

"Seems to me you've already stirred things up," and he leaned over and grabbed the check.

Chapter 10

The image of Jake Kasili standing on a raised platform in a basketball arena filled the screen. "This country is duty-bound to lessen dependence on energy production that ah pollutes our air and water. My policy has been to encourage ah closure of outmoded facilities and emphasize environmentally friendly power supplies such as, ah stressing the development of solar and wind technology."

The follow-up question, if you could call it one came from a woman who was half-hidden behind the cameras of the Albuquerque NBC affiliate. "So, it is your policy to block the Desert Mountain Power Plant, part-owned by the Navajo Nation, from coming online, thus preventing the poverty-stricken reservation a major employment opportunity, dooming them to struggle with a lack of good jobs and worsening economic outlook."

"Ah, don't misunderstand my position. What I have said is ah that we, as a nation, must ah target the development of ah-ah clean energy resources…"

"Isn't that short-sighted when the Native population is reliant on the resources available on Reservation land?"

Click. He couldn't stand listening to it again. It was bad enough the first time, let alone the fourth and fifth replay. It didn't take a genius to know that their candidate was a little less than swift if he didn't have the words printed in front of him or projected on a teleprompter. Whatever happened to the device that was supposed to be implanted? He knew the candidate had balked at the idea, but he had been assured that Kasili had gone along with the plan in order to avoid debacles exactly like this one.

He lowered his head into his hands and just closed his eyes in frustration. There were bound to be ambushes and the candidate was just too green to be able to field questions that came in out of the blue. Oh, he did well enough when he was actually informed about the subject matter, but unfortunately, his scope of knowledge was limited in economics, foreign policy, national health care. Face it, the guy knew a great deal about very little and he wasn't chosen for this because of his outstanding intellect insomuch as his ability to whip a crowd into a frenzy with his charismatic personality, and even that had had to be cultivated. Hell, a lifetime of cultivation and he still crashes and burns on a podunk stage in effing New Mexico.

He stood up, brushed off his pants and left the conference room. It was time to pay the piper and man, was he going to be pissed. Not that he'd show it, unh-unh. No, he will stare you down with those soulless eyes and make you feel as small as an insect, and, he will be right because we failed to keep the man in check. Well, it was too late to trade horses now, it'll just have to work. He straightened his tie and knocked before pushing open the door to the office. *It has to.*

Aysha, Ethiopia – 1968

He just traveled over the border from Djibouti in a beat-up Land Rover that has definitely seen better days, but is still mechani - cally solid. Which is a good thing because the road is barely deserv - ing of the title. It is more of a cattle track, not that there are many of the native bovine in this northern edge of the Great Rift Valley. The few head that wander up and down the dry savanna are watched by dark-skinned herders, ever vigilant for rustlers that steal cattle to feed the growing rebel forces.

This trip is to conclude a transaction with those very same rebels, supplying them Soviet manufactured weapons for a hefty prof - it. Where the scraggly troops manage to scrounge their funds is of no consequence to him, though he presumes it is from preying on the unprotected populace and general thievery. The goods always manage to make it to a black market on the coast where initial sums, earnest money changes hands. It is those down payments that brought him over the poorly protected frontier to where he is sitting today, under the shade of a huge thorn tree awaiting the arrival of his contact.

Within the hour a man dressed as a native herdsman comes into view, walking with a young boy at his side. He carries a curved staff of native wood that stands taller than his own 6'3". The boy is dressed in similar fashion and is pumping his little legs to keep abreast of the man.

The man in the truck, jumping down agilely, meets the herds - man under the outstretched limbs of the tree. The boy, who can now be seen, appears to be somewhat lighter in complexion than the herds - man, whose face and arms that are uncovered have the deep skin tone of dark-roasted coffee, smooth and unblemished. Although he moves with ease through the heat, he doesn't have the weathered look of a man who lives his life outside tending cattle, an occupation that, indeed, is not his. He is a man of growing stature within the diplomat - ic corps of Haile Selassie, yet he plots the emperor's downfall. A trai - tor, but not for gain... for principle. Today, he is here to close the deal for arms that will equip his comrades, the ones that he cannot publicly support.

It all seems rather odd to the gunrunner as the man who stands before him, fairly towering over him, prides himself on his relation to the emperor whose lineage is fabled to reach all the way back to King Solomon by way of Queen Makeda of Sheba. No matter, the gunrun - ner has known the false herdsman for some years and had even bankrolled his degree from the University of Chicago earlier in the decade, an investment that has paid off.

This is the first, however that he has met the man's son, a boy of about five with dual citizenship who is staying with his father for a year before returning to his mother's care.

Husayn places a hand on his son's head and tells him to shake the gunrunner's hand. The little boy looks up without hesitation and complies with his father's command. The man is impressed with the boy's intrepid nature and evident fearlessness and before they finalize their business, the gunrunner quizzes Husayn about his son, his apti - tudes and his quickness. Then he turns his attention to the boy and with Husayn's urging, asks the boy many questions about his life and his experiences.

The child is forthright and appears bright, which gives the man an inkling of an idea, one that he decides to broach at a later date with Husayn. For the meantime, he asks Husayn to keep him apprised of the boy's progress. A proud father, the fraudulent herdsman agrees.

The two men complete the business for which they have met on this desolate plain. Acceptance of funds by the arms dealer is followed with a radio call made to a small convoy of trucks that waits just over the horizon to fulfill its mission – the delivery of weaponry.

A cloud of dust rises in the distance and they wait for the arrival of the vehicles. As the first truck rolls to a stop next to the Land Rover, the gunrunner shakes hands with the herder who then lifts his son into the passenger side of the truck and climbs in after him. The gunrunner boards his own vehicle and spins around to drive back toward Djibouti and the Gulf of Aden while the convoy continues deeper into Ethiopia and mounting conflict.

The meeting between the assistant and his superior went as well as could be expected, which wasn't saying much. He'd been given the directive to call Kasili's campaign and get some responsible answers as to the candidate's apparent inability to field policy questions on the fly.

Reaching for a phone that was not tied into the office lines, he pressed one of the speed dial numbers on the little cellular unit. The phone was answered within three rings with a crisp, "Yes?"

"Can you tell me what happened this last week in Montana and New Mexico? The Man is understandably upset with the abysmal performance that just happened to make national coverage."

"We were blindsided by a Native American journalist," the campaign manager supplied as a poor excuse and he knew it. "No one suspected that she would take a hostile attitude in her questioning. The questions she'd supplied for review were mediocre and unintimidating, more or less what we expected from a backwater news crew."

"Not good enough," the assistant shot back brusquely. "I thought you had all the contingencies covered with the device. Was I wrong?"

"Well, he has to turn the damn thing on," he was as exasperated as the man on the phone. "Most of the time, there isn't a problem and no one suspected that this would be a difficult situation."

"All right, then tell me how the woman got through a *second* time? This, I don't understand."

"Fubars by the staff. The gal running the show hadn't followed up on the last three engagements while she was pulling together the loose ends for the New Mexico appearance." He sighed and massaged his thick, ruddy brows with thumb and fingers of one hand. "The governor's staff was more demanding than anticipated and dragged her around the block on miniscule details."

"The damage is done. Even though we've been able to control most of the major media, the internet crowd is blowing it out of proportion and talk radio is having a heyday. You have to control the crowd more closely."

"Hell, you know there are limitations and republican spies everywhere," he was tired and knew this was going nowhere.

"Right. Republican or Castor spies?"

"Does it matter? They're both impossible to detect most of the time," said the campaign manager.

"Her interference needs to be addressed before the convention," added the assistant.

"Sure, you got any ideas? At the moment I'm fresh out," the exhaustion was making him into little more than a puddle.

The other side of the conversation dried up for a few moments leaving both of them to stew in silence.

The campaign manager finally said, "What do you want?"

"Hey, I don't have to tell you what to do. You're a big boy," and he was gone.

Chapter 11

Feeling rested after a solid night's sleep, Solana swung her legs over the side of the big, heavy-framed bed. Stretching, she took in her surroundings with more acuity than she had before climbing under the covers. She'd been too exhausted to notice the style of the décor, which amounted to mostly solid wood furniture that was well-made but not particularly distinguished in any fashion sense. The couple of prints on the wall depicted high mountain forest scenes and upon closer inspection, she noticed that each was signed by the artist.

Enough lookie-loo. I've got to get a move on. She checked the bedside clock to see that it was almost eight a.m. Rummaging through her bag, she came up with clean clothes, grabbed her shampoo and headed to the bathroom, which was actually part of the guest suite, for her shower.

A half-hour later Sol padded into the kitchen to find it empty except for the morning light sifting through the windows and the skylight. She looked up to see a clear, blue field dotted with a few clouds scudding by. A beautiful day for... what? She didn't know yet and Toddy was evidently a late sleeper, though from what Anthea had said, she assumed that he never slept. *Guess I got that wrong,* she smiled as she started hunting through the cupboards for coffee makings.

Not long after she had coffee dripping through his fancy machine that had an espresso maker on the side, the lord of the manor crossed the kitchen threshold, rubbing the sleep out of his eyes. He was barely dressed in shorts that allowed her to get a good look at a pair of strong legs, probably from all that skiing and bicycling, and a crumpled old t-shirt that was torn off just below his chest, revealing a trim waist and solid abs. Definitely not the computer nerd she had expected.

The coffee dribbled into a sleek looking carafe, half-filling it. Sol had already located the mugs and set a couple on the counter. "Are you ready for caffeine?"

He jumped slightly at the sound of her voice. Apparently, he was still half asleep and had forgotten that he had a guest in his abode. "Damn, you scared me," he said lowering his hands.

"The fact that you were entertaining a houseguest slipped your mind, huh?"

"Um. Yes," and he looked down at his lack of proper clothing. "Otherwise I'd have dressed for the occasion," and his sun-tanned skin took on a slight tinge of pink.

She cocked her head. *Bashful, too. Must have been a long time since he's been around anyone, let alone a woman.* "Doesn't bother me. I don't mind sharing coffee with a man in a state of undress. Makes me think I lead a wilder life than what the reality is."

"And what's the reality?" he asked taking a steaming mug from her after she'd poured.

"Life is actually pretty tame in the so-called wilds of the North." They took their coffee and sat at a polished marble table that served as a breakfast nook, facing the sliding glass doors that opened onto another high mountain vista.

"I've already checked for a newspaper but didn't see one," said Sol.

"Nah, I don't care to have anyone coming up here who doesn't need to. I get all of the news through the on-line services and papers. Oh and the on-air media, too."

"Guess you're just a modern kind of guy," she said. "I suppose that I'm still stuck in the old ways of print. I like to sit and read a paper with my coffee."

"Sorry I can't accommodate you with that luxury this morning. However, I do have an extra computer if you care to surf the news sites. I subscribe to all of them."

"All of them?"

"Okay, that may be an exaggeration. But I do read just about everything, including Al Jazeera." He ran his hand through his hair, which was already standing on end. "Gotta keep tabs on the enemy," he said, winking as he drank.

"Okay, I need to check out what's been happening, so if you'll excuse me for a bit, I'm going to take a fresh cup of coffee into my version of the newsroom." He stood up, refilled the mug and sauntered down the hall toward another part of the house. "You can come if you like," he called back over his shoulder.

Setting his coffee next to one of his three desktop computers, he picked up one remote control after another, flicking on three televisions, only one of which he left the sound on. All three cable news networks were concentrating on the veep choices available to Kasili.

"Don't you think it's a little early to be vetting vice presidential candidates? Okay, not vetting. They have to do that, but making such a great fuss over it," observed Solana as she sat in a chair opposite one of the other computers. "Castor has barely, and I mean barely, conceded and it simply looks like they're trying to rub her nose in it, which, in my humble opinion, isn't particularly smart."

Toddy was typing away at a mile a minute while he answered Sol. "Under the circumstances, I frankly agree with you. However, I believe that they are trying to distance themselves from the primary contests as quickly as possible. They need to get Castor and her toadies as far on the outside as they can."

"Well, what about the fact that the Castor supporters have petitioned to have her at the top of the potential VP list? That 'perfect ticket' propaganda that was getting tossed around earlier in the campaign?" continued Sol.

"You know as well as I do that's not going to happen. She'd try to steal the ticket and considering the almost even split of delegates in the primary races, she'd have a good shot."

"You're not thinking that 'shot' is the operable word, are you?"

He slid her a sideways glance, then laughed. "No, but knowing the history of both these candidates, it's not completely unimaginable. Look at the people who have been close to the Castors that have come to a nasty end, physically and politically." He stopped talking while he pulled up another news website. "But then you have to consider Scirras and his connection to Kasili. This is not a character without a past, either, he's just been far more discreet and, at this point in his life, wields far more power, too."

"How is Kasili connected to Scirras? This I don't think I've heard," she perked up her ears and leaned back in the secretarial chair awaiting another explanation.

Toddy described the pipeline running backward from building-bridges.org, Kasili's major backer and 527 funder, to Scirras who funds *them*. Since federal election law limits how much hard money a member of Congress can raise for their campaign, section 527 of the Internal Revenue Code saw the addition of a new loophole, which allows for the collection of unlimited soft moneys raised from individuals, corporations and unions.

"Now look what I received from Anthea last night. She's been looking into the gold connection…"

"The what?"

"The gold connection. There appears to be an interesting link between countries where gold mining is, or *was*, I should say, a going concern until those same countries ended up dealing with revolts and major unrest. And now each of these countries has a chapter of the Free State Foundation meddling in their affairs." Anticipating Sol's thoughts, he answered her unasked question before she could get the words out, "Scirras formed the FSF as a supposed means to spread 'democratic values' throughout the world, and the organization now has managed to *invade*, if you will, over 50 countries, all third world nations with struggling economies. A number of these nations include the ones I mentioned that mine a fair amount of gold, such as Australia, the Dominican Republic, Ethiopia, Romania, Zimbabwe, Namibia, USA and Uzbekistan. Oh, and we believe he has his eye on South Africa's mineral industry as well.

"Now, not all of these are failing economies, but even Australia and the USA have been battling a media blitz warning of economic disaster, whether or not it's really true. Where there is a connection is this, and it's four-fold:

"One – A number of these countries have suffered a major coup, rebellion or insurrection within the last forty years. Two – We believe that Scirras began his empire building as an arms dealer in the 1950s, later using his ill-gotten gains to fund his international currency trading for which he is now known. Three – Scirras' Herculaenea Fund is the major stockholder in Altamont Mining, which has ownership or major options in gold operations in all of the countries I just listed, and developing others in South America, Africa, Asia, well, everywhere. Four – His Free State Foundation is now entrenched in each of the countries that, the circumstantial evidence would indicate, he was instrumental in bringing about their collapse, thus making them vulnerable to outside economic leverage, i.e. Scirras in his philanthropic guise." He looked over at her from the notes that Anthea had sent him. "Is this making sense?"

"So far, but I think I need a chart to really absorb it all. The visuals help me. Probably why I'm print media and not radio," she added for a little lightening of the atmosphere.

"Okay," said Toddy, "so let's look at the countries that have changed regimes, and not necessarily for the better as far as the people are concerned. Though it was definitely better for someone whose plan it was to come in as a perceived savior. Hungary: 1956; Kenya, the Mau Mau Rebellion: 1952-54; Haiti: 1957. Remember this is part of the island of Hispaniola which the Dominican Republic shares; Czechoslovakia: 1968; Rhodesia, now Zimbabwe: 1974; Ethiopia: 1975; Uganda: 1971; Angola/Namibia: the 1970s-80s; South Africa: the 1980's and Romania: 1989. All the dates aren't exact, but they're close."

Solana had grabbed a legal pad and had been scribbling down the names of each of the countries he'd mentioned, first as gold producers and secondly as war-torn or having had a rebellion or coup. "Not all of these are gold producing nations," she said as she studied the second list.

"Right, but look at the proximity to the countries that are," and he pulled up both a map of Europe and one of Africa. Sol repositioned herself so she could look over his shoulder at the computer screen. He pointed out the countries in Europe first. "See how Czechoslovakia, well now it's the Czech Republic and Slovakia, and Hungary border Romania and all were part of the Communist Bloc." Then he switched to the African map, "Look how Kenya and Uganda close in on Ethiopia, and down here... you have Angola and Namibia stacked one on the other, just north of South Africa and Zimbabwe bordering South Africa here. Anthea thinks that South Africa is the prize that he's trying to corner down here with some of the richest mineral deposits in the world."

Sol just stood there and looked at the maps, her mind whirling with the implications of the whole idea.

"And we didn't even go to gold producing countries like Mali and Burkina Faso which back onto Niger where there has been major problems over the last decade. Nor did we look at Asia or South America. Bolivia is a gold producer and it borders Colombia, and you know what's been happening there for years." He just sat back and felt her breath on his neck as she tried to grasp what he had pointed out. He found her closeness a little disconcerting. It had been a very long time since he'd been anywhere near a woman that he found interesting, and Solana intrigued him. She smelled of fresh rain in the desert, which brought him back to the reality that he was sitting there virtually in his underwear, unshowered and unshaven.

Without preamble he pushed back from the desk, forcing her to step back. "I've got to get cleaned up. Go ahead and take a closer look at her notes. Back later." And he strode out of the room as if the house were on fire.

His sudden departure caught her by surprise, but snapped her out of a daze of disbelief. She decided she needed more coffee and went back into the kitchen for a refill then came back to claim Toddy's chair and study the notes and maps more thoroughly. The whole convoluted concept was almost more than she could digest. She sipped her coffee while she thought about the monstrous association between someone who might be fomenting rebellion in dozens of countries for financial gain and then using that money to back his own private presidential candidate. It made her think about what could possibly be in store for the United States. How far would someone like this go and is it even possible to hurl *our* country into the kind of disarray that these other nations had been dealt?

Solana swiveled the chair to face the soothing mountain scene that lay outside a large picture window and slowly drank her coffee while she tried to make sense of just this part of the puzzle. Because she knew that as soon as Toddy reentered the room there would be even more information that would stand her on her ear and she was beginning to dread it.

Twenty minutes later, Sol heard Toddy's tread coming down the hall. When he stepped into the room the transformation was complete. He'd dressed in casual slacks and an aqua colored polo shirt and even combed his hair, which was still damp from the shower. For some reason, Sol had expected him to arrive in ripped up jeans and t-shirt and turning to rise from the chair to give him back his seat, she decided that he'd probably made a special effort for her. The thought made her grin.

"Have you found something humorous? I rather thought that this information was pretty disturbing," and he nodded in thanks as he resumed his seat.

She quickly brushed the smile aside and sat back into the other chair, swiveling a little while watching him get resettled. "I'm having a difficult time imagining that anyone could be so devious as to pull together the kind of conspiracy you're advocating. You'd have to be practically nuts to believe all this could be possible." She stopped herself abruptly, "Not that I think you and Anthea are crazy, I mean..." She rubbed the back of her neck. "Geez, I don't know what I mean. It's just too incredible."

He whipped his chair around and studied her. "Precisely. No one like you or I would conceive of anything of the kind. The problem is that Scirras' tentacles don't end with gold, that's just a, a *hobby* with him. He sees himself as the next king and we are his subjects and, dare I say? His playthings, his amusement. To be plain, I fought the *con - spiracy* angle as much as I could. I'm a skeptic but," and he turned to sweep his hand around the room, taking in all the screens with images in constant motion, "all of this? It could change your mind. And boggle it."

"Boggled would about cover how I feel at the moment. This is just too much to accept, at least on first impulse."

"That doesn't mean that we can ignore it. The fact is that we don't have a choice except to try to do something about it. Scirras is an economic terrorist using his financial power to cow governments into doing his will. First he brings them to their knees by sponsoring violent overthrow, then he manipulates their commodities and currency, and *then* he brings his philanthropic agency in to offer succor and rehabilitation. *And*, I haven't even started on the environmental angle." Sol looked at him, puzzled, while he shook his head in begrudging admiration. "It's brilliant. And, what's worse, it's working."

Switching his attention to the television, he brought up the volume as the candidate Kasili came into view walking back and forth across a stage with his shirtsleeves rolled up, a microphone in one hand. He was addressing a crowd and talking about his personal legacy as being a man of two worlds, Africa and America. Sketching his history, he talked about spending time as a youngster with his father in Ethiopia learning about his roots. Roots that go back to the Emperor Haile Selassie and all the way to Solomon, as the royal lineage traces their ancestry. He was waxing eloquent about pride in our heritage, whoever we are and wherever we come from… yada, yada, yada.

"Here's another one of Kasili's little not-quite-truth, not-quite-a-lie moments," said Toddy. "Here he is extolling the wonders of his ancestry, stating that he follows it back to King Solomon, when in fact his ancestry is traced through Selassie's *wife's* side, his father being a great nephew of Queen Menen." He looked back at Solana. "Anthea uncovered this one too. It's not such a big deal except for the fact that the Queen traced *her* ancestry all the way back to *Mohammed* not Solomon. His father carried the traditional family name of Husayn and his name, Yakub, is from the same tradition. Although the royal heir must profess the Ethiopian Orthodox faith, most of the Queen's side of the family are and have been Muslim for centuries. So, what does that say to you?" He looked at her expectantly.

"Simply that he is trying to make it seem that he is noble by birth while being just like you and me, except now he's actually drawn attention to the fact that his father is Muslim, which could be detrimental to his campaign because of terrorist implications if he can't convince people of his Christianity. I guess they're banking on the fact that no one will bother to check it out," her voice trailed off.

"They, of course, have not encountered people as diligent as us," he winked.

"And you need me for, what?" she looked across the short space to level her gaze with his.

"To help us uncover and document the truth. Isn't that what you do best?" A slow smile spread across his face.

She just sat back in the chair, letting it take her weight while she stretched out her legs, hoping to relax when she knew that wouldn't be possible. Could people really be as conniving as Anthea and Toddy have been trying to convince her they can? The insanity of it all was that she believed their sincerity but Sol couldn't figure what any of them could do to fix it if all of this *was* true and the country, no, the world, was heading for disaster at the hands of a new kind of megalomaniac. She just felt stumped and overwhelmed.

Gazing back at Toddy, who turned his back to her while he

worked the keyboard at an amazing speed, Sol felt like she'd been swept into a whirlwind. Maybe *she's* the one whose nuts.

Standing up, she said bluntly, "I've got to go for a walk."

Toddy sat back and watched Solana leave the room. He'd only just met her but admired her perspicacity and resolute nature. A little worried about how this last session had unfolded though, he called Anthea.

"I'm afraid that I might have scared off our colleague with too much information too fast," he started before even saying 'hello.'

"Nothing new about that. Where'd she go? I take it you meant 'scared her off' literally."

"Just on a walk," he said. "It may take some time for everything to penetrate."

"Forget it. No one can take in all the data you churn out in one sitting and still be considered sane. Give her a break. Maybe a flow chart would help."

The comment made them both laugh a little. "You know, she actually mentioned that."

"Wouldn't help, the arrows would go every which way and nobody would be able to figure out what's up or down. I'm speaking from experience because I have trouble outlining the concepts we talk about half of the time," she confessed.

"That's a crock. You always catch what I'm saying and Sol did too."

"She'll be back before long looking for more information. I believe you've already hooked her. Then we have to figure out what we can do about it." She sighed. "No one will publish this stuff, you know."

Toddy wasn't put off one bit. "That's why we have the internet."

There wasn't much in the way of a trail near Toddy's house, just mostly deer tracks winding through the pines standing sparsely among the rocks and low lying sage. She was careful not to wander too far afield while her mind sifted through everything she had been learning over the past couple of weeks.

She stopped to study the line of mountains stretching into the horizon, questioning what she was doing a thousand miles from home staying in the house of a virtual stranger. The rallies where she'd had the uncanny fortune to pepper a presidential candidate with queries that she *knew* would never have been made otherwise sent a shiver of satisfaction down her spine.

So what was it about Kasili that really bothered her? The fact that he could appear to be so erudite when pumping up a crowd, unhampered by hard questions or heckling, was at odds with his bungling answers when unprepped by handlers. You'd think that a man with a J.D. from the University of Chicago could field a few inquiries from a small-time reporter. It didn't add-up.

Are these guys really capable of perpetrating the evil and manipulation Toddy and Anthea allege? Even though there was no one else to see, she nodded, knowing in her gut that Scirras was who they portrayed him to be. The evidence might be circumstantial but it was overwhelming when you put it all into context. *None of it would hold up in a court of law.* But then, that wasn't their duty, digging up the information and generating enough interest for the judicial system to follow-up through the proper channels was.

Get the proof and print it, she told herself. *That's your job.*

Chapter 12

"So, what's the plan? I assume that you have one," Solana was leaning against the doorjamb to the media center, as she'd privately dubbed the room where Toddy was plunking away at a keyboard, so completely engrossed in his work that he practically shot out of his chair at the sound of her voice.

"Would you stop doing that?"

"Sorry, didn't mean to disturb your concentration," she said, smiling a little at his intensity. "But you do have a plan, don't you."

He swiveled around in his chair, an impish grin immediately replacing the startle he'd experienced. "I have given it some thought as to what our options are. We already have a head start on some of the research."

"I'm assuming that you want to get this information into the mainstream," she speculated. "To what end? What can we accomplish?"

"Think about it. We have drawn conclusions about Kasili and his connections to a powerful entity who is encouraging acceptance of his skewed vision of the future by misdirecting media as to the state of this country's economy. And he's managing to do it by way of manipulating currencies and certain commodities, most of it through misinformation."

"I don't get your point," she gave him a cross-eyed look. "English, please."

"Okay," Toddy paused to see if he could explain it differently. "The public is listening to Chicken Little. Instead of the 'sky is falling,' it's 'we're destroying the earth with carbon dioxide,' a natural bi-product of the process of life on this planet, which, by the way, man is responsible for only one-half of one-half percent in *everything* that we do, including breathe. But this is the excuse that's used to scare people into accepting whatever the State decrees, including such idiocy as banning incandescent light bulbs," he rolled his eyes heavenward. "Perpetuating the myth has placed the world in a precarious position because now we are using food for fuel. Talk about idiocy," he grumbled. "And this creates an actual hike in the cost of everything, since it is all related to the cost of energy. And the cost of energy is related to the devaluation of the dollar against currencies such as the euro or the yen."

"Back up," said Sol. "How does devaluing the dollar increase the cost of energy? I'm not much of an economic wizard."

"When the dollar loses value it purchases less, and energy, mostly oil in this case, is a commodity with a global market. So, oil is purchased with more dollars because the dollar buys less on the world market, which shoots up the price of just about everything back here in the U.S.," he lifted a brow as if to ask if this makes sense.

Solana nodded in answer and shifted her weight.

"Now, if someone is also manipulating the value of the dollar by hedging their bets on the currency market *against* it by buying billions in foreign currencies and *gold*, the commodity and futures, then the economy here will suffer in the long run because it forces up the cost of doing business. What Scirras is doing is forcing up the price of goods by leveraging other currencies and gold against the dollar. But what keeps the United States in a bind is the fact that the public has bought into the environmental craziness that has kept us from developing our own resources. We are being denied the opportunity to level the playing field and produce our own energy to buttress our economy because we are foolishly listening to Chicken Little."

Solana just stared at Toddy with narrowed eyes. All of a sudden she snapped to attention. "Gotcha. So our mission, should we decide to accept it, is to get the word out that we are being manipulated by an 'economic terrorist,' as you so aptly put it before." She walked into the room and sat down. "There are plenty of alternative media types that have been beating the drum about the global warming hoax, but no one has connected the currency angle into the equation." She leaned forward, elbows on her knees and chin in her hands, "That's our mission." She looked up into his eyes, which sparkled with pleasure. "Am I right?"

"Yup. But there's one more thing."

She dropped her head into her hands and moaned, "I should have known."

"Scirras is using his soapbox of the Free State Foundation, and a reputation for being a master trader on the stock market, to proselytize about creating regulations for trading on the world's stock markets. He wants to limit speculators from doing exactly what he did that almost destroyed the Bank of Britain. Basically, now that he has the upper hand, it's in *his* best interest to make certain that no one can stop him by using the same unregulated trading strategies that he used to create his empire. Destroy the enemy's potential to destroy him. In effect, it will annihilate capitalism as we know it and leave the world in an over-regulated society where the State will control anyone's ability to create wealth. It is the creation of a benevolent dictatorship, i.e. instituting communism by eradicating capitalism."

She looked up again. "Holy moley. You've got this guy ready to take over the world. That doesn't seem possible."

"It is if people don't wake up to recognize the kapos that are herding them into the extermination chambers."

❀❀❀

"Changingwind.org. What do you think of that for the webpage?" Toddy asked Sol without turning his head from his focus on the computer screen.

"Webpage?" She looked over her shoulder only to see the back of his head, thick, dark hair rumpled from having run his fingers through it over and over again while he'd explained his ideas to Sol.

"How else will we get this information out? No one would touch it no matter how much documentation we throw in. We'll have to do a 'Drudge' to get it going. Only difference is that we're going to have to be anonymous."

"I've never operated that way," she argued. "If it's not corroborated then it's not worthy to be published, nor to carry my byline. But if it's correct then there's no reason not to sign it."

"That's not the point," he turned around to face her. "This is a matter of self-preservation." She looked perplexed. "We are not dealing with run-of-the-mill thugs here. These are major players with real guns and ammo. There's no reason to put our necks on the line if we don't have to." He tilted his head to the side. "All we have to do is stir up interest, offer enough real information and let the dogs out. Others will pick-up the momentum and run with it." He went back to the screen. "So, what do you think... changingwind.org or whatnerve.net?"

"Hmmm. I like them both but I think the Changing Wind will be taken more seriously."

"Done."

While Toddy was creating the webpage that would sponsor the blog, Solana had been drawing up a flow chart for her own benefit. She'd been sitting at the kitchen table and letting the soothing scenery framed by the glass sliders take her away from the seriousness of what they were attempting to do.

As she finished the convoluted circles of arrows that even she wasn't so certain she could follow, she heard Toddy call her name from down the hall. Picking up her pad, she walked down to join him in the media center.

He had all three televisions on with two muted and one where the volume had been turned up. What she was seeing was a breaking news flash that centered around Governor Castor. A shot that was obviously being taken by a hovering helicopter, showed a motorcade strewn over a quarter mile of highway that stretched across a wide river. One of the limousines was engulfed in flames and hanging at a precarious angle over the side of the bridge. The whole road was closed down to traffic, orange cones and lit flares fashioned staggered barriers and a number of individuals were huddling in a group about forty feet from the blaze.

Then, as they watched, the burning hulk teetered on the edge of the roadway for a few seconds before pitching forward and tumbling into the swirling waters below.

"What just happened?" said Sol as she stood in the doorway.

"Dunno. Hopefully we'll find out," and he increased the volume even more.

The talking head, an unnatural redhead with a Middle Eastern name and a British accent was describing the scene as the camera swept the bridge from side to side, capturing the image of two limousines, the third one having taken a header into the Susquehanna River after inexplicably exploding into a fireball. The loop kept playing of the third limo caught on the lip of the bridge, flames leaping into the air and no one escaping the inferno before it fell into the dark water of the river's current.

Apparently, the small fleet was returning from the airport, traveling to the governor's mansion after retrieving the governor and her entourage upon their arrival in Harrisburg. They had just alighted after attending a brief meeting with Kasili that had been held in Washington, D.C. to coalesce the plan for joining the two democratic forces. Information wasn't immediately available as to who had been riding in the ill-fated car.

Half talking to himself, Toddy said." Well, what do you know? They didn't waste time."

"Who didn't waste time? What are you talking about?"

"It'll sound crazy." He skimmed his eyes past her own questioning ones. "Kasili's machine."

"Wait a minute, I thought it was the Castors who had a 'machine.' And you're right, it does sound crazy." Her look changed to one of skepticism.

"If you look at the situation from Kasili's standpoint, Castor is a major stumbling block for the continuity of his campaign. She's too strong a personality to stand next to him on a dais and she certainly wasn't going to disappear without a peep. Castor paid for every one of those delegates in blood and she'll be damned before she lets Kasili bask in the limelight without receiving her due."

"But what are her options?" asked Sol. "The party has thrown its lot in with the first black candidate over the first woman." She paused to think, "but she still has control of her delegates and they *will* carry weight at the convention despite her abandonment by the DNC." Her expression changed to one of incredulity. "You can't believe that they would try to get rid of her permanently! That *is* crazy!"

Toddy switched his attention from the television to Sol and said evenly, "Why not? Face it, Castor is now a distraction from the real agenda and she thinks of herself as a powerhouse who doesn't need to share with anyone else. Kasili's handlers don't want two head chefs and Castor, had she been given the DNC nod of approval, would never have relinquished control. In fact, she would never understand that she didn't actually wield much of *any* power and would be a thorn in their side. Kasili, on the other hand, is happy to be a puppet because he's been groomed for this role."

The coverage on the news has changed to a different camera angle and they returned their attention to the screen. The news anchor was saying that the limo that went in the water had been slated to be carrying the governor's son, but he had flown out to Montana to meet friends for a fishing trip at the last minute. Instead, the vehicle had been carrying two upper echelon campaign workers who'd been in D.C. with the governor to advise her on her new role within the Kasili presidential bid and that both the governor and her husband appeared to be unhurt.

A few moments later the camera had panned to where the governor and her husband were being spirited away from the scene in a helicopter that had been flown in for that purpose. The state police kept the remaining limos in place and shut down the bridge to all other vehicles as they continued their investigation. The whole mess was causing a major traffic snarl as rush hour approached in Harrisburg. The anchors on all of the channels were tossing out theories right and left on how a limousine in the governor's train managed to burst into flames while trying to downplay any political implications.

"They're going to have a helluva time trying to explain away an explosion with the excuse of a 'mechanical' failure. Looks to me like someone screwed up." He was quiet for a few moments while they watched the ambulances and police cruisers pile-up on the bridge. "What I wonder," said Toddy absently, "is if this was meant as an assassination attempt or just a 'message.'"

"Yes, but *whose* message?" she paused to think. "I suspect that whatever the message was, the point came through loud and clear because, although we may not know the answer, the target certainly does."

Chapter 13

E-mails flew between Toddy and Anthea throughout the afternoon postulating on the implications of the Harrisburg 'accident.' Solana, needing a break from the constant hubbub of the media center with volume from more than one television turned on and a radio tuned into one of the more caustic talk show hosts, went into the kitchen to see what she could scrounge for a late lunch. It was obvious that Toddy ate well. The refrigerator was well stocked with fresh vegetables, fruits, cheeses and exotic condiments and relishes, and the pantry held quite an array of canned goods of a somewhat unusual variety. It wasn't long before she'd found the makings for salad and sandwiches. She put together a hearty meal since neither of them had eaten breakfast.

Toddy was glued to the computer, informing Anthea of the plan for the website, "changingwind.org" and that he planned on launching it within twenty-four hours. Anthea wasn't happy with the idea and cornered him about the wisdom of a blog. It was one thing for them to be sharing information about their suspicions but why set himself up as a target?

He wrote back that he wouldn't have any trouble setting up a bulletproof site, reminding her that it *was* his specialty. He could make it virtually impossible to trace.

Not liking his answer, Anthea wearied of the argument via the internet and called him. "Are you nuts? You're the one who wrote the best protection program out there. And then what did you do? You went and wrote a better program that allows you to hack into the first. Someone else could do the same. Much as I like to think sometimes, you, my dear, are not infallible."

"Ah, but you forget, *my dear*, that I am so familiar with the software that is available that I am thus the best prepared individual to guard against it. No worries. I teach at the college on occasion and can use their system to set it up. I doubt you want to hear the details, so just be assured that I can protect us well."

He had it all planned out to route the website through the college's mainframe, letting himself in a backdoor to a business located in another state that he'd already pegged as a likely prospect. Using their internet connection as a proxy, their IP address would be the one that would appear to the outside. He was then planning to route the blog through yet another school in Texas as a further proxy. It wouldn't be too difficult to add a couple more proxies on top of that one, since he'd raided any number of college sites in the past for no other purpose than practice and alleviating boredom. He'd spent years arranging a privacy network that gave him access to credit cards that couldn't be traced back to him, so he was all set to be able to use internet cafes as a means to input the blog from anywhere. He would make certain that all the proxies stayed within the United States lest he trigger interest from Homeland Security.

Anthea finally gave in and told him she would provide him with some historical reports that would support the conclusions Toddy's blog would be propounding. He'd already explained that Solana would cover the news end and he would supply the philosophical tie-ins.

"Just be sure you write it in layman's language. You're apt to drive off your readership if you don't. I have a terrible time trying to follow your train of thought and I know how you think, well, sort of." She let out a breath, "It's just that the esoteric concepts you espouse are something of a challenge for most of us average bodies."

He laughed as he typed, "I'll have Sol read it and edit the content for general consumption. Will that help?"

"I'm sure it will. I guess that you two are hitting it off pretty well then."

"I think so. She's a very sharp woman," he hesitated, "but I'm not sure what she thinks of me."

"Hey, what's not to love? Just don't scare her off again," Anthea became serious, "and promise me that no one will be able to backtrack this thing to either of you." As an afterthought, she added, "or, *me*."

"Cross my heart."

After preparing the meal to the best of her ability – Solana usually was not enamored with the idea of chef duties – she had trouble hauling Toddy away from the computer to eat.

"Come on, you haven't had anything today and if you're going to get this thing off the ground, you need sustenance."

Finally, he gave in and followed her to the kitchen where, of course, there was another television that Sol had avoided turning on. He immediately grabbed the remote and pressed the power button.

She just took a long drink from an iced tea and rolled her eyes. *Is there no man who can live without a remote control always at hand?*

The Castor story now had added in the fact that the convention was less than six weeks away and every one of the news anchors and pundits were speculating on how this 'limousine incident' would affect the two democratic camps. Would there now be a strain between them or would they consolidate their efforts behind Kasili's nomination?

It didn't take long before Governor Castor showed up in front of the cameras. They were still seated at the table when her form appeared on the darkened steps of the governor's mansion, high voltage lamps bathing the façade of the building with the intensity of a noon sun in the tropics. Oh, and she was ticked. At least, that was the impression she was giving despite her best attempts to appear distraught and anguished at the loss of two of her senior campaign advisors.

"She's never been a particularly good actress," noted Solana as she pushed her plate aside to lean her elbows on the table and cup her chin, giving full attention to the ensuing circus.

"I'd have to agree," said Toddy, leaning back in the opposite direction, legs outstretched under the table, thoroughly enjoying the show. "That smile of hers rarely looks genuine, but then, when has she really had something to smile about? Particularly being married to that smarmy tomcat hovering behind her."

Sol slid her vision sideways to catch his own enthusiastic grin before shaking her head in disbelief and retraining her attention on the screen.

The governor was standing in front of a makeshift panel of microphones sprouting out of a podium that someone had dragged from the residence and she was preparing to address the crowd, trying her best to plaster a look of tired dismay and sorrow on her face.

Her statement wasn't more than a few minutes comprised of condolences for the families of her co-workers, glowing praise for their attributes and how they will be missed and thanking the efforts of the rescue workers whose rapid response contained the damage, ultimately saving the lives of others. Enough to glean some topnotch soundbites that would cover the news channels for hours and maybe even days.

"You know," Toddy mused from his relaxed posture, "if this was meant as a message for her to take a back seat," Solana darted him with a near deadly glare, "then it really backfired."

"Two puns in one?" she sniffed. "It's bad enough that two people died in that back seat of what could be a bombing." She stopped. "Backfired, huh? You might be right. Look at all the press she's getting and Kasili is nowhere to be found. In fact, no one really cares about him at the moment."

"Hm hmmm. She's busy grabbing headlines when Kasili should be basking in the limelight. Makes you wonder if Castor might have orchestrated this herself to ease him out of the picture."

"No way she's that merciless," said Sol. "How could you even think of something that awful," she said flatly.

"How much worse is that than our other postulation that Kasili's team could be behind the explosion?"

"It's still possible it was an accident," Sol said, not believing it herself.

Toddy looked heavenward and said, "Right. The question is if Kasili could be so dumb or his operatives so incompetent that in their attempt to quiet the opposition they've created a monster instead."

"Okay. Say she didn't do it and the other guys did, then she'd better be afraid of what they'll try next. And if she *did* do it, then she's got to make hay while she can."

"So where *is* the man of the hour, I wonder?" Toddy asked the air.

Practically as soon as the words were out of his mouth, the television lit up with a shot of Kasili himself, who had just landed in Chicago for a campaign engagement. The news crew picked him up as he disembarked from the plane onto the tarmac where he made a brief, and apparently heartfelt, statement of sympathy and commiseration directed to the families of the deceased. In light of the tragedy, he had decided to briefly suspend the campaign out of respect for Governor Castor's loss and return to Washington D.C. for the memorials.

"I'd say it's more to regroup and strategize their way out of this Castor media coup than to share condolences," remarked Toddy.

"Ever the cynic, aren't we."

Toddy eyed her. "We are talking politics, remember?" He got up from the table and began clearing away the dishes. Sol stood and helped.

"What now?" she asked as they worked at the sink, loading plates and utensils into the dishwasher.

He looked down at her, eyebrows cocked in an amused expression. "Back to work, of course. We've got a webpage to launch." He winked, finished washing his hands and went back to the media center.

❊ ❊ ❊

The next morning they had already fallen into a routine. Solana was up making coffee by the time Toddy ambled into the kitchen. This time, however, he'd made an effort to present a better appearance when he arrived. They didn't spend too much time at the table before heading into the media center, picking up where they'd left off the night before… late the night before.

Toddy had just about everything ready to go for the debut of changingwind.org. He had written an introductory blog encouraging readers to learn more about the sordid connections between the Kasili candidacy and a multi-billionaire, international currency manipulator. To draw them in, he followed the line of campaign funding that could be traced through some questionable channels, offering documentation to bolster the claims. He didn't detail everything yet, letting them know that the story was unfolding even as he wrote in hopes of building intrigue.

Solana had combed through his essay reducing some of the hyperbole, double-checking that the implications were pointed and accompanied by strongly supportive cites. Toddy's work was thorough but some of the language needed to be taken down a peg, to accommodate the average person who did not read at a Grade 15 level. That estimation of the comprehension level was according to schooling 60 or more years ago, which is a mite different from present day teaching practices. Actually, Sol found it dismaying that written English comprehension wasn't encouraged more among modern day students, as sloppy grammar and vocabulary use was more the norm rather than uncharacteristic, particularly among young people.

With the blog ready, Toddy turned his attention to one of the areas of interest that he raised in his article – the gold connection. Since his contention was that Herculaenea Fund was central in manipulating currency trading partially through controlling gold production and, ultimately, influencing the price structure, he wanted to follow-up on the activities of Altamont Mining. They had already found connections between solidly producing mines being closed in Romania and parts of Africa, so he located other operations and started delving into whether or not they were under the same pressures.

Talking to himself, Solana, who was working at one of the other computer stations in the converted den, heard him mumble something that sounded like, "Let's see what the goldgrubbers are up to," followed by furious typing.

What he found was an option the company had been pursuing in the region of north Arizona. As all of the online reports of Altamont were vague, he wasn't able to pinpoint much other than a reference to the remote Kanab Indian Reservation. So, following that lead he went to the tribal website and located enough data to pique his interest, which sent him to another site to uncover what he could about large property leases from the tribe.

Voila! There it was. Altamont had a huge lease with the Kanab Paiute where they were supposedly exploring for gold and other minerals, but it looked like the project had been shut down due to environmentalist pressure.

"I think we've got us another gold rush crush," he said as he skimmed through the little bit he could find on the subject.

"A what?" Solana pulled away from her reading to query his odd comment.

"An Altamont specialty. Buy up a promising gold strike and then crush it under the weight of claims from heavily funded environmental lobbies which have ties back to Free State Foundation. The system practically steals a valuable resource from an otherwise poor population." He turned to look at her. "I want to go check this out personally."

One eyebrow shot up. "O-okay," she said, hesitating a little. She was used to running off on her own to do research. That's why she was sitting in a virtual stranger's home creating an odd association that she hadn't anticipated when she'd loaded up her Tahoe. Or had she?

"Prepared for a road trip?" he asked smiling mischievously.

"I thought I was on one," she narrowed her eyes at him.

"Hey, we're partners now and this time we need to go and see what these bozos are doing up close and personal." He cocked his head sideways, hair falling into his eyes. "You're an investigative reporter, right? Let's go investigate."

She gave up. "Oh, why not. Where to?"

"The Kanab Indian Reservation near Fresia, by the Utah border. It looks to me like Altamont is sticking it to the tribe."

"And you said it's environmental lobbies doing the dirty work?" She considered for a moment. "That seems to be a modus operandi for environmental concerns around these parts, preying on the Native population."

Toddy pulled closer to her computer screen. "What did you find? Something related?"

"Not exactly. I want to check out the delay on plans for the new, clean technology coal-fired power plant on the Navajo Reservation that environmental lobbies have sandbagged. The Desert Mountain Power Plant is up north of Gallup. Maybe we can work that into the data gathering mission." She caught his eye with her own and grinned. "Want to see how they're still trying to keep my people down?"

He propelled himself backward in his rolling chair, hands coming up in innocence. "Hey, don't look at me. I've been shouting "state slavery" from the highest hill for years. Color or creed doesn't matter to these guys. It's all about creating victim mentality and a welfare class. Who listens?"

Gold Baron

Chapter 14

After merging on to I-25 from the two-lane highway they'd traveled from Ruidoso, Sol reached back and, grabbing a manila folder, tossed it to Toddy. As he opened it, he saw that she'd printed out what data and stories she could find on the Desert Mountain Power Plant.

"Is this what you were working on yesterday while I finished the website?" He asked as he began leafing through the loose pages.

She nodded. "Take a look. You can't even depend on the liberal press to support the oppressed Native Americans anymore," Sol pointed out. "Take a look at the article from the New York Times, my former employer, and how they're practically demonizing the Diné people for attempting to make a better life for themselves using their own resources."

Toddy skimmed through the article. "I've been reading up on the new technology they're putting into coal-fired generating plants these days. It's some of the cleanest energy production available now. From what you hear in the press one would think that coal is still the filthiest power production existing."

"It is if you're in China," said Solana. "They're still using old technology which is why they're so worried about the smog levels in Beijing for the upcoming Olympics. It's worse than L.A. ever was."

"I see the Farmington News has covered it more objectively." He rattled the sheets as he read. "The Navajo tribal council voted "overwhelmingly" in favor of the project by sixty-six to seven. It's not like they're just handing their resources over to another entity, either. They're solid partners in the project and will reap millions in benefits. Income that's really needed."

"Another thing that irritates me," added Sol, "is that the majority of websites listed on the net, when you input 'Desert Mountain Power Plant,' are almost all national pressure groups like the Sierra Club and Earth First! denigrating the initiative of the people. The stories are all ridiculous assertions about the impact of the new plant, which puts out a fraction of the pollutants that the old Four Corners Plant did." She took a breath and let it out. "There are very few locals that are blasting the plans. Oh, some are complaining about impending environmental devastation, but the facts don't bear out any of it from what I can see."

"You know my opinion," put in Toddy. "It seems to me that organizations that promote environmental extremism are more interested in controlling the actions of others rather than actually doing much good. If we look back at who's funding the loudmouths, millions can be traced back to those who'd rather see the poorer population rely on the government dole, and that includes the reservations. They may be sovereign nations but being surrounded by jurisdictions with more power that have input through the BIA and BLM bureaucracies, it's practically impossible to get anything done without ending up in court to protect their rights."

"That's precisely what they've had to do. The tribe had to threaten a lawsuit to get the EPA to rule by the end of July on granting the permit. It's no wonder this country is suffering under suffocating energy prices," she huffed. "This plant would bring prosperity to the Navajo nation and it would supply," she looked over at his papers and pointed to one of them before rapidly returning her attention to the road, "how much power to the region?"

Toddy checked through the figures, "Fifteen hundred megawatts. Enough for a million homes. That's just about the size of Phoenix's population." His gaze traveled along the desert landscape stretching for miles in all directions. "There's a reason why we're making this trip, rounding up information to feed a blog that will address these issues. Someone has to speak up."

"I just hope it does some good. People forget how we've been locking up our resources for years. Just last decade one of the largest sources of low-sulfur coal was placed off limits to mining by the creation of that new national monument not far from where we're going."

"Yup, I remember. The Grand Staircase-Escalante National Monument." Toddy supplied the name. "Thank you, President Clinton."

"There are some people who believe that was done simply to increase the value of the Indonesian coal by locking up this source and decreasing the overall supply," said Sol. "And now they're doing their best to keep the Diné from developing resources on their land."

"All in the name of supposedly reducing carbon dioxide emissions which have zero to do with global warming," added Toddy.

"Ooooh, I wouldn't say that aloud in some circles. Could get you into hot water," she said, smiling.

"I think I've already stepped off that cliff, don't you"?

"You and me both."

They continued to drive along at a good clip, Solana not being one to stick too closely to speed limits although she always had a watchful eye open for that lone highway patrolman lurking near some underpass.

There wasn't much on the radio and both of them seemed content to travel in silence for a while, a comfortable sense of calm disturbed only by the steady road noise of the blacktop passing beneath the Tahoe's tires.

A half-hour or so later, Solana, her mind wandering back and forth between the two tribes – the Kanab Paiute and the Navajo – comparing the situations, asked Toddy if he thought there was anything relating the two projects they were planning to check-out.

"Other than a concerted effort to keep both from developing their own resources? There might be." He fell silent again while he cogitated on the question. "Let's see. Both of the tribes suffer from a depressed economic condition. Agriculture, raising stock and so on has been a declining proposition considering the arid nature of both reservations. The casino trend that so many tribes have followed hasn't really been an option, particularly for the Kanab. They're too remotely located."

"From what you'd said, it sounds as though the pressure to derail the gold exploration is coming from environmental activists, same as the Desert Mountain protesters."

"Yes. The Kanab have been fighting a legal battle that they can ill afford and are losing. Though it sounds as though the power plant has a higher likelihood of prevailing, at least for the time being. I saw a brief story that said a group called Earthfair is gearing up to fight for an injunction if the EPA grants the permit." He looked across the cab to her, noticing her clear, attractive features offset by large, expressive eyes that were trained on the road ahead. "Makes you ponder who is bankrolling all of these expensive legal gymnastics."

"Do you think it comes back to that foundation? That one that resembles a Hydra with heads popping up in every corner of the earth?" She flashed him a quick glance.

"It'll take some work to trace funds directly back to them, but I'd venture to say 'yes' because they *are* directly behind the slapped together environmental groups that are making trouble in places like Romania. And the Sierra Club is the ever-present body that appears around the globe to fight local resource development operations. Them, I really wonder about, especially the fact that they simply can't mind their own business. They seem to make it a mission to pressure poor communities into junking economically advantageous industry, leaving them to loll in poverty." He ended up mumbling about having some gall.

"So you think the foundation might be funding the so-called local environmental activists to keep these poor communities under control by basically, keeping them poor," she ventured.

"Well, it's easier to direct people who have no wealth or resources. They have a tendency to be more tractable because they have needs that they are unable to fill themselves, creating a system of dependency, i.e. slavery in an economic sense."

"That is so utterly misguided, cruel and unjust," said Sol.

"You think so because you don't happen to believe that you are wiser than people who have lived and cared for their own land for, in some cases, centuries. Perhaps it's because your culture has suffered under a heavy-handed elitist attitude and you can see it from the underside looking up at the oppressor, if you will," said Toddy

"I'm just disgusted with the fact that there's always someone around who is so damned certain that they know better, even if they base their conclusions on faulty facts."

"Or, how about no facts at all? Because it isn't about truth, it's about power, pure and simple."

The Castor incident was still keeping up a head of steam in the news. The man was stretched out on the motel bed using the remote control to flick between the cable news stations checking the reports, which were sparsely peppered with any real information. He really couldn't figure out how the empty-headed desk blotters (some of the anchors had as much brain power as a blotter, in his opinion) could manage to spew more tripe about so few actual facts for hours on end. On the whole it was a good thing for his bosses. They seemed to consider all the ruckus as something of a smokescreen for following up on other areas of interest to the opposition.

Since he'd been there for the last couple of days awaiting instructions, he'd been amused to see the stories that have popped up on odd channels about Kasili being taken down, not once, but twice, by some Indian chick at these rallies that were supposed to be a walk in the park. *Right.* He'd been on duty with the guy and was still astounded at how he'd managed to spirit away the nomination from Governor Castor.

He'd been e-mailed the less than flattering article that had run in the Boise Statesman after the blindsiding in Montana at Little Big Horn, which led to an increased interest in the Greyfisher woman, particularly after she managed to slip into UNM and catch Kasili off-guard *again.* Thinking about it, it didn't make much sense that they'd expend any energy on her. It's not like the story had been front page, but the fact that there were still video clips circulating on the internet after it had met a quick death in the national media, kept his boss' interest alive. He figured it was a waste of time and so, here he sat, watching TV and waiting for someone to decide what to do.

Shaking his head at the stupidity of it all, he flipped channels again.

His cell rang just as he was examining the legs on one of the counter girls in a skimpy skirt who was reiterating the same old stuff.

"What's the scoop?"

"We want you to keep after Greyfisher."

"That'll be tough. I have no idea where she is…" The truth was that he'd lost her after the rally at the Pit, a few days ago. No one had thought to keep tabs on her until after the rally. By then she was long gone.

"We want to make certain that there is no recurrence of the earlier situations and the best way is to know where she is."

"I have no leads, so what do you want to do?" *Gee, I wonder if anyone checked to see if she just went home?* He thought sarcastically. It always amazed him how some of these guys thought that everything needed to be cloak and dagger. No, make that more like the idiocy of *Spy vs. Spy.*

"She's not an unknown and we have a line on her cell phone, so we'll give you coordinates as soon as it's activated long enough to locate her." The man on the phone directed him to stand by for them to feed him information.

"No problem. I've no place to go." The connection went dead.

It wasn't long before he was called back with a target.

"We got a triangulation on her cell. It was just activated outside of Las Lunas on the I-25 corridor. She appears to be traveling northwest on a cutoff road to I-40 west. Pack up and move out."

The communication was ended before the recipient of the orders could answer. Not that he really cared.

Rolling down the off-ramp to take a little two-lane road that bypassed Albuquerque, Solana's cell phone went into its rendition of "Home on the Range" causing Toddy to quirk his lip in a barely perceptible smile. She reached into a side slot on her capacious purse and pulled out the palm-size device, pushed the button with her thumb and held it to her ear as she expertly negotiated the left-hand turn onto the highway.

On the other end of the line was her editor from the Statesman offering some merited kudos for garnering national attention with her meaty questions to Kasili. Kathy became fairly loquacious, a first for a woman who mostly grunted in lieu of an answer, always having her head either buried in research or cutting inches from an article that some reporter would cry that they had sweat blood over – and later bitch that the heart of the story had been sacrificed to make room for some worthless ad.

"Aw shucks, ma'am. It warn't nuthin,'" she drawled in fun.

"That's what you think," replied Kathy in all seriousness. "Fox and at least five talk radio shows are using cuts from his answers in non-stop loops demonstrating his lack of preparation and so forth and so on."

"Oooh, maybe I'll get an offer from the big boys. You know, go to *Noo Yoark City,* get my shot at the big time. Oh, wait. Been there, done that."

They both laughed. Kathy comes back with, "Except for the fact that those 'big boys' are all lining up and falling all over themselves to crown Kasili as the new emperor."

"Well, he *is* related to Haile Selassie, after all," quipped Sol. "Wait a minute. I thought *you* were in the Kasili camp. What are you doing slapping me on the back for making your boy look bad?"

"News is news and I'm not about to hand in my journalist's credentials and play favorites. Unlike some, I have standards. When are you getting back?"

"Don't know. I'm off to see the wizard and I may have lost my ruby slippers. Why?"

"It wouldn't be a bad idea if you want to do a follow-up story and," you could hear the approval in her cigarette roughened voice. Kathy had been around the newsrooms in the east for decades and was actually past retirement age. But like the old-time reporters, she just couldn't shuffle off to some senior village to play pinochle, she'd be chasing a story until she dropped dead from a heart attack. "I owe you a drink."

"You're on, sister."

"Hah! *Sister,*" she cackled. "Just call me 'grandma.'"

The man was kicked back in the driver's seat of his sedan, cruise control engaged and one hand draped across the back of the passenger's headrest when his phone started vibrating in his shirt pocket. Pulling out the cell and flipping it open, he answered with a simple "here" and just listened.

"She's booked into a motel in Gallup for tonight," said the disembodied voice, a different one from the Boss, but not unexpected. Directions could come from any member of the management team in this outfit, though there were only two supervisors who were on his detail. This supervisor gave him the motel information as well as the make, model and license number of Greyfisher's car, which the man committed to memory. He didn't need to hear how they'd tracked her location through her cell phone and hacked into her credit card accounts to get information on hotel registrations. Nor did the supervisor offer any of that up for his consumption. He knew that was how they operated and it wasn't any of his concern, anyway.

Hanging up and dropping the phone back into his pocket, he punched the accelerator of the turbo-charged engine in his nondescript 2002 Toyota Camry and continued tooling down the interstate.

They arrived late in Gallup, exhausted and hungry. Not being interested in doing much more than eating and sleeping, Solana and Toddy pulled through a fast food joint for something to tide them over before going to the motel.

Sol didn't have any trouble finding the inn and parked her rig under the portico that extended from the cheery and brightly lit lobby. The receptionist managed to be pleasant despite the late hour and her own evident fatigue. Textbooks piled next to the computer terminal, it didn't take much to reach the conclusion that she was a student.

Neither of the two travelers really paid that much attention. Solana informed the girl of her reservation and was checked in quickly. Toddy registered under an alias that was matched with a credit card and ID and obtained the key to the room adjacent to Sol's.

Having no energy for more than dragging their bags into their respective rooms and saying good night, that's precisely what they did.

Chapter 15

The sun had risen hours ago and the man was reclined in his seat, a Styrofoam cup of coffee purchased from the convenience store down the street cooling in his hand. He was dog-tired and bored. Checking his watch he saw that it was just after nine a.m. Obviously, the Indian reporter wasn't an early riser, but he wondered what she was doing out here. Operations had given him some background on her and 'home' was up in Idaho not western New Mexico, though apparently she had graduated from UNM. Even so, that's a distance from Gallup. Oh well, he just sipped on the tepid liquid wishing that she'd make an appearance to alleviate the tedium.

Not a few minutes later, she finally exited her room and deposited her bags in the car. He watched as she turned to greet a man who came out of a room next to hers, pulling a rollaway overnighter. Stepping aside, her friend lifted his bag and settled it next to hers in the cargo compartment after which she closed the back and they climbed in and drove off.

The appearance of a traveling companion was news to him, so he speed dialed operations and informed them of the man's existence, giving a quick description and informing them of what room he had occupied. He flipped the phone closed and stowed it in his pocket as he waited a bit, then pulled out a distance behind them.

He didn't have far to follow the Tahoe as they just went up the road half a mile before stopping at a coffee shop, getting out of the Tahoe and walking inside. The man parked at the other side of the lot and entered a few minutes later, taking a booth where he could keep an eye on them. At least he'd have the chance to get a fresh cup of coffee while they ate breakfast.

Toddy and Sol hadn't noticed the man who trailed them into the restaurant. They sat down and ordered breakfast, accepting coffee from a waitress who had a huge smile that didn't reach her eyes. It already must have been a long morning.

Toddy rubbed his eyes and peered across the table at Sol, bringing the mug to his lips for a, hopefully, life renewing shot of caffeine. "You have no right to be so perky in the morning," he grumped.

"I would hardly call this 'perky.' I could have slept another two hours," she said.

"Why? Didn't you sleep well?" His forehead crinkled in concern.

"Oh, I slept fine once I got to bed. I spent a couple hours going over some information on the Diné Power Agency and the Navajo Environmental Protection Agency presentation to try to get a handle on the Desert Mountain project," she yawned.

"So how come I look the way you feel?"

"Because I have a certain ability to cover the tracks of fatigue with a glowing personality and deception," she raised an eyebrow playfully.

"Deception, huh," he said. "And what would that be?"

"The expert application of make-up," she replied without inflection.

"No wonder I can't keep up."

"They make cosmetics for men too, you know."

"Are you implying that I need a makeover?" he asked, eyes widening.

She studied his face. "No, just a more careful job of shaving. You missed a few spots."

"I'll try harder next time."

Their meals were delivered which they ate while going over a simple strategy for the day, finishing and leaving a half-hour later to implement those plans.

Tribal headquarters was little more than a forty-minute drive from Gallup, where they looked up the administrative offices of the Diné Power Agency to gather more information on the current development of the power plant. Although Sol had been able to download a fair amount of data from an official site, the agency official was very helpful in explaining about the project. The Desert Mountain Energy Group was the subsidiary of a privately held, independent power company based in Houston, Texas that partnered with the Diné Power Agency to build the plant, an enterprise of the Navajo nation that was organized by the tribal council to promote the nation's development of economic and energy resources. The proposal was to build a hybrid, dry cooled, pulverized coal-fired electric power-generating plant south of Farmington in northwestern New Mexico but before they could even break ground they needed an air quality permit from the EPA, which was pending. The land where the plant was sited, being held in trust for the Navajo by the federal government, also had to go through an approval process by the Bureau of Indian Affairs before the long-term lease between the project partners and the Navajo nation to be accepted.

The EPA had been dragging its feet for two years without making a ruling on the PSD (Prevention of Significant Deterioration) permit which is necessary before the Operating Permit could be granted. Earlier in the year, the partners had sued the EPA to force a decision on the permitting process. As a result, a settlement occurred guaranteeing that the Environmental Protection Agency would make a determination by July 31, which was coming up soon. The other hurdle that the Desert Mountain project was running into were the numerous national environmental groups that had been blanketing the internet and the media with slanted arguments against the project. One of those articles that had run in the NY Times was the one that Sol had handed to Toddy to read during their drive to Gallup.

Although the Environmental Impact Study indicated that the proposed Desert Mountain Power Plant would be well within the guidelines of the law, the opposition from outside the area was heated. In fact, the new technology incorporated into the project was the most advanced available, creating one of the cleanest power generation facilities to be built to date.

What Toddy and Sol were told was that complying and surpassing the guidelines of the law simply wasn't enough to please the activists. Instead, lawsuits to force injunctions blocking the plant's construction were already in the works should the permit be granted. The official, a woman of short stature but solid with a thick, grey-shot twist of hair secured at the nape of her neck, explained that the $3 billion project could generate $50 million a year in taxes and royalties selling power to Phoenix and Las Vegas and create 400 permanent jobs. This kind of income would be an enormous economic boost to the Diné people who are the most populous of the Native American groups in the United States, numbering 250,000 on the reservation. Even the governor of New Mexico had taken sides against his own constituents, making statements that placed him in the same category as the environmentalist critics.

"You know that the other two coal-fired plants in the area, the Four Corners and San Juan power plants provide almost no benefit to the Navajo economically and they are older and produce pollutants, whereas the new Desert Mountain plant will be exceptionally clean burning. With 1500 megawatts, it may take over for the plants that will probably be phased out eventually as obsolete," said the official. "It's important that we keep continuity of power generation for the southwest region and the opponents to this project are not promoting any viable alternatives."

Sol finally spoke up, "I understand that the environmental groups are buying the story that CO_2 is a contaminant to the atmosphere, but I hope that the Indians aren't falling into that trap. It seems to me we have enough trouble without non-Natives trying to shovel that um, manure onto our plates." She looked at the woman, "I mean, if there were any merit to the argument that humans had any effect on the CO_2 levels, that would be one thing, but there is no scientific proof for such an assertion."

"Not that I would disagree, but what is it you're looking for?" asked the DPA official.

"Just trying to see what the dynamics are of the permitting process, the true specs of the project and how much input the activists really have on halting the construction."

"Well, it looks good that we'll finally have the go ahead for the construction permit, but the environmental groups have been throwing up legal barriers wherever they can."

"Is most of the opposition local or national?" asked Sol.

"The local groups are small but vocal and we believe they have financial support from nationally and internationally funded organizations to make it look like there's a larger grassroots resistance to the plant than there really is," she said in answer to Sol's question.

Toddy added his own thoughts, "The money has to come from somewhere to pay for the legal fees and it's doubtful that the locals could raise enough, don't you think? Anyway, if they sue for an injunction it will all come down to the political leanings of the judge that hears the argument. Whether or not he, or she, caters to the global warming cant."

The DPA official just nodded her head in agreement. "It will be hard to know which way the wind will blow on this, but we certainly hope the plant will be built and allowed to come online for the benefit of the People."

Sol and Toddy thanked her and asked for directions to the site. They were interested in getting a look at the location of the Desert Mountain Power Plant.

Driving out towards Burnham where the Desert Mountain project partners had leased the land for the power plant, the two surveyed the raw desert vistas stretching away for miles in all directions. Rocky formations shaped by the elements standing forlornly, dotted the landscape.

The location was isolated and little was to be seen of what would one day be a power generating plant that could supply electricity for a million homes in the southwest while bringing prosperity to a people who have struggled with an unforgiving terrain with little water for agriculture or raising livestock. The days of the daunting Navajo horsemen were long gone but the future held promise through the development of other resources yielded by their ancestral lands.

As they traveled the only things they saw were a few roadrunners, a coyote darting across the road and a little traffic consisting of a few pick-up trucks and mostly older model American cars. Throughout the trip they noticed a dirty white car, it might have been more than one, that kept its distance to the rear and came into view off and on, but not much else.

Late in the afternoon they came into Farmington and found their way to the newspaper. The editor was good enough to spend some time with them to give them background on the local organizations that had been active in the debate over the new plans for the power plant. He gave them printouts of some of the articles that had run over the past months regarding the EPA debacle, the lawsuit that finally forced them into setting a decision deadline and local sentiment about the whole situation.

He was only able to set aside about fifteen minutes before he was called back to work, having a paper to put to bed. Solana and Toddy thanked him for his time, gathered up the sheets he'd supplied, and went to look for a motel for the night.

Chapter 16

The next morning they regrouped and headed west across the Navajo Reservation taking a short detour to drive into Monument Valley a little way since Toddy had never seen the majestic buttes other than in photos. The dramatic landscape was well worth taking a diverted route for a few miles and he pulled out an old 35mm Nikon camera. Being immersed in the digital world hadn't lessened his appreciation of photography and, although he was shooting color film, he enjoyed taking the time to develop his own black and white prints.

They weren't in any particular hurry so they ambled across the desert at a fair but not breakneck clip. The fact that the state of the roads was somewhat less than optimal with potholes and asphalt buildup over the cracks made by time and weather, encouraged Sol to keep the speed down.

Even with traveling at a slower pace they entered Page, Arizona by late afternoon. It didn't take long to locate a motel that overlooked the Colorado River, the dam forming a backdrop across the waterway. Exiting the car they were struck by the intense heat of an early summer day chasing them inside the lobby where they registered and went to their respective rooms before meeting to go to dinner.

Toddy spent the extra hour going online to check how many hits the new blog had gotten over the last couple of days. He was pleasantly surprised to see the number hovering in the low thousands, assuming that the keywords he'd placed into the search engines were doing their job to direct people to the site. *Not bad.*

Afterward, he dug into a little research on the Kanab Paiutes' gold operation, or *almost* operation since it was at a virtual standstill, again courtesy of the environmentalist lobby. The information was spotty but he located a little data on the lease agreement between Altamont Mining and the Kanab Indian Reservation. The only other information he could find was that exploration had been shut down six months ago because of a temporary injunction order levied by the court after a lawsuit was filed by a local activist group. *How local can that be? Nobody lives out there.*

Toddy downloaded information on the prospective gold operation to find that the exploratory efforts had located a rich vein under the Paiute land near Fresia. Finding information on the lease, he saw that Altamont held the upper hand in that they would glean a clear profit in exchange for developing the undertaking. The Environmental Impact Study was actually fairly positive on the production procedures and management of the air and surrounding land. However, that hadn't halted the efforts of the conservation groups to put the kibosh on the whole plan. In fact, the pressure applied by the environmental lobbies had been accepted by Altamont who, by all accounts, pulled the plug, packed up and left. He even found an article where the lead complainant, a nationally known eco-organization, literally told the Kanab Paiute, a very poor nation, to stick to cattle grazing.

He shut-down the laptop, disgusted by the high-handed attitudes of the so-called conservationists, wondering what they would do if some outsiders told them to curtail their ability to make a living and go back to gathering nuts and berries.

The next day Toddy and Solana drove the couple of hours west to the small Kanab Indian Reservation, a spot on the map that few travelers visited most of the year, it not being a direct destination nor lying along a main route to any of the area's well-known vacation spots. Tribal headquarters was located in the small town of Fresia and consisted of little more than a few manufactured buildings set back from the highway that served the 320-member tribe. The small government was also the major employer of tribal members.

Pulling into the parking area that was large enough for a big-rig to turn around, Sol and Toddy climbed out to find the Tribal Department of Natural Resources. It turned out to be something of an overstatement as the department consisted of a cubicle in one of the office buildings that was manned by a single official, Noah Roanhorse.

Roanhorse was a middle-aged, bandy-legged man of medium

height who sported a long braid of black hair woven with silver strands that hung to his waist. He was sitting at his desk, reading some paperwork and entering data into his antiquated desktop computer. When the two strangers arrived at the open door of his space, he looked up without expression although the interest in his eyes sparked briefly. He was unused to receiving visitors of any kind and was wary of those who did drop by.

The department director stood up, pushing his chair back as he did so and offering his hand to Sol and Toddy who introduced themselves.

"Noah Roanhorse, director of Natural Resources," he stayed standing since there weren't any guest chairs and his visitors were forced to remain standing also. "What can I do for you?"

Toddy answered him, "We're interested in the Kanab Mining Works, and we've been told that you're the man to talk to."

"Well, I would be if there were such a thing, but at this stage it looks like the operation no longer exists."

"I'd read that Altamont may have moved out, conceding to environmental pressure groups." Toddy considered hi next question. "Why would they hightail it after all the preliminary work? The injunction is only temporary. Surely they could have mounted a good defense with a positive EIS behind them."

"Cutting their losses, is my guess," said Roanhorse. "They weren't interested in a prolonged legal battle." He settled a hip on the edge of his desk.

"What I read, it sounded as if the mineral deposits here would justify hanging in for a long run, particularly since the Environmental Impact Study seemed to bear out a pretty clean operation that wouldn't stress the area's resources or endanger any flora or fauna."

"Apparently, that wasn't enough for them to continue with the project despite the profit projections for both Altamont and the tribe."

"How far did they go?" asked Solana.

"Well, the initial planning and infrastructure work had already commenced since the permits were issued. Altamont had fifty-six tribal members employed for a year doing the work of laying in roads and constructing the offices, but none of the actual operation ever reached the point of ore extraction. They say they spent $21.2 million on the work and planning stages, though our office can account for only $3 million spent on fees, permits, payroll, etc. Our people were laid off six months ago and Altamont is somehow showing that they have $18 million outstanding that was put toward operations design, employee housing, community improvement and infrastructure."

That's all it took for Toddy's mind to start seeing the possibility of a money-laundering scheme. "The tribe would have made out pretty well if the gold mining had begun in earnest, from what I gathered."

"It's no secret that the tribe would have been bringing in thirty-five percent of the net profit and the employment would have been a huge boost to the area. I'm sure that you've noticed there isn't much out here and the mine would have employed over a hundred people, eventually. That would have fed a local service industry, housing... been good for everybody." He shook his head in frustration.

Toddy stood there in thought and Solana noticing his silence, looked over at him to see him staring into space for a minute. Finally he piped up, "How does the lease stand now?"

"Why?" He gave Toddy a look of skepticism. He didn't know these two people despite their introductions and the obvious fact that the woman was Native. She still wasn't from around here. Her speech was different and she certainly didn't look Diné or Paiute. She seemed more, what would you call it... citified. Yeah, that's it. She was more sophisticated than most of the people he knew, not that that should make a difference, but, well, it did when it came down to the basics. He'd gone to Arizona State University and had come across Indians who didn't think like Indians anymore and he wondered if she was one of those. "What's your interest?"

"I was curious as to whether the tribe is still able to access the mineral rights," replied Toddy. "It seems from what you've said that Altamont may never have intended to develop the mine at all. Like they used the tribe as a shill to move funds around, though $18 million isn't that much for a conglomerate like that. Wonder if there was more somewhere..." his voice trailed off with the thought.

"As in 'illegal' transfers?" Roanhorse was taken aback at the implication.

Toddy almost jumped at the question then just shrugged his shoulders. "I suppose it's possible. Either way, the tribe may have been taken for a ride, and a very long one depending on the lease."

Roanhorse thought, *oh, why not...*

"It's ironclad," he admitted reluctantly. "Our attorneys have been through it a dozen times and can't find an out. If we could remove ourselves from the lease we can hunt for another mining firm to develop the deposit and bring some real prosperity to the reservation. But for now, our hands are tied."

"So, essentially, the tribe got a measly $3 million and a few amenities while the rest of the money is gone, poof?"

"That's about the size of it. We lost control of the biggest break that's ever come our way and don't have the resources to fight. Essentially? We've been hornswoggled. Plus, most of the money went to non-recoverable improvements at the site." He sighed and looked up into Toddy's earnest face. "We got squat."

"On top of which you're locked out of your own land. Cute."

"Wouldn't the BIA have to have overseen the lease agreement?" said Solana. "I mean, don't they hold the land in trust for the tribe?"

"They were involved in the negotiations of the transaction, more as a committee than anything else."

Toddy looked at her and his eyes lit up, "I see where you're going. If the BIA had input and gave their approval to the lease, then they could be held liable for the tribe's loss. Well, at least the tribe could make the case that the BIA is liable for allowing a fraudulent action to take place, loss of income and autonomy."

"And that would do what?" asked Roanhorse.

"Force the government to take action on the tribe's behalf." He lifted his shoulders, looking very much like an ingenuous teenager. "Maybe put pressure on Altamont to settle the lease if they were facing criminal charges."

"Now, that's an idea that may have some merit," and he smiled for the first time since his two visitors entered his cubicle.

Toddy and Solana were interested in seeing the site if Noah had the time to direct them. Since he had little going on that afternoon, he volunteered to drive them out there since it was a little difficult to find.

Once they reached the mine, they were greeted with eight-foot high chain-link fencing capped with concertina wire. They were blocked from getting anywhere near the mine offices, which were empty in any case. The gate was locked and an armed guard ensconced inside a little air-conditioned shack made certain that no one entered the site. It was obvious that the guard was not a tribal member, an observation that Solana remarked on, "Couldn't even hire local security, I see."

"What did you expect? They don't trust us, not after they shafted us," said Roanhorse. "Okay, poor choice of words," he chuckled a little despite the irony of being locked out of ancestral Paiute land. It only reminded him of the fact that the current reservation encompassed just a fraction of the land that his forebears had once traversed freely as theirs.

They didn't even bother to get out of the Natural Resources vehicle, a ten-year old Ford 4x4 Explorer, a sandblasted buff color with the tribal insignia affixed to the driver's door. Noah just steered the truck around the western perimeter of the property on a dirt track that hadn't been kept up, the rig bumping rhythmically over the washboard. He decided to give them a bit of a tour of the rough and desolate terrain.

Noah pulled up short of a trickling stream that cut across the road, the little bit of water rapidly drying up in the early summer. Getting out of the truck, he walked over to the threadlike brook and, kneeling down, sifted around in the sand, bringing his hand up dripping with the last of the spring runoff slipping through his fingers.

Toddy and Solana walked over to join him and bent down to watch as he used his forefinger to push around the little bit of sandy mud resting in his palm. They noticed the glittering metallic specks mixed throughout the wet earth in his hand, catching the sunlight.

"Gold?" asked Sol.

"Yeah, but we can't get to it. This gift of the earth could mean a real life for our people," he raised his eyes to theirs. "Instead they tell us to go back to rustling cattle, like we're outlaws." He stood up, brushing the dirt from his hands.

"They never planned to open the mine," said Sol, solemnly.

"Nope," he said bitterly. "Got us Indians again," he added with restrained venom.

On the way back to the tribal offices Toddy peppered Noah with questions about the land transaction, trying to tie down some details on the lease agreement.

"There may be more than one way to resolve this in favor of the tribe, particularly if Altamont acted with intent to deprive you of your mineral rights. And if the BIA is involved, even inadvertently, pressuring them may create an opening for the tribe to force reassessment of the situation. The document and the lease process would come under review." He stopped to think, his mind whirling through the possible tactics available. "We may even be able to get the eco activists to back off if it could be implied or demonstrated that they were working in collusion to defraud the tribe."

"Now, wouldn't *that* be a story," gloated Solana.

Roanhorse wasn't convinced and gazed over at his passenger with a jaundiced eye. *He is white, after all.*

Solana saw the distrust in their host's face and although she didn't blame him, she said, "My companion is a legal researcher with an unsullied reputation and frankly, he's just plain brilliant. If anyone can find a way to crack the lease, I believe he can."

Toddy didn't move a muscle. Rather, he froze slightly at the compliment, uncertain what Solana intended by the remark because now all he could think was that he had no choice but to perform unerringly.

✾ ✾ ✾

Roanhorse pulled up in front of tribal headquarters just as the sun was beginning to dip toward the horizon. As they were climbing out of the truck, he asked them what their plans were for the night.

"We hadn't really planned that far in advance, not knowing how long it might take to gather information about Altamont and the Kanab Mining Works," answered Sol. "Is there a motel anywhere nearby?"

"Not really. That was one of the things that had been in the plans for Fresia, a good quality inn to help build the tourist trade. As it is, you have to cross over into Utah for a place to stay, unless you have camping equipment?"

Toddy jumped in, "No, we're not prepared to rough it."

"We haven't got much in the area," he considered for a moment. "But you're welcome to come home with me and stay the night." He suddenly smiled, "My wife would be pleased to have company."

Toddy was stricken dumb with the offer, which Sol decided was a blessing before he said something that might get them in trouble, like politely refusing. She knew it would be best to accept the invitation. "Thank you," she said. "We'd be honored to be your guests."

Noah looked pleased and told them to follow him home. The offices were already locked up and he had no reason to go back inside tonight, so he got back behind the wheel and waited until they were strapped in and the engine of the Tahoe turned over and was ready to move.

The two vehicles didn't have far to go. The Roanhorse household was only three miles out of town on a small bit of acreage with a couple horses in a corral and an old style windmill slowly grinding in the evening breeze.

Hearing two vehicles pull up, Noah's wife, Joey, came out onto the porch, wiping her hands on an apron she had tied around her waist. A huge grin split her genial face, skin slightly weathered by the sun but still displaying the beauty of her youth. She was a small woman, not much more than five feet tall with delicate bones to match, though she exuded a solid energy.

"Good, you brought guests," she said. "This place sees too few visitors." As Sol stepped onto the porch, Joey came forward and gave the younger woman a hug that practically squeezed the stuffing out of her. Solana was a little surprised since most Indians weren't exactly effusive in their greeting until they'd gotten to know you. She was even more surprised when Joey hugged Toddy as well.

"Don't let her scare you," said Noah. "She just gets a little lonely out here in the sticks."

Joey waved her hand at her husband, "Don't believe him. It's hard to get lonely when you teach school all day. Of course, school's out right now so company is refreshing." She pushed them toward the door. "Come in. I held dinner for you."

"How did you know we were coming?" Toddy asked with a slight suspicion.

Joey's eyes twinkled. "I didn't."

Noah just shrugged and went inside, smiling as if he were in on a secret.

Gold Baron

Chapter 17

They spent the night in the small house, Solana sharing a room with their teenage daughter and Toddy sleeping with his feet dangling off the end of the couch. The other two children were away from home, the son working in Vegas while studying law at UNLV, and the middle daughter spending the summer with the forest service between school terms at Diné University.

By eight a.m. they were back on the road heading toward Phoenix. Sort of. They first had to backtrack 100 miles before catching the southern route. Once they were heading toward Flagstaff, however, the road was clear and relatively free of traffic allowing Sol to speed through the desert highlands without much fear of being sidelined by highway patrol.

Their plan was to pay a visit to the federal courthouse to fetch all the pertinent documents regarding the suit filed by the environmental coalition against Altamont and the Kanab Paiute. Making good time, they arrived downtown before four p.m. and were able to locate the federal buildings without too much trouble, discounting traffic of course.

Toddy knew his way around courthouses pretty well and located the offices they needed in quick time. He had already received the case file number from Noah and was able to look it up on the computer rapidly, order the printouts and collect everything but the transcripts within the hour before offices closed. Noah had also met them at the office early in the morning and made a copy of the lease for Toddy. In fact, they had everything in hand within forty-five minutes, record time to Sol's way of thinking. But then, She didn't care for courthouses and stayed as far away from them as she could. Generally, she had managed to avoid being assigned many legal stories over the years where hanging around listening to testimony and waiting for juries to deliberate was the majority of a reporter's day.

They gathered up their booty and slipped out of the air-conditioned cool into the energy draining heat of the Sonoran Desert sun.

The man was stiff from having spent the night in his car. The desert had too many night critters to even consider taking a sleeping bag and camping in the open, leaving him with the remaining option of sliding back the driver's seat and reclining. The whole of the way down to Phoenix he was leaning forward and rubbing a cramp out of his low back, a residual problem from a nasty ending to a high speed car chase years before. His only thought was that he hadn't signed up for this kind of duty, but then he didn't have much choice anymore. His glory days were long gone and so was the pension he would have had to go with them.

Once he got into Phoenix, he had followed the Tahoe around the downtown area, watching his quarry find a space to park in a near-by garage. There were some spots on the street with coin operated meters and he pulled into one where he could see both the pedestrian entrance and the driveway. He stayed in the Toyota until he saw the two emerge from the garage and make their way down the street toward the courthouse, at which point he opened the door and trailed them to the building, trying not to kick his legs out to relieve the discomfort of the extended road trip.

He passed by the big glass doors opting not to enter since he was carrying a small gun strapped to his ankle, it being too hot to wear a jacket to obscure the contours of a shoulder holster. The last thing he needed was to draw attention to himself at the security check. Instead, he decided to walk back to the car and await the pair's arrival knowing that it wouldn't be that long considering it was already just past four p.m. Federal offices closed at five on the nose and he figured he even had time to get a quick cup of coffee at the corner before they came back.

While he waited for Sol and her companion to finish their business, he called in to headquarters to give his report, brief as it was. He gave the supe a rundown on the visit they'd made to tribal offices in Fresia and their visit to an abandoned industrial complex, Kanab Mining Works, outside of town. That they'd spent the night at the private home of the Director of Natural Resources for the tribe and then headed down here to the federal courthouse.

No, he didn't think he'd been spotted on the reservation, though it was iffy because of the tiny size of the town. The fact that he was dark-complected helped to keep him low profile. Had they gotten any inkling as to who her traveling buddy was?

The supervisor told him that they'd only tracked him to a dead-end identity with no real address other than a couple of post office boxes in two different states. They were still working on it.

Fine, just keep him informed when they find something.

After retrieving what documentation Toddy needed from the court, Sol was back on the freeway driving east or trying to, they were locked in bumper-to-bumper traffic and moving at a snail's pace. Wanting to catch up on events, he called Anthea to see if she'd found anything on the Kasili money trail.

"Not that I've been able to locate, but that's not my area of expertise. What are you thinking?"

Toddy gave Anthea a rundown of what they'd uncovered in Fresia about the strange allocation of Altamont funds and his loose theory on where they went.

"I'll call my friend Rennselaer at the San Francisco paper, he's good at this stuff. But you suspect money laundering, huh?" she asked.

"Who knows. Maybe this is about injecting international funds into political campaigns by filtering it through a big conglomerate like Altamont to a 527. Just look at the fact that the liberal 527s have out-spent similar conservative non-profit orgs at the rate of two-to-one. Where is all that cash coming from?" threw out Toddy. "I don't think anyone has done a thorough investigation of the 527 collection practices and I seriously doubt that the money is all $5, $10 and $50 donations from itty-bitty individuals," he sneered.

"Hmmm," considered Anthea. "We are talking about millions of dollars that are being collected online through 527s like building-bridges.org. It has to come from somewhere and you think that maybe some of the cash is funneled through scams like this Kanab Mining Works?"

"Could be. If Kasili is the puppet we think, then there has to be a way to sling money into his campaign without raising suspicions. Look, we have the union PACs out there infusing money into the democratic candidacy. Just look at the major union website. The ads are all about supporting Kasili against big, bad corporations when it's those very same corporations that the pension funds are investing in to rake in billions of dollars, which they turn around and give to supposed anti-corporate candidates." He was getting exasperated with the whole concept of deception. "The unions put the dues into political action committees and pension funds. The members have no input on where any of their hard-earned dollars are invested. They're told that the oil companies and big corps are evil and yet their own dues are being invested in them hand-over-fist by the hedge funds where the pension money is invested. These are the speculators driving up energy prices and yet the worker whose money was used in the first place sees no benefit except for a small retirement. I would hardly call higher gas and commodity costs, since one feeds the other, to be a *benefit.*

"Those funds are controlled by the union officers who also direct the Political Action Committee funds and send accumulated money from both to campaigns that support their socialist interests."

"It hardly makes sense to be making money off of the very corporations that the unions are practically trying to break through contract demands," said Anthea, slightly bewildered.

"In some ways it doesn't. What it's about is redistribution of wealth, or 'equity' as the unions term it," replied Toddy.

"Well, 'equity' can also mean 'justice.'"

Toddy sighed, "Same thing in their minds. However, although the party line is that the little guy, the worker, will receive 'equity' through the renegotiated contracts and the pensions, what's really happening is that the union bosses are taking them all for a ride. And they're supporting the candidates that will give them what they want like, for instance, the eradication of closed balloting at union elections. Talk about intimidation."

"Okay, let me get this straight. You're saying that money from Scirras goes through his many corporate stocks, like Altamont, into 527s like buildingbridges.org, some of it legitimately given and some of it laundered, to end up in the campaign basket. Then the union PACs send donations to 527s and directly to the same campaign basket. Also, the union pension funds are making a killing in offshore hedge funds, some of the profit then being diverted back to the PACs and other 527s to end up in the campaign fund. And all of these campaign funds fuel an agenda that drives up energy costs that builds profits for the hedge funds and thus making Scirras and the union bosses even richer and more powerful." She was out of breath and only partially convinced.

"In a nutshell." Toddy thought for a second. "It's all about control. Using the workers to create wealth for those who already wield it and the power that goes with it. The more the worker is dependent on the union for their livelihood and the government for succor in times of trouble (which will become more frequent because the controllers drive the energy prices up and down), then the less they worry about individual freedom. They are inundated with the need to feed their families and that becomes their purpose in everything they do. They study less and accept what they're told more, creating an easily guided populace that will do anything for 'change' when 'change' actually means more of the same."

Luckily for Solana, the whole of the conversation had been on Toddy's speaker feature on the cell phone, otherwise she would be utterly lost in the one-sided conversation. As it was, the concept was still too convoluted to completely seep into her mind, yet.

As quickly as they'd gotten into the money trail conversation, Anthea switched gears with the most recent news tidbit. "Have you heard the latest slipping through the cracks about Kasili?" she asked.

"No, we've been traveling and out of the loop for a day or two," said Toddy.

"Someone's brought up a discrepancy with his birth certificate. It looks like he has two of them."

"So? I do too, the original and an official copy from when I couldn't locate the original," he said.

"But I assume that both of yours were issued by the same state," she expanded.

"Of course."

"He apparently has one from Minnesota, his mother's home state and another one that says he's an Ethiopian national. It's not certain where he was born."

Toddy thought for a moment. "It could be more of a problem publicity-wise than anything else. Even if he was born overseas, his mother is an American who was attached to the diplomatic corps unless the Ethiopian certificate states that he is an Ethiopian citizen, in which case, if I remember correctly, his parents would have to submit paperwork to the United States asking that he be recognized as an American citizen. If she failed to do so, he would be a naturalized citizen and not a natural-born American. Sounds like it could be red herring, but it's worth looking into."

"I think the thing that is more disturbing to some is that the Ethiopian certificate plainly states his religious affiliation to be Muslim and a half-brother who was located in Africa states Kasili was raised in the faith," she said.

"Yes, the problem with that could be that someone raised as a Muslim has their allegiance to the faith first and country second. It's already evident that he lacks loyalty to the Constitution simply because of his socialist policies and his apparent acceptance of international law as a superior authority over that of U.S. law…

"But I'm thinking we need to stress the money ties."

After hearing the debate about union ties to liberal political campaigns and the bit about Kasili's multiple birthplaces, Sol added to the mix after Toddy hung up, "Maybe there's two of him."

Toddy laughed, "Lord, isn't one enough? Trying to figure out where he was spawned is someone else's job. It'd be hard to prove and only fuels the discrimination factor. But I wouldn't be one bit surprised if he *had* been born in Africa and his mother neglected to file the proper paperwork, in which case he would be ineligible to run for president."

"What we need to do is decide what our next move is. What we should post on the website."

Toddy's hands went up in the air with frustration at the sheer volume of information, and innuendo that was likely factual, that they'd been uncovering. "Everything, dammit! There's just too much here to let it slide without pointing it out to someone, and soon."

"What about the consequences of getting this all online," Sol wondered. "Don't you think they'll track the origin of the site and try to close the pipeline? What you've posted so far is fairly tame. Some of this stuff is getting down and dirty."

"I think we need to find a nice place in the middle of lots of internet traffic where I can start compiling some of this ASAP. On top of everything else, the convention is coming up and I have my reservations as to whether Castor will make it to the floor to address them," conjectured Toddy.

"I know you mentioned it before, but you can't seriously think they'd contemplate her, um, removal."

"Unfortunately, I can. I have my suspicions about Olin Girard as it is. It was just too convenient to have the one strident and independent voice in the mainstream media silenced just when Kasili might be challenged." He looked out the window and up at the sky. "Just look at the state funeral they had for the guy. He was a nice fella and all but why the pomp and circumstance for a member of the media? To make others recognize their own mortality?"

"Oh, like Castor, perchance?" said Sol. "Is that what you're implying?"

"He'd have been bound to be on the debate panels, likely even the moderator. You and I both know he'd have pressed for answers unlike the old liberal hack they replaced him with. Face it, Kasili can't withstand the strain," He turned to look at her, "He couldn't even handle your questions. In their eyes, they had to drop Girard. Would they drop her too? In a heartbeat."

Gold Baron

Chapter 18

Feeling pressured to get something accomplished on the blog, Solana and Toddy decided to find a hotel in Mesa for the night. As soon as they registered into adjoining rooms, they set-up their laptops in Toddy's room where he immediately flipped on the television to a cable news station. From there on out there was nothing but the sound of the droning anchors and typing as they worked on their respective stories.

The first thing they heard was that Kasili had decided to forego public funding, which he had promised to use, in favor of being able to collect money from private factions.

"We aren't even at the conventions and already he's opted to pursue private financing," observed Sol.

"So what's *that* tell you?"

"That he expects to have a non-stop flow from an unnamed source." She peered across the room at him, "Back to the old adage, 'follow the money?'" She stopped and stared at the screen. "Listen to this..."

A picture of Dean Castor leaning toward the microphone, speaking at a forum of supporters who aren't ready to concede in their home state of Pennsylvania.

"Let's talk about funding," says Castor, giving the cameras his well-known hangdog look of reproach. "How does one work their way through the University of Chicago with a couple of summer jobs. Is that even possible? A world-class university is vastly expensive and I wonder where the money came from. He had loans but no scholarships or grants. Who could have paid off the loans?" He stopped to look at the crowd, which had a good showing from the press, who he had been working for years, as well as constituents. "Nowhere in his financial history does it show that they were reconciled, and yet they disappeared. It seems a fair question to wonder if Kasili has had a benefactor all these years."

"Oh man, this is getting downright dirty. Castor is evidently not ready to capitulate yet. Not after the limo incident. Is that what brought this on, you think?"

"Whatever the point is, she's smart to get hubby to do the dirty work since he's already been pulled onto the carpet for talking out of turn. It gives them an out later with a disclaimer," said Toddy, who'd briefly looked up from his work to catch the fireworks.

Sol brought him back to attention, "Look there's more." The voiceovers cut to someone bringing up the issue of the conflicting birth certificates. It looked like the first may have been issued in Ethiopia and his mother may have renounced U.S. citizenship to marry Kasili's father but was then reinstated as a citizen at a later date.

Sol asked, "Is that possible? The whole thing seems an unlikely scenario."

"Don't know about the circumstances. I never researched it. Never needed to. Maybe... she was born here, but if her citizenship was forgiven and this has an ounce of truth, it would make Kasili naturalized and not eligible to run for the presidency."

"This will just be labeled another form of discrimination," said Sol.

The talking heads at the studio were going back and forth about the legalities of dual certificates, discussing the possibility that one is not legitimate, etc. In any case, there wasn't a living witness since both parents were dead. The woman in the red scarf and helmet-hair simply stated, "It must be a fluke."

"Oh that's a good objective statement," Sol said with disgust. "Where do they get these people?"

"If Castor's machine is attacking that hard, I'd guess that there may be some weight to the charge. If it could be proven it would remove Kasili from the running and allow her to usurp the nomination."

"Well, there are weeks left until the convention and things are getting rougher day by day. This is beginning to look like a dogfight."

Toddy slid back in his chair to contemplate the TV screen. "Senator Eddinger just needs to sit back and watch the fun. It looks more and more like the democrats could implode if he were lucky."

"If we want to prove who's really pulling the marionette's strings, we have to find out who has backed him all these years. And

Castor may be correct in that the financier of old may have been grooming him all along, even to the point of scripting his appearances, because without that teleprompter he's not so confident," Sol added.

"You would know," his eyes twinkled in humor. Toddy then said more soberly, "They must be worried enough that they think the only thing that can save Kasili's campaign will be orchestrated media exposure, and for that you need a ton of money."

"And private funding."

Gold Baron

Chapter 19

Seated behind the arced surface of his expansive desk, he ran his hand through his springy, cap of gray hair that showed only remnants of the brown it once was. He was reading through the latest reports from the Zimco Mine that an Altamont subsidiary, RioMata, operated in the mineral-rich Midlands district of Zimbabwe.

Altamont had closed down the mine earlier in the year, purportedly because the central bank failed to pay gold miners what was due for gold deliveries made to its subsidiary, which was to be tendered in foreign currency – inflation making the Zim dollar unreliable. However, under threat of state seizure of the mine by President Mugabe, RioMata reopened the operation at a much-diminished capacity.

Although Scirras would have preferred to keep the mine closed for now, loss of control of the operation to Mugabe was not an option. Better to function on a miniscule level, the numbers in front of him bearing out the wisdom of that decision.

He turned to gaze out of the window at the bay where sea traffic moved at a steady pace, and reflected on the news coming out of Zimbabwe. Mugabe had forced his opponent from the presidential race, who'd decided to protect his life rather than buck a virtual dictator who had been in that office since 1990. The result was an unsanctioned runoff election after which Mugabe declared himself president, again. The upheaval in the country was growing rather than lessening after his show of force to retake the office, a situation that wasn't unhealthy for Scirras' bottom line. It actually assisted in its own small way.

Scirras turned his attention to the mining situation in South Africa and contemplated how the unrest in its northern neighbor could be used to his benefit, if there was any way he could manipulate a mine closure or two in one of the largest gold producing nations. The thought brought just the hint of a smile to his face.

*ZANU (Zimbabwe African National Union) has just re-cement-
ed its partnership with the Zimbabwe African People's Union, which
had suffered the initial split into the two factions in 1963, one year
before both leaders, Joshua Nkomo and Robert Mugabe, were impris-
oned for anti-government activities.*

*Upon their release in 1974, Mugabe and Nkomo took up arms
against the Smith government, waging guerrilla warfare while battling one another for supremacy among the black nationalists. It was
a toss-up in the eyes of the world as to who would take the lead, but
one intrepid investor anted up by betting arms and cash on Mugabe.
It turned out to be a shrewd gamble.*

Butawayo, Rhodesia - 1974

*The arms dealer and the head of ZANU were meeting in a small
hotel situated in the center of Butawayo, upon the latter's discharge
from government detention. Under dark of night, the arms dealer finds
his way to a second floor suite, though that description is probably
overrating the accommodation, after entering through a rear access.
Mugabe is prompt, knowing that it would be unwise to make his contact wait. He is gearing up for the skirmishes he had to fight with both
the government and his rival party, and for that he needs ammunition,
literally. The man occupying the suite is his ticket to success, a man
who has been supplying revolutionaries all over the world for twenty
years, with special emphasis on Africa and Eastern Europe. And
today, the ZANU leader has cash. Enough cash to arm his guerrillas
for the next year with ease. But he is also expecting to cut a deal with
the gunrunner and pocket a goodly percentage, something to put away
for his escape should that become necessary.*

*Mugabe knocks to announce his arrival and, straightening his
makeshift uniform, opens the door and enters with an air of authority.
The arms dealer is seated as comfortably as possible in one of two
worn wingchairs that flank a threadbare settee. Primly poised with a
bottle of lukewarm Coke, a luxury in the beleaguered south, on the end
table, the man calmly examines his protégé, for that is how he views*

the rebel, as he deposits himself in the other chair.

The greetings are almost nonexistent, being glossed over by the dealer's need for haste in concluding business and the haughty attitude of the rebel. An attitude that the gunrunner finds amusing, though he doesn't allow his face to display his humor. In truth, the dealer would not even be bothering with ZANU and its leadership were it not for the potential Rhodesia posed in its geographic location and the rich mineral deposits that lay beneath the topsoil. He decided it is worthwhile to indulge the self-important rebel knowing that he is laying good odds on the probable outcome of the enmity between par - ties, that the man sitting across from him will win the day.

With that in mind, he allows Mugabe to open the negotiations, which he does by offering a ridiculously small amount for the arms that are, even then, waiting in trucks just a few miles outside of town by a large barn. The arms dealer eyes him thoughtfully and counters with a purchase price that he knows will give the rebel leader enough to line his pockets and make his own delivery very profitable, for he knows exactly how much funding Mugabe has to play with. He sips some of the beverage that is rapidly going flat and waits for a reply.

The rebel nods sagely before accepting the offer without fur - ther bandying on the price. He cannot afford to let the arms fall into the hands of Nkomo and he is certain that the dealer will waltz the goods to his rival without blinking an eye.

They both rise at the same moment, shaking hands to seal the bargain. The arms dealer, gripping the larger man's hand with strength and holding him in his place while he stares meaningfully into the rebel's eyes, letting the rebel know that this is just the beginning of his recompense for today's delivery. He will be called upon to pay his due at a later date. The leader of ZANU doesn't show it, but he shiv - ers ever so slightly at the menace such a seemingly small man can convey.

The news moved through the stories of the hour, one of which was the ongoing intimidation of the man challenging Mugabe for the presidential office in Zimbabwe. Solana was interested in that it sparked something in the back of her mind, the list of gold producing countries that Anthea had forwarded to Toddy just a few days ago, though it seemed like weeks with all that had occurred.

With that thought she started searching out information on gold mining in Zimbabwe to see if there was any connection to the Altamont conglomerate. It didn't take long before she found that the one-time largest gold operation in Zimbabwe was the Zimco Mine owned by RioMata, lo and behold, a subsidiary of Altamont.

"I was listening to the report and got curious," said Sol, "and look what I found." She told him of the connection and the fact that the Zimco Mine had been closed and why. "What are the odds that RioMata is part of the overall gold price manipulation you and Anthea had been talking about?"

"In my conspiracy-trained thinking," said Toddy, "highly likely. Even though you said Mugabe forced the mine to reopen, they've drastically reduced production, keeping the market tight where they have the capacity to do so.

"So, let's see… if they are able to drive the price of gold higher which weakens the value of the dollar, then Altamont benefits. And if Altamont benefits so do the major stock holders, which would be Herculaenea Fund, which benefits the partners such as union pension funds, which in turn benefits the PACs who receive funding from the pension funds, which in turn funds Kasili."

"Herculaenea is Scirras as well, right?" proposed Sol. "So he makes hay off the rising gold prices and then sends money through the 527s that support the same agenda as the unions who are also making money off the very same hedge funds invested in the gold market, no?"

"Yes."

Sol was sketching out a flow chart while she listened to Toddy make the connections and then added her own understanding of the directional current of funds, despite how far-fetched it appeared. "What do you think of Altamont's hopes that the unrest in Zimbabwe could overflow into South Africa, unsettling their gold production and influencing the price further?"

"It's a possibility," considered Toddy, "though a long shot despite the fact that South Africa has had its share of problems over the past decade since the change in government. All of it comes down to funneling more money to the unions' choice for president in the

States."

"I think we need to make the connection and post this," Sol said as she followed the arrows circling around her page.

"It's practically impossible to prove," Toddy pointed out.

"Hey, it's a blog. It isn't meant to be solid journalism, it's meant to raise questions. It can all be couched in the proper language alleging that these things are happening." She looked over at him. "Let them prove us wrong. You and I both know they won't go there because I think we're right and you can't scream libel if it's true."

Gold Baron

Chapter 20

Always keeping an eye on the internet to see what new references popped up relating to their candidate, a couple of the Kasili campaign workers devoted hours to web searches at headquarters. During one of these sessions a young part-timer, a computer technology student at a local college, started reading something that caught her attention and called over one of her superiors.

"Take a gander at this junk," she pointed to the screen while sitting back and pulling on her ponytail which was getting oily after a long day in front of the computer. The man, who managed to keep a dapper look despite the heat of a summer day in D.C., bent down to peer over her shoulder at a website he hadn't seen before: changing-wind.org.

"Is this new?" he said as he started to scan down the page. Slowly, his jaw clenched and his cheekbones took on a crimson tone with the anger that was rising in his gullet.

"I haven't seen it before today, so I think so. We've been pretty diligent," she said as she tried to move back some, his demeanor darkening, frightening her a little.

"This is unadulterated crap," he sputtered. "E-mail the info to my account," and he walked away heading for an office where he could close the door while he made a phone call.

He sat at his desk and checking his e-mail, got the website pulled up on his desktop while he dialed a number on a throwaway cell phone. Being one of the top advisors at headquarters, he was aware of some of the more intimate details of the campaign's funding and connections – the information that was not publicized, nor would it be. While the phone rang on the other end, he was shocked and dumbfounded by the accuracy of the allegations in front of him.

The call connected and a voice answered. He told the other person to check the website immediately.

"We need to find out who's behind this webpage today. Hack

it and kill it… FAST."

Chapter 21

Toddy's computer sang a little melody when an e-mail from Anthea was deposited in his inbox. Opening it, he glanced over at Sol who was typing rapidly, finishing up her second part of the saga about the Desert Mountain Power Plant.

The message was an outline of the stock ownership in Herculaenea Fund that her friend in San Francisco had supplied, probably through illicit means. He had also managed to get a donor list for the Kasili campaign that was shunted through a couple of the visible 527s. On top of that there was a list of other politicians who had received large gifts from 527s that were earmarked for re-election funds. He began cross-referencing the lists and it was providing quite an eye-opener to Toddy, even though he had suspected as much in the way of financial incest.

When he noticed that Solana had apparently finished her work, he called her over to take a look at the beginnings of a pattern, intricate as it was. The 527s were tied to the Free States Foundation by way of donations received from the foundation. Then, they were tied to politicians that had taken intense environmental stands against virtually every domestic energy-producing endeavor, and some foreign ones, that had been proposed in the last ten years. There was also a list of extremist environmental groups that had received funding from the FSF during the same time period. The one thread that was woven throughout the pattern was the fact that much of the funding was initiated from Scirras-backed foundations and business affiliations, i.e. where he or his proxies held major blocks of stock.

"Ooooh," cooed Solana, "let's see who's on the payroll."

The list was long, but at the top of it was Yakub Kasili, good ol' Jake. Familiar names popped out: democratic senators from most of the western states along with a number of congressional representatives; a few jurists; practically every liberal governor, including Castor; and even a lengthy list of foreign dignitaries from Ethiopia,

Romania and Zimbabwe just for starters. There were even a fair number of republican recipients of Scirras roundabout largesse.

"Lord, just look at all those folks. Do you think they all know where the funds originate?"

"I suspect that a few may not but that most have a good clue," said Toddy. "It's their business to know and other than what funding has been funneled in from overseas, most doesn't appear to be illicit though the amounts are obscene."

"We can even backtrack from the stalled energy projects to the non-profits that weighed-in against them and the amounts received from FSF, etc." noted Sol. "This is amazing and it certainly gives us plenty of fodder, not that it's evidence that could be used in a courtroom."

"Nope, to the judge it's all hearsay, but the folks mentioned wouldn't even want to deny it since it would raise some pretty ugly details that I'm sure they'd rather ignore.

"It's getting late and, I don't know about you, but I'm famished. I want to check something on the blog and then let's go get some grub, okay?"

Before Sol could agree to his suggestion, he groaned aloud and started furiously typing, intent on his screen.

"What's wrong?" She dropped what she was doing and came back to look over his shoulder. She couldn't understand what was going on with the website. While he was inputting data streams, the screen would flash black and then come back up. It happened a number of times during the few minutes that she watched him work.

Finally, he punched a few keys and sat back, exhausted and slightly paled by the intense mental effort.

"What happened?"

"There was an attempt to hack into the website and shut it down. I was able to defeat them but it was close and I couldn't backtrack it to see where they were coming from. They disappeared without a trace, dammit!" He slumped in his chair and crossed his arms over his chest in a huffy pose, enough anger emanating from him so that Sol took a step backward. "I don't think they got through all the IP proxies but someone is doing a damn fine job of trying to trace us."

"I thought you said your set-up was foolproof, that no one would be able to find us."

"Well, they haven't yet," said Toddy, "and it is proofed against fools but not some of the geniuses out there." He looked over his shoulder at her. "I'm good but there are others out there who are better. What's frustrating is that I can't get a line on the origin of the hack attempt," he fumed.

"They may know more about us than we think," Sol thought aloud. "Could there be trouble?"

"Oh yeah. You're already on their radar after those two aberrations at Little Big Horn and UNM. That made national news."

"Hey, when you're good, you're good," she smiled trying to lighten the mood a little.

"But now we've got a potential problem. They know who you are and they may even know that you now have a partner in crime, so to speak," he smiled back.

"So we're going to have to be extra cautious. Can we still go get dinner?"

"Let's. Take your laptop and anything essential. We'll keep them with us just in case. "

"Fine," she began, tongue-in-cheek, "we'll guard them with our lives, park in open spotlit lots and carry uzis under our trench coats so we can ward off the orc army that'll be lurking behind SUVs."

Toddy grinned, "Just so long as you don't miss."

Sol gave him a dangerous glare. "I *never* miss." She winked and slung the strap of her computer case over her shoulder and walked out the door.

※ ※ ※

The phone in his pocket began vibrating, tickling his chest. He pulled it out and flipped it open, "Here."

"I want you to find out if the fish woman is part of a cabal behind a blog that's trashing the candidate."

"So? What's new about that? It can't be the only blog out there."

"That's not the point," said the supervisor. "You need to find out what they're doing."

"Follow them or go through their possessions… which is it."

"Get inside their rooms and see what you can find," he paused to think. "Just call me when you know something."

"Will do." For some reason he missed them exiting the room, almost as if his eyes had glazed over for a few moments. He shook his head to clear his thoughts as they climbed in and closed the doors of the Tahoe behind them, then he watched the truck pull out of the motel lot. He must be more exhausted than he thought.

"Don't get caught."

"Hasn't happened yet," he said, not certain as to whether he was reassuring the supe or himself.

It was just after ten p.m. when they arrived back at the motel. Toddy walked Sol to her room and stood with his back to her, surveying the parking area while she unlocked her door. She flicked on the light and just stood there, unmoving and speechless at the scene that unfolded before her as she pushed the door all the way open.

"What?" Toddy turned around sensing her immobility. He peered over her shoulder to view the mess that confronted her. "Someone isn't particularly tidy," he said in an amused voice.

"I hope you don't mean me, because I left this place spotless."

"Uh-oh. I guess I spoke too soon," He didn't walk in, but pulled her out instead. "Let's see if they got to my room," and he moved to his own door and slipped the keycard in the mechanism. Pulling a clean tissue out of his pocket, he wrapped it around the door handle and pushed it down when the light showed green.

His room was in the same state as Sol's… it had been tossed by someone who was hunting for, what? He had no idea.

"I guess it was a good thing we took our computers with us, after all," said Sol. "You must be prescient."

"Hardly. I had a very real 'heads up' with that hacking attempt." He glanced over the damage without entering the room. "They inadvertently gave us a warning."

He pulled out his cell phone and dialed a number he had committed to memory a long time ago. "I think it's time to call in reinforcements."

Sol rolled her eyes at the melodramatic statement before asking, "I thought that maybe part of our problem might be the use of our cell phones. Can't they track us through those?"

"Probably yours since I assume the plan and number are licensed to you. Am I right?" He was listening as the phone began ringing somewhere more than a thousand miles away. "This one isn't traceable to anyone let alone you or me."

"How is that?"

"I have my ways," he said, waggling his eyebrows comically as the phone was answered on the other end.

Gold Baron

Chapter 22

Toddy hung up the cell phone and dropped it into his pocket. "Now what?" asked Sol.

"We wait. Zeke is sending someone out right away."

"Zeke? You actually know someone named Zeke?" She looked out at all the cars in the parking lot and said distractedly, "My uncle had a dog named Zeke once."

"Well, I wouldn't mention that to Mr. Arris if you meet him. He might take offense." He started to move back towards the Tahoe. "We'd better wait in the car so they can go through the room before we mess anything up."

"If I remember right, the place is already a mess. I doubt we could do any more damage," said Sol.

"Come on, you watch those crime shows. Zeke just wants them to check through the rooms to make sure that nothing untoward is awaiting us."

"What are you thinking? Bombs or booby traps?" she almost laughed until she noticed the serious expression on his face. "I doubt someone's going to trash a room and then set a bomb when the quarry has been alerted to danger. Personally, I think we'll be fine and I'm bushed. Tell me though, who is Zeke, anyway?"

"Someone I met when I was doing contract work for NASA. He was with the NSA, um, in management," he ended lamely.

"I get it. Only so much information can be imparted. Fine." She leaned on the windowsill outside her room. "How long do we wait?"

"I don't know," said Toddy. "He has offices in Phoenix so I expect they'll get here in a couple hours from what he said about pulling people from home or other duty. Then, they'll probably be staying to keep an eye out since I don't have any protection."

"Well, I don't leave home without it," and she revealed a gun in the side pocket of her computer case.

"Toddy's eyes grew wide then melted into smiling respect. "You're just full of surprises. I never figured you for a girl who packed heat." He added with a joking lilt.

"I grew up in the country. We hunt, fish, ride and pretty much take care of ourselves. I don't travel without backup."

"Good thing because I don't know the first thing about guns. L.A. had enough pitfalls without winding up on the wrong side of a gun muzzle," he leaned against the wall. "It was easier to distance myself from the gangs in every way humanly possible and the low profile I keep these days prevents me from applying for a carry permit."

"Look, I don't want to stand out here all night. I think we'd be safer inside. Why don't you book another room and we'll grab what we need from the car since you never bothered to move in and I have my big bag there. We'll make it simple and share."

He stared at her half in shock.

Sol just patted the side of her bag. "Security in numbers."

Fifteen minutes later, Toddy had secured a room two doors down, informed Zeke Arris, and moved into the accommodations with Solana. He was strangely nervous being alone with Sol even after having spent the better part of a week in close proximity working and traveling. This situation shifted the dynamics of their casual relationship, at least in his mind. He peered surreptitiously past the open overnight bag that lay on the counter next to the television, catching Sol as she settled her laptop onto the tabletop and wondered if he was the only one who felt any tension.

"So which is it, do you like the wall or the window?" he asked, hoping to dispel the uneasiness in himself.

"I'm a fairly light sleeper. I'll take the window," she looked over at him before hauling her suitcase onto the bed. "Unless you have a preference."

"No. I do like some fresh air though."

"Sorry to disappoint, but under the circumstances, I think we ought to leave the window locked, don't you?"

"Yes, actually. I'd already forgotten the danger skulking in the shadows," he quickly agreed.

"Distracted are we?" she almost laughed.

"What makes you say that?" he queried self-consciously.

"You've been digging through that bag for five minutes. It can't be that hard to find what you're looking for in that little bit of luggage."

He arched his brow in defiance. "You'd be surprised what an efficient packer can stash in a case this size. And I am nothing if not efficient," he added defensively.

"Whoa, I wouldn't dare to insinuate otherwise. Efficiency is your middle name."

Under his breath he said, "and yours is 'trouble.'"

"How'd you know?" she smirked.

"You weren't meant to hear that," he backpedaled.

"I have unusually sharp hearing and, if you hadn't already guessed, my spirit guide in the Tasmanian devil."

He dropped what he had in his hands laughing at her remark.

She bent over to pick up his briefs and hand them to him, mischief sparking in her eyes. Giving them back to him she said, "Would you like first use of the bathroom? You know how women always get lost in there. I'd hate to put you through hours of an agonizing wait.'

He snatched his underwear out of her hands and said, "Sure, I'll go first."

As he started for the door she added, "You may want to wear sweats to bed just in case we have to evacuate. It would be unseemly to run outside in our undies… or less, depending on how you sleep."

He sighed and went back to snag the pair of sweat pants that dangled from her hand after she had plucked them from his belongings. She just grinned, knowing that she had succeeded in embarrassing him.

He looked back over his shoulder, "Are you sure you don't have any brothers that you teased into submission?"

"Nope. Had to hone my skills on cousins. Just as good for practice."

He didn't bother to answer and closed the door with finality.

He emerged bare-chested not ten minutes later, looking scrubbed and pretty appealing to her tired eyes. The fleeting thought caught her by surprise. She averted her gaze, grabbed her own nightclothes and closed the bathroom door behind her.

By the time Sol finished her ablutions and headed toward her bed, Toddy was sitting propped up by pillows bathed in the eerie glow emanating from his computer screen, the television emitting a low droning of voices.

She crossed in front of the never ending news cycle, placed her folded clothes in her suitcase and climbed onto the other bed, reached across the gap and pinched the remote control that was lying next to Toddy's thigh. Before she could retract her hand he caught it with his own.

"Don't you just want me to turn it off?" She lay in an awkward position, half-on half-off the mattress, stretching across the little chasm. His eyes became smoky with his little game.

Clearing her throat, she squeaked out, "Sure," and she whipped her hand back across the space, just catching herself before she lost her balance and tumbled off the bed.

"Are you going to be comfortable over there or do you want me to rig up a privacy blanket, ala "It Happened One Night?""

"Oh, so now you're Clark Gable? I hate to tell you but I don't resemble Claudette Colbert one whit and no, I don't think it'll be necessary to hang a blanket between the beds." She arched an eyebrow, "I trust you to stay on your side of the room." She crawled under the covers as he switched off the TV. "I didn't know you were such a movie buff."

"What else do nerdy kids do except read, watch the tube and play video games, except they weren't very sophisticated when I was in high school. I had to invent my own."

"I should have known," she grumbled as she pulled the blankets up to her chin and turned toward the window.

He closed down his computer and checked his cell phone for messages. There weren't any so he turned out the light and lay on his back, arms akimbo with hands behind his head. Sleep wasn't going to come easy tonight.

It seemed to take forever to drop off, and Toddy could have sworn he'd only dozed for a few minutes when he was roused from what couldn't be described as anything other than a dead sleep. He rolled toward the small table that separated the two beds to strain his eyes at the red numbers of the digital clock's readout. Three-ten.

As his eyes focused he saw Sol crouched down by the window, her gun in evidence, muzzle pointed to the ceiling.

"Whaa...?" he began before she shushed him with a finger to her lips.

She spoke in a low tone that was almost inaudible. "Heard a noise. Could be the neighbors but I don't think so."

He scrubbed his hand across his face. "I'm a big help. Slept right through it."

She quieted him again with a wave of her hand. Listening hard, they both heard movement outside. Car doors closing and a vehicle peeling out of the lot.

They just sat there staring at each other, tensed and waiting.

Toddy just about shot out of his skin when a knock came at the door. He managed to rise from the bed and cross to the door while Sol leveled her gun at the entrance. When Toddy reached her, he put his hand on hers and lowered the firearm, "You think the bad guy's going to announce himself?" he said sotto voce. Speaking up, he addressed the door, "Who is it?"

"Alejandro Rey."

Toddy went ahead and unlocked the door while Sol leveled her gun at the guest who appeared in the opening.

"Whoa," said the new guy. "I wasn't told you had a body-guard." He smirked slightly. Tall, thirtyish with a blond brushcut, he stood in the doorway with his own sidearm pointed at the ground. "Friendly presence here. You can lower your weapon."

Sol looked at Toddy for confirmation. "You didn't recognize the password?"

She looked puzzled for a moment and then dropped the gun, shaking her head in amazement at the silliness of it. "Geez. "The Flying Nun" to the rescue, huh?" She stood up, checked out the man in the doorway, "Where are your wings? No, wait, Rey was the Latin lover." She scanned the blond hair and light eyes. "Well, you don't quite fit that description either."

"Latin or lover?" he tossed out as he peered through the opening.

She just shrugged and let it slide, it was too early for her and she wasn't in the mood. "I guess the password was your idea," she accused Toddy as she went to put the gun away. "You watched way too much TV as a kid."

"Hey, you recognized the name, so who is it who watched too much boob tube," he asked rhetorically.

"It's just a part of modern culture that, as a journalist, I would familiarize myself." She looked over her shoulder at the obviously good-looking man who hadn't moved from his stance at the door. "So who are you really, señor?"

The beefcake grinned, slid his gun into a shoulder holster and walked inside, "Russ Tarlington, Blade Security. And you are?" he asked, making eye contact with Sol that heightened her senses and made her take notice.

"Solana Greyfisher, bodyguard extraordinaire," said Toddy before she could answer. She cocked her head to scrutinize both him and Tarlington, wondering at the stiff attitude Toddy had assumed. Realization of the jealous streak that suddenly appeared in Toddy's features before he schooled them back to a blank expression brought a brief smile to her lips. *Well, well, will wonders never cease.*

Visibly relaxing, Tarlington gave them a quick rundown of his arrival and the rapid departure of the watcher who apparently had had Toddy and Solana under surveillance until he realized that the new-comers were backup.

"Since we weren't sure if you were okay, my partner followed him and left me to check on you two." He turned as a dreary looking sedan drove back into the parking lot and pulled up next to Sol's Tahoe. Tarlington did not look happy to see his partner so soon returned. "Must've lost him," he said flatly. "Damn."

He twisted back to engage Toddy and Sol's gaze. "We'll be out here for the rest of the night. Thing's are quiet now so you may as well get some sleep," and he walked out to the car while Toddy watched, then closed and secured the door.

Chapter 23

The blackout curtain was rimmed with bright light when the knock startled both Solana and Toddy out a solid sleep that had finally descended on them just before dawn. As Sol reflexively stretched through feline moves, Toddy threw back his covers and jumped up to answer the door. Unwilling to get up just yet, she sat back against the pillows rubbing the sand from her eyes as Toddy blocked her view of the person standing in the thin crack of an opening that he had allowed.

He didn't talk long before shutting the door. "Gotta get ready, Sol," he said as he headed over to grab his bags. "Twenty minutes to departure, I'm told."

"What? I didn't sign up for any tours. What's the hurry?" She pulled herself out of bed and starting rummaging through the case for clean clothes.

"Blade Boy wants to get on the road before the surveillance team from last night picks up the trail again."

Blade Boy? "I thought we were just heading back to your place since our little reconnaissance mission is pretty much completed." She stood up with her shampoo in one hand and in her other hand, a khaki colored outfit with some lacey underwear in plain view on top.

The underwear caught Toddy's eye for a brief second and then he rapidly switched his attention to the querulous look on her face that was framed by an appealing sleep rumpled look that at any other time would have given him thoughts of doing anything besides preparing to *leave* a room with a bed. Instead, he explained the situation in as concise of terms as he could.

"Zeke doesn't think this is just a fluke and he's concerned enough that he wants to get us out of here and someplace safe, which is not my house. So, we've been directed to get our things together and meet at the car in twenty minutes," and he started for the door.

"Where are you going?" she asked before he pulled it open.

"Back to my room to shower. They went over it last night, early this morning, rather. They found what they needed, which, I gather was a whole lot of nothing."

She lifted her shoulder in defeated acceptance, "that's pretty much what we expected... just a mess and no leads."

Toddy barely answered, "yup," before closing the door behind him.

It didn't take Toddy long to run through the shower and haul his gear outside. Tarlington called him over to the large American made car parked in front of the room they'd stayed in the night before.

"What is it with feds and Fords?" he said as he loaded his bags into the back. "At least it's not a Crown Vic. All you'd need is a neon sign to make identification complete."

Russ just grinned as he helped Toddy toss the overnight bag inside. "This is a step up because we're a step away from being feds. These days an SUV blends in better than a big sedan, don't you think?"

"Hmmm. Right," agreed Toddy, checking first Tarlington's smirk and then seeing how his expression changed to a genuine look of approval as he watched Sol emerge from her room. That set Toddy's teeth on edge, just a little.

She started toward her Tahoe when Russ moved quickly to intercept her progress and redirect her to the Expedition where Toddy stood at the back, the rear compartment open and ready to receive her luggage. He could see her face change from incomprehension to indecision to slight annoyance as the security specialist took the suitcase from her hands and led her to the SUV. Not sure what else to do, she followed, laptop case in hand.

When she arrived next to Toddy, he could see the burr of irritation that hovered around her pursed lips when she noticed that the overnight bag that had been in her original room was already settled in with the other luggage in the cargo bay. Toddy stepped back to give her space before he became a target of her evident displeasure, while he tried to cover his own grin.

"So tell me why I have to leave my car here?" She aimed the

question at both men who were standing close by, Tarlington lifting the suitcase into the back.

"We're not leaving your vehicle here," answered Tarlington over his shoulder as he settled the bag then stepped back to close the tailgate. "We have two operatives who will be leaving soon to take your Tahoe to a predetermined location," he paused slightly, "as bait."

That's when Sol noticed a woman opening the door of her old room and leaning out while Russ mumbled an "excuse me" and went over to meet her. She appeared to be a tall woman with dark hair cut about the length of Sol's. In fact, she resembled Solana somewhat except for the fact that she appeared to be Hispanic. From a distance it would be hard to tell the two apart.

Tarlington came back toward them and gave a signal to Toddy to load up, which he took seriously and jumped into the shotgun seat before Sol could even think about it. A very ungentlemanly move, she thought, but not unanticipated considering that he seemed to feel the need to run interference between her and "Blade Boy" as he'd called the interloper, since that was obviously how he perceived the new man. The thought actually gave her the first smile of the day even though she was pretty putout that her car was being driven by someone she didn't know. She was not happy at being relegated to a position where she lacked all control and was forced into a role of dependence. The circumstances did not agree with her nature, not that she could do anything about it at the moment. So she buckled herself into the backseat and tried to let it go while she took in the new dynamic that was developing between Blade Boy and Toddy. She gave herself over to a self-satisfied smile.

"I know this is not what you expected," began Tarlington, "but we felt that the circumstances required that some action be taken to identify the persons watching you two. So we have Linda Rincón and her partner taking your place to see if we can draw them off."

"How sure are you that they haven't been watching this whole charade?"

"One of our guys spotted the watcher down the road where he can see the parking lot exit but not the rooms. He's switched vehicles and this car isn't familiar to him, so he'll pick-up the Tahoe pretty quick when she pulls out and then we can leave the back way." They all watched as Linda put the Tahoe in gear and headed toward the street. It wasn't but a few seconds before a nondescript car followed at a safe distance. Russ looked over his shoulder and gave Sol a knockout smile as he backed out of the parking space. Toddy just crossed his arms over his chest and tried to ignore it.

They drove northwest up US 93 as the most direct route to Las Vegas, neither Toddy nor Solana understanding why the destination had been chosen, both having given themselves over to the supposedly more capable hands of professional security.

After making the second pit stop along the way at a fast food joint in Kingman, curiosity got the best of Sol and she finally asked no one in particular, "So who's paying for all of this? It feels like a government operation but, not to sound offensive, Toddy," she added tongue-in-cheek, "I don't see how you or I rate this kind of protection."

"No offense taken," replied Toddy. "You're correct in your assessment of the fact that as far as the government is concerned, we're not much more than a blip on some obscure screen. Zeke may owe me but not this much, so I'm footing the bill."

"But do we need all of this? It seems rather over the top 'cloak and dagger' stuff." She could she the corner of Tarlington's mouth lift in a furtive smile.

"Look, I had an idea that our little blog might raise some eyebrows, but I hadn't really expected to be followed around during our fact-finding mission. And I certainly hadn't thought that someone was going to go through our possessions looking for, God knows what." He sighed and settled back into his seat. "I started this whole thing so it's my responsibility to make sure that nothing happens to you. Well, or me either if I can avoid it."

She didn't have any response for that and just chewed on the fact that this whole thing seemed to have been blown up out of all proportion. All they were doing was a little investigative reporting, right? Nothing new there, or, at least there shouldn't be.

"I just think we need to find out what's going on and I prefer to have professionals handle the job that they're trained for. You and I are just going to have to go along for the ride for now," said Toddy.

Great. All I wanted was a vacation with a little travel and a little intrigue. I didn't want to end up in the middle of a damn spy novel.

The Expedition came down out of the surrounding heights of Boulder City just as the sun was lowering toward the western horizon. *If nothing else,* thought Sol, *at least we got to take the scenic route over Hoover Dam.* She'd never taken the time to drive this way into Vegas, but then, she rarely went to Vegas, not being a girl to gamble or get caught up in the glitz of a place like Sin City. New York had offered enough pitfalls of its own for a young woman feeling her way around non-stop action. She'd found early on that she wasn't cut out to be a party girl, so leaving the lights of Broadway behind was no sacrifice and Vegas didn't excite her any more than did the Big Apple.

As it was, she didn't have to worry about being tossed into the churning mill of the strip's nightlife. Before long, Russ guided the Ford off the freeway and down an off-ramp turning into a south side, suburban tract not far from Henderson. Driving past a couple of strip malls, he wound his way through a quiet neighborhood to a cul-de-sac that ended on the crest of a small rise that had a bit of a view of the surrounding terrain. The only thing that blocked visibility of part of the horizon was a neighbor's stand of junipers on the southern perimeter of the property.

Tarlington hit the remote garage door opener that was in an overhead center console and rolled the car inside.

"Wait a minute while I check out the premises," he said as all three started to exit the vehicle. "It'll only take a minute to make sure no unauthorized people have been here." Both Toddy and Sol stood by the side of the vehicle while Tarlington went through the house and eventually came back around, entering through the open garage.

"Looks clear. Let's unload."

It didn't take long to bring the luggage in through the side door leading from the garage and to have their guide take them down the hall of the rambler and show them their rooms. Solana gave Toddy a wearying look when they were assigned specific rooms, as if they were receiving bunking arrangements at summer camp. He just gave her a self-conscious grin and pushed his gear through the door of his new quarters, as if he had no input on the matter. She thought, why make a fuss? These guys are supposed to know what they're doing so may as well let them follow their plan, and she dropped her own bags inside the door.

It wasn't much later when Russ knocked on each of their doors and invited them to come in to dinner. They both emerged from their rooms at approximately the same time. Sol noticed that Toddy had taken the time to clean up and shave whereas she hadn't done much more than splashed water on her face and laid back on the bed, which she'd found to be more comfortable than it looked. Of course that could have just been the exhaustion talking. As a result, when the door rattled under Russ' knuckles, she was jarred out of a nap that she hadn't intended to take.

Toddy followed her down the hall and into the dining room where their host had laid out a gourmet Italian meal complete with a vintage bottle of Chianti. Sol's eyes widened in surprise but Toddy just settled himself into a chair as if he'd been aware of the upper-class treatment. She gave him an inquiring look and he answered her thought, "I'm paying for the best," he winked as Tarlington played along and offered the wine as if he were a maitre d' at an exclusive restaurant.

"I hardly thought Mr. Tarlington here was a chef as well as a security expert. This must be the new world of multi-tasking," she said as she raised her glass to take a sip.

"Sorry to be a disappointment *ma'am*," he said as he sat down next to them to eat. "But I can't cook. The company supplied the vittles. Dig in and enjoy."

"At least I'm not the only one," she said and did exactly as she was asked… she picked up her fork and ate.

During dinner Russ filled them in on the specifics of the safe house and the rules, of which there were many and none were to Sol's particular liking. No communication, no travel, pretty much, no nothing. "For how long?" she had to ask.

"Hopefully, not long. We should know who these guys are by tomorrow and be able to lay out a real plan of action."

"Terrific. I'm going to need to let someone know back home when to expect my return."

"Don't worry, we'll set it up for you to get in contact with family, etc. soon. Just make sure that you don't use your cell phone or your wireless computer connection. We're pretty sure they can track you." Russ stopped to take a bite and savor the food.

"What about Toddy," she gazed across the table at her traveling companion. "Are your communication privileges revoked too?"

He nodded. "For now. I think we'll be able to get back to work soon, though."

"Good," she said aloud. *Because I'll go nuts if this lasts longer than one day...*

After dinner, Toddy and Solana were so fatigued from lack of sleep the night before that they weren't able to go directly to bed. They sat up to watch an old flick on the movie channel, settling in for Hitchcock's classic "North by Northwest" and wondering if it was a particularly good choice of viewing material.

Around ten p.m. Tarlington's relief arrived. Just as the two were extracting themselves from the plush cushions of the couch, a burly, seasoned looking character in his mid-fifties walked into the living room. Tarlington introduced the 'night patrol', Eric Nolan. Nolan, who stood about 5'10" putting him at eye level with Sol, shook hands with both of them.

"I'll hold the fort while you three get your beauty rest. Russ, don't forget your night cream, those crow's feet are etching deeper into that silky skin of yours every time I see you."

Sol laughed and slid out of the room before the other two could follow.

Chapter 24

For once Toddy was up before Solana. She saw him ensconced behind a miniscule computer desk, laptop open and working online as she wandered into the kitchen seeking caffeine to bring her back to life. As she was pouring the rich liquid into her mug it struck her that they had been told not to tap the internet. Taking the cup with her she walked up behind her partner and leaning in close to his ear she said, "What is it about "no internet" that you didn't understand? Or is it that I missed something?"

He grinned without turning his head. "You didn't miss a thing. They have a cable connection here and I talked to one of Blade's communications specialists. He gave me a protocol to use that works with my proxies to get me under any watchful eyes, or ears. So, ta-daa, we're online."

She stood up straight so she could actually enjoy her coffee while she peered over his shoulder at the latest headlines. What showed up on a couple of different sites was news about a fire bombing at Kasili campaign headquarters in Ohio. The story stated that a radical wing of Castor supporters had taken responsibility for the destruction. They'd even issued a press release to explain their displeasure at the 'dissing' of their candidate.

"Oh, the natives are restless," she deadpanned.

Toddy chuckled and scrolled down to read the rest of the story. The Cleveland office had anti-Kasili slogans scrawled in red on the outside walls that called him a crackhead. The pictures indicated that they weren't content with trashing Kasili. There were denigrating remarks scribbled about the republican candidate Eddinger as well.

"Well, they're certainly not giving in gracefully," he said.

"Bet she raises a ruckus at the convention. There are too many people who think the nomination was stolen from her. I'm not so sure I'd roll over and play dead if I were her, either. The delegate count and the popular vote were too close to just hand everything over without some acknowledgement. And this fella has far too many strikes against him." She stopped to read and sip her coffee. "Got anything we can use to stir the pot?"

"I've been checking on a non-profit that appears to have financial ties to buildingbridges.org. It's called the Crescent Group and is affiliated with a well-known Islamic apologist organization that is more militant than it proclaims itself to be, collecting funds for probable terrorists. It looks like it has a funding relationship with some mosques in the States, which isn't a crime, however these in Saudi Arabia, Chechnya and Pakistan are dubious, to say the least."

He pulled up a worksheet on the screen. "It looks like the Crescent Group has contributed some $2.3 million, in small donations of course, to our friends at buildingbridges.org, which has made significant contributions to Kasili's campaign. And it appears that one of Kasili's half-brothers is on the board, and surprise-surprise, serves as an advisor on the international board of the Free States Foundation."

"Isn't that a tad too obvious?" she said, gazing at the funding chart on the screen.

"You'd think so, but it took an awful lot of hacking into the two websites to dredge this up."

"All that matters is, can you prove it?" she said.

He looked up over his shoulder at her as she closed in again to read the screen. "It'd be a little tough since the money trail leads to a couple of Caribbean waystops and then back to Dubai," he grinned slyly. "But that doesn't mean we can't create a 'stir' as you said."

"If it's not hard copy documentation it's not what I like to rely on as solid evidence when writing a story, because connections via the internet can be erased as well as traced," she thought for a few seconds. "It's a blog and they'd have to prove you wrong."

"The trail is there. If they even bother to answer the charge they lend credence to it and someone might actually get a warrant if they think there's probable cause to investigate further. I don't think they can afford to acknowledge the illegal contributions charge one way or the other."

"It's a no-brainer if the funds are coming from international sources, let alone ones with terrorist ties. I think you have to run with it, Toddy."

"Well, then, best get started with today's 'connect-the-dots,'" he grinned.

Toddy had hunkered down and was oblivious to the outside world as he typed away ferociously on the connections between the Crescent Group, buildingbridges.org and possible terrorist ties in the Middle East when Nolan walked out of the kitchen to announce breakfast.

"If anyone is hungry," he added, his own coffee mug in hand.

"Is this a convention of men who cook?" Sol asked disbelievingly.

"It's an occasional stress reliever for me. Helps me refocus my thoughts." He quirked an eyebrow, "You don't like men who cook?"

"Actually, I love the idea, I just don't trust men who bake. But I thought you were supposed to be watching the perimeter, not flipping flapjacks."

He laughed as he headed back toward the kitchen. The levity seemed almost out of place on his careworn features. "I'm off duty. Russ has taken over. Come on and eat."

Sol followed him out of the den while Toddy finished up and closed the computer in order to join them.

Omelets prepared with tarragon, tomato and Parmesan cheese disappeared without a morsel left on any of the plates. They all relaxed at the table, relishing a second cup of coffee before cleaning up. It was a few moments of peace that evaporated into a question and answer session led by Sol who wanted to know exactly what was going on.

"I'm assuming that since Toddy is footing the bill for this, there's no need to keep us in the dark. It's not like this involves national security," she said, pressing for information.

"No. We just didn't want to say anything until we had some idea as to who's sponsoring the surveillance team," replied Nolan.

"And?" asked Toddy when he didn't seem inclined to continue.

"The trouble is, we're getting mixed signals. It almost appears to be a government operation except no government agency has any reason to follow you two. So far as we can tell, even if they had traced the blog changingwind.org to you two, which we don't believe they have, that they only have suspicions, there's nothing on the site to implicate anyone with that kind of access."

"Look at your organization," said Toddy. "You're not government but you sure can appear official in your operations."

"Because we're mostly retired feds and military, which is why we believe these folks are the same and kind of narrows the field of usual suspects, so to speak."

"Are you going to give us an idea of who those suspects are or do we have to torture you?" Sol sat forward with her hands wrapped around her mug, a menacing look on her face.

"You *are* frightening me," conceded Nolan, with a quarter smile that said the exact opposite.

Tarlington chose that moment to reenter the house, closing the sliding glass door behind him, he jumped into the conversation. "Don't be too hasty, Eric. I've seen her with a gun and I wouldn't be quick to discount her ability to intimidate."

"Right," she said disgustedly. "You were shaking in your boots, as I remember."

"Nah, I just cover my fear well," and he disappeared into the kitchen for coffee.

"We need to find out what's going on because I have information I'd like to get to the Kanab Tribal Council. I think we located some documents that will help them in their legal struggle with that mining group," said Toddy.

Nolan appeared confused about the change in subject but let it pass without comment.

"This whole episode has interrupted some of our investigation into the long reach of lobbyists and backers funding Kasili," added Sol.

"Odd you should say that since we have reason to believe the Kasili camp may be possible suspects for keeping tabs on you. They're the only ones with any motive."

"Don't jump to any conclusions on that," mused Toddy. "We've been going after Scirras' organizations pretty hard."

"I hate to burst your bubble, but it'd take a lot more than a website to capture the interest of a billionaire with business tentacles of his reach and strength." He stopped for a moment to think, "and it's not like there aren't a lot of other blogs out there also attacking him. He's fair game."

"True," agreed Toddy, "except that none of them are delving into the truth with real facts and irrefutable ties to political thuggery and extortion around the world. So far as I know, none of them has found the Kasili connection either."

"You're that certain of your sources?" he sounded unconvinced.

Toddy and Sol both nodded their heads. "Oh yeah. My sources are *his* sources," said Toddy.

"Meaning… maybe I don't want to know," his voice trailed off.

"I mean that I've hacked his records on a number of different sites and it's *his* information that I'm using."

Nolan said, "He's got to know that."

"Oh, he knows the information is factual, he just doesn't know how we got it." Under his breath he added, "I hope."

Nolan heard him. "You better hope, all right."

Gold Baron

Chapter 25

They'd been stuck in Vegas for four days and Sol was antsy. She'd finally been able to talk to Drury to let him know that there was an emergency and she wasn't going to be back for another week at the latest. The news didn't seem to bother him since things were pretty slow. With school out there wasn't anything in the way of sports. No politics and everyone was out on the powwow circuit for the summer. "Not to worry" was all he really said, so, she didn't.

They also let her check in on Lainie who, according to Anthea, was getting bigger by the day and missed her auntie but was fine otherwise. Sol had nothing to distract her from the home front and that soothed her anxieties by a mile, allowing her to focus more attention on the website developments with Toddy.

It didn't, however, dispel her boredom. Toddy could spend a whole day in front of a computer without getting up to eat. She often wondered about all the sporting equipment she'd seen in his garage and if he actually used any of it. The fact that he appeared to be in pretty good condition would attest to the fact that he did, but watching him become utterly absorbed by his research made her doubt her conclusions.

She, on the other hand was dying to get outside more. It was hotter than Hades during the day, being Vegas in summer, and the 'Blade Boys" didn't like her going out at night to walk around the neighborhood. In fact, she'd only been able to talk Tarlington and Nolan into allowing her out for a stroll for the first time, the night before. Since it was Russ who was going to accompany her, Toddy immediately popped up to come along. It surprised her that he heard any of the conversation when he'd been so buried in his work. *Proof positive of men's selective hearing.*

They had been able to go into town to visit a couple of internet cafes so Toddy could upload the blog twice since they'd been there. Nolan did not approve of the breach of security measures in order to do so but since Toddy was essentially the boss, he hadn't any choice but to comply.

That afternoon, Sol had finished with her article and had already read and edited Toddy's work that he was going to upload the next day. She was standing at the back window gazing through the sliding door at the view to the east, the mountains creating a harsh backdrop of sizzling heat waves rising off the rocky planes, creased with slashes of black shadows between the granite outcroppings. The flat rise of the land was dotted with the spreading neighborhoods of tract homes sprawling ever closer toward the mountain vista. The beauty of the desert, sprinkled with the fragile green of sage and junipers was a whole different landscape compared to the lush grasses of home that lined the creeks and river valleys. As much as she enjoyed road trips, this one had turned sour with their compulsory incarceration. She was beginning to wonder if she would ever be free to wander the open road again.

As she stood staring at the view, Russ came by to check in from his rounds. Nolan was sleeping, catching up on some rest before he went on duty later in the evening. Toddy, who had finished his work, was just scanning through some news channels on the television to see if they'd missed anything important. He looked up as soon as Tarlington entered the room, as if his radar pinged every time the man was physically near Solana. The obvious reaction of her blogging partner fascinated her and she figured that Russ managed to find a reason to close his distance with Sol just to make Toddy bristle. The whole of the situation caused her to smile, which was answered with a wink from Russ as he crossed the room, knowing full well that Toddy had witnessed the interchange.

It took a fantastic effort for Sol not to burst out laughing.

It was just about six p.m. when Linda Rincón arrived, somewhat unexpectedly by the look of Nolan who had just risen from his off-duty rest and hadn't taken the time to address his attire. He caught Russ and Rincón with their heads together and joined the little confab.

Sol went into the den to grab Toddy who'd been checking more websites, as usual. "Something's up. My look-alike is here and it doesn't appear to have been a scheduled visit. Come on."

The two of them stood at the end of the hall trying unsuccessfully to hear what was being said.

"What do you think's going on?" said Sol.

"Don 't know. My guess is they'll tell us soon. Come on."

Seeing them step from the shadows of the hallway, Tarlington came over to get them.

Sol was a little brusque in her first encounter with the other 'Sol.' "We haven't officially met, but since you're here I thought I'd find out how things are going with my car. Did you bring it back?"

"Sorry," Rincón smiled ruefully. "It's not here but it's safe."

"What's that mean, 'safe?'"

Russ cut in. "Don't worry about your Tahoe, Sol. It's still serving as a decoy. You'll have it back in no time."

"Forgive me for sounding dense, but if she's the decoy along with the car, what's she doing here? I'd think that they'd follow her as well as the vehicle."

"Evidently, the two of you are pretty much alike in more ways than one. Linda was suffering from cabin fever same as you and slipped out. But she's delivering information at the same time."

"Yeah?" Sol and Toddy both looked expectant.

"We got a line on the guy who was following you. It seems that a couple of folks on the Kanab reservation saw him and were able to give descriptions of him and the car. Even got a plate number," said Russ.

"That sounds promising," offered Toddy.

"The unfortunate news is that it dead-ended at a private investigation firm out of Los Angeles."

"Damn," spluttered Toddy. "I'd lay money that there's a connection to Kasili. What's the name of the PI company? Maybe we can hack into their records."

"Sorry again," Tarlington said reluctantly. "We tried that. However they're working, they're not keeping records in a computer that's linked to any online service. It must be a closed network they keep separate from their internet network." He took a breath. "Just sit tight, we're going after the offices tomorrow. They'll find something.

Everyone looked a little glum as they realized that they were going to be stuck in Vegas a while longer. Linda made a comment about being in Sin City with 24-hour entertainment and they can't leave the house.

Sol cocked her head. "You managed to escape."

"Get used to it," said the ever-sensible Nolan. "We don't know the implications yet, but it's likely that you two have stepped into a deeper pile than you thought." He yawned. "I'm going to get cleaned up," and he sauntered toward the hall.

Just as Nolan was walking toward the bedroom he got a phone call and stopped in his tracks as the voice on the other end obviously arrested his attention. "Shit," was what the foursome in the living room heard as Nolan turned around and confronted them all, hands on his hips looking pissed and a little concerned.

"The diversion didn't work. The place was broken into and Linda," he stopped to draw a breath, "your partner was tortured and killed."

Toddy and Sol were rooted in place, stunned to their core. Rincón held her ground but was shaken despite her unchanging visage. Russ raised a hand to her shoulder, but she didn't even notice his grip.

Nolan raked a hand through his close cropped graying hair. "What the hell have you two gotten into?" His face was blank but his eyes were distantly accusing.

Toddy just stood there, shell-shocked, but Sol sat heavily on the sofa. "Oh God," her voice was small, and she looked across the room at Nolan. She asked as if she hadn't heard him the first time. "He's dead?"

"That's what I was just told. On top of that, they gutted the place."

"They burned it?" Toddy finally came out of his stupor. "Could they know about this place?"

"It would seem unlikely," said Russ. "I'm pretty sure he didn't know the location. You should be safe for now."

The graveness of the situation was settling in on all of them. But the two researchers weren't convinced that everyone in the house *was* safe.

Before he turned back to go get his shower, Nolan caught Sol's notice with his eyes. "Oh, not that this will make any difference to you now, but your Tahoe? It didn't make it either."

Chapter 26

There was nothing that they could do, but they also couldn't concentrate on anything except what had happened to the agent who had been Toddy's double. They hadn't met him and didn't even know his name, but the thought that someone had died because of their actions was a burden that neither Sol nor Toddy knew how to handle. Instead, that sat at the kitchen table, drinking coffee and feeling completely inadequate, useless and buried by guilt.

"What do we do now?" Solana verbalized her thought without expecting an answer.

"We can't go home. They may know who I am by now, and even if they don't, they *do* know who you are," answered Toddy.

"I can't even report the vehicle loss to the insurance company. Nolan says that they can track us through that, too," she was sullen. "He's right, you know. We're pretty much stuck."

"What really threw me is the fact that someone would go so far as to maim and kill for, what? A blog?" He wagged his head in disbelief. "This makes no sense. Even if they managed to get to the right people and dispose of them, i.e. you and me, the blog disappears. Although there's been some interest in the website, no one knows who's sponsoring it and it doesn't have any credibility *unless* they do away with it, bringing attention to the fact that it's *gone*."

"We need a plan that protects us and whoever we work with by creating a backup," said Sol, thinking aloud. "You need to put a device into effect that will take over if either one of us are unable to upload for a certain period of time. Something that will let the public and authorities know there was truth behind the blog and that's why it dropped out of sight."

"A failsafe device."

"Yes. That's the only way that this could end up being worthwhile. Otherwise, if they dispose of us and changingwind.org drops off the map, then no one will miss it and the bad guys get away with their evil plans once again." She looked across at him, "I know, I know, a little melodramatic, but you understand what I'm getting at. We can't have anyone die in vain and if it and we disappear into the internet ether, then that man will have lost his life for nothing." She slid back into her chair, chin on her chest. "I don't think I could live with that."

"I'll work on that right away. We'll have a failsafe in place before things get out of hand."

Sol looked up, her eyes brimming with dismay. "It already has."

Nolan walked into the kitchen, replenished his coffee and sat down at the table with them. "You two have got to go get some sleep. We're swinging out on a limb right now and there's no telling what the big boss will have us do next. Not to insult you, but you understand that you hired us to make the security decisions and we may need to move at any time." He gazed at them over the lip of his mug. "You need to be rested."

"How soon before you think we're going to be told to pack it in?" asked Toddy.

"We'll see in the morning. They'll be poring over all of the data now to devise the best strategy. You need to be alert and prepared or you'll hamstring the operation." He took a sip. "Your prerogative, but as you've seen, other lives are involved now."

"Okay, we're going to bed. I just hope we can sleep. At the moment, that's not too promising a notion."

Sol collected the cups and put them in the sink, then they left the kitchen and went to their separate rooms where neither one was able to drop off to sleep for a long while. Each was plagued by images of burning buildings and flames climbing toward a ceiling, enveloping the figure of a man, tied to a chair, unable to escape an excruciating death.

In response to the tragedy that had engulfed all of the members of the detail, they were working in teams, hoping against hope that the culprits who had murdered their colleague had not uncovered the location of the safe house. Nolan was dubious of the probability of their safety and was on edge. He'd been in similar situations plenty of times throughout his career, but rarely were civilians at the heart of it. He paced the living room, listening and waiting.

Linda Rincón reentered the house after taking the tour of the grounds. Tarlington was catching a four-hour rest before they switched duty for the staggered watch.

"Everything appears to be clear and quiet," she said.

"Good. Coffee's in the kitchen."

"Thanks, I could use a cup," and she strode toward the opening off the dining area.

Nolan sat on the couch and contemplated the options that would probably be offered in the morning light. The lamps in the house were being kept dim so as not to attract too much attention, but he wondered if it would almost be better to have the place lit up like a stadium to ward off the attackers. He shook his head. Second guessing their tactics wouldn't help at this point. Just go with the plan.

At one-thirty a.m. Nolan did his walk around the perimeter, keeping his ears open for any telltale sign of intruders. He saw and heard nothing, but his senses were heightened and he *felt* something, a presence though he couldn't put his finger on anything and there was no evidence of anyone. Maybe it was a coyote or a cat. He crouched down and scanned the edges of the property, keeping himself as invisible as possible considering there was virtually no place to hide. A fact that both worked in his favor and against him as he could be seen, but he could also see whatever was out there.

Satisfied that there was nothing there, he came to his feet and finished the perimeter trail.

Three a.m. and a concussive explosion tore through the kitchen as a flash-bang was shot through the sliding glass door, lighting up the interior of the house, deafening the two agents inside.

Fast on the heels of the blast, shots rang out, sounding as if they were coming from right outside the sliders, which stood as empty sockets, open wounds in the side of the house.

Rincón ran blindly into the living room where Nolan caught her as she stumbled over the back of the sofa. He felt a wetness on his hands as he lowered her to the ground, knowing instantly that it was blood, that she'd been hit by either flying glass or a bullet.

He'd been looking toward the front of the house when the flash-bang had detonated, so he was still able to see as he checked Linda's wounds while drawing his gun. She was conscious and, although hit in the upper arm and dealing with a steady flow of blood from her scalp, she was ready with her gun in her hand, waiting to regain her vision. Both of them knew that their hearing would be a long while in coming and they'd have to rely on what sight was left them.

As Nolan and Rincón were hunkered down behind the sofa, Russ had his gun out of his holster and was leading Sol and Toddy down the hall staying back from the corner, keeping cover as quiet ensued. Russ stretched his arm to the side, blocking the two neophytes from crossing into open fire and Sol had her gun out and trained on the floor, unable to see anything but the wall in front of her. They waited for instructions.

"Get down!" Nolan let out a harsh whisper while he dialed for backup on his cell phone, causing them to crouch in the hallway waiting for the attackers to make the next move.

All of a sudden the silence was split by rapid-fire originating from automatic weapons positioned in the backyard, slicing straight across the dining area and into the living room, peppering the wall just above the heads of Linda and Nolan who had flattened themselves behind the couch.

"We've got to get out of here. Grab your computers while I cover you," Tarlington instructed his charges in a low voice. "Stay low. Hurry… now!" They ran into their rooms, snagged their computer cases, Sol also catching her purse as it lay on top of the laptop bag, and returned to file in behind Russ.

"Follow me." Tarlington led them to the end of the hall, which verged on the dining and living area. He had to get them across the space and to the other side of the kitchen where the side door was located. Although there was a free-standing wall separating the kitchen from the dining room, part of the kitchen was open to the living space and fire was blasting in through the busted out glass doors, keeping Nolan and Rincón pinned behind the separating wall where they'd crawled, the sofa having offered no barrier from the hail of bullets.

Nolan waved Russ and his charges to stand behind them and get ready to make a dash for the garage while he and Linda prepared to lay down covering fire through the kitchen.

Sol knelt beside Linda in an attempt to tend to her wounds but was waved away. "I'll be fine. Got to get you out of here."

Nolan signaled them to run and as he and Rincón began firing a barrage at the attackers, Russ dashed along the backside of the wall and across the short kitchen space to fling open the steel side door, which added a shield for the fleeing researchers who were right behind him. Toddy and Sol flew through the opening followed immediately by Russ.

"Hold on to your bags and get behind that cabinet," Tarlington pointed out a wide metal four-drawer file cabinet that was pushed up against the inside wall. "Stay put until the garage door is up and we can clear the exit. Be ready to jump in the car. Sol in the front and Toddy in back. Keep your gun drawn, Sol."

Tarlington made sure the side door to the yard was locked after checking to ascertain that no one was hiding near the side yard. Then he depressed the garage opener and waited by the growing gap as the segmented door slowly slid up the tracks, constantly peering around the corners, expecting an assailant to come out of nowhere. The noise of the shooting seemed to cover the sound of the motorized retreat of the door, a concern that Russ had when he first pushed the button to activate it.

At first it continued quiet and then gunfire exploded into the open space, forcing Russ back behind the lip of the garage and pray that the shots missed the tires and gas tank while he returned fire into the night, aiming for the sparks emanating from the gun barrels as they ignited behind each bullet sent his way, and hoping that the neighbors were keeping their heads down.

Not many shots were expended before sirens blared and flashing lights careened around a corner a few blocks away. A couple seconds later, car doors slammed and a vehicle peeled away from a nearby curb, headlamps black.

"Get in the car!" yelled Russ as he ran, jumped into the driver's seat and shoved the key in the ignition. Toddy and Sol scrambled over, opened the door, tossed in their bags and climbed in, banging it closed just as Russ dropped the transmission into reverse and roared backward into the street. The Expedition was out and gone before the first of the police vehicles could pull in the driveway, leaving Nolan and Rincón to contend with the authorities.

Chapter 27

A few miles away, a man parked in a lot at a strip mall on Maryland Parkway that housed an all-night laundromat, a copy center and a Winchell's Donuts. Exiting the gray mid-90s model Taurus SHO, he closed the driver's door and leaning against it, pulled the throwaway cell phone out of his shirt pocket and dialed.

"What news?"

"Nothing good," he said as he combed his fingers through his dark mop of hair. He'd grown it out since being unofficially assigned to this duty, trying to look less like a fed. "We cleared the decoy and found the main camp but were unsuccessful in taking out the perps. Had to abandon the objective."

"Are they lost to you?" asked the disembodied voice.

"Only temporarily. They'll be moved after tonight but we managed to tag the vehicle with a GPS tracking device." He inhaled and let his breath out slowly. "Can't follow them yet. They could have extra eyes and we'd be too obvious at this time."

"You have a plan." The voice made a plain statement expecting a detailed answer.

"Yes. We'll catch up to them in the next hour after the initial heat dies down. They won't be going far at this time of morning and the device is already activated. We know where to find them."

"This is a priority," he was told in no uncertain terms, making it plain what was needed without using direct language. "Keep me informed."

The man flipped the phone closed and slid it safely back inside his pocket. Looking over at the donut shop he decided that he was hungry. Poking his head inside the window he nodded at his partner to join him. The two ambled at an unhurried pace to the glass doors, pulled them open and walking over to the counter, ordered two coffees and devil's food donuts to go.

The neighborhood behind him in a shambles, reflections of red and blue flashing lights streaking across the windows of the homes in the lonely suburban tract that had been quiet until half an hour ago, Russ checked in with Nolan for an update on the situation and Linda Rincón's injuries. He wasn't on the phone long since Nolan was trying to juggle conversations with the local authorities and headquarters. Russ hung up, thankful that he was the one driving off into the dark with clients rather than having to fend off unhappy police officers who would be dissatisfied with any explanation offered about the pyrotechnics that had split the night.

He punched in the number for Zeke Arris to get instructions while looking over at Sol and Toddy, who were both quiescent and, to his reckoning disassociating with the events of the last few hours. They had been too disoriented to follow instructions and both were seated in the back, which, to his mind ended up fine because Toddy had his arm around Solana's shoulders, offering some support even though they both looked emotionally drained.

The conversation with Arris was brief, trying as he was to go back and forth on another line with the local law enforcement agencies. Arris' attempts to smooth over the unholy mess that presented itself after the blow-up at what had turned out to be a not-so-safe house, were meeting limited success.

Tarlington hung up and Toddy, who was paying more attention than he had suspected, asked, "Where to now?"

"Good question. We're heading to the federal building downtown to reconnoiter. Zeke will meet you there and advise you."

Toddy looked out of the window at the dancing multi-colored lights from the Strip that brightened the pre-dawn sky. "Whatever you say. At this point I'm blank and completely out of ideas."

Depositing the vehicle in a space on the first level of the parking garage attached to the federal offices, Russ assisted his passengers from the rear seat and pulled their few belongings out after them.

Handing Solana her handbag, he shouldered her laptop case and gave Toddy his, then led them to the elevator where they traveled up to the lobby and were hustled through security. Russ' credentials were already in the system, so he handled Sol's bag, indicating the case was his in order to get her gun through without being confiscated.

"Carrying back-up, huh?" The guard inquired rhetorically before letting all three pass the gate to reach the main bank of elevators that would take them upstairs.

After they boarded the car, Russ told them that Nolan would bring the rest of their things from the safe house.

Sol, who had appeared almost catatonic throughout the whole drive downtown and the processing at security, muttered under her breath, "Some safe house." Adding volume to her voice, she said, "Speaking of being safe, how is Linda? Is she all right?"

"Yes," he answered. "An ambulance took her to St. Rose Dominican in Henderson. She suffered a bullet wound to her upper left arm and another one to her scalp, just skimming her hairline. That one will be a couple of stitches. The other was a through-and-through. Clean." As they exited the lift, he added, "She'll be fine."

"Thank God," said Solana. "I feel terrible. She was hurt because of me."

Both Toddy and Tarlington looked at her as if she'd grown a third eye.

"A decoy, meant to be mistaken for *me*." She said to Toddy, contrition in her voice. "I never imagined this could be so volatile, did you?"

He shook his head enough that his hair fell into his eyes, "I knew it could get hot but I didn't think we'd touch off a firestorm."

Ever the journalist, Sol said abstractedly, "Wonder how they'll spin this one in the news."

Both Toddy and Russ crossed glances and Toddy held back a knowing grin.

Tarlington led them down the corridor to an unmarked door and rapped on the solid core barrier. The door was opened by Zeke Arris himself, who greeted Toddy with a hearty handshake and a slap on the back that just about knocked the wind out of him.

"Man, do I owe you for this," said Toddy.

"You got that right," began Arris. "Except it probably is more like making us even. Besides, it's not like this is a free service."

"Yeah, well, worth every penny. I think," he added as an afterthought. "I really would have preferred to avoid all the excitement. It's not really my style."

"So I recall."

Introductions were made all the way around. Zeke was a tall, broad-shouldered man with skin the color of espresso, his unrevealing countenance topped by gray hair cropped close to his head. He had added some inches to his middle, detracting from his onetime taut boxer's build to resembling more that of an aging heavyweight. His ham-handed grip could crush bone and he could narrow his gaze to strike fear into a seasoned agent, a trick he'd used to his advantage often in the past when espionage had been his daily bill of fare.

Toddy and Sol slumped into two of the chairs that encircled a large conference table, Tarlington conferring with Arris about the vehicle and the need to have it thoroughly checked before choosing to stand practically at attention close to the entry. Arris made a call to another operative to follow-up on the vehicle after which he took to pacing the front of the room. The brief camaraderie of the greetings vanished as Arris resumed the brooding quiet he'd had before their arrival; a mood dictated by the circumstances.

Silence ensued except for the steady tread of footsteps back and forth across the industrial carpeting until Zeke received a brief call. He was informed that a tracking device had been attached to the vehicle the clients had driven up in. He gave instructions to leave it in place for the time being and turned abruptly, capturing Toddy's eye.

"Any contribution to make at this stage of the game?"

"Nada. That's why I called you in the first place," replied Toddy. "Not that we expected anything so bizarre as to be chased and attempts made on our lives." He dropped his head into his hands, elbows propped on his knees. "I still can't fathom that someone has lost their life because of this effort to uncover the truth."

"Now, *that* surprises me," said Zeke. "You, of all people, know how unpredictable politics can be, and how the quest for power can overwhelm even the most noble sentiments of an otherwise upstanding citizen, not that I'm equating these thugs with any such decent intentions." He stood up tall and, placing his hands at the small of his back, stretched in an arch that thrust his solid chest toward the ceiling. "I've been privy to some dirty tricks politicos and power brokers have engineered in the past which only makes me more wary of this maelstrom you've instigated." He trained his eyes back down on his friend and client. "We're not left with a lot of options at this point. Someone is after the one or both of you and we're going to have to stash you somewhere safe until we figure out who's behind the hit."

"Hit?" asked Sol, incredulously. "You think this is an execution or assassination attempt? That sounds pretty overblown, don't you think?"

"Well, 'hit' is probably too colloquial a term. But, yes, I think someone is out to put you out of their misery. You must be exposing something particularly sensitive that they would rather keep under wraps."

"Great. What's the likelihood of them going after family?" asked Sol. "I'd hate to think that we've endangered anyone but ourselves, though," her voice dropped solemnly, "I guess we already have."

"No," Zeke dropped his hands to the tabletop, resulting in a thunderous boom, and said almost belligerently, his voice low and pointed. "Blade is hired to deal with this kind of thing and if one of our people is endangered, hurt or even loses their life, it's because we didn't do our jobs well enough." He stood up again and began pacing. "It's our duty to keep our clients and our operatives safe. No one's life should be forfeit."

Tarlington had gone to an adjoining room and returned with coffee, which he handed all around. He then turned one of the armless chairs around and sat with his arms across the back, a concerned look on his face. "Brian's death is a tragedy for all of us, but we still have to face the fact that you two appear to be a target." He looked over at Arris who was pacing again and rubbing both hands over is shorn head, almost as if he were working up static electricity to jumpstart his brain. "Boss, it doesn't look to me like any of our safe houses will be suitable. We need another plan."

"I agree," he didn't elaborate, however, seemingly stumped for the moment, which, to Toddy's mind was completely out of character.

"Somehow, I don't think they've yet identified me," he said. "It looks like they tracked Solana and stumbled over my presence. So

I don't think I'm in any danger other than having been seen with her."

"You're still buried in some data base somewhere from years ago… if they have access to government files," said Zeke. "And I think they do. This operation is a little too slick. It was too easy for them to find you," and he looked directly at Sol whose eyes widened in worry.

Toddy added, looking at her as well, "Face it, you're easy to find. You show up at two rallies, an Indian journalist who skewers Kasili both times and they had your name from the press credentials, right?"

She just nodded in resignation.

"But they only have a suspicion that you're related to the blog, *if* that's what they're after." He pinched the bridge of his nose. "And I can't think of anything else they could be looking for, can you?" He directed the question to Zeke.

"No. No other explanation comes to mind."

"Well, I blocked their intrusion into the website and altered the proxies keeping them at bay, but they must have a pretty sophisticated connection in order to get as far as they did. To me it looks like there's a government connection somewhere because I'm the one who provided them with the best hacking programs available and they came close before I shut them down. Which, by the way," he added smugly, "I can do again. Now that I know they're trying, I can continue to evade them without much problem."

"That's good to know. So the question is, where do we take you next?"

They all remained quiet pondering the options.

Zeke finally spoke up. "We need a location that's accessible yet somewhat remote; that can be protected, i.e. see the bad guys coming and be prepared. It also needs to be a place that some one of us knows the area well in order to make preparation for any contingency."

"And we need internet access for monitoring the web. Plus we need to be able to get to a relatively close suburban area where I can upload the blog," put in Toddy.

"You're not going to continue this mischief after all that's happened?" Arris' jaw would have dropped in disbelief if he weren't stoic by nature. Instead, his jaw jutted a little and a vein throbbed in his temple, anger at Toddy's foolishness close to the surface.

Sol had never seen Toddy dig in his heels, but he did now. He was adamant, "We have to continue the blog. It's our duty to keep disseminating information, especially if it's hitting home." He stabbed Zeke with a hard stare, "If someone, and we think we know who, is trying this hard to suppress the website, then we're far too close to the truth and *must* keep the pressure on.

"We have a country to wake-up before it's gone. Congress is already legislating citizens out of work through overregulation." He went into a minor tirade about how the State is destroying the productivity of the people by limiting their earnings through licensure, taxes and driving up basic living costs. "The blog is bringing out how we're on the verge of losing everything that our forefathers established. This is how ancient Greece died – not allowing the people to keep what they earned until no one would or could work," he looked hard at Zeke. "These people are Marxist to the core. It doesn't take a genius to see that they want to gobble up the productivity of the people and enslave them to the State, which is nothing more than a new name for the Prince or the Monarch. The State then divvies the spoils collected from the serfs, via taxation, etc., between the Politburo, or the Nobility by another name. We don't have a choice. No one is going after the perpetrators of this reintroduction of the feudal system, which is all that Communism is. Hell, we're already half-way there!"

Toddy was on his feet and, while he vented, had taken over the pacing from Zeke, who had found a chair and dropped into it. He stopped and just fumed for a minute while everyone kept to their seats.

"Okay," said Arris. "Got it. There is an agenda that is being promulgated and, apparently, you just happened to push the right button while uncovering the facts. I understand your passion for keeping the information in the forefront. But, frankly, I'm a little stymied that one blog could be so dangerous."

"Think about it," inserted Sol, "Dramacrats…"

"Dramacrats?" repeated Tarlington, amused at the term.

She just waved aside the comment and continued, "… are so frightened of conservative talk that they're trying to reinstall the Fairness Doctrine to shut down as much opposition as they can. The First Amendment is being attacked on a daily basis by those who want only their opinion voiced, because, as they continually yell at the top of their lungs, hence '*dramacrats*'," she shot Russ a look, "their belief system can't possibly be contradicted. Think about it. If you refute their logic, and I use the term loosely, you are a 'deny-er' and a liar." She shook her head, "Welcome 'Pravda', the State-run press."

Zeke brought them back to the present situation. "We still have the problem of where to place you for the time being."

"Okay," said Toddy, visibly calmer after Sol had interjected her piece. "What are our choices?"

"Protective custody…"

Toddy and Sol answered in unison, "No."

"Okay, then back to where we were. A place that isn't overly populated and we can set-up a real perimeter that can be protected."

There was a long silence while everyone contemplated the dilemma. As they sat hunched or slouched or paced, Nolan arrived hauling a cart with the rest of Sol and Toddy's belongings stacked on it. Despite the fact that he looked tired and beaten up, witnessed by the traces of blue shadows that underlined his eyes, they tossed questions at him about Linda's condition. He lowered himself into a chair and answered what he could while Russ grabbed some coffee for him.

As he handed him the Styrofoam cup, he said, "You're gonna need a lot more than this to get you going again."

"True. The city cops are an unforgiving bunch and they weren't happy about a safe house being set-up under their noses," he said as he sipped after giving them the lowdown on the investigation into the assault. Nolan didn't have any great revelations to offer, the cops hadn't derived any different information than what he'd already told Arris over the phone, so they lapsed into silence once again, trying to figure a solution to where the couple could be moved to be protected without further incident.

�֍ �֍ ✖

Sol had assumed a resting position at the table, her forehead propped on her crossed arms, looking to be half-asleep, which at this stage of the morning she wished she were. After some time she sat up, a little twinkle appearing in her eye.

"I think it's time I went home."

Russ came out of his reverie. "What the hell are you thinking?

That's the first place they'll look, if they haven't already."

"Home, but not my personal house. As you point out, they will already have been there," she said. "Look, we need someplace secluded but not too far from civilization that has a perimeter you can patrol and internet access, right?"

At first there was no answer.

"Okay," Zeke said calmly. "Where is home, exactly?"

"Back on the rez. My grandparents have a place that backs onto the river, sort of, if you take into account a sheer, 300-foot drop. It's about five miles from town, up a gravel road where you can see anything coming in. The area was logged years ago and the trees don't encroach too closely onto the property, except for a few small stands that couldn't really hide anyone. And it has satellite internet. Would that work?"

All eyes scanned one another for protests or better ideas.

Zeke shrugged his big shoulders and sat back, folding his hands across his belly. "It's as good a suggestion as any, and so far, we haven't had another one."

Gold Baron

Chapter 28

The gray Taurus was parallel parked on the street near the Federal building, close enough to see the garage entrance without raising any suspicions. The two operatives inside the car were dressed like average businessmen, easily fitting into the crowd, which was comprised of a cross-section of Americana since offices in the vicinity served all types of citizens' needs.

Sitting back in the driver's seat, the team leader looked out the window. "Didn't take an astrophysicist to find them this time. But it looks like all we can do is wait… again."

There wasn't any activity at the building until after offices opened around eight a.m., after which they spent time moving back and forth, covering the entrances to watch for their targets, should they leave by some other means than the vehicle they'd tagged.

Nothing was happening and they checked in once with supervisors to inform them of the location and the fact that the couple they were following hadn't left since arriving just before dawn.

Foot traffic was heavy with weekday business to be conducted, same with vehicles entering and exiting the parking garage, but no sign of their quarry. A helicopter took off some time around ten a.m. and the two continued their surveillance without drawing attention to themselves, patiently watching and waiting. About noon another helicopter landed and lifted off shortly thereafter.

Nothing.

Three p.m. came around and the team leader spotted movement on the tracking device. He signaled his partner to stay and continue surveillance while he hopped in and fired up the engine just as the Expedition finally rolled down the ramp to turn onto the street.

Keeping his distance, the Taurus tailed the SUV to a body shop, where just one man opened the driver's door and walked into the front office. The leader, having the time during his wait to examine the vehicle more closely, realized that the car had some bullet holes riddling the body. Evidently this was the reason it was now sitting in front of a repair shop. He was beginning to think that they'd botched the assignment and combed his fingers through his hair, the only sign of his agitation. Not ten minutes later, while another car, a mid-sized black sedan, pulled up in front of the business to pick up the Expedition's driver, the team leader called in to report.

"I don't know how it happened, but we lost them," he wasn't particularly excited about having to report failure for the second time in twenty-four hours. "Could be they're still inside the building since my partner hasn't seen anyone exit. I'll call you back," and he punched the 'off' button. Without a minute to spare, as he followed the black car which was heading back to the Federal building, he speed dialed his partner and gave him the news of nothing more than auto repairs. Silence on the line.

"What about the helos?" asked the man still standing on the street, watching the steady flow of people in and out of the building.

"Shit," he muttered, half under his breath. "I'm picking you up," and he closed the phone while drawing a cleansing breath before calling in the screw-up.

Chapter 29

Solana was no longer concerned with boredom. Truth be told, she was almost fantasizing about the dull routine she had fallen into at the tribal paper in Idaho. The few hours spent at Blade's official, unofficial offices in the Federal Building hadn't prepared Toddy or Sol for dealing with the chaotic, uncontrolled spin their lives had veered into over the past week. The melee of the night before was still too fresh in their minds as they disembarked from the helicopter, the flight from downtown to the airport having taken less than five minutes once they were airborne.

It was a rapid development of plans as soon as they'd opted to implement Sol's idea of transporting them to her grandparent's lodge in Idaho. The corporate Hughes was the one that Arris had flown in on not ten hours earlier. He had made the decision to keep it at the helipad knowing the potential for circumstances to devolve at a moment's notice, particularly as they closed in on the identity of Toddy and Sol's adversaries.

For only the second time in her life (the first being a few minutes previous) Sol ran under the wash of the rotors swinging overhead, feeling a little disconcerted by the blades chopping the air just above her head. As if the rest of the night's experiences hadn't already been unsettling enough, jumping in and out of aircraft wasn't helping her equilibrium any. Toddy, on the other hand, seemed comfortable with the whole whirl of events – dodging bullets, speeding cars hurtling down the streets, hustling in and out of helicopters and now being herded aboard a small jet almost as soon as they'd touched down on the tarmac.

Zeke guided them up the steps and through the open hatch in quick time, settling them into their seats rapidly while their gear was stowed.

"You'll be flown into Spokane instead of the local airport," explained Zeke. "An aircraft like this coming into a small field attracts a lot of attention. Something we don't want right now."

"Who owns this little baby?" asked Toddy, taking note of the luxurious surroundings. "It doesn't look like government issue to me."

"It's not, though we have a lucrative contract with the NSA. This is a Blade Security jet. It's not exactly a cheap ride, but it'll get you close to home quickly and without fear of tracking," answered Zeke. "A company car will meet you in Spokane and the four of you will drive from there. Good enough?"

"Four?"

"Yes. Tarlington and Nolan will accompany you as security detail." He turned to question Sol. "Do you want to inform your family that you'll be arriving?"

Sol shook her head 'no.' "It'll be better if we just show up. I don't want them jumping to any conclusions or getting worried ahead of time."

Toddy looked at her, inquiringly, "Conclusions? What kind of conclusions would those be?"

"Driving up with three men in tow. What would you think?"

"A male harem?" Zeke quipped as he prepared to leave.

Sol cocked an eyebrow. "You don't know much about Indian culture, do you," she shot back with humor.

They buckled in as Zeke deplaned and Russ and Nolan came aboard, greeted them and settled into their seats for take-off.

Just as the jet began to taxi down the runway, Toddy turned to ask her what she meant by her remark about Indian culture. "Did I miss something? I hadn't heard that multiple husbands are acceptable in Native American society."

"Nah. We usually take them home one at a time." He looked deep into her eyes to fathom them for sincerity and was rewarded with a golden glint of laughter. Shaking his head at her teasing, he readjusted his view to take in the swiftly miniaturizing buildings and crosshatch of roadways dropping into the distance as the jet leapt off the runway and rose into a cloudless sky.

The plane was equipped with satellite TV and as the flight progressed, the two passengers flicked through the channels to check in on the current state of the presidential campaign.

While they watched, a report came over one of the networks that the Kasili camp had inadvertently leaked that his campaign had redesigned the White House seal. The insignia now sported two ceremonial spears with African motifs crossed in the background.

"This, I don't believe," said Sol, aghast. "What kind of arrogance does this man possess if he not only presumes to be the president-elect before he's even tied down his party's nomination, but his toadies have the gall to redesign the seal of the President?"

"Castor hasn't even fully conceded yet," added Toddy. "And it looks to me like she's going to take the challenge to the convention floor. It's not going to be a cakewalk for Kasili. Black heritage or not."

"This character needs a reality check. She's not going quietly, nor should she. Her delegates are raising a ruckus, and rightly so in my opinion. He hasn't walked away with anything, no matter how overconfident he acts."

"I don't understand how his followers seem to feel that the rest of their party is superfluous," said Toddy. "Let them keep it up. Kasili will alienate the Castor voters if he continues with this attitude."

"The denigrating comments about Eddinger's status as a Viet Nam vet could backfire on him, too," added Solana. "It's nonsensical to place your bets on the fact that having an African father will give him more standing than someone who has served their country and been a P.O.W. If his campaign is assuming that all minorities will automatically flock to their banner because we are 'downtrodden,' it's not likely to happen that way. People forget the proud heritage Native Americans have of serving as modern day warriors. My grandfather, many of my uncles and some aunts served this country. The democratic mantra disparaging the armed forces goes against a proud Native legacy of fighting for freedom, first against the U.S. in the past and then as part of this country's citizenry.

"Sure, we're sovereign within the borders of the United States, but we are also representatives of this nation's history, creating a strong link between the ancestral heritage of the land and modern times.

"You know what really ticks me off is the mantra that simply because the man is African-American, anyone who dares to vote for someone else is automatically painted as a racist," she fairly seethed at the presumption. "Skin color hasn't a damn thing to do with whether or not someone is qualified for a job, let alone the presidency. If that were the criteria then I'm just as qualified to run this nation."

"Don't underrate yourself," smiled Toddy. "I'd venture to say that you're far more qualified than Kasili if it came down to basics of understanding what this country stands for and what real freedom is." He reclined in the seat. "I'll bet you can balance a checkbook, too and I'd lay money that Kasili probably hasn't even had to do that much in his stunted experience. I'd vote for you any day."

"Well, I'm not crazy enough to run for high office. I sometimes wonder if you have to be pathological to want that kind of power. Who needs the scrutiny and headaches? You have to have the hide of an elephant to take the battering the media would give you. Although, Kasili has been their chosen one, so he hasn't suffered the 'slings and arrows' that every other candidate has undergone and he whines if they give him a tough question. It gets really tiresome how he is treated as if everything is off limits… his past, his buds, his experience, or lack thereof, even his father's name. He needs to grow a pair, in my book."

Toddy chuckled. "Bet on it, the people propping up Kasili are pathological about running everyone else's lives. Liberal elitism is an aberration of normal thought and environmentalism is little more than a pagan religion."

"Ooooh, you'd better watch who you say that to. Them's fightin' words to those folks." She winked before turning on her side to take a nap while there was time to catch one.

Chapter 30

The few hours of flight time passed uneventfully during which all four of the cabin's occupants were able to get some shuteye. The plane's descent woke everyone except Toddy who had to be shaken out of his slumberous stupor to prepare for landing.

The jet rolled to a stop at a private airfield where the security could be overseen without the excess worry of dealing with the general public milling around. The empty tarmac held only a couple of airport vehicles and the ubiquitous Ford, a hunter green Excursion waiting for them to deplane.

It didn't take long for the four of them to climb down with their carry-on items while Blade Security staff loaded the rest of the luggage into the rig's cargo bay. Within ten minutes of arrival, they were underway, Tarlington at the wheel and Nolan riding shotgun. Sol didn't even have to give the driver directions to US 195, since he'd apparently boned up on his geography before landing.

Driving south across the Palouse, the vast farming plateau that was named for one of the local tribes whose numbers had dwindled over time and pressures from the influx of the pioneer population of the last two centuries, Toddy asked question after question about the area. The trip turned into an educational tour for him as Sol explained some of the history of the local tribes, the largest in the area being the Spokane, Coeur d'Alene and Nez Perce, where she was an enrolled member. She talked about the seasonal rounds of hunting, gathering the fruits of the earth, fishing and storytelling that are important to a transhumance lifestyle that belonged to the Plateau Indians. Sol related the history of the horse in the region and how important it became, particularly to the Nez Perce who still took great pride in their Native breed, the Appaloosa. She told some of the old tales and war stories tied to a few of the geographical landmarks they passed, for the countryside was rich with the history of the Plateau peoples who had roamed the land long before the white trappers and settlers had come.

Toddy was mesmerized by the accounts she shared as they passed a creek or a butte, the history coming alive just as he imagined it had for her, hearing the tales from her grandparents and tribal elders. It was an open door into a culture that, for most mainstream Americans, was glossed over in the schoolbooks or misrepresented in popular culture. The average person might recognize the names of explorers like Lewis and Clark, Jedediah Smith, or Kit Carson but they wouldn't have heard the legends as they had been handed down from generation to generation among the first inhabitants of North America, whose perception was quite different.

He was impressed, not only with her knowledge of her heritage but with her ability to objectively paint the historic panorama, at times telling the Native perspective and at other times shifting into that of the newcomers who quickly displaced her own people, changing the landscape to fit their own vision of property ownership which vied with that of the Indians. In the end, sheer numbers and government policy overwhelmed the Native population, relegating them to small reservations that covered only a fraction of their ancestral lands. It wasn't a pretty tale but she also didn't dwell on a bitter attitude. Instead, the way of life now was different and she accepted the changes while acknowledging how important it was for her people to remember their heritage and pass it on to the children.

"This is why I tell you and share with the babies as they grow, just as my parents and their parents did," she said, staring out the window as they rounded a long curve bringing them down into a populated valley carved out by the Palouse River. "We all have stories of our past and perhaps that's why I became a journalist, was to make sure that the stories of today are conveyed to future generations with impartiality. Making it easier to understand why history will develop as it does. Too much of the world's history has been written with a biased hand. I can only try to report the facts and hope that I have done my job well to ensure there is a posterity that can understand how it all occurred." She turned to look at Toddy, an underlying passion revealed by her voice. "You know, so those generations will have a clue, and an opportunity to uncover the truth even when it is being hidden from them by those with agendas of their own. Just as has happened before, as is happening now and will happen in the future." She broke the eye contact and looked back out the window.

Toddy didn't have a response, nor did he feel that she needed one. This was one of those times when he felt privileged by the peek he was given into the heart of someone he was growing to like and respect more with each day they spent in each other's company. He'd met women of all kinds over the years but very few who could affect him with their words.

Less than an hour later they started down a seven-mile grade into the Lewis and Clark Valley. Peering over the edge of a deep cleft carved out by the confluence of the Snake and Clearwater Rivers, Russ took the rig down the highway that rolled through rounded hills that fell away into more than a two thousand foot descent. Toddy had traveled a fair bit but, even so, the road seemed more like a downward plunge than a four-lane highway sculpted into the steep mountainside.

"Pretty spectacular view for the uninitiated," said Nolan as Tarlington took the truck out of overdrive and shipped it into cruise control to keep the speed at an even 58 mph without riding his brakes.

"Have you ever been here before?" Sol asked.

"Yeah. My brother-in-law and his boys have been up here a couple of times steelheading. Excellent fishing and terrific scenery to boot. I can see why you'd want to come home. I would too if home looked like this."

Toddy was curious now, "Where's home for you?"

"If you want to know where I grew up, that'd be South Philly. Not the most picturesque place but I still have family there."

"You don't sound like you're from Philadelphia," observed Sol. "I remember most people I met from there had a distinct accent, in some cases harsher than Brooklyn."

"I left that back by the Schuylkill. Some people hold a Philly accent against you. Sometimes, I think the only thing tougher is listening to someone from Trenton. One of my teachers in high school disparaged Trentonites for murdering the English language and *she* talked with a Boston Southie twang," he laughed. "It's hard to hear your own voice, you get used to the cadence, but there are those who can certainly be quick to judge someone else by pronunciation and word usage."

At the bottom of the hill they turned east onto US 12, heading up the Clearwater River for another forty-five minutes before reaching the turnoff outside of Lathrop. The winding road quickly devolved from pavement into gravel that was only one and a half lanes wide with occasional turnouts for passing oncoming traffic. The road was little traveled and at this early evening hour they met only two vehicles heading down the mountain. Both drivers gave the fancy SUV long looks but did the pinky wave from the steering wheel to the passing truck. Russ picked up the greeting and returned it each time accompanied by a grin.

If Toddy was uncomfortable on the grade coming into the valley, this made him even more uneasy. The road was tight, twisting and narrow, three elements that stuck in his gullet, making it a little difficult to swallow.

Sol noticed his slight discomfiture and commented, "Just a couple more miles to go."

Russ asked her to direct him when they were approaching the turnoff for the property. Five minutes or so later she complied with his request by telling him to turn left at the mailbox that was painted with a blue feather. Of course, there was no way to go right without taking a header over the cliff, so telling him which direction to turn was probably unnecessary, a point he couldn't resist making as he steered onto the crushed rock lane. The long driveway skirted flat hayfields and a fenced area where a couple of Appy mares and a cow munched placidly on the lush grass, the pasture stretching away for acres before abutting a forested mountainside that climbed steeply upward another hundred feet or so.

They arrived long before dark, it being the height of summer the sun wouldn't set for more than two hours. As they pulled around the circular drive, a tall man, easily in his mid to late seventies, with a thick shock of white hair came out of the house, his face an emotionless mask until he saw Solana climb out of the back seat. He yelled for his wife, Millie, as he walked forward a little stiffly, the arthritis in his hip causing him some trouble, to hug his granddaughter. He stood a good four inches taller than Sol, even with the slight stoop that had taken hold of his shoulders, and gave the other three men a good staredown as they followed in her wake.

"So. Solana. This is unexpected. Who are our guests?"

"P'lahka, these are my colleagues from Arizona." She greeted her grandmother as she came out of the door tugging on one of her favorite vests, a sign that they were preparing to go somewhere. Sol introduced her grandparents, Lester and Millie Greyfisher, to the three men standing somewhat awkwardly beside her. Lester invited them all inside, got them seated in the living room and after a comment, simply waited for her to talk.

"You're always welcome but this is an unusual entourage you have," he said as he studied the men who all looked as different from each other as night and day, plus the fact that two of them had a military bearing that was unmistakable to the old man who was a veteran himself.

"I'm afraid it won't be easy to explain the circumstances that brought me into the company of these honorable men, and I see that you were preparing to leave," she said, somehow feeling the need to be formal in her explanation.

"No matter," said Lester, "we have time." He sat down in the worn leather recliner that was obviously his chair. Millie claimed a corner of the sofa and pulled her granddaughter down next to her. "Go ahead. We want to hear the story."

Sol tried to simplify the tale so her grandparents could get down the road before dark, and she was fairly successful in detailing the reason for the four of them showing up on their doorstep, not that it was unusual for family to drop in at odd moments.

Lester simply nodded his head while listening as she recounted the occurrences of the last week, understanding without questioning. He knew his granddaughter and her passion for truth. "So, you will need to stay here for a time. That will suit fine." He was quiet for a few moments. "Your grandmother and I were just leaving for a trip and will be gone for a few weeks. Like usual this time of year." He looked at Sol. "You remembered that when you made the suggestion to bring your friend here for safety."

At this, Toddy wanted to break in to explain that *she* was the one in danger, not him, but he realized before he opened his mouth that she was diverting the issue in order to avoid the older couple deciding to stay and protect her.

"Yes," agreed Sol. "It seemed a good place to come in order to keep him safe and these two men provide security professionally."

241

"They work for the government," Lester stated.

"We have worked for the government, yes," said Nolan. "But we are under private contract and pledged to protect Mr. Johnson and anyone with him. It is actually quite opportune that you will be traveling. We greatly appreciate your willingness to accommodate us in our duty."

Lester just nodded acquiescence then deliberately stood up and crossed to Toddy and his two guardians to shake their hands, officially welcoming them to his home.

"Grandma's sister is expecting us tonight so we will leave you to care for the house. You should call Angie to tell her that she doesn't need to come and feed the animals." He then addressed Eric Nolan, who was obviously the senior member of the group. "You will prefer to keep visitors limited in order to ensure Mr. Johnson's security. Solana can handle the place on her own, but you keep her safe." It was evident that he hadn't bought the story of Toddy being the target.

Millie had gotten up to gather her things and was standing by the door waiting for her husband to join her so they could leave. Sol embraced her grandmother and then turned to her grandfather before he left her in his home with three strangers. He looked into her eyes and then nodded once more, giving her a solid hug. She walked the old couple out to their Dodge pick-up and watched them climb in and drive away.

After Sol's grandparents started down the mountain, she turned Toddy loose in the kitchen to whip up dinner while she called her cousin Angie to inform her that the animals would be cared for by another friend of her grandparents to save her the need to truck up the hill to see to them. Angie was a talker and although Sol tried to extricate herself gently from the conversation, it was a full eighteen minutes later when she had to get aggressive saying she had another call that needed immediate attention.

She finally hung up the phone and massaging her ear, told Toddy she was going out to feed the horses. As soon as she pushed open the screen door, Russ Tarlington was on her tail as she left the house.

She gave him a glare, "Where are you going?"

"With you."

"No need. There are only five horses. I'm perfectly capable of handling them myself, thank you." She turned on her heel and climbed down the front steps. Hearing his clomp right behind her, she said over her shoulder, "What now?"

"You forget that I'm on duty, and hard as it is to accept, that duty is to keep you in view and safe," he said as he trod in her wake.

"Psshaw, I hardly think we need to go to all that trouble up here. No one knows we're even in the state, right?"

"Doesn't matter. Letting things slide just a little is why Brian lost his life. We won't be making that mistake again," he said solemnly.

Putting it into that perspective, she kept her thoughts to herself and went out to the pasture where the horses were milling around by the fence that backed onto the haystack. They knew where dinner was and stood quietly in anticipation of their evening feeding. She approached the small herd and scratched the necks of the two closest horses, a mare and her two-year-old colt. The other three were hanging back a little, reticent to approach the newcomer who followed Sol to the fence line.

Sol separated a couple of flakes off the end of one of the rectangular bales that had been left in the weather beaten, but still functioning, wheelbarrow that she'd played in as a child. Walking back to where the horses stood, she distributed the hay among them and stayed to pat their necks and scratch their haunches before heading back to the house.

Russ just hung back while she took care of the animals, keeping an eye on the perimeter and noticing Nolan as he made his way around the back of the property, circling the house from the other side to familiarize himself with the general lay of the land. Russ scanned the horizon, realizing that the acreage was going to take more than the two of them to keep under constant observation.

Sol finished with the horses, all who had their heads bent busily consuming the hay that had been strewn for them, and started off toward the house after checking to be sure the trough was full with clean water. Russ fell in beside her as she strode across the grass that was beginning to lose its verdant color, ripening to gold as the summer heat moved up the mountainside. Sol stopped to check the sprinkler system that she would need to put into operation soon, examining it to see if her grandfather had prepared it for use. Satisfied that all was well maintained, she continued on her way back to the house, Russ tagging along like a little brother, despite the fact that he stood a few inches taller than she.

As they sat down to a meal that Toddy had assembled with relish, he commented on Sol's preference for enjoying someone else's cooking rather than being saddled with the duty herself.

"Is that some kind of crack about me choosing to feed the horses as opposed to feeding three men who cook quite competently?" she mocked.

"Nope," he smiled. "Not everyone is meant to be a Julia Child."

"Hey, this is the new generation," cut-in Tarlington. "You mean Martha Stewart."

"No, I don't. Julia Child was the French chef's chef. Martha is the matron du jour. Competent but no panache."

Sol just laughed. "I'll never measure up to either one. It just isn't in my genes."

Toddy looked at her with an unusual warmth. "We all have our strengths, and yours is in dogging the iniquitous to their downfall. Who needs to cook anyway when there's always the Colonel?" he grinned.

She just rolled her eyes and began listening to the other two as they had fallen into a conversation about the problems they foresaw in trying to provide security for their clients with the extensive acreage that needed to be covered.

"We need back-up," said Nolan, shaking his head. "There's no way around it."

Toddy hearkened his ears to the conversation, too. "What are you saying, that it's too much for just you two up here?"

"In a nutshell. We're going to need to call in the troops," said Tarlington pushing his chair back from the table and stretching his legs out in front of him, crossing them at the ankles.

"So what are you planning to do?" Sol queried as she rose to clear plates.

"Well, I don't like how long it'll take to pull in more men. The closest office is in Los Angeles and even if we fly them in, it'll be a full day of travel what with driving on top of it," explained Nolan.

"You can bring them in by helicopter after their flight," offered Toddy. Then he thought. "Maybe not, we don't want to draw too much attention."

"No, we don't. Even though there is some helicopter logging around here, the curiosity factor is something we need to avoid." Tarlington fell silent for a moment.

"What about local help," Sol offered as she walked out of the kitchen wiping her hands with a dishtowel.

"Are you kidding?" said Nolan. "That's the next best thing to using a bullhorn."

"Unless you happen to have family on the local police force," Sol hiked up an eyebrow. "Indians can be the most industrious gossips around if it suits them, but when it comes to protecting their own, you couldn't pry open a mouth with a crowbar."

"You have family on the force?" Nolan was interested.

"My nephew is with the tribal police." She looked at the men seated around the table. "He can be pretty intimidating," she baited them.

It was Nolan's turn to cock an eyebrow. "Is that so?"

She shrugged her shoulders and started back into the kitchen.

Nolan and Russ considered the option, communicating with their eyes across the empty table.

"How soon could he get here and does he have friends?"

She smiled to herself as she continued walking toward the kitchen. "I'll call."

Two hours later Cisco Rafael appeared on Solana's borrowed doorstep with a cousin and Gary Mathers in tow. Of the three, Cisco was by far the most imposing, standing at 6'5" with a broad build to match. Tarlington, who flanked Sol, could picture how impressive the young man would be in uniform and that he'd be apt to put the fear of

God into any lawbreaker who crossed his path. He was happy to be on the same side of right as Sol's nephew.

The security detail stood to the side as Sol hugged each one of the new arrivals as they came through the door. Russ' eyes opened even wider at the sight of the more mature man with graying hair who shook him down with a searching steel-eyed gaze as he walked into the living area. Russ gave Sol a questioning look and she introduced each of them, explaining that Seth had just been hired by security at the casino and had served in Iraq until six months ago. He wouldn't be starting for another two weeks. Gary, she said, was retired from the Portland police department, to which both Nolan and Tarlington nodded in understanding. Cisco may have been the largest of the three, but Mathers' demeanor made it clear that he'd be the one who'd be hard to bulldoze. They were pleased with the new recruits.

Mathers' made quick work of making the Blade men's acquaintance before he went hunting for Toddy, who hadn't been at the door to greet them. He was interested in meeting the man who had stirred up all the ruckus. He wasn't exactly overjoyed about the turn of events knowing how his wife, Anthea, could be sucked into the treacherous vortex that Toddy had generated. It was bad enough that Solana was in so deep that she needed professional protection, but now, with Cisco coming to their aid, even Lainie's future was endangered along with the baby she was carrying. He wasn't exactly incensed, but he wasn't in a mood to let his wife's friend off the hook too easily either.

He found Toddy in the kitchen making another pot of coffee and pulling some cinnamon rolls out of the oven, an apron tied around his hips. *Great, a kitchen maven on top of being a freaking genius.*

"You're Toddy," he said flatly in lieu of an introduction.

Toddy could hear the disapproval in the man's voice as he straightened up with the pan of baked goods in his hands. As soon as he got a look at the man who stood in the kitchen doorway, he knew who was addressing him from the picture that Anthea had e-mailed of their wedding more than a year before. Although he had been disposed to like the guy from Anthea's descriptions, it was obvious that the feeling wasn't reciprocated, though he wondered at the hostility. It was unexpected.

"Yup, that's me," he said in an attempt to be jovial, knowing that the circumstances surrounding their meeting weren't exactly the most auspicious. He put down the baking sheet, took off the oven mitt and held out his hand to shake Mathers'. "You must be Gary."

At first, Gary was disinclined to take Toddy's proffered hand but, deciding that he was being a little judgmental, set aside his attitude and accepted his grip, which was stronger than he'd anticipated. He didn't let up his hard stare, however.

At that moment Toddy could only speculate as to how Anthea had connected with such a hard-ass. He certainly hadn't been prepared for the third degree burns he was receiving under Mathers' glower. It was just at that moment that Sol walked into the kitchen, interrupting the uncomfortable meeting, Cisco right on her heels like an overgrown puppy. She could feel the tension but decided she'd make an effort to disperse it even though she wasn't sure of its source.

"How's the coffee coming, Toddy?" she asked brightly. "We've got reinforcements to nourish."

Cisco brushed past her and didn't wait for an invitation to reach for one of the sweet buns. "Thanks," he said. "These are for the hired help, I presume." He grinned as he took a huge bite out of one. "Hmmm, not bad. I didn't know Auntie's man was a pastry chef," and he grabbed a napkin before heading back out the door to the dining area before she could deny the assumption that Toddy and she were a couple. But it put another thought into her head as she witnessed the barely concealed animosity from Gary.

Oh... jealous? Anthea had said he didn't like Toddy. Maybe it was because Toddy's had a soft spot for her all these years. The idea swept over her like a brief wave of sorrow, thinking that maybe the man she was growing so fond of might be carrying a torch for another woman, and that woman just happened to be her friend. *Can't any - thing be simple?* She let a few injudicious expressions fly through her mind without voicing them as she went to help place the rolls on a plate and tried to lighten the atmosphere.

"It's about time you two met," she cringed after the words had escaped her lips. *Stick your foot in it, why don't you. You can corner a presidential candidate and you can't even diffuse a little tension between current husband and past admirer.* She wanted to bang her head against the cabinet. Instead she opened it and, grabbing a couple of mugs, said, "Who wants coffee?"

Finally the standoff ended, Gary's features softening as he realized that Sol was trying to put a normal spin on things despite the clearly abnormal situation in which she and Toddy had found themselves. He let the resentment dissipate and turned a smile on her as he accepted a cup.

"Tell me what you know," he said as he poured some of the aromatic black brew from the carafe and then leaned back against the counter. "I think your security specialists are filling in Cisco and Seth so why don't you give me your take."

Sol poured herself a cup as Russ came in to inform them of the fact that Nolan and the two young recruits were going to do a walk around while he stayed with her, Toddy and Mathers, further dissolving the tension that had prickled in the air a few moments before.

"These two were just going to tell me what all this is about. It couldn't hurt if you had your say as well." He took a sip as Russ, a dominating figure in his own right, found himself yielding to the authority of the new arrival and nodded in compliance.

The three of them took the next half-hour to sketch out the events of the last two weeks beginning with Sol's brush with celebrity. After the tale was completed, Gary was quiet while he considered the implications and the predicament that now embroiled them all. He sighed in defeat.

"Damn, Toddy, when you muckrake, you don't do a half-assed job, do you?"

"I think I have to take some credit for this mess, too," Sol added guiltily.

"I'd agree except for the fact that you were lured to your demise by the siren song of this man," he allowed himself a half-smile. "If it weren't for the ceaseless efforts of Toddy, here, to ferret out the truth, Anthea wouldn't have dragged you into this whole thing," he said ruefully.

Tarlington finally spoke again, "We still have a protection detail to execute, no matter what caused the turn of events that have placed their lives in jeopardy."

"Right you are. And for now I think we should concentrate on that dilemma and deal with the machinations of political skullduggery on the morrow."

Sol shook her head at the poetic twist the two protectors had employed, wondering what Toddy had put in the cinnamon rolls.

The contingent of three returned from their rounds and Tarlington went to join them for a briefing by Nolan. He and Gary would take the same tour with Nolan later in the evening.

In the kitchen the conversation devolved to Toddy's blog. Gary brought up the fact that Anthea had been keeping abreast of new developments in the news that related to what Toddy had been addressing in his almost daily postings.

"She's filled me in on a few ideas over the last couple of days and suggested I raise them with you since you hadn't yet mentioned them on the website," he looked across the room at Toddy who was feeling a bit nervous under the scrutiny. "Though she assumed that you would probably already be working on the connection."

At that point he began discussing a comment that Kasili had made about how shocked he was at the speed at which fuel prices had risen in a matter of a couple of months. Anthea had also noticed the simultaneous increase in the price of gold along with the precipitous drop in the value of the dollar, deciding that it was likely related.

"Yeah, I noticed his gaffe. Even a few of the talk radio guys picked up on it," said Toddy. "What they *didn't* pick up on was the fact that in order to say what he did was to *admit prior knowledge*. He *knew* the prices were going to go up, he just hadn't expected them to skyrocket so rapidly. What else it points out is, *how did he know* that oil and gold prices were going to climb so high?" he gave them an intent look.

"There's one way that makes sense... Scirras," Toddy elaborated.

"Scirras? How? Why?" asked Gary.

Sol answered. "Scirras has been manipulating the price of gold for a while through cornering the market as much as possible and controlling new ore supply."

"*And,*" added Toddy, "he's been leading the speculation in oil futures which has been driving up the price. The question is... how did Kasili know this was going to happen, because that's essentially what he admitted." He paused briefly. "I'll tell you how. Kasili has been a puppet of Scirras for a very long time and Scirras had told him how he was going to maneuver him into the presidency quite a while ago. He was going to do it by manipulating the markets to see sky-high prices, which would strike fear into the average voter. You see, according to Scirras calculations, they would panic assuming that the current administration was to blame for the volatile rise in prices. The concept was to paint the administration's party with the same brush of evil purpose, i.e. to rake in corporate profits at the expense of Joe citizen. What Kasili unwittingly let out of the bag was the fact that if he knew prices would go up, then he was also privy to the scheme that forced them up in the first place. If that was so, then the culprits couldn't be the republicans and their so-called corporate gangster associates," he shook his head. "Unh-unh. It means Kasili was in league with whoever was pushing the prices up and who has he been in bed with? Buildingbridges.org and the Scirras gang of speculators who have the means to leverage *hundreds of billions* of dollars of commodity shares."

The other two had nothing to add to his monologue until Sol held her head sideways and finally said, "So, the mantra of 'change' is all about creating a scenario where essentials are forced out of the reach of the citizens by outrageous price leaps that have been engineered by the very people who are acting as if they are the saviors. In this way, Scirras creates a personality who epitomizes the forces of 'change' to supposedly sweep evil from the presidency that was never there to begin with. Letting fear maneuver Kasili into office by creating havoc and blaming the opposition. History repeats itself."

Toddy looked at her, "What?"

"Nero who burned Rome and blamed the Christians. Hitler who burned the Reichstag in Berlin and blamed the Jews. Scirras who manipulates fuel and gold costs to extremes and has Kasili blame the republicans," she shrugged. "Same thing."

"We all thought that Kasili was so sharp," said Gary. "Makes you wonder how he could blunder into making such a telltale statement in the first place."

"I think I can speak from experience," said Solana. "His intellect may be overrated. If I can trip him up, anyone can. What should really concern us is why Scirras would place confidence in someone like that."

Chapter 31

There are three TVs in the house and each one is tuned to a different channel, Fox, CNN, CNBC. As always, if there is some way to tap into the news cycle, Toddy was doing it and Solana could only marvel at his ability to pay attention to all of the competing voices at once. To her it was a huge distraction as she attempted to focus on one screen at a time, trying to relegate the overall cacophony to the back of her mind. It was enough to give anyone a splitting headache. But when all three channel anchors moved to the stock market, describing its current dive while gold topped a thousand dollars an ounce, her ears perked as Kasili announced another of his plans. This one was to increase the taxes on capital gains, dividends and gas.

The stories moved swiftly through the two camps of the presidential nominees and it wasn't long before Eddinger came out swinging on the foolishness of Kasili's economic scheme.

"They may be selling him as an old coot, but he's bashing Kasili for promising to up the tax burden by hmmm, twenty-two percent on capital gains," a questioning lilt in her voice, "and a pledge to increase gas taxes shows that he's not going to let the freshman congressman slide," commented Sol.

"Think about how moronic the concept is to place more taxes on an already inflated price of an essential commodity," said Toddy as he typed, forever-working on the computer. "Why not just burden average people with so many costs that they can't afford to get to work in order to pay the taxes that this guy thinks will provide relief to the very same folks who are being squeezed by those high prices. Circular thinking.

"Oh no, wait… he wants to tax the *rich* who provide the jobs that will become non-existent because they can't afford to keep their doors open due to the costs of goods, fuel and services, so the workers lose their jobs on top of not being able to pay for household needs. Still circular thinking."

"… Which only proves how this guy is not thinking at all, or simply doesn't understand how the market works," added Sol.

"Well, how could he? Kasili's a Marxist to the core and their idea of economics 101 is to tax the productive to pay for the unproductive." Toddy's fingers punched the keys with more pressure than usual, indicating his seething at what he considered stupidity. "As if the State ever produced anything. All it can do is usurp the acquisitions of workers to redistribute to those who don't. It creates programs to support the earnestly lazy, which, if you think about it could be anyone in office. What do they produce? Laws that restrict others from producing the ultimate funds that pays their salaries?" He continued his little diatribe, "We need to get back to where average citizens went to the Capitol for a couple of years to serve with the wisdom they'd gathered by working for a living and then return home and their productive lives. The fact that being in office has become a career, is a statement unto itself as to the demise of our country."

Not that Sol didn't disagree, but her attention was drawn back to the television where they were airing a clip from Eddinger's recent response to Kasili's tax plan.

"It's one thing to provide services for the people, but to tax them into oblivion in order to fund expansive programs is not beneficial to the productive health of our economy," said Eddinger as he stood tall at a podium, his white hair stark against the backdrop of an American flag as he spoke at a VFW convention.

She sat back in a chair and turned the volume down on the TV in that room.

"You can't elect a candidate with guilt, which is precisely what they're trying to do. Everyone should feel guilty if they vote against a black man. They should feel guilty for earning a good living. They should feel guilty for destroying the earth (which we're not doing). They should feel guilty for having a work ethic that has made the gross national product in this country higher than most every other on the planet." She sighed. "That's right," Sol spoke to the air rather than Toddy who was sitting a few feet away. "We work too efficiently, so we should support others who do not rather than instill the competitive spirit that will make them better producers and give them a higher standard of living? It's demoralizing."

Toddy added, "Charity should be from the heart, not compelled and not overseen by bureaucracy which produces nothing, wastes resources, energy and the human spirit."

"Spirit is what infuses life. Partaking of the gifts of the earth and giving thanks to keep the gifts from disappearing. It's not about despoiling, it's about wise usage. Even my ancestors understood that.

"And what about trying to make everyone dependent on government? They've been doing that with Natives for years. Take by taxation, or other means, then dole out everything according to a State plan. It strips the individual of their will to produce. It's been happening on the reservations forever. Sovereign, but not sovereign... the reality is so twisted, it's a wonder any of my people feel they have power over their own lives. The frustration gives me a headache." Toddy set his laptop aside and standing behind Sol, began to massage her neck, an action that was as reassuring as it was startling. Yet, even as he manipulated the muscles to relax, he was acutely attuned to the lowered voices being emitted by the television, sounds from the ones in the other rooms easily heard in the background.

It wasn't much later when Senator Eddinger was quoted with a statement condemning the European Union for raising interest rates in an effort to undercut the dollar even more. He pointed to hedge funds wagering against the dollar in favor of the euro and gold, which had risen to an all-time high.

"And guess who's behind that little maneuver?" Toddy had returned to his work and Sol, not knowing what else could be done, had begun compiling some thoughts for an op-ed piece. "It's not as if Scirras hasn't instigated something like this before," he stopped to listen for a beat. "Do we never learn?"

With that, Toddy continued on his tack of demonstrating a possible connection between Scirras using leverage tactics to increase speculation in order to force up energy prices, thereby creating a scenario that people might swallow – a belief that his protégé Kasili would be able to control costs by regulating the speculation. Speculation that he placed in motion to promote the problem in the first place.

The lines he had drawn were traceable but came up in a strange warp and weft. Scirras was funding buildingbridges,org and other 527s which were freely funding Kasili's campaign. The 527s were receiving their funds from Free State Foundation and political action committees. The Free State Foundation received funding from the Herculaenea Fund and what had become Scirras holdings, which were strongly involved in the energy and gold speculation growth. The PACs were receiving funding from the union pension funds, which were also heavily invested in oil and gold futures and were based off-shore with mostly offshore investors holding the paper. It came down to this, a lot of the money that eventually made its way to back American candidates originated from foreign interests that were work-ing toward the devaluation of the dollar through those same hedge funds that were speculating against it. And the ones really raking in the dough were the union bosses, offshore investors and Scirras.

In Toddy's estimation, it all added up to a twisted road that pressured the American people to think that by voting for a Scirras sponsored candidate – Kasili – they'd be instituting change, when in fact, they would be lessening their influence on their own government. Scirras and Kasili's purpose was to increase government control and 'beneficence' creating a subservient and dependent populace.

When he'd finished writing the blog, he went looking for Nolan to let him know that he needed to get to the college to upload his posting for the day. Sol had told him that the local college was actually about forty-five miles away but he didn't want to chance accessing the website from his host's home.

The idea met with a great deal of resistance from his security crew but since it was Sol who was the one of the pair that was identi-fiable in the area, Nolan finally relented. They decided that Russ would meet with them and collect Toddy after Gary took him to the college, since he had access as adjunct faculty and was needed back in town for a couple of days. Sol would have to stay on the hill, a plan that didn't make her particularly ecstatic. First, for being left in the sticks and secondly, after witnessing the tension between the two men the night before she thought they could use a buffering agent. After the arguments were raised and qualms were assuaged, she just raised her hands in defeat and walked away deciding that Gary and Toddy could work out their differences on their own.

"Let's go." Although Gary was still unhappy about the circumstances surrounding the arrival of his wife's friend, he'd decided to suck it up and help however he could to make sure Anthea and the other innocents didn't get caught in any crossfire.

Gold Baron

Chapter 32

Leaving the unofficial posse behind, Gary and Toddy took off down the mountain in Anthea's Expedition, his Chevy pick-up not being conducive to hauling three tall men up to the Greyfishers' the night before.

The drive was only occasionally broken with stilted conversation at first, Toddy feeling the underlying antipathy from his traveling companion. He still wasn't sure what the cause was behind Gary's attitude but he was determined to ignore it as long as possible by gazing out the window at the river running high beside the road, the spring runoff having reached its zenith.

Finally, Gary just asked him outright, "Are you that obtuse as to not have realized what the consequences would be of creating this blog of yours?"

Toddy was a little confused at the question and the flat tone of voice in which it was delivered. "The possibilities crossed my mind, if that's what you want to know, but I never thought anyone would truly come under fire."

"And why not?" He speared Toddy with an accusing glare before returning his attention to the road. "You've not only dragged Sol into this bedlam but Anthea and now even Cisco's pregnant wife are at risk."

Oh, now I get it. "Because I'm damn good at what I do. I *wrote* the proprietary software that the government uses to catch would-be hackers and I can deter the most prodigious bugs," he bristled with the impugning of his ability and, in his mind, character since he related the two.

Gary just kept looking at the road as he said, "they got past your defenses anyway."

"Actually, they didn't. What they *did* do was identify Sol and assume that she was connected to the blog. It was an effing lucky guess." Under his breath he added, "Not that it matters. Blog or not, they want to take her out. I think more to appease Kasili's fragile but monstrous ego than anything else.

"The fact is," he raised the level of his voice a bit, "that they came so close to cracking my proxy trail indicates a government connection."

"What, you don't think anyone else out there could be as smart as you?" said Gary snidely, surprising himself at his unnatural reaction.

Toddy sighed. "No. It's the fact that the government snatches up anyone with a particular gift in that regard faster than a frog can catch a fly. How do you think I ended up working with them, however briefly?"

Gary didn't have an answer and just stewed for a while as he continued around a bend and onto a straight stretch of road just before crossing a bridge over the roiling water. He let his frustration out in a breath. "Fine. We've succeeded in trimming the possibilities down to government related operatives that are hunting down Sol. All in hopes that she will lead them to the webmaster, i.e. you, their nemesis."

"That's my guess. What's odd is that Kasili and, in association, Scirras are the two who would most benefit by the disruption of a blog that hones in on the truth, and I'm not so sure how they are related to the government."

Gary considered the question. "We might be dealing with a rogue agency. Money can buy loyalty and the people you're talking about have an enormous amount to toss into someone's retirement fund."

Toddy didn't have an answer for that and continued along in silence until Gary drove into the parking lot at the student union building.

❈ ❈ ❈

It didn't take long for Toddy to make the new posting on the site. In the meantime, Gary just waited outside in the shade by a fountain that was in the middle of campus, letting the irritation flow out of his system. As much as he worried about the safety of his wife, her friends and the young couple that occupied the apartment next to his home, he knew that his anger was irrational and needed to be set aside.

He was trained to deal with nasty situations and although he'd retired some years ago, his instincts were still solid. He'd do what he could to assist the security delegation that was now formed of professionals and family, all strong and committed individuals. What he prayed for most was that Toddy would find a way to defuse the state of affairs so the danger would lapse and everyone would be able to go home. In his heart, he knew that wasn't likely to happen anytime soon. Toddy had prodded a sleeping tiger.

Before Toddy's re-emergence from the building, Gary looked at his watch and, realizing they a good hour and a half before they needed to catch up with Tarlington, he called Anthea and suggested they meet in town.

When he told Toddy what they were doing, Toddy jumped at the opportunity to see his friend since it had been such a long time. It also presented a respite from the stark disapproval he felt from Gary, not that he really wanted to drop Anthea into the middle of it all. On second thought, he acknowledged that she'd probably soften his attitude just by her presence.

Everything was within a few miles' proximity in the town of approximately 30,000 souls and it didn't take long to reach a local coffee house which neither Gary nor Anthea frequented. Toddy's own town of Ruidoso was small, but the population was spread all through the mountains adding travel time between destinations, here the population was far more condensed.

The two men walked in and as they ordered, Anthea was dropped off by a friend and entered the establishment greeting first Toddy and then her husband. Gary stayed to pick up the drinks while Toddy and Anthea found a table against the back wall.

The whole outing was a treat for Toddy who'd been under pressure of being on the run for more than a week. He was a little guilt-ridden knowing that Sol was stuck up on the hill while he had the freedom to travel, but knew that it was for her own protection. He was also beginning to feel culpable after Gary's lambasting because, despite the danger she was in, he still felt compelled to continue the online assault.

For the moment, he decided to put on a more cheerful face for Anthea as she sat down opposite him. Gary joined them, setting the cups down on the polished wood surface.

It had been well over two years since they'd seen each other so there was a fair bit of ordinary chitchat that needed addressing. When Toddy and Anthea spoke on the phone the conversation almost always revolved around the greater doings in the outside world rather than their personal lives. It was funny that, although they were friends, they rarely shared the inner workings of their hearts. Toddy had had no clue that Anthea was on the verge of marrying until after the fact. He found it odd how close they could seem to be and yet share so little of their innermost thoughts and feelings.

It didn't take long before they had brushed past the mundane and moved on to the events that had landed Sol and Toddy in such hot water. As they were in public, details were glossed over but Anthea reveled in Sol's accomplishment in stumping a presidential candidate with little more than a few words.

"Frankly, I was shocked at how easily she managed to make him look ignorant," she said.

"The sad thing is that it wasn't hard, according to her, because he is."

"And this is the best that party has to offer? We're in for a hard time if people don't start paying attention, but then isn't that what we're doing? Trying to get their attention?" she asked rhetorically.

"What's most worrisome is the fact that they zeroed in on her and have been tracking her movements with the intent to... well, you understand what I'm saying."

Gary gave him a hard look that diminished as he saw the remorse that was carving new lines across Toddy's forehead. "It's likely that they've had her under surveillance since she showed up in Montana," he said with concern. "At least she didn't use her cell phone or credit cards while she was up at my place, so they may still not know of our connection. Not that that makes me feel any better, the fact that she's definitely the target."

"You can bet they've seen you, though, and they're moving heaven and earth to find out who you are," said Gary somberly. "These forays into town are going to have to be few and far between for now until we can devise a plan to get them off of her back."

They finished their coffee and packed up to take Toddy to the predetermined rendezvous point knowing that Anthea and Toddy wouldn't be seeing much of each other this journey, making the reunion bittersweet.

Once Toddy returned from town he went to find Sol to tell her that they were back on track and that he'd had a chance to see Anthea.

"Sorry I missed the get-together," she said with a tinge of disappointment in her voice. "Did you and Gary work out your tiff?"

His eyes widened in surprise. "I didn't know we had one."

She gave him a shrewd look that made him wince a little. "Uh, yeah, we got things straightened out," he admitted.

She stood waiting for an explanation. "And?"

"And nothing. It was just a little misunderstanding." He brushed his hands together as if to sweep away dust. "All gone," he smiled, engaging what he thought was an endearing guise.

She laughed at the comic face, and let it go realizing that she wasn't going to wheedle anything more out of him.

"I was just going to go for a walk now that it's cooled off some, why don't you come along," she nodded her head toward the door.

"What about the ever-present guards. Will they let you out of their sight long enough to take a stroll around the property?"

"What about them? It's my home and I know every nook and cranny. I need to get out for a while." As she started out the door, she gave him a direct look. "Coming?"

For some reason her gaze made him swallow involuntarily. "Absolutely, I could use some outside time."

They followed a path that skirted the precipice, a wall of rock tumbling away beneath their feet toward the rushing water. After about fifteen minutes they stopped at an overlook where a large boulder formed a perfect bench wide enough for both of them to sit comfortably. Well, it was comfortable for Sol. Toddy, being slightly acrophobic, was doing his best to keep a healthy distance between himself and the edge so when he sat down, he scooted as far back in the depression carved out of stone as he could manage.

"You live in the mountains," said Sol. "I'm surprised that this makes you uneasy."

"I don't generally make a habit of walking along the lip of a cliff. I have just enough respect for myself to avoid unnecessary peril.

Sure-footed as a mountain goat, I am not."

He spotted a hawk floating on the updraft. "See him? That's how I imagine myself if I approach the edge too closely. Heights like this make me imagine that I could step off the edge and fly. It seems more prudent to step back instead since Superman and I have virtually nothing in common."

"That's all in how you look at it," she laughed.

He studied her sideways, wondering what she meant by that remark. She likes him? But in what way, he wondered. He tried to defuzz his brain and concentrate on the view and the simplicity of Sol's company. The last thing he needed was to start reading things into off the cuff comments.

They sat there contentedly for some time watching a couple of boats that were anchored midstream with fishermen kicked back, lines working the depths three hundred feet down from their cozy perch. The sun had left the little cove in shadow, giving them relief from the heat that had climbed into the mid-nineties during the afternoon.

After a bit they stood up and continued down the trail, Sol regaling Toddy on the stories of some of her mostly well-spent youth wandering the hills framing the steep valley that stretched below.

This farm was a contrast to her mother's family ranch in Montana where she lived during most of her teenage years. Here, though, the Clearwater Valley was where her parents lived when she was a child. Her dad had been a logger and a firefighter, one of the elite smokejumpers who would battle the backcountry blazes throughout Idaho and Montana. That was one of the reasons they split living between the two states.

"You couldn't ask for much more as a kid, not that I understood that then," she said wistfully. "I can certainly appreciate it now, especially when I see what our current crop of young people have to deal with. Drugs, alcohol, outside cultural pressure. Some of it wasn't as evident to my parents' generation because they didn't travel outside the rez as much."

"I thought these kinds of problems have been plaguing the reservations for years."

"In a way, they have. And I may be wrong but it seems like the hurdles have gotten to be greater as popular culture has made deeper inroads into our traditional life," she explained. "I grew up during the beginnings of a cultural crisis. The old ways were being lost and television and radio were accepted vehicles of delivering the 'new' culture, the American mainstream. Trouble was, and still is in some places, the mainstream doesn't account for social differences. Acceptance is still difficult here and there, but I believe that it's improved hugely even in the last twenty years."

"Okay, I understand the problems of melding cultures and I would probably agree that it can be more of a challenge in rural areas than in metropolitan places. Unfortunately, just about every area has got a problem of trying to bring the old and the new together," Toddy started on a tangent. "The old could be the Native Americans or it could be the established Hispanic population in a city like Los Angeles where they preceded the white influx. And then you have the *new* immigrant Mexican population that shuns the old one along with the Caucasian, African-American and Asian groups that have lived there for generations. Inequity comes in many forms and, it seems to me that could we inspire everyone, no matter what their background, to aspire to create and produce for themselves, the rest would work itself out."

"Talk about idealism," Sol grinned. "Not that you're far off. When I worked in the city, I stood out less and judging me and everyone else usually had more to do with how much you made rather than what you looked like. Face it Toddy, there are double standards everywhere. All we can do is try to expose them in order to expunge them."

"Well said, but I want to get back to your formative years. You talked about the cultural barriers yet you told me before that you were a rodeo princess. Isn't that kind of an oxymoron, like participating in the antithesis of Indian culture?" he was perplexed. "You talked about seasonal rounds and gathering the gifts of the earth according to season. In a way, doesn't rodeo represent ranching and property ownership which is counter to the old ways?"

"Hmmm, I suppose you could look at it that way, but remember I grew up in both worlds. My grandfather was a white rancher in Southern Montana who married a member of the Crow tribe. His life was built around cattle and working horses. Not so different from the Nez Perce whose horses carried them from place to place throughout the year. Still working horses, just a different job description," she smiled and he chuckled.

"Okay," he sobered a bit. "How does the development of natural resources fall into the traditional mold, like the Kanab Paiute mining gold to sustain themselves?"

"Don't you think that you pretty much answered that question?" she asked. "It's about survival and most tribes work hard to make sure that their needs are met without defiling the earth, but they are pragmatic, which is something that the environmental lobbies are not," a cloud of indignation crossed her features. "Indians have been managing resources for thousands of years and the attitude of modern day environmentalists is nothing short of simple impudence.

"According to their standards, Natives do just fine when our plan is acceptable to the environmental lobbies, but deviate one iota from their agenda and they turn on the Indians as quickly as they will anyone else.

"Take the struggle to maintain salmon runs and actually reintroduce them to waterways where they've disappeared. You have out-of-place sea lions sitting on the fish ladders in the lower Columbia River, catching and gorging on the salmon as they climb the ladders to reach the smaller streams to spawn. The environmentalists scream bloody murder when it's proposed that they should be removed in order to give the fish a chance. Which is more natural, that the salmon make it home to spawn or that the huge sea lions, that aren't even usual denizens of the Columbia a hundred or more miles upstream, are provided a free lunch?" She had stopped to watch the activity on the river. "Personally, I vote for the fish and chase the sea lions off to where they can feed themselves as the earth intended."

"What about the argument that the dams should be removed to restore the salmon runs," said Toddy, playing devil's advocate.

"The world is changed. Removing the dams would only create extreme hardship for millions and economic collapse. You can't ignore the truth of that." She appeared tired as she allowed the corruptness of some factions to permeate her thoughts. "There is no going back to the ways of our fathers.

"As soon as the environmentalists decide that Natives are at cross-purposes to their hallowed view of the world, we are vilified as much as any big corporation. They fight us when we try to exercise our treaty rights, whether its selling our water rights to farmers, or simply hunting, fishing and gathering on traditional lands. They'll battle us when we want to build casinos or resorts and as you've seen, they'll condemn the construction of needed power plants that provide *them* with the very electricity they need to fight *us* via e-mail and the media.

"Their agenda is the same for everyone: no one should be allowed a better life if it means encroaching on anything they decide needs their protection. Trouble is, they're not protecting it for the sake of the animal or plant's ability to reproduce unimpeded but as a tool to block others' access to the earth's gifts.

Her features hardened a little as she described the battle lines.

"It's about control. And they hide behind the buckskin of the Native American, and other indigenous peoples, to promote their agenda. We're used for our ancient wisdom, but they eschew that same wisdom of the elders by assuming that their superior knowledge overrules that ancient understanding of earth's harmony. Under the guise of environmentalism, all humanity is facing the arrogance of one small group who are attempting to make us believe that *we* can change the overall course of this planet; that *we* have the power to destroy it," she sighed in frustration.

"If nothing else, Coyote taught us the folly of thinking that *we* are smarter than mother earth. These people are dangerous to everyone's spirit of freedom, not just Natives. The difference is that Natives the world over have already experienced the arrogance of usurpers. We, of all people, should know better and be working the hardest to protect freedom."

They continued down the trail in silence. It was Sol's historical perception that opened his vision a little more. Even though he'd known repetition of history was in play, which she pointed out the night before in another context, he hadn't seen how minorities and indigenous people around the world should be the ones leading the pack to protect freedom. She clarified how all humanity is now in danger of encountering the same disaster that has been suffered by Native people throughout time. Although he had long agreed with her stated views, he hadn't heard it from a personal perspective. He'd tell anyone that he's a theory and practice guy. He understands serfdom, the true white slavery and how a privileged few were reintroducing feudalism to the world at large. The fact that this was deeply personal for Sol made him even angrier at the blatant use of racism by liberals in order to 'guilt' people into voting for their shill… a man who sold his skin color to the highest bidder.

They quietly contemplated the landscape, its beauty and how a relative few arrogant, self-ordained elitists were working to withhold the bounty of the earth from its rightful heirs: all of humanity.

Having received a memo from his assistant, the market mogul logged onto his PC, which had been vetted with better than state of the art security precautions and anti-viral protection. He pulled up the website that was listed in the note and was amazed at the accuracy of the information that the author had managed to uncover. Whoever was investigating the lines of funding, convoluted as they were between his holdings and some of the more subversive political activism, was doing an excellent job of closing in on the truth.

He smiled however, when he thought of how impossible it was to prove, despite all the precision of the inferences made in the blog. *Even if any evidence were uncovered, the vastness of the plan would make it virtually incredible to the point that no one would believe any - one capable of such intrigue. It's inconceivable that anyone would destroy the faith that fools had placed in him as a market guru. No one would ever think Warren Buffett could be deceitful, and neither would they doubt the guru's equally upright reputation.*

Smugness might be an unflattering trait to some, but it didn't prevent him from briefly indulging in it. He knew well that the perpetrator's identity would be discovered soon, and the verbal rampage would be curbed. Then the website would disappear and simply be forgotten, Americans have such short memories.

His mind drifted toward whether or not this person had yet connected the environmental lobbyists with the diminishing supply of energy resources and metal commodities that influence the world currency markets. He couldn't see how they would have found a link between the Foundation presences in certain countries to any of those machinations, their offices numbering beyond fifty in the far-flung hell-holes of the world.

Why would anyone expend effort looking into backwaters like Uzbekistan, Namibia, Ethiopia and Romania?

And even if they had? Who would believe it? No matter. They'll be out of the picture before any of it ever reaches the internet.

Gold Baron

Chapter 33

They were almost a quarter mile from the house when Cisco found them.

He had a rifle slung over his shoulder and a two-way radio clipped to his belt, which he picked up and, flicking the button, said simply, "Found 'em."

As he readjusted the radio on his belt, Toddy said, "Isn't that a breach of security? Anyone can pick up the bandwidth."

"No. Those guys you hired are on top of things and it's a secure channel." He answered without preamble and was stern in his approach, which seemed odd coming from a young man in his early twenties. The fact of his youth didn't stop him from scolding his two elders as he reached them.

"You two know that you're not supposed to wander off without protection," he said, a determined cast to his features.

"No problem," she answered blandly, not to be cowed by her bullish nephew. "I have protection," and she turned sideways, lifting the tail of her shirt to indicate the gun tucked into her waistband at the small of her back.

Toddy smiled at the thought that this woman had been looking out for him rather than the other way around.

Cisco's attitude dropped a little to more resemble contrition, but didn't change his stoic expression, which his auntie outdid in response. Dropping the visual standoff, he thumbed the radio and called in that they were on their way.

As they got close to the barn, Tarlington advanced on them, getting a little testy in his confrontation. "What am I supposed to do if something breaks and I don't know exactly where you two are at any given moment," he delivered it in an undertone and not as a question.

Sol had apparently had enough from Cisco and shrugged off Russ' recriminations, continuing on her way back to the lodge. At the moment she was thinking that it was his problem. She'd decided three could play the grumpy game.

Out of character, Russ just threw his hands up in the air, letting his irritation show, "What did you hire us for if you don't plan on cooperating," he grumbled.

Toddy just lifted an eyebrow and fell into step next to Sol, Cisco on her other side and Tarlington following with an eye on the growing shadow of the mountain behind them.

Sol said without looking at her nephew, "Is that what you wanted?"

He let his composure slip a little, "No, we couldn't locate you and Lainie got upset. She's here to see you."

"What? It could be dangerous up here. What's the matter with her?"

"Besides being pregnant and hormonal? Not much," said Cisco with a straight face. "She got ticked when she found out you were back and didn't come to see her."

Sol shook her head. "You explained the situation to her, right?" He glared at her as an answer. "She should know it's only for her protection. We can't endanger her or the baby."

"Since when could anyone tell her what to do? I can't. I wouldn't even try."

Toddy and Sol both looked up at this 6'5" mug who wouldn't cross his pregnant wife, doing their best to control their smiles.

"Come on, you can mellow her out," he told his auntie. "She won't listen to me."

"Yeah," she said resignedly, "we know who's more dangerous here. Not the death threats but little Lainie."

They came up to the lodge and saw Lainie standing outside on the front porch, hands on hips, stomach distended with almost seven months pregnancy. Face blank of expression.

The slightest wisp taller than Sol, she was anything but petite in stature.

" 'Little' Lainie?" said Toddy.

"Compared to Cisco, she's demure."

"Hell, I wouldn't cross her either," he added, assessing the strength emanating from the mother-to-be's authority.

"Keep that in mind for now," said Sol quietly, out of the side of her mouth.

Cisco walked ahead of the other two and greeted his wife who presented her cheek to allow a quick peck. Standing side by side, they resembled two Indian sentinels at the gates.

Not to be intimidated by her niece, Sol asked bluntly, "What are you doing here?"

There was to be no backing down from this foot soldier. "You're back after weeks and don't come see me," she accused with an almost imperceptible crumb of hurt in her voice.

"Of course not," countered Sol. "They've made attempts on my life. Why would I lead assassins anywhere near my favorite niece?"

"Your *only* niece," she corrected. Then, slightly placated, she said, "Well, I can get away with coming up here. It's only natural to visit my grandparents."

Sol nodded her head in temporary agreement and hugged Lainie. "Until someone figures out that they're not home. You should-n't come up here again." Sol embraced her niece and rubbed her belly, then led her over to sit down in two of the chairs on the deck, allow-ing them to talk while they looked out over the river valley.

"We'll think of something for next time," said Lainie, not to be contradicted as she settled into the cushions.

Toddy and Cisco just looked at each other bemused and walked inside.

❋ ❋ ❋

Toddy wandered into the kitchen, where he found Nolan seat-ed at a laptop computer reading information forwarded by Blade on the private investigation firm in Los Angeles that was connected to the Las Vegas debacle.

Looking over his shoulder to see if he could make out what was on the monitor, Toddy walked past to start checking the pantry for meal preparation.

"I'm going to start dinner. What've you got there? Or can't you divulge the secrets of protection magic," he said blithely as he began rummaging through the cupboards.

"Not much. That investigation company in L.A. that was tied to that tail car seems to be a dead end. Looks like a front for things like car rentals, credit cards and travel, but no individual names of employees or clients which gives us any motive," said Nolan, disregarding Toddy's attempt at humor.

"No connection to any of Kasili's known associates or backers, huh?"

"Not that we can tell. Of course that doesn't mean the ties aren't there, it's just that someone did their homework in setting up this operation without strings. No evidentiary trails." Nolan rubbed the heels of his hands into his tired eyes.

Cisco, who had followed Toddy into the kitchen, was a little confused at the conversation. Nolan cocked his head at Cisco while catching Toddy's eyes, as if asking for permission to talk in front of him.

Toddy nodded his consent. Cisco was family and his wife was at risk now. "He should know what we're dealing with here since he's heading up the Nez Perce arm of our protection," he said.

Nolan acquiesced to Toddy's suggestion and went into describing what little information he had on the men who seemed to be hunting Solana, which amounted to about a thimbleful of nothing. "At this point we have no other indication that the pursuers know anything about who you are or even why they've been put on a detail to follow Sol.

"All we have is a car registration traced back to this P.I. company in L.A. It looks like they do a lot of contract work for corporations, celebrities and political groups. Mostly investigative, but they might be strong-arm types. They may even specialize in providing independent muscle or work the blackmail angle or be a shell company. Whatever it is they do and who they do it for, they hide their trail very well. We can't even locate a list of employees, just the owner which is an offshore corporation."

"Yeah? Where?" asked Toddy.

Nolan consulted the computer documents he had printed out and were laying in front of him. "Let's see... Aruba and Turks and Caicos."

Toddy's eyes widened with illumination, making Nolan curious as to what he was thinking.

"You've got an idea?"

"Scirras."

Nolan frowned. "Why do you say that?"

"Herculaenea Fund is out of Aruba and Scirras has another headquarters for his personal holdings in Turks and Caicos. I think buildingbridges.org receives funds from that operation."

By now Cisco was really mystified. All Nolan could say was, "Cute."

Toddy went back to poking through the contents of the fridge. His voice muffled by the fact that his head was buried in the icebox, "You should have someone check to see if there could be some secret service ties to this PI office."

Now Toddy had captured Nolan's attention. As he emerged from the interior of the refrigerator, turning around with a couple of onions, some mushrooms, asparagus and a butcher paper wrapped package in his hands, he said, "I think the tie might be to Kasili protection and who better to undertake knocking out a potential threat than the Secret Service?" He offered a chilling grin.

Nolan just stared him down, pissed off at Toddy's presumption. "I know those guys. I worked with far too many of them while I was with the NSA," he shook his head, negating Toddy's postulation. "No way any one of them would be involved."

"You'd bet your life on that?" He said with a serenity he didn't feel.

Nolan kept quiet, steaming at the implication. Then, simmering, fingers flexing as he miserably but realistically looked at Toddy's assessment, he rasped out, "No."

Arms full of dinner makings, Toddy walked to the counter and set the food down. "Look at it this way, uncomfortable as it is, who better to sidestep privacy issues? Who could get their hands on confidential information, hack into private internet sites and follow cell phone triangulation bypassing a warrant? Who can get information in the name of security for a presidential candidate? Remember, Kasili had Secret Service protection from the outset. Why?"

Nolan looked vanquished by the logic of Toddy's argument and sat back in his chair. Cisco, who had been absorbing everything, was stymied at the implication.

Finally, Nolan conceded and shook his head in dismay. "You may be right, damn it all." He looked across at Cisco. "Keep this to yourself. I have a hell of a lot more checking to do. It may take a while before, or even if, we can confirm anything." He stood up and ran his fingers through his gray hair, "I didn't think this could get any uglier." He walked toward the front of the house to find Tarlington who was keeping an eye on Solana and Lainie.

While the ladies were deep in their téte-a-téte, Nolan approached Russ and they had a head-to-head of their own.

Chapter 34

High above Elliot Bay, the man watched a supertanker as it crawled through the water, resembling a giant sea turtle with pesky little minnows flitting in all directions around its durable shell, keeping a healthy distance but unworried of the behemoth's ability to block their path because of its plodding progress. He was as unconcerned about the ship's location as were the small craft that went about their business, avoiding its hull as they dexterously maneuvered through the sea on their own missions. He even allowed himself a fleeting smile as he thought of the outrageous fortune that was floating in the monster's holds, a fortune that he had helped increase in value to levels that even he hadn't expected to see for months yet. His smile dissipated as he thought about how someone had gotten greedy and overplayed their hand, jeopardizing the program. He turned away slightly disgusted at how he could obviously trust no one but himself.

He went back to his desk, resettling himself behind his computer when his assistant called to alert him to a new posting on the infamous blog that had been receiving so much notice. He had not been pleased to learn that other alternative internet sites and radio talkers had been accessing changingwind.org and using it as a directional resource for research on schematics that had been well buried until now. Although there were articles posted, the website had been developing into a reference center that was steering the general public too close for comfort. Not that anything was provable, a point that was in his favor.

When he went online this time, he was stunned to read the new financial connections that the author had revealed. The money trail in the new posting went backward from buildingbridges.org to the Free State Foundation to the Herculaenea Fund, and from there he or she drew correlations to terrorist and socialist or religionist nations. Not good.

The connection of funding from nations with an anti-capitalist agenda would hurt the candidate that was buildingbridges.org's presidential pick in this election. There was already enough gossip roaming the web about Kasili's family ties to Ethiopian Muslims and his own stupid slip when he commented on his Muslim faith and the interviewer actually corrected him with "your Christian faith."

More controversy was not needed and yet this blog appeared and started going through the full list of the non-American investors in the Herculaenea Fund, other than the founder, and the fact that they were European and Arab nationals, none of whom had an interest in preserving Americana. He couldn't fault the blogger who also did a splendid job of tying the investors to terrorist groups in Sudan, Syria and Pakistan as well as Saudi Arabia. On top of that, the blogger followed the funding for supposed education and environmental programs being funneled through the FSFoundation to former Eastern Bloc countries like Hungary, Romania, Moldova, Slovakia; the Balkans including Bosnia, Kosovo; and rim countries with large Muslim populations such as Chechnya, Albania and Bulgaria as well as a number of the Asian 'stans' such as Uzbekistan and Kyrghyztan.

He knew as he read the list that the blogger had only touched on the lengthy directory of Foundation influence. It was apparent that he was most interested in drawing the line between the American presidential campaign and Muslim terrorism by means of tracking the movement of money.

The website blog clearly defined how countries where the Foundation had a presence had most all been in a constant state of flux and unrest for years, some for decades, the strife being spurred by the alleged sale of arms through his own machinations either directly or indirectly. The blogger was making a point of an ulterior design to usher in socialist reconstructions under the guise of 'democratic reform.' All of them were governments with corrupt leadership that could be manipulated by, what else but, money.

As he read on he found that the blogger then brought up, yet again, the connection of Kasili to the Ethiopian Muslim community where Kasili's father, and later his half-brother, were involved in Muslim separatist politics. The blog even made note that one of Kasili's family members was on the international FSFoundation board.

That wasn't all. The author even managed to correlate the

upheaval in Zimbabwe, where Mugabe refused to give up his 'throne,' to the likely exportation of destabilization across the border into South Africa, contending that influencing gold and mineral production was the probable intent.

He had to admire the spunk and organization of the blogger and the fact that he managed to come so close to the truth.

Not being a man who was prone to anger or emotional outbursts of any kind, he sat back in his chair and contemplated the consequences of this having already been posted on the internet. The number of hits on the website were growing daily, enough to cause him some alarm, even though he realized that the absurdity of the charges would deter most people from accepting it as factual. It had served well that the average person could not imagine the existence of a maleficent intention behind a scheme so daring, and even now, they would reject the hypothesis because of that.

However, that did not mean that something mustn't be done to quell the reaction that was due to arise if the blog continued. Already, other websites had begun digging on their own in an attempt to prove and disprove the assertions. A groundswell could occur and someone may be talented enough to locate evidence, though he doubted that possibility. He had laid the groundwork well and properly.

After a few moments he called his assistant.

When the assistant answered, he inquired as to the progress of locating the origin of the website.

He was highly disappointed to be informed that there had been no breakthroughs. The trace jumped from ISP to ISP, crisscrossing the nation making it impossible to pin down.

Curtly, he told his managing assistant to inform him directly the moment anything developed. He also gave the assistant directions to rein in the candidate's foolish activities. The leak of a newly designed White House seal was an utter disaster and spoke to poor judgment.

The assistant paused before hanging up to tell his superior that they were having an increasingly difficult time controlling the candidate's actions and responses. The general consensus within the operation was that they were dealing with a runaway train.

If nothing else, the man behind the desk said, ensure that he chooses a vice presidential nominee from the short list he'd been provided. No argument will be brooked. He cut off the connection unceremoniously.

Ethiopia – 1975

The little boy has sprouted tall as he reached his eleventh year. Staying with his father for a summer between school years, he stands at his sire's shoulder now while he was sitting in a village coffeehouse, staring across the tiny table at a man the boy has only met once before. Between the two men, one tall and sinewy, the other almost squat but trim, are two small cups of thick, sweet and aromatic Arabic coffee.

The arms dealer is there to make the last of his deliveries to the socialist insurgents who are attempting to shore up their power base after the assassination of Emperor Haile Selassie earlier in the month.

He sips the strong, sugary brew as he studies both the man and the boy, considering his plan and whether these two are the right choices to implement it. He knows the father's tremendous ability to focus and coordinate others to achieve his goals. He is a man of charm, intelligence and action who has proven his worth over the years. The boy, however, is young still and although he has spent much time during these formative years with his father, the mother is a weak woman of indiscretion and indecisiveness. Stock that is not promising.

He takes another drink from the diminutive cup, weighing his options. The time must be now. He is not getting any younger and this boy meets the criteria he has devised.

The arms dealer sets the demitasse down and looks deep into the man's eyes trying to fathom his soul.

He decides.

He maps out a years' long plan for the man who sits with such strength and dignity opposite him. He will finance his son's education at all the best American schools, including exclusive American col - leges and groom him for a career in American politics, with a future of powerful stakes. He has been a strong and stable supporter of the man's cause to change the course of Ethiopian history. It is time to pledge to participate in the cause to influence change around the world and his son will be the harbinger of that cause.

He sits back, cradling the dainty cup in his thick fingers, the hands of a man who, under other circumstances, would have been the worker rather than the executive.

The man mulls over the proposition, his son still standing by, attention wandering to watch two oxen being herded with a long staff in the stockman's hand. He lifts the cup for the first time to drink some of the now cooling liquid and carefully constructs the agreement in his mind before voicing the words.

He looks out the door at the dusty plain as he speaks of mak - ing the commitment to direct the boy's mother in the details of the plan for her son's future. They discuss the candidates among whom the boy's surrogate father should be chosen. The arms dealer has already done his background investigation on the men in the mother's life and one contender stands out above the others. There is no debate as to the selection of the man who should guide his son in his American upbringing – he fits the bill perfectly as a privately leaning, revolu - tionary socialist holding a career position within the diplomatic corps of the United States.

Their business completed and the coffee drained, they arise from the table, the boy stepping back to give his father room. The boy is a little dazed from what he could glean of the conversation when his attention would drift back toward the dialog. There was talk of a new father and great American colleges, the first of which frightens him a little and the second holds no interest for him. Right now, he is look - ing forward to going home with his father and regaining the freedom that will be his for what little remains of his holiday.

The arms dealer climbs into the waiting Land Rover, and takes a last long look at the boy with whom he is entrusting the future.

Time had plunged ahead and the man who had shared coffee with a backwater revolutionary in a dusty village now sat in the midst of wealth and power, pondering his decision of decades past. For the first time he questioned whether he had chosen the right boy.

Chapter 35

Kasili was on a roll.

It was a spontaneous remark at first, reveling in the adulation that was being heaped on him with every appearance he made. The swooning and screaming, almost as if the original Beatles had been reincarnated in a tall, gangling African-American lawyer, was interfering with his more rational side. He wasn't giving his words proper forethought before making statements that would eventually come back to haunt him as the campaign became more heated. This time what he said would only make for a security nightmare that, when his secret service detail heard about it, instigated a surfeit of off-color language.

Taking his celebrity a little too far, in the opinion of some of his staff, loyal as they were, Kasili stated during a nationally televised interview that he would be making his acceptance speech as the party's nominee in a sports venue rather than at the convention hall.

He told the news anchor that it was only fitting that he speak, not just to the party delegates, but to all of America and in order to open the process to the populace of this country, he needed to be accessible to everyone. So, before the newsman could interject a question about a possible problematic arrangement, Kasili announced that the DNC would engage the baseball stadium as the scene for the speech, allowing 90,000 people to be a part of the historic occasion.

"Of all the self-aggrandizing, overconfident jerks," said Solana. "He must think he's a rock star."

"Yeah, at least Clinton could play the saxophone," smirked Toddy. "It looks like all the orchestrated swooning of adoring fans went to his head. Evidently he has come to see himself as the redeemer of humanity, the rock star of ages."

Sol rolled her eyes. "What's so very presumptuous is that Castor *still* hasn't conceded and is keeping her delegates as an ace in the hole. How can he arbitrarily announce where he'll make his acceptance speech when it seems all but obvious that she's going to challenge him at the convention?" Sol was practically agape at the sheer nerve of Kasili's declaration.

"I'd like to think that he's giving his handlers fits," said Toddy. "Not to mention the big money backers."

"It's all fodder for another post to the blog. This guy can't keep his mouth shut long enough to give us any rest," she said. "Between the way you've been tackling the issue of foreign funding slipping into the campaign coffers, tying it back to terrorists and the usual, run-of-the-mill union, political and Wall Street bosses, there's far too much information to dispense."

"What's most frightening is the pressure being applied to drive down the dollar to create the impression of a wallowing economy, all to make Kasili appealing. It gives him a handle to press forward with his socialist agenda and tax hike plans using crybaby vindication as the hook. This guy can't look good unless the economy is painted with the brush of dysfunction and impending collapse, which has been so far from the actual truth that I am amazed at their audacity to try to create the impression of doom and destruction." Toddy leaned back in his chair and glued his eyes to the ceiling, tracing miniscule cracks in the paint. "Let's just hope that the alternative media is doing its job to raise the hackles of the average citizen and that they are finally beginning to pay attention."

"All we can do is keep working and pray the message gets through."

At the Castor nerve center, the lead players were in the midst of a strategy session. Discussion was all over the map trying to draw up a viable plan to inject the governor's message into the convention rhetoric. Looking over the platform as it seemed to be coalescing at party headquarters, she was not happy with the overly radical turn they were adopting. Even she knew that the party couldn't haul their own centrists on board when the opposition had promoted a moderate of their own. Her face, which she had tried to keep schooled, was quickly twisting into an expression of disgust. This last gaffe of assuming that "all of America" would tune in to listen to the man with the golden tongue, as the media had dubbed him, was nothing more than offensive in its arrogance.

"This is an appallingly stupid move," the campaign manager was leaning over a file folder that lay open with newspaper clippings and computer printouts spread across the low table in front of her. She had one hand riffling through the sheets and the other at her neck, massaging the base of her skull, vainly attempting to keep an approaching migraine at bay. "Why would he want to polarize the party and assume that the rest of red state America is the least interested in watching him make bombastic remarks for the better part of an hour?"

Castor laid her head on the back of the couch across from her CM and stretched out her legs, nylon encased feet crossed on the edge of the coffee table. "He keeps showing how inexperienced he really is. You can't keep blurting out statements and opinions that will lock you into an untenable position. Even announcing that your *acceptance* speech will be made in a stadium to better address the *world* is foolish. He keeps underestimating the opposition, and I don't mean me."

"No, he's alienating your followers, the millions of voters who almost knocked him back into the north woods," said the manager, examining one of the sheets with another thoughtless quote blazing across the headline. "For all the talk of unity, this guy has got to be the most divisive character I've seen in American politics since George Wallace."

"You know," Castor lowered her eyes to connect with her subordinate, "you've really hit the mark with that one. Every time you turn around, he's injecting race into the conversation. It's a toss-up to choose which is the stronger victim standpoint, race or sexism," she grinned a little wickedly.

The manager pulled up a printout that was from a website and handed it across to the woman who, even in her effort to relax, looked ready to strike with the speed of a viper. "Take a look at this blog," she said, "it's been receiving a lot of attention from conservative talk radio. Looks like the information is pretty well vetted."

Castor scanned the article about Kasili and her eyebrows began to rise in wonder at the data that was literally dripping from the page. Funding that definitely occupied a gray area in the whole scheme of things. She looked at her campaign manager.

"So, where's this going? It could damage him irreparably if it's proven, but it seems pretty implausible. We had our own run-in with funding scrutiny a few years back and survived." She reread some of the charges. "Except they never connected us to terrorists that are bent on destroying the Great Satan. This is very nasty stuff." She stared off into space for a moment. "Is it true? Have you any idea who's behind this blog?" Her eyes sparkled a bit with renewed hope.

"No idea. I hear the Kasili camp has been trying to ferret out the culprits behind this "scurrilous attack" but I don't believe they've made any progress. And if he keeps opening his mouth without thinking, it only gives this blogger," and she stabbed at the sheet held by Castor, "more material than he could ever use. Might be good for us in the long run."

"Just so long as nobody thinks we're behind the smear, it's fine by me." She tossed the paper back onto the table and took a deep cleansing breath. "As for it being in our favor, I'm not so sure. The DNC has dug in their heels to support this upstart despite the constant barrage of misfires from his campaign. He's a more charming speaker than I am. I'll give him that, but that's just not enough to get the job done." She leveled her eyes at her campaign manager with the tenacity she was known for transmitting through the air. "We intend to keep the challenge alive for now."

"Smart to hedge your bets. We might be able to land the second seat anyway."

Castor's stare became more intense with resolve. "That's not the plan."

Chapter 36

Two weeks had past and the blogging duo were still technically incommunicado with the rest of the civilized world. Toddy made his forays into the outside world to periodically post to the internet, but otherwise they had been holed up on the side of the mountain overlooking a river valley deep in the throes of a summer heat wave.

Toddy had been surfing the net gleaning every little bit of detrimental data he could find on Kasili and Scirras. The televisions produced a constant buzz of background noise as the news channels relayed the latest of political hay that was being reaped by Kasili's opponent each time the democratic candidate spoke without a handler or teleprompter to guide his thoughts and his tongue. There'd been a growing trend among conservatives to 'Kasili watch,' a newly coined term that had taken on the meaning of just waiting for another misspoken word to fall from his mouth. Some more unforgiving critics had begun to refer to it as 'manna from heaven.'

With the convention just one week away, the price of gold had leapt yet again, and the value of the dollar was taking another beating in the wake of the rising gold market.

"Apparently no one but Kasili," blurted Toddy.

Sol, who had been seated nearby keeping half an eye on the television while reading and sipping iced tea, put her glass down and turned her attention to her partner. "What are you talking about?"

"Didn't you just hear what he said? I'll Tivo that. Man, these things are great," he said as he leaned over to snatch the control for the digital recorder. "It's terrific that your grandparents are real electronics buffs." While he said that, he recaptured the image that had been onscreen moments before in what amounted to an instant replay of the comment Kasili had made.

"Just listen to this."

The video image caught Kasili in the midst of a charge that the United States economic woes stemmed from the country's overuse of petroleum products. He forged ahead even further to say that should the country take the initiative to change its gas guzzling ways and embrace energy alternatives, the economy would boom. *And...* by installing more taxes on gas it would discourage energy *over*use.

"What could he possibly be basing that conjecture on?" Sol asked incredulously. "We don't have any alternatives available that don't cost far more than oil to process for fuel. Everything else, such as wind and ethanol are sponsored by government subsidy, which by application in itself multiplies the cost to the taxpayer. So, on top of the indirect charge of subsidizing alternative energy development, he wants to add another outright tax at the pump." She was too astounded by the asinine suggestion to say anymore.

"He apparently never passed Economics 101. What can you expect from someone who was raised by a card-carrying communist? Not only do they not understand the essence of capitalism and the motivation to be productive, but they have an utter disdain for it as being an unworthy endeavor, as if it is more commendable to live off the fruits of other's toil." Under his breath he muttered, "Effing lawyers."

"What have you got against lawyers?"

"Just that, for the most part, they only know how to make money off the backs of others. Think about it, would you? The democratic party office holders, which holds the majority in Congress right now, are almost exclusively comprised of attorneys who know nothing except how to write legislation. Legislation that *restricts* the ability of citizens to earn a good wage and produce goods or supply services. It creates *license*, which is nothing more than a charge for what has essentially been redefined as an illegal or illicit activity. Once it is designated as such then the activity requires a permit, thereby creating a tax on virtually every productive endeavor that a person might undertake in order to feed and clothe their family.

"Lawyers posing as legislators remove rights but reintroduce them as privileges, or said licensing, making it something that can be retracted by dictum as opposed to a right granted by Providence or God, as this country's, *our* forefathers recognized." He turned the television back to the current newscast.

"Compare that to the opposing party. The majority of republican legislators are business people and, as such, understand the workings of capitalism and how well it can drive an economy, fuel and feed a nation. The motivation to work, produce and be efficient in one's efforts is inherent in the system. Communism and socialism promote non-productive members of society and even rewards them for being non-productive with welfare and other social services and entitlement programs. It encourages indolence. The propagation of a system that strips productive human beings of their justly earned gains leads to the demise of the society and utter corruption of the State. It all crumbles upon itself, just as Athens did. There was nothing left to steal from the productive citizens because they simply stopped producing realizing that they could no longer keep what they made and that instead, whatever they created would be taken to support those who made nothing, i.e. the bureaucrats. They were literally taxed to death."

He sat back and rubbed his forehead with the back of his hand. Sol watched, taking in his despair at the thought of how most people she knew already struggled to provide for their families and knowing that further burdens would break them.

"This is Kasili's plan," continued Toddy. "Tax the successful to subsidize ineffectual and uneconomical enterprises such as ethanol, wind power, solar, etc. All nice ideas that couldn't be developed in the private sector because they're not cost effective, yet. It's a return to serfdom, slavery. Do as you're told and only the new nobility, otherwise known as bureaucracy, live comfortably and are well fed. Innovation be damned."

"Well," said Sol, "There's your next posting."

It didn't take long for Toddy to whip out the next rant, a term he stole from a comedian-cum-political satirist, and he pushed himself away from the makeshift desk where he had set-up his laptop. Stretching his long arms overhead, Solana walked back into the room and suggested that they get out for a while and enjoy the afternoon, which a brief thundershower had cooled down some from the sizzling heat that had been engulfing the canyon walls.

Over the weeks that the two had spent in such close company, Sol and Toddy had established a friendship that was growing stronger with each passing day. In many ways they had become almost inseparable, discussing concepts on ever-deepening levels and even arguing the minutiae over long days that were brightened with daily outings within the confines of the Greyfisher property and surrounding tribal lands.

It wasn't long before Sol even had Toddy saddled up and riding trails that wound along the steep sides of the valley and across the fields that terraced the mountainside. Personally, Toddy had never imagined himself sitting astride a horse, having grown up an urban urchin who had spent his time escaping the drugscape of the city and the gangs that roved the streets near his home. Always something of a nerd, he'd been taunted and baited by the 'cool' crowd, who, in his judgment, had been anything but. Losers all. And to prove it, the majority of them had ended up in juvie or doing hard time in the county lock-up. He'd been ecstatic when his father, a closet philosopher – you couldn't be vocal about such things in that neighborhood – had found a way to extricate the family from that jungle and relocate to a lower middle class neighborhood not three miles away. By that time, however, Toddy had already turned seventeen, graduated and had left the drug-sodden haunts to find his own way in the larger city. At least his younger siblings had been given a chance to attend better schools and eventually move on to college, but in so doing, they had abandoned Toddy to his own fate, seeing him as too eccentric for the rest of them to associate with.

So, horses had no place in the childhood dreams of Toddy's past. He had always equated them with a romanticism that would never be related to his existence. Yet here he was, now in his forties and riding comfortably beside a beautiful Native American woman who had taken the time and effort to teach him to sit in a saddle and, much as it still bewildered him, seemed to enjoy having him tag along on the trail.

Sol, for her part, had been surprised at how well Toddy had taken to the horses. He'd been a little reticent in approaching them at first until she had shown him the basics of patiently waiting on them to get accustomed to his company. It hadn't taken long before he was assisting her with their care and, when he was in a quandary about some data that he'd uncovered and was trying to assign it a place in the overall puzzle, she would often find him out in the pasture, communing with the big animals as if they could give him new insight or direction. The fact that he had chosen to live outside a mountain community, isolated from his neighbors and the rest of society, bespoke a deep loneliness that she saw him giving up a little as he'd sit on the fence deep in thought, the horses nuzzling him as he'd comb his fingers through their manes. When she'd met him, she hadn't expected to find him engaging her more than just intellectually, but he had rapidly gained a place in her heart that she was beginning to recognize as being more than just a slight attraction.

As their mounts walked side-by-side along the trail, their legs occasionally brushing up against each other in the narrower passages, she became aware of the fact that she had crossed the line of simple friendship. She looked over at his profile as he leaned down to scratch the gelding's neck and wondered if his feelings had taken a similar turn during the weeks of enforced solitude and increased dependence on one another for support.

Shaking off her idle thoughts, she just settled into the quiet of a pleasant afternoon's ride in the silent company of a friend.

It was late afternoon when Toddy and Sol turned their two mounts back out into the pasture and closed the tack room door behind them. As they were heading back up to the house, they saw Anthea's Expedition round the corner and drive up to the front porch.

"What brings you two up the mountain today?" asked Toddy as they approached the lodge. "Gary, I thought you weren't doing guard duty for another couple of days?"

Over the past weeks, the two men had managed to work out their differences and had even become philosophical sparring partners, much the way Anthea and Toddy had been for years, except for the fact that Gary tried hard to hold the non-conspiratorial line of thought. It was a difficult position to keep amid all the evidence to the contrary that Toddy was constantly unearthing, but it made for fascinating discussions, even if Gary was apt to roll his eyes on occasion.

"We're not here on official business," said Gary. "My wife had another motive for dragging me back up this forlorn mountain."

"Oh?" asked Sol, cocking her head at her friend who was just climbing down from the rig's cab.

"I'm going to push Nolan around a little," announced Anthea as she brushed the wrinkles from the lap of her shorts and straightened her blouse, preparing for a standoff.

Toddy's grin was half-hidden as he watched his small friend march off into the depths of the house to confront the head of the security detail. "She thinks you need a break from this place," clarified Gary, "and I believe that Eric is about to get an earful."

"I wouldn't get in her way when she's made up her mind about something," said Toddy. "So, do you think we should gather our gear? Where are we going?"

Gary smiled. "Just to Spokane for the evening. She's got a plan."

"Never knew her to not have one," said Toddy as he and Sol followed Anthea into the house.

The three of them trailed Anthea at a far slower pace to ensure that they weren't singed by any sparks that were sure to be flung wide of the sizzling discussion. No voices were raised but the tone was heated as Nolan vainly tried to hold his ground, that the danger was too real to let Sol leave the plantation for even one night's outing. In the end, he caved. There was a reason that Anthea had earned the tag 'Whiplash Annie' during her years as a publisher. Not that anyone had ever called her that directly, but she'd always been aware of the epithet and was just a little proud of it.

They loaded up and drove to town to enjoy an evening of freedom for Sol, who hadn't been allowed off the property since arriving, and now the first political convention was only a week away. The conversation in the car was fraught with speculation on Kasili's tactics and how Castor's cronies were planning to counter them, or even if they could or would.

"What I wouldn't give to be part of the press corps covering the events," mused Sol later as they enjoyed a lavish meal overlooking the Spokane River and the falls not far away.

"Hmmph," Anthea eyed her friend, amused. "Like Kasili's gorillas would let you anywhere within a hundred miles of the 'uh-uh-uh' train. He has enough problems without having to beat off some Indian reporter who's already managed to catch him with his pants down."

"Please, I'm trying to eat here," said Toddy around a mouthful of some savory dish that, until then, he was thoroughly enjoying. "That image is not conducive to proper digestion."

"I am anticipating some real fireworks," said Anthea, ignoring Toddy's comments and leaning back to watch the water flow past the deck, sipping a little from her wine glass. "I haven't seen a good ol' knock-down drag-out at a convention in years. It's just the ticket for this campaign, I think."

"Don't hold your breath. If there's anything the democrats know how to do, it's shore up the bulwarks to try to present a solid front, no matter how fractured the foundation," said Toddy.

"Which, of course, is also they're downfall," observed Gary. "If there's too much turmoil that's being covered over in favor of a unified display, the rotten floor boards will collapse from the heat of the friction. The term 'crash and burn' comes to mind."

"It could happen. Kasili is too apt to say something he'll regret in an unscripted moment," said Sol. "What I mean is that he's apt to say something his *handlers* will regret."

"Which is why nothing will be left to chance and it will all be drafted ahead of time and carried out accordingly. They can't afford a gaffe when all the world is watching," noted Toddy. "They're probably praying that there aren't any teleprompter miscues."

"Now there's a simple answer to the opposition's dream… screw with the teleprompter and let the candidate flounder on national TV," chuckled Anthea.

Lifting the receiver of his phone and punching the button that would connect him with his assistant, the executive scanned the relatively empty seas and watched the final rays of the sun cast a deepening reddish glow over the sharp pinnacles of the distant Olympic Mountains that rimmed his view to the west.

When the call was answered, he bluntly asked what progress they had made to find the wayward blogger. It had been weeks and he was becoming irritated with the constant barrage of information and 'lies' that were streaming from the changingwind.org website.

His assistant was reluctant to give his superior the only answer that he had, which was that they still had been unable to unearth the origin of the blog. He prepared himself for the quiet rage that would seep through the phone lines. He had never seen the head of this vast financial empire lose control, but the impatience was stinging in his periodic silence.

The assistant was informed that all stops should be pulled to locate and remove the threat. The convention was opening in less than a week and Kasili's position as unassailable was becoming more tenuous each day.

Puzzlement at how this person, the blogger, had found a way to pierce his, until then, impenetrable veil was not evident in his soft voice as he urged his underling to direct their operatives to greater effort and implement a final solution.

The phraseology chosen by his superior to describe what was needed had not been inadvertent. The assistant knew only a little of the man's history, since it was closely guarded for the most part. Yet, the market wizard's Eastern European accent told it's own tale of midtwentieth century experience, whether it had been as a perpetrator or a victim, the assistant did not know. What he *did* know was that the man meant what he said.

Chapter 37

The Staples Center in Los Angeles was the focus of every media hand available. The liberal press was tripping over itself to run after the Kasili procession as he arrived amid fanfare that had the appearance of a royal reception for the acclaimed monarch. When Castor arrived amid an impressive entourage that bespoke the power she wielded with nearly half the delegates securely in her camp, the media made passing mention of it, giving her short shrift in the coverage cycle. The slight did not go unnoticed and although she kept her smiling game face on, her husband was not so easily persuaded to look the part of a vassal.

There were a few rogue news agencies in the crowd that speculated on the virtual face-off that could occur should Castor not feel inclined to stand aside and allow the party hierarchy to dictate the convention outcome. The fact that her stubborn feminist backing was leaning toward mulish support of their candidate was a cause of some consternation and worry among the DNC board. The race between parties was far closer than had been anticipated and any sign of weakness could undermine the united front they wanted to show at the convention's conclusion.

Despite the hubbub about factions and the fawning over Kasili, the opening ceremonies at the democratic convention went off without so much as a burp. Everyone was playing nice for the time being and the cameras picked up numerous instances of the delegates exchanging back and hand slaps that practically resembled an adult version of patty-cake. The first night of static speeches by boring Washington hacks interspersed with a few incendiary calls to arms by party firebrands ended without problem or confrontation, much to the DNC's relief.

The friendly lull didn't last long.

Toddy and Solana could be found ensconced in the den, computers within easy reach for quick reference searches on the web and note taking, when they witnessed the first signals that contention was deeply imbedded on the convention floor.

One of the stable party spokesmen approached the podium. A senator from the 'Eastern Bloc,' as Toddy had named the liberal north-eastern quadrant of the country, opened the day's event with arms raised in a victorious gesture that, instead of receiving raucous approval from the delegates, was greeted with an overwhelming sound of 'boos' and catcalls. To his credit, he kept his smile in place and began his opening address for the evening's agenda, speaking over the noise until it subsided in grumbling and hisses.

Solana looked over at Toddy. "Do you think Kasili can pull this off? I've seen better welcomes for chum in a shark colony. He's being eaten alive."

Toddy lifted an eyebrow at her comparison. "With Scirras' money driving the cause, he'd be tough to beat within the party. Castor has a shot if Kasili opens his mouth sideways and lets fall some idiot-ic responses, which, looking at recent history, seems inevitable. Castor's ties haven't been strong enough to withstand the pounding so far and there's no reason to think that she can pull a rabbit out of the hat at this late date. But," he shrugged with slight indecision, "it's hard to know where the real power stands. Scirras has unlimited funds and has been able to direct the party and union bosses, but Castor has had support from the old school democrats who still wield plenty of clout, despite all the sleight of hand Scirras has used.

"It all weighs on the backs of the super delegates and how far in the bag they are with Kasili designated money. They are not going to jump ship unless they're convinced that he simply can't claim the prize. Being able to read a speech with verve and passion is turning out to be not enough of a character reference with the public. Or so the polls indicate."

"With as many ridiculous mistakes this man has made, I am at an utter loss to understand how he made it this far. I know that people are blinded by their need to believe, but to listen to the emptiness of his promise of 'change' and the complete lack of any kind of econom-ic plan, border protection or foreign policy is simply frightening."

"You know, for those who like to harp on religionists for hav-ing faith in their beliefs, this is tantamount to as baseless a faith as there can possibly be. Especially if anyone actually looks at the facts of Kasili's life and so-called accomplishments. They are placing faith in something that is counterintuitive, unlike religious faith which stems from an intuitive understanding of a greater being or force of the universe."

Turning back to the television screen. They see that Solana's description of the senator's reception was not so far off the mark. The convention floor, which was equally split between the purple and yellow banners of the two candidates, was in motion like a seething ocean in a rising storm. The underlying thunder was scarcely being held at bay while the man was virtually under the siege of a barely contained anger on one side and an insufferable superior attitude on the other.

The cameras of a few of the cable stations were able to sweep in any direction to find delegates with their mottled faces up against one another, hardly constraining themselves from coming to blows.

"This is better than the WWF," said Sol completely absorbed by the dissension on the convention floor.

"World Wildlife Fund? I knew Lord Snowden was a radical about offing humanity, but…"

"No," she said laughing and unbelieving of his disingenuousness. "Wrestling. The wrestling federation." She caught his snicker as she glanced in his direction and shook her head in disgust while redirecting her attention to the convention coverage.

There were a couple of different reporters, harping on the anger and mayhem roiling around them, who ducked signs that almost whacked them as they were being waved through the air like weapons.

As the night dragged on, speaker after speaker attempted to quell the crowd with appeals to the factions to work together and to combine support for Kasili as the candidate of compromise. They addressed the crowd to no avail as Castor supporters vocalized their disenchantment with the system.

"It's not looking like the party muckety-mucks are going to get much cooperation from the floor. This is probably the most contentious convention since Chicago in 1968 when the yippies were hauled off for inciting to riot," said Sol as she watched the drama unfold.

"Yeah, I remember my dad telling me about a quote from John Chancellor, the NBC reporter who ended up in the middle of the mêlée. Apparently, he made a comment describing the plank negotiations as "sie-de-die, la-de-da and boop-boop-be-doop." Toddy grinned as he recalled seeing the back of the envelope that his father had saved with that line scribbled on the back. "What a quote. I've always loved that. You know, if I remember right, even Chancellor ended up behind bars for a night while the police sifted through the crowd they'd arrested without bothering to check credentials."

The convention trials continued on as they watched. The polling of the delegates was brought to a halt, supposedly by some accord between the candidates since the overall atmosphere had only gotten more divisive rather than settling down. Castor had wanted to prove that she was a force to be recognized within the hall, but it still gained her nothing as the super delegates were sticking by their guns and backing Kasili all the way to the wire.

"There are going to be a lot of unhappy campers at the end of this little soireé," said Toddy as he tuned into the dais, noticing that Castor was approaching the podium, raucous yells of approval coming from all corners of the convention hall.

She settled herself behind the microphone and addressed the crowd.

"We are millions strong," at which point she was shut down by the noise level of voices and feet pounding in agreement to her statement. "But we are a part of a universal move toward implementing true change in this country." And here, the other half of the hall opened up with stomping and yelling. "It's time to set aside our differences and focus on our unity of purpose, combining our prodigious voices to speak for the good of all…"

"I'm just waiting for the clarions and cherubim to descend from the heavens," said Sol snidely.

"Sorry, that's tomorrow night when Kasili addresses humanity at large from the baseball stadium. If we're lucky, we may glimpse God Himself."

"Ooooh, and I thought I was mean…" she smiled.

Castor continued on trying to soothe the spirits of her aching followers who were finally being shown the door. Her husband was standing to her rear and slightly off to the right, camera angling him in and out of the shots. His face said it all. No matter how big Governor Castor's olive branch was, Dean Castor was not ready to throw in the towel, and his expression was as dark as a storm cloud, proving it. The underlying grumbling that mirrored his look was rolling back and forth among the crowd, reaching a higher pitch and then fading into the background again. The problem was not gone no matter how much Castor tried to placate her troops.

"This is probably why Kasili isn't seated in the gallery," said Sol. "I bet he'd be lynched by a bunch of menopausal delegates."

Toddy looked at her askance. "'Lynched' is probably not the best word to employ in this instance."

"I'll make note of that next time I have a similar observation to make in public," she sniffed. "Damn, if people aren't touchy."

He lifted his shoulders in a 'whatever' gesture. "Just a thought in these days of PC."

"PC verbiage is the last thing I'll worry about at home. Anyway, she's managed to rein them in for now, all glowering by the Dean aside." She looked at Toddy. "Have you had enough for one night?"

"Absolutely. We still have the nominee making his acceptance speech tomorrow night. That's enough anticipation for me," and he flicked off the screen.

❋ ❋ ❋

Yakub Hamid Kasili ascended the dais to face tens of thousands of 'fans' who had stood in line for hours in order to gain admittance to the momentous affair. The security was indeed a nightmare, just as the head of the nominee's secret service detail had predicted. Every contingency was covered by trained officers of the law, imposing men both in uniform and muted suits. It almost appeared that the streets had been emptied of men in blue in order to supply security at the stadium, a circumstance that did not thrill the mayor of Los Angeles one whit.

Silence descended on the crowd as the presidential nominee took his place behind a Plexiglas lectern that was flanked by Doric columns that made the stage look more like a Southern antebellum estate than Olympus; a definite blunder in décor...or was it?

He began his address with platitudes that were meant to declaw the Castor faction but, ringing false in her ears, only riled her instead, as she, her husband and entourage sat in a place of honor before the stage. She struggled to keep a smile on her lips as Kasili offered backhanded appreciation of her efforts to bring women's rights to the fore, as if her credentials to run for office were beneath his own.

Turning back to the business of accepting the support of Castor, however grudgingly it was given, he declared, "The underdog is here! In this stadium and, even, on this stage." He tried to sound as if he was including all the overworked and underpaid victims of society, but the gist became obvious – he was invoking race as the trump for leading the throng. Expanding on the issue, he exhorted the disadvantaged, the disenfranchised, the minorities to take up the cause and follow his march out of the vestiges of slavery, which he will champion via the institution of 'change.'

"Oh, that's rich," commented Sol. "If anyone read your postings they'd see your point about how he is actually advocating the exact opposite, the reinstatement of the institution of slavery, only this time to the State rather than individual plantation owners." She nodded at Toddy. "See, I read your stuff," she gave him a half-smile.

"I hope that you're not the only one."

The speech stretched on for forty-five minutes exhaustively repeating the same cant without giving any actual plan of action by which he expected to achieve the resultant change he so passionately said the country needed. Sol was bored and Toddy was making notes for another posting. When he finally brought the talk to a conclusion and raised his arms in the signal of victory, the crowd disintegrated into a screaming mob of sycophants, chanting the mantra of 'change for our future.'

Castor rose and applauded with reserve, stone-faced at having to accept the unacceptable. Her following did not appear to be among the throng. In fact, there were television correspondents making the rounds of the conventioneers' haunts immediately after the rally, where they found hundreds of delegates that had not attended Kasili's acceptance party. They were disgruntled and offered little in the way of encouraging words for their party's nominee. The press quickly discontinued the interviews in order to focus on the praises being sung back at the stadium where the party was in full swing. Kasili was in savior mode.

As the coverage was rapidly digressing into a revival atmosphere, Sol and Toddy discussed the direction for the next blog and how to approach the disrespectful junking of the Castor candidacy. The week had been one of high drama within the ranks of the democratic party and they deemed the need to derail the Kasili freight train was more important than ever. Tired as they were, they were loath to leave one another's company, even to catch some sleep.

The hunt was still on.

Chapter 38

The convention was done, finished, kaput and the delegates had torn up the town after the acceptance speech Kasili had delivered at Dodger Stadium.

"I still don't see how anyone could have thought that acting like a superstar could possibly be beneficial to a presidential campaign," said Sol the next morning over coffee. "It demeans the whole process. Whatever happened to 'looking presidential?' Isn't that supposed to indicate dignity? Celebrity and dysfunction go hand-in-hand anymore, which to my mind, is the exact opposite of dignity."

"You forget that you're talking about democrats," pointed out Toddy. "They are enamored with celebrity. Face it, that was Castor's downfall. She simply didn't have the celebrity look or personality and presidential politics has become all about personality and less about character."

"No joke. This guy has proven that the less character you have the better. I don't even like Castor but she at least had more substance than Kasili who's about as transparent and stalwart as a jellyfish."

"Hmmm. I kind of like that. I may have to use it in one of the articles," smiled Toddy as he gulped his coffee before getting to work.

"Is that how you request permission for stealing my ideas? I think I ought to copyright this stuff. Maybe collect royalties."

"On to the next point to be made on changingwind.org… the running mate," said Toddy, moving along to another subject.

"Now, whose idea was he? A former senator from South Dakota? Even if he was popular at one time, hardly anyone remembers his name. Why not a sitting office-holder? That would make more sense to me. Not to mention the fact that this has-been is from one of the least populous states in the union. What's all that about?"

"My guess?" said Toddy. "They don't want to give up any seats in the Congress or gubernatorial assets. The split in the senate is too close to pull a sitting senator from office and there isn't a state officer that would put Kasili over the top. But it's not a smart move to pull in someone who hasn't been in the headlines for two years. Guess we'll see where this goes and check the polls later today to see if he's getting any kind of post-convention bounce. So far there's been nothing of significance," concluded Toddy.

"I don't think they're going to get anything near what they'd hoped for a pop in poll numbers. They made a serious mistake in not drafting Castor as his running mate because her folks are seriously peeved and may abandon ship."

Scanning the websites and television news for poll numbers, the two are taken by surprise as Eddinger made his own surprise move and grabbed the headlines by announcing his running mate before the convention the following week.

Normally, the announcement of a vice presidential candidate wouldn't be all that stupendous except for the fact that the republican candidate stole Kasili's thunder by naming a woman to the ticket.

Both Sol and Toddy sat up, ears perked to catch every little bit of news coming over the airwaves. Not only did Eddinger find a woman to fill the bill, but she happened to be a woman of diverse ethnicity and the mayor of a large metropolitan area. Since Eddinger hailed from a Midwestern state, he scooped up Risa Cristóbal, the mayor of Phoenix, Arizona, a city that surpassed a million population with the last census.

Not only was Cristóbal a conservative republican, she had made her mark as a Hispanic who sponsored a proof of citizenship campaign for potential voters in a state where illegal aliens had become a strong contingent in the population. Her own family had been landed gentry at the time of the Gadsden Purchase and she was fiercely loyal to the Union, having seen the abject poverty that her long-lost cousins were subjected to south of the border. She had also gone to Washington to fight the growing INS policy of turning a blind eye to the steady stream of poor Mexicans crossing the border only to become victimized by coyotes dealing in human misery. Her city was being inundated by people who needed health care and services that were breaking the municipal budget. She understood that there were limits to charity and her constituents were overburdened.

Cristóbal's stance on illegal immigration was somewhat different from Eddinger's as he had taken a more moderate position. However, this strengthened his candidacy among conservatives by placing a solid border protectionist in his camp and one that was not anti-Mexican American since she was one herself.

"Looks to me like Eddinger trumped Kasili's super speech," gloated Toddy. "No one even knew Cristóbal was in the running. I'd never have guessed it."

"It was a damn smart move on his part and it doesn't hurt that she's easy on the eyes as well. She may be in her fifties but she's a classy woman with solid credentials. I like the choice."

"And so much for Kasili's post-convention bump. Looks like the polls are staying flat." He looked over at her as she gripped her coffee mug. "That the ten point pop they expected just didn't materialize. Eddinger has got some smart advisors working with him. I'm impressed."

Toddy started flicking through the channels to catch a taste of what the different pundits had to say about either the acceptance speech or the VP candidate that Eddinger had unveiled. This is where Girard would have been an asset to the television line-up, he thought. Instead they were stuck with the usual talking heads and the old coot they'd wheeled out to take Olin Girard's place, none of whom were thrilled with Eddinger's coup. In fact, they had already begun denigrating her experience as nothing more than a mayor of some arid southwest retirement center and a baseball mom before that, which wasn't exactly the whole story. Cristóbal's son played with the hometown team of the Diamondbacks and she had been an emergency room nurse and supervisor for twenty years before deciding to get involved in politics. Definitely not the average political resumé.

"Already they're in attack mode with the new VP candidate while they literally stumbled over themselves to flatter Cameron Van Schaal. And what did he do besides spend thirty years in the senate before retiring to take a cushy position with some Washington think tank that lobbies for environmental issues, i.e. global warming." Sol sighed with despair. "These people who call themselves journalists give the rest of us a bad name."

"Unfortunately, Sol, there aren't many of you left," commiserated Toddy. "Hardly enough to complain that your reputations have been damaged."

"Fine, make fun. My trade is dead."

"Don't take it personally. You're still carrying the torch, remember?" And he got up to give her a consoling hug, which took on a little more intensity than he had intended. Pulling himself away before she felt awkward was one of the hardest things he'd ever done. He found that he wanted to hold onto her as long as he could.

A little flustered at the warmth of the embrace, Sol reseated herself on the couch before answering. "How can I not? You work overtime to be objective in your coverage, no matter what your personal views and these jokers waltz in and then tromp all over the concept of objectivity with personal agendas." She looked over at Toddy, a thought crossing her mind. "At least, I assumed they were personal. Maybe it's more than that."

"It's unlikely that the positioning of so many in the press is due just to personal bias. I wouldn't be surprised to find that many are in reception of varying kinds of gifts." He re-attuned his focus to the original point. "You still have work to accomplish to keep the bad guys from winning. Dejection and depression are counterproductive."

"Well, it doesn't help that we're stuck here on the mountainside literally hiding out from those 'bad guys.' How long do you figure this is going to go on?"

"Could be until the election…"

"Oh, don't tell me that," she interrupted.

"The blog will get more attention now and we can't afford to let the truth be buried," he smiled wanly. "You know, beat the drum and all."

"Right," she said glumly.

Every once in a while, Solana would get a brief respite from the overwhelming boredom of life on the farm. She had trouble seeing the forced isolation as anything but incredibly dull, being a woman used to finding herself regularly surrounded by news maelstroms when she'd been reporting in the metro centers of New York and Denver. So when the visiting angels, embodied by Anthea and Lainie, came up the hill, Sol was ecstatic to have some female companionship. With all the men constantly hovering in her peripheral vision, the testosterone levels were practically suffocating. When Lainie would arrive, the mother-to-be swinging the hormone balance heavily to the other side, estrogen and progesterone temporarily overwhelmed the opposition.

Today, Lainie was feeling the midsummer heat, the weight of her advancing pregnancy making her uncomfortable in the rising humidity that would get trapped between the valley's rock walls. Cisco hung around just out of earshot in order to keep a protective eye on his wife who had been under watch for high blood pressure. Toddy and Solana had been at the Greyfisher property for nearly a month and nothing untoward had occurred, shifting the worry of a possible attack further to the rear of Cisco's mind, far behind the concern for his wife's health.

Actually, the most threatening problem the security detail was having to deal with were the vociferous complaints from Grandmother Millie who was making noise about being kept from collecting her berries now that they were coming into season. Lainie brought up the subject as she lowered herself into one of the chairs on the front porch.

"I feel awful about Grandma not being able to come home right now, but I'll go out and collect what I can, if the army we have roaming the woods will allow me," said Sol. "Maybe you can get up to the mountains to collect some huckleberries with her to make up for the loss."

"Right," said Lainie. "Have you taken a good look at me lately? Like I could haul this bulk up a trail to pick berries." She laughed. "And even if I could, Cisco would have a fit."

"Well there isn't much we can do. These guys," and she waved her hand to include the numerous male guards wandering the perimeter of the property, most not visible to the three women on the porch, "think that we're still in danger. Though, personally, I think the evil empire has forgotten about us."

"Hardly likely," Anthea put in. "Not with the content of Toddy's blogs. He's been furiously writing about Scirras' fingers in just about every pie around the world. From fomenting unrest in so many backwater regions to seriously funding Kasili support through obscure channels and even manipulating gold and dollar trading. Even if he's off the mark, which doesn't appear likely if you really check the research he's done, it's enough to cause some real consternation in the Scirras and Kasili households." She shook her head in acceptance of the facts, "You're still in danger."

"I know," Sol said a little dejectedly. "He's right to keep up the pressure and he seems determined to save the world all by himself, if he has to," she added the last with a fond little smile tweaking her lips.

Looking at Anthea and changing the subject she asked, "So how did you two manage to make it up here if the risk is so high? I'd have thought that Gary would have pulled the plug on your plans." She arched an eyebrow at her friend who sat smugly sipping an icy glass of tea.

"I suppose if I'd told him, he would have raised hell." She paused for another drink. "But I didn't. I'll see him later and Cisco's here. He wouldn't allow anything to happen to Lainie."

"True enough, and for the moment I could use the luck," she reached over and warmly rubbed her niece's expansive belly, "and the company. A house full of men gets to be rather tiresome." She sighed. "At least they can cook."

Both Lainie and Anthea laughed knowing how little pleasure Sol took from working in the kitchen.

"See? Something good comes of all things," said Lainie as she held Sol's hand over the side of her stomach where the baby was kicking.

"You know," she continued in a different vein, "I find it hard to understand how fired up people are about Kasili. He has virtually no credentials and as much as the press is trying to make him out to be this incredible speaker, I just don't see it. In fact, I don't hear it either. He says virtually nothing with so many pauses I lose patience waiting for the next word. How does that make for a great orator?"

"Well, it doesn't. We in the press understand that the repetition of a statement seems to validate it, even if the statement is untrue. Göebbels figured that one out." She looked at Lainie. "You shouldn't have to worry about your baby's future, unfortunately we're faced with an important turning point for this country and Kasili is at the crux of the problem. He is a pawn for an ambitious and ruthless financial terrorist who appears to want nothing more than to control as much of the world's economic structure as he can, and he will do it by undermining economies through violence or engineered collapse." She shivered with the thought of such a formidable power. "It's frightening to think anyone could want so much and seem to be within grasp of achieving his ends."

"Until people are informed enough to understand the Scirras – Kasili connection and the incredible manipulation of the candidate, we are facing a silent coup of huge proportions," said Sol.

"Actually, I begin to wonder about that. Kasili seems to have become something of a loose cannon, fueled by his outrageous ego," sniffed Anthea. "I still can't believe he was so dense as to snub the other half of his party at the convention. All the supposed hand wringing aside, he was inconsiderate of the Castor backers and, if we're lucky, may pay the price."

"We can only hope. But it makes you wonder by what means his handlers will bring him under control, because I don't think that 'the boss' will sit idly by much longer and suffer Kasili's antics to continue." Sol shrugged.

Lainie picked up her train of thought. "Maybe it will all work in our favor, like you said, Anthea." She paused a little and looked out over the cleft in the mountains carved out by the swift flowing river below. "Funny how a man of color is actually blocking the way for us to continue handing down the heritage of our people to the children. Maybe he's too dense to understand that the life he wants us to accept is the *denial* of freedom not the continuation of it. For Indians, we'd lose what little sovereignty we still have and what's left of the treaties will be abrogated completely, all in favor of the *common good*. Oy."

They both look at her. *Oy?*

"I always knew you were a smart girl," said Sol, confused by the expression. "But *Oy?*"

"Hey between you and your New Yorkese and Anthea, I've been corrupted."

Chapter 39

An important development occurred in Europe that had managed to avoid major media attention.

Within the last seventy-two hours authorities had interrupted a very private party that was being held at an exclusive London dining establishment that catered to the privileged and politically connected. The host was a Romanian national by the name of Antonin Vescu who had achieved minor fame among the moneyed elite as a man who was able to provide just about anything for which the rich and famous might have a penchant, including items that would not be considered legal among most of civilized society. The man had been erroneously considered a lesser actor in the area of small, illicit acts fending for the wealthy classes and Scotland Yard had had no idea the size of the crime ring they had tripped over until they were dealing with the actual arrest of diplomats and international businessmen. The whole state of affairs was in danger of taking on a life of its own and they were anxious to bring the whole mess to the attention of an agency used to dealing with the possible political storm that could ensue.

They called Interpol for assistance.

The revelry that Scotland Yard had cut short had been an understated affair attended by men and one woman representing government bureaucrats and business officials from an odd collection of countries: Vescu's fellow countrymen from Romania and the others were from Australia, Namibia, the United States, Dominican Republic, Burkina Faso and Yemen. All of them had rapidly been supplied with high-powered advocates, all but Vescu who had been caught with his hand buried so deep in the cookie jar that he had no avenue of escape.

It was Vescu, a sleazy thug in the assessment of the lead Interpol investigator who had been invited on board and had just left the man's presence, who was now wallowing in a cell in London awaiting arraignment. The sweep of the allegations had ballooned quicker than the investigator had anticipated because Vescu decided that he needed to share the blame. He was, if nothing else, a complete coward who began trying to broker a deal as soon as he was in a confidential situation with someone he assumed was empowered to speak with authority.

The Interpol detective unconsciously wiped his hands on his pants as he finally escaped the company of the disreputable Vescu, whose attention to hygiene was faultless and his appearance impeccable. It was his character that sullied the atmosphere and after hearing the sordid details of his trade, the investigator was as close to becoming nauseated as any case had ever taken him.

He was leaving the holding facility now, walking beside the Yard detective who had observed the interview, in order to confer with their superiors about the results of the interrogation – a tale of international trafficking in narcotics and human flesh, the little London soireé having been just a peek into the grandiose operation. Heroin, cocaine, methamphetamine, arms dealing and the peddling of pre-teen sex slaves. Although Interpol had been following cold trails for years in the drug distribution and the pedophile rings, no one had seen the possibility of Romania as being the heart of the prostitution venture, specializing in both teenage and underage girls and boys. There had been rumors of an Eastern European connection in the sex circles but until now, Bucharest was seen as a city reinventing itself for the 21st century, not a center for vile and corrupt criminal activity.

What truly sickened the investigator to the point of his muttering oaths under his breath in his native French as he exited the building, were the ties Vescu made to the philanthropic Free State Foundation. It turned out that every one of the individuals apprehended at the London restaurant was somehow linked to the organization, either by family on one of the national boards or being directly connected to commerce that was conducted with it. Funds, according to Vescu, flowed freely between the FSFoundation and the businesses and organizations that these, and many other individuals like them, represented. He hesitated to use the term that clung to the end of his tongue. It would be up to the prosecutors to verify the evidentiary trail that pointed to money laundering, but the conclusion seemed obvious in his mind. The political trade-offs for the cash to support candidacies in so many countries, most without solid regulatory oversight to discourage payoffs and collusion, were far more common than he'd ever imagined.

If Vescu had even a fraction of the implications correct, the FSFoundation was going to be branded as a front for political payola to look askance at the illegal activities crisscrossing many of the countries' borders where it's presence was felt. It could also come under a microscopic examination for its role in suppressing free market growth in many of those nations, applying pressure to restrict business and resource developers in the name of environmentalism. Vescu's naming of each of the now-freed offenders from the London incident drew one more link that confused the investigator – he said that they, all but one, represented countries that were gold producers, and had some connection to a corporation by the name of Altamont.

He scrubbed his hand through his thinning brown hair as he made his way to his colleague's offices where there would be days more of compiling information for the prosecution.

The director's office in the financial center overlooking the Puget Sound was abuzz with tension despite the fact that only two people occupied the tastefully decorated, understatedly elegant space.

The second in command, which in this particular business ultimately meant that he wielded little or no power – the owner trusted no one – was informing that same owner of the turn of events in London. The CEO sat back in his leather chair, looking outwardly calm while the atmosphere crackled with his unvoiced fury. The assistant was uncomfortable under the beetling gaze of his boss who seemed to look more through him rather than at him as he detailed the incident according to his informant. That Vescu was attempting to forge a deal for lesser charges, in what could easily lead the way to the death penalty if taken to the World Court, was evident.

Composed in his response, the executive simply stated that Vescu would not have the option of avoiding his meeting with mortality.

The answer caused the second in command to furrow his brow in question at the declaration of his superior, but all he replied was, "As you say."

The CEO stared off into the blue of the vista that filled his office window, dismissing his assistant without words, who understood and silently left the office.

After a few moments the leader of the financial institution that had such high stakes in so much of what Vescu was implicating in criminal activity, turned back to his desk and unlocked one of the drawers. He removed a small personal telephone directory along with a cell phone and leafed through the book searching for a number.

He was seriously angry at the recent betrayals from men to whom he had given so much opportunity. They had squandered that wealth with the foolish activities of men drunk with their own importance. First Kasili, by flaunting the unity he needed so badly to enforce with members of his own party, and now the puffed-up Vescu. A small man with an oversized ego.

Just another stupid criminal. Vescu would never amount to more than an immaculately clad crook. He was exasperated with himself for not seeing the potential of both these men to let their ego surpass their brains. What was it about little men who came into a little power? As yet he had not found one who could manage the responsibility of wielding real power. That was for the very few. Those who had the ability to anticipate the direction the herd will move and can understand what is beneficial for the herd. Those are the shepherds, he thought, the ones who can direct and train and guide the masses.

He mused over the fact that there was always a suitable stand-in for filthy vermin like Vescu and it wouldn't be long before the incarcerated parasite was replaced and had indeed found his peace.

Finally a small smile crossed his lips as he placed a call to the Bucharest office. No time like the present to take action.

Chapter 40

Always scanning the internet for relevant information, Toddy caught an odd reference to an arrest made by Scotland Yard in a London bistro. It didn't mention any names of the johns (and one jane, apparently) but it did note the host, Antonin Vescu, a Romanian player that Toddy had come across in his research about FSFoundation activities in that country.

As he read the brief article, he saw that the others who had been apprehended were traveling under diplomatic papers and their identities were being closely guarded. All he could find, as he swept through his search engines, was what countries they hailed from. Even the charges that had been set aside for these 'diplomats' were only vaguely referred to as 'drug-related' and 'averted possible sex scandal.' Both of those references however, clanged a bell in his head when he put it together with other obscure articles he had stumbled across in the last few months relating to widespread criminal activity stemming from a base in Bucharest.

What he'd read, and hadn't been able to verify, were the extensive rumors that Romania had become the obvious hub of an international prostitution ring that specialized in underage flesh and the name, Vescu, had recurred in a few of the stories he'd uncovered. Not that any of it was provable, yet.

It was evident that the illegal activity in an exclusive British establishment was somehow connected to the Vescu interests in prostitution and narcotics trafficking, which according to other news sources, had been expanding exponentially throughout Europe and Eurasia. The trail also led to corrupt governments, particularly in Eastern Europe, parts of Asia and into Africa, where officials turned a blind eye to the lucrative business of drugs and arms dealings and the sex trade. Interestingly, each of those countries staffed dynamic offices of the Free State Foundation that were hip-deep in the political process of fledgling 'democratic' governments.

Toddy examined more closely the representative states of the protected individuals involved in the London exposé. Something about them struck a chord... what was it? He sat back in his chair and stared at the screen, mulling over the names of the countries. Australia, Namibia, the United States, Dominican Republic, Burkina Faso, Yemen... There was a tie between them that he recognized.

Wait a minute.

They all fit except one. Yemen. What was he doing there? Because the link was gold.

He bolted upright in his seat and looked harder at the screen, then began typing away, pulling up lists from his research on gold and gold mining.

There it was... Altamont. It had major ventures in each of those countries, except Yemen. Yemen didn't produce anything except sand. Their oil reserves depleting rapidly, the few wealthy had been shifting their fortunes over to gold.

Maybe that was the connection.

He jumped up and hanging his head out of the door of the den, he called for Solana to join him. When she walked into the room she could feel the excited tremor in his actions as he sat at the computer and pulled up all of the different articles that substantiated his premises for tying FSFoundation to the scandal in Britain. He began explaining about his little discovery as she leaned over his shoulder to study the articles he had opened.

"Wait. You're moving too fast. I can't see what you're doing."

Unable to slow himself down, he just pulled his fingers away from the keyboard and turned to tell her what he located instead. She came around to the sit on the couch and listen to the semi-convoluted train of events that brought him to recognize the Romanian vice lord and how it connected in to the influence of the Scirras empire.

"Philanthropic organization, my ass," she spewed with indignation. "What kind of man sets up a foundation to support the development of newly democratized nations only to undermine them for the purpose of gain?"

"Someone like Scirras," said Toddy more calmly than he felt. He agreed with Sol but was a little stunned by the vehemence of her response. "He never was about helping people to achieve higher levels of self-determination. He's always been about instituting ways of exercising power." He took a deep breath which seemed to encourage Sol to do the same. "There's something in his make-up that makes him believe he has the far superior intellect and should use his vaunted intelligence to guide humanity toward his vision of what is right and proper for society. The guy never did believe in an open society except for himself."

They were both quiet for a few moments.

"So, what do you think?" He asked her.

"What I think is that you need to go forward and make all the connections. And refer back to the information about the Rosalia Monteyn gold operation in Transylvania. It all points to throwing the weight of big government around in order to bring the small communities into line, even if it means financial ruin and suffering for individuals, because to someone like Scirras, they are only there to serve, not be served. And certainly not have a voice in what their lives should be like." Sol paused, then said, "If it's at all possible, you have to reach as many as you can through the public forum. As big as he is, you may not be able to touch him but you may be able to cause him some discomfort."

Taking Sol's advice, Toddy penned a vituperative dissertation that demonstrated how the prostitution and drug trade ring in Romania was operating under unrestricted protection due to the influence of the FSF funds wending its way into official pockets. The 'free state' or open society was a misnomer for deregulating vice while enforcing restrictions on individual productivity. It was all tied to control… controlling people through their tendencies toward indulgence and controlling people through their need to provide a living for their family. By either route, freedom was limited – substance abuse and sex was thralldom for some and restrictive measures limiting a productive life enthralled others. It was all slavery in Toddy's estimation.

This posting caused more of a stir when it came up on the computer's desktop confronting the CEO at the Seattle headquarters making connections to organized crime that went beyond the pale. His assistant took his time entering the finance guru's bastion, hoping to allow a little breathing room before he was cornered on the subject of the offending website. He knew what was coming and he knew that he didn't have a satisfactory response for the quietly seething man who had called him on the carpet.

The interrogation began with a simple inquiry. Where did this blogger get all this information?

The answer was only going to fan the fire but he had no choice.

The information came out of some obscure news stories that ran in Britain and Europe, he told his boss. It's all over the web because more than one researcher unearthed the stories. The assistant informed him that they had managed to disable more than thirty sites that were carrying the Vescu story as a headline, cutting off further dissemination.

The CEO asked simply, "What about this one?" while punching the air toward the computer screen.

The second-in-command sighed and confessed that this particular website had been much more of a problem. They've been after it for weeks and unable to shut it down.

The man behind the desk was emotionless as he told his assistant to put all their resources on it. "Find this man."

Anyone else would have considered his turning his back on his assistant as rude. The assistant understood how that was just his way and left as the CEO brooded on the corollary effect of the website's influence while gazing into the depths of the waters below.

Even Nolan was taken off-guard.

When Zeke Arris drove up and lumbered up the front steps no one knew he was coming.

Realizing that his clients were probably getting antsy at being stashed away on a lonely mountain in the middle of Idaho, Arris decided to pay a call to make certain that they were behaving themselves. He also wanted to check on the current security measures personally, understanding how even the most vigilant operatives can become lax when nothing occurs to keep them on their toes. What really put him on the track to drop in, however, had been the fact that he had been keeping abreast of Toddy's postings to the website and the last one had him worried.

Walking straight past the duty guard with only a brief nod of acknowledgment between them, Zeke found the den without any trouble. The noise from the television and talk radio filtered through the doorway at once, all of it overlaid with the tap, tap, tap of a computer keyboard, fingers constantly in motion.

Standing in the doorjamb, both hands on his hips and looking as imperious as a former boxer could, Zeke stated without any niceties, "What the hell are you thinking going after Scirras like that?"

Without even looking up, Toddy replied over his shoulder, "Hey, Bubba, nice of you to drop in, say 'hi' and all."

"Bubba? You are out to get a good ass-kicking, aren't you."

"Me? No way, man. I would never taunt a guy like you with fists that are bigger than my free weights," he grinned into the computer where Zeke couldn't see him.

"Fine, you idiot. Just tell me why you did such a moronic thing as to goad the devil," he sauntered in and sat heavily on the couch.

"It's my job?" Toddy offered pathetically.

"Well, you're making *my* job damn near impossible."

"Nah. You can keep us safe. It's working so far."

"That was before, when you were just a small irritant," said Zeke pointedly. "Now, you've gone and equated one of the most powerful men in the world to that of a pimp and a drug pusher. You don't think that's gonna push some buttons?" He settled back into the cushions. "I think you just crossed the line. If he was willing to come after you when you had just gotten this thing started, I'd say that the effort will be magnified a thousand percent, boy. You just upped the ante."

"How do you know it was Scirras who came after us the first time? Personally, I think it was the Kasili protection squad." He stopped what he was doing and looked Zeke squarely in the eye. "You're probably right about this, though. Scirras will be on the warpath."

"And that makes you feel, how? Good? Important? Like the utter ass that you are?" Zeke sat forward and glared at Toddy who didn't shirk.

"None of the above. I'm doing what I'm supposed to be doing because nobody else will take on the Great White Shark, gnashing teeth and all." He sighed and sat back. "I have the resources to do this when no one else does and certainly no one else is willing." He looked deep into his friend's eyes. "If not me, then who?"

"Oh, hell," said Zeke as he relaxed into the sofa and ran his hands over his bristly hair. "It's just that I'm concerned not so much about you but everyone else who is in the ring of fire."

"They've made their own decision as to where they will stand on this issue. I haven't forced anyone into this situation. They all came willingly."

"Fine. Get up and come with me. I'm going with Nolan to check the property and want more information from you on this whole set-up. This can't go on forever."

As they were exiting the house while Nolan went to get the truck, Cisco drove up with his wife.

Zeke went ballistic when he saw the very pregnant Lainie clamber down out of the cab of her father-in-law's rig, the little Honda they owned had become uncomfortable for any distance travel. He drew them both aside and read them the riot act about allowing her to visit at a locale that was dangerous to both her and her child. When he tried to forbid her to stay, she dug in her heels, crossed her arms across the top of her belly and stared him down with a look that simply made him throw up his hands in defeat and follow Toddy out to where Nolan waited.

"You're all nuts," said Zeke as he climbed in the truck, "the whole lot of you."

Nolan just grinned as he put the vehicle in gear and headed out to the perimeter track.

Chapter 41

Toddy returned from town with Russ after having made another posting to the website, only to find Sol slumped on the sofa, channel surfing and seriously bored.

She'd been following developments in the campaign and was slightly amused at the attempts Kasili was making to appear that he was edging toward the center of the political aisle.

"Right," she mumbled under her breath, "like anyone's going to believe that."

It wasn't but a few minutes later she had to laugh outright as she caught him in a blatant denial that he was doing exactly that, trying to look more like a centrist.

"What's so funny?" Toddy asked as he came into the room.

"Listen to this," and she 'rewound the tape' via Tivo.

"People keep saying that I am moving to the center. Not just from the right but from my friends on the left. Those people haven't been listening to me," said Kasili. "I am definitely progressive."

She went back to the current news.

"Uh huh. He has waffled on foreign policy, calling enemy states non-threats one day and "grave threats" the next. Who would think he was moving to the center?" She stopped for a second to catch another statement before moving on. "But he's right. No matter how much he tries to sound moderate, it's not going to work. He's not only liberal through and through, he's a Marxist when it comes to fiscal policy. The more government the better."

"You ought to write a piece for the website. We could use some more from another viewpoint."

"May as well, I'm not getting anything else accomplished here. Even checking in periodically with the tribal paper has been nothing but depressing. Drury hardly needs me except for the pieces I submit to make sure they have some real news in there."

"You're kidding, right?" said Toddy as he came to sit next to her and put his arm around her. "They're suffering down there, which is why he's always hounding you via e-mail to decide what to run and who to assign where." He kissed her forehead as she laid her head on his shoulder. "Drury knows his way around the hardware and the software but he's not a newsman. They'll be glad to have you walk back in that door."

She almost collapsed with the fatigue of hiding out day after day, she wanted to just say the hell with it all and go back to being a normal human being. Instead she allowed herself to take in a little bit of the determination that Toddy conveyed, and let herself be held for a while, enjoying the close relationship they had forged over the past month.

Pulling herself out of the comfortable embrace, she went over to her computer to compose something addressing how minorities should beware the snake charmer. Her points resonated on how Kasili didn't actually represent minority equality, that instead his pet policies would gut minority progress as reaching the level of truly competing in a capitalist society, creating even more dependence on government programs for support.

She pointed out that his attempts to garner support by infusing the guilt factor was a racist strategy. She delineated his differences from the true minority experience in that he had lived a privileged existence of private schools and exclusive colleges, that he hadn't struggled to get ahead through competing in the classroom or the work force.

Further attacking his favored policies, she painted Affirmative Action as a backfired program that created an underclass of lackluster achievers who were denied the opportunity of learning how to compete in the free market by, instead, being sponsored through school and job hunting – that quotas defeat the purpose of pitting experience and ability against those of other contestants.

She addressed how 'green' policies quash business potential and growth, placing minorities at an even bigger disadvantage when they can't develop a financial 'stake' in order to compete. For example she used the Native Americans who were working to develop the resources they had at hand but were being deterred by 'green' policies that blocked their endeavors. The environmental lobbies were breaking the back of clean coal and mining that would benefit tribal populations and their governments.

Further 'green' policies were forcing up the price of fuel and food, restraining forward economic motion by costing citizens more for the basics of life, thereby hamstringing the progress of every citizen, not just the minorities.

Sol concluded by tying it all to the liberal agenda of Kasili's wish to apply heavy-handed entitlement programs that would pressure the individual citizen to meet requirements to the point of losing the drive to be productive at all. Using guilt to acquire votes because he is a man of color had no place in today's political spectrum. Individual character of the candidates and the policies they have supported in the past are what she said should draw a voter's attention. Let their record be the basis of deciding how to cast a ballot, because even listening to what the candidate said did not ensure that they would follow through, in fact, it's most likely that they would not, particularly if the story changed with each speech. Look to their history for the true tale, she said.

Toddy took the piece and lauded her for giving an opinion expressed from that of a minority perspective.

"I think we need to include this in the next posting. Maybe it will resonate with minority voters and whites who are clamoring for 'change' but haven't taken the time to challenge what Kasili is really saying, that he would institute policies that will plunge the country into an economic bust by breaking the backs of the producers to support the growing phalanx of non-producers... his cry to tax the rich even more while giving tax-breaks to 95% of the people, all those who pay little or nothing as it is. The guy needs a math lesson.

"Yeah, well, Ayn Rand would be proud," she smiled weakly.

Russ and Toddy left for town so that he could upload the new posting at the college. Sol was envious as the two drove down the mountain leaving her abandoned in a deck chair with nothing to do other than read a book.

Beyond following the campaign and trying to keep up on the more unsavory activities of some of Kasili's cohorts and backers, all Sol was able to do was ride, walk and read. So, as Toddy was heading out she gave him a list of favorite authors in order for him to pick-up a few novels to keep her occupied during the long, long days of solitude. She was going stir crazy not having left her grandparents' lodge but once over the month since they had fled Las Vegas, and it was a trial to be stuck in the boonies with so little to keep her busy.

Sol jumped up when the two men returned from their foray into civilization, meager as it was in North Idaho. They pulled some groceries out of the rig and traipsed into the kitchen to set down the special items they'd purchased for dinner that night.

She started unpacking one of the bags, curiously rummaging through the contents to see what Toddy had planned for supper. "Maybe I can help with dinner tonight," she held up a jar of marinated artichoke hearts to examine the light filtering though the liquid. "What have you got planned?"

"I thought you didn't like to cook?"

"Yeah, well, sitting on the porch all day makes me feel like an old granny, rocking and knitting socks for the babies," she said with slight scorn.

He turned to her. "Where are your needles? In all this time you could have knitted me a sweater by now." Examining her more thoroughly, he added, "Forget it. You hardly look like someone's grandma."

"Don't worry. You're not going to get one, either. I don't knit and I'm not domestic." She looked over her shoulder at him from her position of checking through the other grocery bag. "Maybe I'll get you a deer this season and you can make jerky. Hunting is my idea of domestic activity. Hmmm, and you cook, so, sounds like teamwork to me," she snickered.

He just shook his head and pushed her away from the sack to continue unpacking the ingredients for dinner.

Chapter 42

Checking on changingwind.org had become a habit among the managers of the Kasili campaign. There was a constant worry that the blogger would reveal some new and possibly devastating information that other internet researchers would tap into and circulate through their own sites. So far, headquarters had been able to counter most of the moves on the side of those hoping to trip up Kasili's rise in the polls, and although his numbers had not skyrocketed meteorically the way they had expected, they had been able to counteract much of the harmful information. The ties of Scirras to organized crime rings in Eastern Europe had been steadily dropping off the internet, although some sites were more diligent than others. The fact that Scirras' money was feeding Kasili's campaign was considered common knowledge by this time, so the information could be deemed as injurious to the candidate.

This morning, the campaign manager read through the article that was obviously written by another person. The style was different making it evident that it was composed by someone who was not only a member of a minority group, but who was vociferously calling for minorities to shy away from the siren call of Kasili. The author was clear in leveling charges that Kasili had sold his minority status to the highest bidder in an attempt to conjure up a race loyalty and a white guilt vote based on his color and not on his abilities, which they found to be seriously lacking.

He was livid and his face matched the color of his flaming red hair. The last thing they needed was for more minorities to skewer Kasili for not being representative of their cause, even though he wasn't.

He called the committee in for a meeting.

"We need to outline a strategy to counter allegations like these that our man is insensitive to the causes of minorities despite his heritage." He leaned back into the cushions of the couch. "Ideas. Give me some."

The room fell quiet for a few minutes while the group pondered the problem.

A young woman who had been hunched over a copy of the offending article, reading the content asked without looking up, "Did anyone notice the specific allusion to Native American issues? Whoever this is didn't harp on African-American or Hispanic concerns. Those were generalized… but the Indian tack…"

A light went off in the campaign manager's head. "Native American?"

"Yeah, Rick. Read it again."

"No need. I think I just solved this little quandary," and he shooed everyone out of the room to go make a call.

A telephone receiver stuck in his ear as he scrolled through the changingwind.org website past postings and comments, Kasili's campaign manager was asking his contact in Seattle if he'd read the most recent article posted at the site.

The second-in-command at the financial center moved to his computer and pulled up the story in question. He was tired of hearing about this turkey who kept driving new nails in his coffin. With each new complaint his stomach reacted with an eruption of acid that was sending him to the doctor more often than he thought possible, and he popped another Maalox as he read the page. He knew he was going to die of a burst colon or something equally as ugly and painful. That is if his boss didn't dispose of him in his own nasty fashion, not that he had any real evidence that the man did that sort of thing. He just assumed so, by what he said. And he specifically remembered the "final solution" comment.

A shiver ran down his spine and he read on.

He asked Rick what the problem was, aside from the usual vicious diatribe.

Kasili's manager noted the fact that the author seemed to be writing from the perspective of a member of a minority, Native American in particular.

Hackles went up on the assistant's nape and he asked if Rick thought this might be the Indian journalist that dogged Kasili weeks ago.

"That's what my gut tells me."

"So you're thinking that she may be the connection for tracking down the blogger." His hopes were raised just a bit. "Do you know where she is?"

"Not a clue. We lost her weeks ago in Vegas."

"Good enough," he replied, hopes dashed again, and hung up. Of course, now he had to tell the old man about the connection, a duty he definitely wished that he could avoid. *May as well get it done.* And he popped another antacid, leaving the office with as much alacrity as he could muster, which was none.

The timing of the article's release on changingwind.org couldn't have been more ill-timed. The polls had stayed flat since Eddinger had introduced his running mate, the vibrant mayor of Phoenix, Risa Cristóbal. The fact that she was in her prime, popular at home, a woman *and* Hispanic was hurting Kasili who had snubbed his sure-fire trek to the White House when he bypassed Castor for the number two spot on the ticket. Anytime his team made mention of it, the candidate shut them down with a solid, "no way in hell" would he have surrendered his campaign to the overbearing witch, saying that she would have run roughshod over his agenda with her own. There could be no compromise where the governor was concerned.

Not that it mattered now.

It was too late for regrets, but this new blog that painted him as actually being supportive of programs that hinder the ability of minorities to achieve real success, despite his background, was supplying ammunition to the opposition. Even Dean Castor, who had been something of a schmoozer in the previous democratic administration and well loved by the general populace, was throwing fat on the fire by obviously taking the rebuff personally.

The result? His numbers were slipping and Kasili's campaign manager was adamant that he swallow some of that pride and call in Castor for help.

Kasili was too stubborn and had reached a point where his ego trumped his good sense, though his lead advisor was beginning to doubt that Kasili had ever exhibited any such thing.

Taking his unwelcome advice with him back to his own office, he placed another call to the Seattle office, this time to plead for help, a slight case of panic slipping in under his not-so-calm exterior.

Once again chatting with the office director, he laid out the problem clearly and concisely. The election was less than two months off and the republicans were gaining more than was comfortable. He just asked point blank, "What can be done? We have too much invested here."

"I'll talk to the CEO about the problem," he promised and ended the call while deciding when to approach his superior about this new angle on the same dilemma. He knew that he couldn't wait long.

Still dealing with the first aspect of the website riddle, the office director followed through by placing his own call to a man in the organization's employ who had returned to D.C. weeks ago to regroup and rejoin the Kasili security team.

They discussed the fruitless search that had been conducted so far to locate the origins of the maverick website. The operative commiserated without stating anything other than concurring that the blog had become a thorn that was burying itself deeper than ever into the side of the campaign hierarchy. Although he didn't say as much, he'd been getting tired of the constant bellyaching at headquarters. No one would take responsibility for anything, least of all Kasili.

The Seattle finance leader's assistant told him that they might have a lead on a cold trail.

The operative said nothing, though his eyebrows went up in question, the man on the other end of the line couldn't see it. He volunteered the information anyway since that was the reason he called the operative in the first place. The speculation was that a posted article was actually written by the Indian journalist the operative had been tailing weeks ago until the search had been let go as unimportant. Find her and they may find the blogger.

The operative replied with a brief, "We're on it."

Chapter 43

The basement office that was no larger than a tennis court had the feeling of dusty air-conditioned drear. A drab grey coated every-thing from the walls and cabinets to the myriad of computer terminals that bulged from every conceivable cranny, most sitting unused and unoccupied by operators, many which were ignored as out-dated. Spread among the flotsam were six techs typing at the speed of light, hunting up whatever information they could on their different quests for truth and the American Way.

Entrenched in a cubicle that was tucked in the far corner sat a skinny kid with lank hair, a nose ring and a tattoo with the word 'Mom' inscribed on his wrist. He had three monitors surrounding his miniscule space and he constantly scanned the swift changes that slipped across the screens, seeking a hint for what he was hoping would appear. He hit the 'return' button on his keyboard after rapidly typing in another lengthy command.

Watching the main screen directly in front of him go through what looked like a minor glitch before settling on a visual that made sense to no one else but himself, he let a loud whoop of exultation escape his mouth while circling his fist in the air.

The noise stabbed through the otherwise quiet room, disturb-ing only the team manager. Everyone else was too absorbed in their work and ignored the disruption simply because they hadn't noticed it. He looked up from his own workstation and saw the kid, who wasn't a kid at all but a graduate from Georgetown University who had just celebrated his thirtieth birthday, he just didn't know how to dress like an adult. Not that his personal style meant much where they worked. The 'kid' was a wiz on the computer and that's all that counted in this office.

The team manager hefted his bulk from his chair and trundled over to check out the reason for the merriment. Overweight and exhausted by high blood pressure that was a result from too many stressful years as an underpaid government drudge, he positioned himself behind the kid's shoulder.

"What's all the excitement about?"

"I think I located an upload point for the website you've had us trying crack forever," he said proudly.

"Yeah?" The team leader tried to sound interested, but frankly, the rationale behind hunting down some idiotic political blog was lost on him. Waste of time, in his opinion.

"Took a hell of a lot of tracking. This guy is good and usually brief in his work, but this time he was online longer than usual," he started to explain his methodology, not that his superior really cared all that much. "I was backtracking through the ISP's and found one that is pretty close to the region that was given us to check out. You know that directive that just came through about a subject that might be in Idaho? I think we received a home and work address that came up empty, but I used them as a starting point for the search anyway." He started typing in some more commands while he talked. "You know sometimes it's the obvious answer staring us in the face."

"So, what did you find?" He was getting a little exasperated at the explanation.

"I found a college near the two locations. Even if there's no one home, so to speak, it looks like someone is still hanging around the area and uploading the blog.

"Look here. This is the home address and there hasn't been any phone or internet activity at that location, but," and he keyed in some new commands bringing up another screen with address listings. "The subject has relatives in the area. The name Greyfisher is pretty uncommon and easy to trace. See this place? It's outside of the town by quite a few miles but it has satellite and according to the log here, the uplinks are almost constant."

The team leader hunched over the kid to look at the log-on file from the address. "Whose place is it?"

"Looks like the grandparents. How many grandmas are that internet savvy?"

"You'd be surprised but it looks like they're connected continuously. Someone's doing research," he said confidently. "Good work kid."

Chapter 44

Everything seemed to be moving along at a dull clip. The weather had been sultry and no one had been particularly energetic. No changes in the situation had occurred and everything was fairly tranquil.

Taking advantage of some quiet time, Russ Tarlington booted up the communal computer and decided to check out the website to see what Toddy had been up to. Reading through the newest article he noticed that the style was different, more coherent in his judgment since Toddy had a tendency to run-on sentences that often lost Russ' attention, no matter how cogent his arguments. As he continued through the piece, he hadn't noticed anything much except for the writing technique as being more objective in word usage. Before long he realized there was a little bit of a change in the direction of the article in that it appeared to be written from a Native viewpoint.

He muttered a few choice expletives as he went to find Toddy, remembering as he was halfway down the hall that he and Solana had gone out for a ride.

He dashed out the front door and hopped on a four-wheeler that was always standing by, taking off in the general direction he believed they had gone earlier.

How long have we got? He was going through his mind the fact that the posting was made to the website the day before yesterday. If Toddy and Nolan's intuition was correct and it was rogue Secret Service behind the first attack, they were facing a real problem. Those people likely were tapped into government resources with an unlimited database at their disposal. This was not good.

Bouncing down the trail, he grasped his radio and thumbed the switch bringing it to life. Nolan came up on the other end where he and Cisco were out doing a perimeter check. He asked them which trail Toddy and Sol had followed, quickly explaining that they may have a situation on the horizon. Nolan picked up immediately on the possible breach of security that had occurred and closed the connection in order to organize the crew that was on the hill for maximum protection.

As Tarlington said, "Out," he allowed his temper to briefly get the best of him, shaking his head in disgust. He was pissed that everyone, including himself, had gotten so lax in their vigilance. *Vigilance? What Vigilance!* And he angrily accelerated in the direction Cisco had supplied, hoping to reach the two before his worst fears became a reality.

Sol and Toddy had been out just half an hour, meandering at a slow pace along the rim trail, their two mounts measuring their strides as they sauntered along abreast of one another. It had been a pleasant day with the overall temperature dropping ten degrees from the heat wave they had been enduring. A good afternoon for a calm ride overlooking the river as it moved more sluggishly now that they were well into the summer doldrums, the high water having passed its crest a couple weeks ago.

The conversation was as blasé as the day, maundering from how they would usually spend their summers to family and who was where, doing what. In that regard, Toddy didn't have much to offer, his family having pretty much written him off as too eccentric, which was a point of some pain for him although he'd accepted it years ago.

Sol, on the other hand lamented the fact that she wasn't able to spend the time she liked with her family being spread out in Montana and, for now, banished from their own home.

They chatted about what they planned to do as soon as they were freed from their voluntary exile. They were just reaching the subject of steelhead fishing when they heard the roar of a two-stroke engine approaching from behind.

The noise spooked Toddy's gelding, but Sol reflexively grabbed his reins before the skittish horse could escape the increasing noise by shooting off down the trail. She pulled them to the side of the track and calmed the horses while Tarlington pulled up next to them.

Staring the newcomer down with a look of reproof, Sol continued to soothe the mounts as Toddy's gut told him that something was definitely amiss.

Attempting to sound lighthearted he asked Russ what all the fuss was about.

Setting aside any greeting, Tarlington went right to the meat of the matter. "Who wrote that last article on the blog?"

Sol arched her brow, curious now rather than ticked.

"Was it you?" He looked directly up at her as she sat astride the Appaloosa mare.

"Yes. What's the problem?"

"Not much aside from the fact that you just waved a huge red flag," his voice was measured in his irritation.

"I don't see how," said Toddy, feeling protective and a trifle guilty for what was looking to be a mistake in judgment by the look on Russ' face.

Frustrated at the denseness of such a smart man, he explained, "They're looking for the known entity and that's Solana. That article is so obviously written by someone with ties to Native Americans it wouldn't take any leap of genius to connect her to the website. Particularly if they had a hunch there was one in the first place."

"So what's the trouble? You're not making any sense to me," retorted Toddy.

"Shit, you two." He took a deep breath in order to gain a little composure. "They probably weren't looking too hard for her because she fell off the map, dropped out of sight and wasn't causing any more trouble, figuring they'd scared her silent. But you," and he skewered Toddy with his glare, "they've been trying night and day to shut you down. You saw that when they tried to hack into your system."

"And they couldn't get in, either," he replied proudly. "I've got it set-up so they'd have a damn hard time closing me down. They still can't get into the site."

"How sure are you?"

"Well, I can't be a hundred percent but the odds are in my favor," he was beginning to back down a little.

"Well, now they know who to look for... Sol. They find her, they know they'll find you. You just let the cat out of the bag and they're gonna shut you down the hard way."

Toddy crumpled under the weight of realizing the enormity of their blunder. "Oh, God. We didn't think..."

"Damn right, you didn't. For such a damn genius you may

have compromised our position," spat Tarlington. He was beyond furious now when he saw the look of shock on Sol's face.

Toddy was distraught and the feeling was telegraphing to his horse who until now had become fairly calm. The uneasiness of his rider was causing the gelding to become restless. Toddy sat up and firmly took the horse's reins, trying to console his mount with determined action. It seemed to be working.

"What now? Any reason to believe we're in danger?"

Russ looked out over the valley as evening began to fall. The two had ridden out to watch the sunset over the river but the news had changed their plans as Tarlington radioed Nolan with their position and to get an update.

"It's all clear here. Bring in the errant riders immediately so we can assess the situation further," ordered Nolan through the crackle of the radio.

Russ looked over at the two riders. "Good. I see that you have your shotgun," he said as he noted its placement in the saddle holster. "Small arms too?"

Sol patted the gun that was stuck in the waistband of her jeans at the small of her back.

"Even better. Give the pistol to Toddy in case we get separated, but stay close."

Toddy looked perplexed. "But he said it was "all clear," right?"

"Right, but that doesn't mean we shouldn't be prepared. They've had two days to try to locate Sol and if you and Eric were correct in your assessment, we've got potential trouble from independent operators within the Secret Service. We shouldn't underestimate them."

Sol and Toddy both blanched at the thought of the danger they may have brought down on everybody. First one and then the other reset their features in a hard cast and Toddy accepted the gun from Sol, sliding it into his own waistband.

"All right," said Russ, approvingly. "Let's go."

Leading the way, Tarlington motored back down the trail toward the house. Over the past month they'd been staying at Sol's grandparents' she'd been tutoring Toddy in riding skills and he'd become fairly proficient on horseback, which came in handy now as they picked up the pace to a trot and then a canter.

They had just reached a stand of pines before the fields opened up toward the house and the barn when they heard the steady whomp of helicopter rotors chopping through the air.

"Time to move!" yelled Russ.

The track had widened out and the horses were side-by-side picking up speed as they felt the riders lean down and grip their thighs into their ribs, urging them faster, Toddy's horse just naturally following the gait of the mare slightly ahead of him. Toddy had only been at a gallop a couple of times but didn't have the luxury of feeling panicked about making the run for the barn. He just grimaced and hung on with everything he had.

They followed Russ as he gunned the four-wheeler for the weathered old building that sat on one end of the five acres of pasture surrounding the lodge. The corral where the horses were usually penned was empty and a helicopter, clean of any distinguishing marks, occupied the abutting front lawn, rotors continuing to swing at a steady pace.

They rode toward the door of the barn as the dusk faded toward black. They could see that the house was dark, the only flashes piercing the shadows were those following the staccato blasts of gunfire that appeared to be aimed at the front door.

The din of the helo turned out to be opportune in covering the racket of the ATV as Tarlington drove up to the barn. He jumped off the quad and swung open the oversized gate built to accommodate horses and farm equipment, standing aside as Sol and Toddy rushed inside. Having made it to relative safety without incident, Russ rolled the ATV into the barn and locked up behind him, indicating that the two of them take care of the horses who were on edge from all the noise and anxiety.

Sol quietly settled the mare as Toddy did his best to soothe the gelding while removing the saddle. Taking them to separate stalls, Sol went back to the saddle and slid the shotgun from its place and pumped it. Toddy followed suit by reaching behind his back and pulling the unfamiliar weapon from his waistband. Russ gave them directions to take cover behind a stall door while he kept his position by the man door.

Gunfire erupted from closer to the barn and muzzle flashes could be seen through the window coming from both the front and rear of the house. More shots were coming from the trees. None of them could make out who was who and they simply stayed quiet waiting for some indication as to where the assault team was and whether they were advancing on their position in the barn.

Toddy was stiff with fright and anxiety over Sol's safety as the two of them crouched behind the stall door. Although she had never been under fire before other than their experience in Las Vegas, Sol had her face in a stoic mask, clasping the shotgun in readiness without clamping down on the trigger. It was Toddy that Russ was concerned about since his knowledge of handguns was almost nil, though he had insisted on a few lessons since their arrival in Idaho. It was kind of funny that Toddy had actually turned out to be an intuitive marksman. Maybe it was all the years of playing video games, thought Tarlington incongruously as mayhem reigned all around.

The view out of the barn window indicated that the house was surrounded by a gunfight that was beginning to look like the OK Corral. Tarlington was able to make out some figures in the trees who, when they fired, he was able to see that they were part of the local posse of tribal members. They all carried rifles and some had pistols as well, Russ knew. What he didn't know, was that Cisco had called in some capable neighbors as soon as Russ had radioed them about the breach in the website's anonymity and the recruits were in the trees flanking Cisco and Seth.

Looking toward an outbuilding, Tarlington saw Nolan make a dash to crouch behind it, rifle drawn and leveling it to fire toward the idling helicopter. The home team was cautiously surrounding the assaulters who had found the house empty upon entry.

Acting in desperation, two of the attackers peeled off from the main assault detail and ran toward the barn, thinking to find their quarry holed up inside. Luckily, one of the men, who was outfitted wholly in black, held his rifle low and in front of him as he sprinted across the open field. The first layers of stars had emerged, and in the depths of the country they emitted a fair amount of light, enough to flicker off the metallic length of the rifle barrel, giving away his position. Tarlington found him in that sliver of light and pulled the trigger, felling the assailant. The other one dove for the ground and fired into the barn, hoping to catch the sniper in retaliation.

Realizing the cause was lost, the two that were caught in the open began crawling back toward the helicopter, under the covering fire of two of the team standing near the aircraft. As soon as they deemed it safe enough, they jumped to their feet and began running for the chopper, the wounded man holding his side and loping awkwardly.

The rest of the assault team darted from the house and climbed aboard while the helo began lifting off the ground. Two of Cisco's crew dashed from the trees to take a couple of shots at the bird as it pulled up, hitting the skids and the fuselage. The shots didn't slow the ascent of the helicopter as it banked and was gone.

Gold Baron

Chapter 45

The relative silence in the aftermath of adrenaline pumping mayhem left the subjects of the attack upset and bereft of a connection to reality.

Toddy and Sol made their way back to the horses to finish taking care of their needs, brushing them down and just handling them with a gentleness that soothed both the horses and themselves. The routine activity was cathartic after the staccato blasts of gunfire and the constant whup-whup-whup of the helicopter rotors slicing the air, standing ready to depart. Now all they heard were the low voices and subdued calls of the survivors as they walked the grounds to ascertain that all of the assault team had been extracted and no one was wounded or lying in wait.

Nolan entered the rear man door, rifle slung over his shoulder and holstering his handgun as he pushed the door open with his hip. He made note of the two writer-researchers as they tended to the horses, fetching hay and hauling the saddles back to the tack room. Gesturing Tarlington to the side, he spoke in an undertone about the rebuffed attack, while keeping a wary eye roving from Sol and Toddy to the clean-up activities outside the barn.

"We got off easy with that one," said Nolan as he fastened the holster closed, assuming, he hoped correctly, that there would be no more need of his gun for at least the rest of the night. Even so, he had the rifle ready for battle.

"If you say so," answered Tarlington as he glowered in the general direction of Sol and Toddy who were mechanically going through the motions of tidying up the barn. They obviously weren't ready to deal with anything outside of the confines of the secure building.

Nolan looked at him curiously. As well as he knew Russ, he hadn't expected him to be sullen about the incident. It wasn't like him to take a job personally, but then the passion of these two crusaders had sort of grown on everyone. Even he'd blurred the lines of friendship and employment over the weeks of forced seclusion. Mentally shrugging, he realized the impossibility of staying detached in such circumstances. Although this was a protective situation rather than hostage, it shed some light on the concept behind Stockholm syndrome.

"Look at the facts. There was no real damage to the house and no casualties on our side. So, I'd say yes, we were lucky." He looked up at the taller man, "Wouldn't you?"

Tarlington slid his left hand through his short hair, trying to wipe away some of the consternation and let out a breath that he didn't know he'd been holding. "Yeah, yeah. You're right."

"It's a damn good thing that you were checking on Toddy's blog, otherwise we would have been blindsided and this could have gone very differently," said Nolan. "We could all be dead." He dropped his hand on Russ' shoulder. "Thanks," he said sincerely.

Tarlington looked him in the eye. "You were right the first time. We were lucky." He switched his attention over to Toddy, who acknowledged him with a nod of thanks and Sol, who was avoiding looking at anything other than the horse she was petting.

Just when it seemed as though a calm were beginning to settle, Cisco barreled through the main entrance and ran over to Sol, grabbing her hands and, checking her up and down for injuries, breathlessly asked, "Are you okay, Auntie?"

Sol hadn't uttered a word since the noise had abated. She appeared to be a little shell-shocked so he just gave her a big hug, gripped Toddy's shoulder before leaving her in his arms and turned his attention to the detail leaders standing by the rear door.

Walking across the old wooden planks that had some hay strewn about here and there, Cisco approached and asked Nolan. "What now, boss?"

"We should button down the homestead." He looked out the open door. "I take it your cohorts are all fine. First report I got said everyone was unscathed."

"Yup, unless you consider a bonked head on one of the guys who collided with a tree branch in his hurry to get cover to shoot. Knocked himself cold and missed all the fun," he smiled mischievously, knowing that his buddy on the force would never live that one down. "It was pretty hard to see anything and a low hanging branch wasn't in the plan."

Russ smiled despite himself as he and Nolan continued conferring after the brief casualty report, Cisco listening in.

"It shouldn't take much to get everything tidied up. These guys aren't coming back after that aborted mess." Almost to himself, Nolan added, "Heads will roll for this fubar."

Tarlington heard him and agreed, "Bet on it."

They heard sirens pealing through the air and saw blue and red flashes from the light bars of the local police vehicles stabbing through the trees as the troops drove up the winding road from the valley.

"Well, here come the reserves," said Cisco, ironically.

"Better late than never," added Tarlington as he hitched the rifle further up on his shoulder and walked out to meet the new arrivals with Nolan. Cisco, glancing back to see that Toddy and Sol were managing all right, followed to meet his fellow officers from the tribe.

☀ ☀ ☀

Two of the neighbors came through the unlocked barn door leading the other three horses that they'd rounded up, having bolted when the assault began. The cow had been far enough from the action that she hadn't bothered to move and was still standing in the fenced pasture chewing passively on the grass. Sol came forward, thanking the men for catching the horses and led them to their stalls, locking them in for the night before feeding them.

Finally steeling themselves to face the rest of the crew, Toddy and Sol led the cow inside, closed up the barn and called the dogs who, being smart cowdogs, had disappeared during the firefight. They came running from a distant quadrant where they'd been hiding in the trees and circled Sol's ankles before settling down to follow them toward the house.

The little entourage of two humans and the dogs right on their heels, took their time walking the distance between the barn and the house. Sol was reticent to see what damage had been inflicted on her grandparents' belongings and the guilt she felt was nearly overwhelming her good sense in knowing that no one had been hurt.

Toddy sensed her discomfort and took her hand in his as they continued across the grounds. He could feel her relax just a little as he clasped her fingers with a gentle grip. Climbing the steps up the front porch, they could see that the front door had been busted in and the windows were shattered. A few bullet holes pierced the wood siding, though most riddled the door that was hanging at an odd angle.

Sol just stood there, gazing at the gaping wound in the front of the Greyfisher's home, the door looking like a twisted tongue lolling inside the open mouth of the house, the fragmented glass in the windows creating the look of a jack-o-lantern as the light spilled out from the living room, bathing the porch in an peculiar warmth that belied the violence of the scene.

The dogs just dropped themselves onto an outside rug that was near the deck chairs that were eerily undisturbed. They'd had enough excitement and were ready to lay down, though their eyes kept a cautious watch on all the activity.

After viewing the damage inflicted on the entry, Sol was prepared to encounter the worst scenario as they came through the gaping hole that used to be the front door.   She was surprised at the lack of harm that had been incurred on the interior of the house. There were a couple of bookcases overturned and some papers and magazines flung across the floor, but nothing of note except for a chair that lay on its side, the arms detached and partially crushed.

"Oh dear," said Sol, "Grandma's going to be upset that they broke her favorite rocker. That's where she sits to do her crosswords and knit."

Toddy gave her an odd sideways look when she mentioned knitting, wondering if Solana would ever see herself as following in her grandmother's footsteps of even semi-domesticity. *Nah, it's not in her make-up.* He smiled in spite of himself. He moved over to the crumpled piece of furniture to examine it more closely.

"I think I can fix this," he said as he pulled it upright and checked the construction of the armrests.

"Really?" she asked, beaming. She came over and hugged him in gratitude for just being able to make one thing right again. He returned the hug and they held on to the moment a bit longer than necessary, regaining some of the strength that had been missing a minute before. No one took any notice as Toddy backed off a little sheepishly even though Sol continued to smile and thank him for undertaking the repair.

Nolan came forward then and asked Toddy about the laptops. "Where did you leave them? I want to know if they removed them from the premises. They took the one that was in the kitchen."

Before Nolan finished asking his question, Toddy was off like a shot and into the den where he had been working most of the time. The televisions and other electronic equipment were untouched, but the household computer had been disconnected and removed, leaving the monitor sitting alone on the desktop.

Toddy ran into his bedroom and opened the closet door. He pulled a backpack from the shelf, looking for all the world like nothing more than a college kid's book bag, and unzipped it. His laptop was inside, along with a thick file of sheets that had been run off the printer.

"Looks like they grabbed the wrong computer," he said as he checked to see that it hadn't been touched.

"They didn't have enough time to comb through the place and just grabbed the obvious stuff," said Nolan as he sifted through a few things that were on the floor. "What about Sol's computer, where's that?"

"She kept hers in a suitcase under her bed. Have her check to see if it's still there."

"No need," Sol called from the doorway. "I already looked and they hadn't had time to disturb anything in the room, really. Pulled out a few drawers and tossed my underwear, but that's about it." She looked puzzled. "I can't imagine why they wouldn't have looked in the case."

Nolan shook his head with the same question. "No time, I guess. They were pretty hard pressed to get out once they got themselves pinned down without any hostages or coming anywhere near being able to complete their mission. I'd say our boys did a fine job of forcing them on their way empty-handed."

"Yes, thank God," said Toddy, running the fingers of both hands through his unruly mop in relief.

"Well, so far, so good," said Sol. "I need to do something normal so, I'm going to make coffee. You can deal with the police, or the sheriff, or whoever's out there, in getting the incident reported. I'm done for now," and she headed back to the kitchen, ignoring the officers who were trying to get a clear picture of what had occurred less than an hour ago.

With Solana in the kitchen and Russ handling the authorities with Cisco, Nolan closed in on Toddy, confronting him with the stupidity of his actions.

Hands on his hips, the shorter man was bristling with barely concealed fury at the danger that was scarcely averted through good luck rather than planning and preparation, making Toddy inadvertently take a step backwards.

"Have you any idea what your little stunt could have cost in lives?"

Toddy visibly slumped as he stood in the middle of the room, feeling trapped, more by his own thoughtlessness than by Nolan's fitting anger. "I hardly thought of it as a 'stunt.'" He answered lamely.

Nolan walked in a circle near the bedroom doorway. "That's the problem with you geniuses. You so smart, you don't think." He stopped in mid-track and speared Toddy with a look that was a cross between wrath and acceptance. "Common sense doesn't appear to be one of your strong suits."

Toddy lifted his shoulders with hands spread in surrender. "I thought that's why I called Zeke in the first place... to protect me from me."

"Oh hell," he barked a laugh. "It's impossible to stay angry at an idiot."

"I guess I earned that."

"Yeah. In spades," agreed Nolan.

"So, what do we do now? Move again?" asked Toddy, hoping against hope that they wouldn't have to go through the whole thing all over again.

"No. We have the cops up-to-date now that the bad guys have shown themselves and we're well situated on the reservation. No way are those clowns going to try it again since we'd be prepared this time. Even though we still don't know who authorized the assault, they'd be crazy to try anything again. They've lost the only advantage they had... surprise."

Toddy's face showed his relief in not having to pack up and move again.

"We're okay for now," added Nolan. "Particularly after Sol

does her job."

Toddy was perplexed. "Her job?"

"Yes. She's going to call the media and clue them in to what happened here. She's got to write an exclusive for that paper she strings for. What is it?

"The Statesman," supplied Toddy.

"Right. They'll love it. It'll be picked up nationwide that she was attacked at her family home *on the reservation* because of what? Her public scrutiny of a presidential candidate? Her posting of an article criticizing him on a website that's been going after Scirras and Kasili? No one's going to be able to prove any of those allegations but the fact that she has no ties to any criminal activity or major stories will narrow the field." He studied Toddy. "The press will have a heyday or they will do everything in their power to bury the story since they're in Kasili's pocket. Either way, it's the best protection you could get."

Toddy sat on the bed, thinking about the implications for Solana with all the attention that was going to be aimed at her. "How is this going to play out for the website and my identity. I don't really want to be worrying about coming out of the closet, so to speak, but which way should we play it? Should I come forward? Will it take the heat off of her?"

"I don't think it will compromise your identity and I'm not sure that it's necessary for you to step up yet. It would probably only cause more confusion and perhaps give them someone else to come after. This way, if Sol is the only known connection to the website, the visible front, if you'll pardon the expression, then it's easier to keep tabs on her family and ascertain their safety." He leaned back on the doorjamb and mulled it over some more. "I think what this does is legitimize the website without compromising the webmaster. For the time being, you're still anonymous. We'll see if that can be kept up as we go along."

"If it would be safer for Sol, I could move again."

Nolan shook his head, negating the suggestion. "Not yet. If you move, you'll be a target again and they may be able to track you if they keep their eyes on movement from this location. It'll probably make more sense for you to wait it out here. Besides we can beef up security, though they'd have to be total numbskulls to try anything here again." He motioned for Toddy to follow him out to the living room where he was going to need to talk to the local police. "Whoever sent that assault team out here has got a PR disaster on their hands. If they had pulled it off, the only thing that would be known was that there was some kind of raid and no one would have been alive to tell the tale. As it is they left a very able newswoman alive and well and ready to tell a helluva story." He walked down the hall. "Someone did not think this through and they are going to end up paying for it."

When they entered the living room, there were at least five officers from the tribal police, the county sheriff and one deputy milling around the overturned furniture. Tarlington and Cisco were keeping them at bay while Nolan shooed Toddy into the kitchen with Sol, keeping them away from any questioning for now.

By the time any kind of crime scene unit could arrive there wouldn't be any real evidence to gather. Not that the perpetrators had left much in the first place. Russ and Nolan had looked things over and already determined that the sortie had been extremely professional in their raid, not leaving anything behind that could be traced back to them. So Nolan was unconcerned whether or not a unit came to comb through things or not. It would be a wasted effort, in his opinion.

Cisco ran interference with the locals, being a member of the tribal force. He'd been instructed by Nolan to keep the police away from both Toddy and his aunt due to the sensitive nature of their identities. The sheriff didn't have any real jurisdiction on the reservation but was in attendance out of courtesy. Even so, he was a little put out at not being able to interview all of the individuals on the property and was making something of a fuss. Cisco and his fellow officers however, were very diplomatic in assisting Nolan to close up the report and conclude the second invasion for the night. Although the raid had been made by air, the fact that the property was so far away from neighbors and possible witnesses, there wasn't much the sheriff could do. All he really knew was that a helicopter had been seen coming into the area and then leaving not twenty minutes later. No one heard anything unless they were part of the piecemeal security force and none of them were talking tonight. In fact, by the time the authorities had made it to the site, most of the volunteer force had dispersed back home before they were embroiled in something that could get out of hand.

In the end, the tribal police had their way and the initial report was concluded, the sheriff headed down the mountain with fewer answers than he liked and a crime scene unit due to appear the next day. The sheriff made it clear that he would accompany them back up the mountain then, which 'suggestion' Nolan encouraged whole-heartedly.

After they finally left, Nolan had Sol call her grandfather to inform him of the 'problem' they had encountered so he wouldn't hear about it on the news since it had been broadcast across police bands in the area.

While Nolan, Tarlington and Cisco was keeping the police occupied, Toddy had tossed together some dinner for everyone who was left behind. By ten-thirty the house was quiet except for Cisco and Seth putting together a makeshift door for the front entry and taping plastic over the broken windows. They knew the sheriff would object when he arrived in the morning, but there was no help for it. Sol and Toddy couldn't leave the premises without putting themselves in danger, so they had to make do with the temporary fixes to keep the bugs out.

After the police left, Cisco called a few of the local crew back to pick up where they left off, patrolling the perimeter even though they were fairly certain the attackers wouldn't attempt a return foray.

While Toddy finished cleaning up in the kitchen, Nolan gave Sol her instructions and escorted her to her computer to fulfill her duty. She called her editor, Kathy, at home to inform her of the events of the evening and ask if she wanted a story for the next edition.

"Are you crazy? One of our own is under attack in the mountains by a paramilitary assault squad and I wouldn't want the exclusive?" Kathy's hoarse smoke-riddled voice came back over the phone line. "Chickie, you get that story written and get it done ASAP. I want it for the morning edition! Call me as soon as you're ready to e-mail it. I assume you can e-mail from that God-forsaken place you're inhabiting."

"Actually, yes," answered Sol. "For some reason they didn't take out the satellite dish. For professionals looking to shut us up, they managed to overlook the obvious avenues."

"Lucky for us. Stories like this don't fall into your lap every day," she said exultantly, then backpedaled. "Hey, hon, I'm sorry. I don't mean to sound insensitive. It's just… well, you know," she left off lamely. Something that Kathy would never do under normal circumstances. "You are all right, aren't you? You sound okay. I mean, I've never been shot at or anything."

"Yes, I'm fine. Sort of," said Sol unsurely even as she tried to sound positive. "I guess it's hard to say how I feel. I think I'm still in shock."

"Writing this will put you right back on track. You know how it is with news gals like you and me. Work puts us to feeling normal, even if you're smack in the eye of the storm." This, Kathy understood, having covered the disastrous Hurricane Camille almost forty years back when she was just a pup.

"All right, boss lady. I'm on it."

"Good girl. Call me when you're done. I'll be waiting."

She hunkered down to the task of describing the attack and the assumed rationale behind it. Solana kept tight rein on the personal perspective in the piece, determined to be unbending in her objective approach to a story where she was the main character. It was a tough job but she felt she had the competence to carry it out appropriately. This would become a major story by noon tomorrow and she had to place her personal feelings aside in order to portray the facts in the clearest light possible because she knew that she would be the one to suffer scrutiny. Once the mainstream press got wind of the fact that she was the author of the article on the website that continually criticized Kasili and Scirras, she'd be toast.

Oh well, someone's got to do the dirty work. And she continued typing her livelihood away.

Toddy heard the rapid clicking of the keys as Sol worked in the den, rapping out the story to get it sent off to her editor before midnight. He poked his head in the door and before he could ask how she was doing, decided that he didn't want to interrupt her train of thought. The evening had been nerve wracking enough, he didn't need to disturb her, possibly even startling her.

As he turned to leave, she looked over her shoulder and caught his eye. "I'm okay," she acknowledged somewhat wanly, but it was a positive answer all the same. What really knocked him for a loop was the fact that she had sensed his presence and knew what his inquiry was before he asked.

He just nodded in understanding and went back to the kitchen to make another pot of coffee for the crew that was on duty for the night. Though everyone was running in epinephrine overdrive since the assault. The whole of the incident had taken place in less than half an hour and yet the feel of the house and its occupants was an edginess that would keep everyone up for much of the night. Even knowing that the invaders wouldn't return wasn't enough to allow anyone the luxury of relaxing. Instead, Toddy was starting at any odd noise he heard. The professionals were less jumpy but even they weren't likely to let their guard down.

On top of it all, Toddy felt demoralized and dejected at having allowed their little stronghold to become a target. Flopping down at the kitchen table, he just leaned over and put his head in his hands, not exactly feeling sorry for himself but definitely feeling like an ass.

He looked up when he heard a full mug plunk down next to his elbows. He saw Nolan sitting down opposite him, a mug of hot coffee in his own hands as he indicated that Toddy drink some of the liquid he'd placed in front of him.

"The last thing that crossed my mind was that the *content* of the blog would give us away," said Toddy as he picked up the cup and sipped coffee he didn't really want.

"I can see that. You're busy writing political opinion and although it's personal because it affects you, the overtones don't indicate who you are or where you come from. You have a tendency to take the philosophical high road and point out the facts, although you can get a little emotional. But you don 't let on *who* you are. Solana's piece was unique because she'd already become a target and the website was under surveillance. Taking a look at the issues from the viewpoint of how they affect minorities, in particular a small one such as Native Americans, was like running across an orange buoy in an otherwise ordinary sea. It was conspicuous," asserted Nolan.

"Our passion sometimes takes us further than we expect to go. Like a riptide that catches us unaware and pulls us inexorably away from shore. We can stroke and stroke trying to regain our place, our equilibrium, but the strength of our beliefs takes us to new shorelines. Sometimes to places we'd rather not be."

Toddy looked at Nolan with an amazed expression. "Geez. You should be writing this, not me. I'm dull and boring trying to make a point. Maybe people would be reading more of what we post if it were stated a little more poetically."

"Yeah, well, I read a lot of different work and I do write some, but I'd never be able to verbalize the concepts that you're uploading every day." He drank some of the coffee deciding whether or not to let Toddy in on a secret. "The first book is with an agent now."

Toddy was fascinated and raised an eyebrow as he relaxed a little. "Tough guy turned writer, huh?"

"Hemingway, I'm not, but we all have dreams of retirement. Writing could be a good retirement plan, don't you think?"

"There are worse ideas. Like selling condos in Lake Havasu," said Toddy.

"Finish up. You need to get some sleep and Sol too. She can submit in the morning."

Toddy shook his head negating Nolan's idea of packing her off to bed. "Oh no, she'll finish the story first. Her editor's chomping at the bit." He got up. "I'll go wait for her in the den. She's fast and will probably be done before long. Good night and thanks for being our guardian angels. Heaven knows we need a few."

Chapter 46

It was late in the morning when Solana was finally able to pull herself away from the mattress that kept inviting her back for a little more rest. Instead of hitting the mental snooze button again for the fourth or fifth time, she dragged her feet out from under the covers and forced herself to stand up. She was as ragged as if she were climbing out of the depths of a hangover, something that she'd been smart enough to avoid throughout most of her life. *Man, if this is what comes after an adrenaline crash, I'm going to avoid that as much as overindulging in alcohol.* With that thought, she sent up prayers for a return to the dismally quiet existence of hiding away from society at large as well as potential assassins.

Looking over at the clock, Sol knew she'd be the last one up, despite Toddy's notoriety for being a late sleeper. She had managed to get the story written and e-mailed by 12:15 in the morning and after finishing she was too wound up to go to bed, no matter how much nagging she got from Nolan. Toddy had stayed in the den, keeping track of the news via the internet while she typed and when she'd punched the last button to send it on its merry way to Boise, he pulled her onto the couch where they just sat in silence, watching the muted images on the television until they both feel asleep. It had been a real comfort to both of them to linger in the den instead of facing the lonely specter of their separate rooms right away. They finally woke up to wander off to bed around three a.m.

Carefully dodging the mirror in her room, she decided to forego dressing for her audience, of which she hoped there wasn't one, before claiming a cup of coffee in the kitchen, which she hoped there *was* some.

Moving at a fairly slow clip, contrary to her usual level of energy, Sol rounded the corner into the kitchen only to be confronted by a very awake and convivial Toddy, a circumstance that actually didn't improve her mood.

"'Bout time, sleepyhead," he greeted her smiling. His eyes moved over her with appreciation and interest in her general dishabille, something he didn't see very often even though they'd been constant companions for over a month.

"Right," she replied unenthusiastically. "Coffee please. Is any left?" she asked afraid that the answer would be 'no.'

"I made a pot just for you. Figured you'd be up and about soon, so it's actually fresh." He wasn't lying. The coffee maker was still burping and gurgling with the dark black liquor only half-filling the carafe. Studying her tired eyes, he motioned for her to take a seat while he got her a cup and set it in front of her.

"I hope you're hungry because I have the makings ready for your breakfast. After yesterday's near fiasco, I owe you at least a hearty meal, and frankly, I think you could use the nourishment. You ate almost nothing last night." He was preparing the pan on the stove to start an omelet, feeling really guilty about, well, everything.

"Sure. I ought to eat even though hunger is pretty much the last thing on my mind."

He went to work in silence at first, but couldn't keep his mind on breakfast preparation for long so he finally spoke up.

"You know, Sol. I feel absolutely terrible about letting this get so out of hand. Yesterday and Las Vegas and this whole month of hiding out should never have happened." He turned to face her with eyes as wide with culpability as a puppy that had been swatted for teething on someone's new hat.

"Quit, already. We started this together. As to the blog, I wrote it and didn't think either. Besides, it may be a blessing in disguise." She perked up a little. "Look at the publicity we'll get for the website and the microscope it'll put Kasili and crew under."

Toddy didn't have a rejoinder to that assessment and turned around to give his attention to breakfast.

Russ strolled in while Toddy was whipping herbs into the eggs with a fork. "Glad you feel that way, because the media is on its way."

Both Toddy and Sol reacted in unison, "What?"

He looked at them slightly baffled by their expressions. "You must have expected this." He put his hands on his hips as if chastising a couple of wayward children who should have known what their actions would trigger. "They got wind of the 'events' and are sending crews from Spokane and Seattle. Even Missoula's getting in on the act and bringing in correspondents. You still have some time since most are driving down." He gave Sol a once-over and a grin. "Better freshen up, my flower," he chuckled.

Toddy checked him for ulterior interest, deciding that he was just yanking Sol's chain, but she shot Russ a deathray before taking another sip of her coffee.

"I'll freshen my cuppa joe here and go get dressed. Hold breakfast for me, will ya doll?" she bussed Toddy's cheek as she left the room, making him actually color a little and Russ cock his head in wonder.

"She's hardly awake yet," supplied Toddy as an excuse as he returned to pouring the egg mixture into the pan.

"Hm hmmm," said Russ as he abandoned Toddy to his thoughts and the omelet.

Getting dressed turned out to be more of a chore than Sol had expected. Having media arrive to interview her made her think about appearances and she was almost overwhelmed with the simple task of deciding what to wear. By the time she emerged from her room, her breakfast was cold and her stomach was unsettled, but she sat down to eat anyway and actually felt less shaky afterwards.

As she finished up, Nolan came into the kitchen to go over the situation and how best to handle it. He'd already sent Cisco to man the front door and worked with the tribal police to assign officers to contain the press who had a bad habit of ignoring ordinary rules of civil behavior, particularly if they smelled blood. And in this case, Nolan knew that they were sure someone was going to be hemorrhaging, he just hoped it wasn't his clients in the end. Already the cameras were roving as far as they could without being rebuffed by the intimidating officers cordoning off the area open to the press, panning the landscape for background shots of the majestic views of the river and the mountains. A few reporters were standing on boxes for added height and had begun beaming their spiel back to their home markets. They weren't concerned whether or not they had their facts straight, and since no one had spoken to them or handed out any kind of press information, it was all blather anyway.

Nolan sat down at the table with Sol to settle on how she should tell the story and how much she should reveal. She was on edge about the whole thing. She was a journalist, not a news story and certainly not a victim.

"Look at this mess." She was worried about the trampling of her grandparents' privacy and quiet way of life, watching the camera crews and correspondents rove around the fields, trying to stay out of each other's shots. "Lord, what a zoo. What have we done?"

"Perhaps saved your lives," said Nolan softly.

"How?" She was incredulous as she saw two cameramen arguing over who got in who's way. Under any other circumstances it could almost be considered entertaining.

"For one, now everyone knows that you're here, though they still don't really know about Toddy." He sat back and crossed his ankles in front of him under the table, ignoring the free-for-all outside. "They may even think that you're the one doing all the blogging and you may want to keep up that façade. Just because the bad guys know you have a partner, though I'm sure they think of him as an 'accomplice,' the media doesn't need that information. Staying here with the camera lens trained on you may help your cause in the long run and even keep you alive."

Sol just nodded in understanding.

He leaned forward to look her straight in the eye. "Are you ready to get this done?"

She swallowed her nervousness. She was unused to being the focus of the camera. "Yes. What do I do?"

"You are going to give the barest details of the raid. Here, I've written up some points for you to cover. You already wrote the story and it's in print by now in your home paper, which is how these guys got it in the first place. Remember, you know these rats. Your style of journalism is long dead and they are only after one thing, a sensation." He paused for a full minute. "You are the underdog here. Kasili conceded the title by going after you, an unknown Indian journalist just trying to do her job when the press has so changed that telling the facts is not only unpopular but practically forbidden. He has now become the overlord, or overseer, if you want to play the race card against him. I don't recommend that tack, yet." His eyes glinted impishly.

"We're going to push the minority button though, by having your nephew at your elbow the whole time. He has an imperious air that will only bring home the victimology."

She started to interrupt. The idea of being perceived as a victim was anathema to her, but he put up his hand to stop her.

"It's the image of the proud warrior who has fought hard but been forced from his home." He put out his hands as if asking for words to explain. "We want to use their ploys against them without actually saying anything. The fact that you were attacked *on your land, on a reservation* is monumental. What is it you have been saying about Kasili being the front for stripping the American people of what they have earned? You and Cisco are the epitome of that very argument." He stopped for her to take in his reasoning.

"Russ will also be beside you to show that this is a united effort of all Americans to stand up for what's right. He's about as mainstream looking as you can get and it brings it all into the realm of America as we are now, not a hundred and fifty years ago." He sat back again, "What do you think?"

"I think you missed your calling and should have gone into marketing," she said.

"This is good. I can do this," and she bobbed her head up and down a few times, approving of his staging. "What I hate is that we have to think like this at all."

"It's all in appearances anymore. You know that. Its exactly why you and Toddy are doing what you're doing, trying to get people to look beyond that. This may just help… I hope."

❋ ❋ ❋

Solana walked out the front door dressed in ranch chic, looking a little down home but prosperous… someone successful in her career, which she was. Cisco stayed close by as she approached the line of microphones and the reporters brandishing them from a carefully enforced distance.

The stations and newspapers represented were from a number of major sources including a few national networks. Although she was surprised to recognize the call letters in the front row, her face didn't give it away.

The correspondents started throwing questions at her as soon as she had opened the door, but as she approached the edge of the porch, Cisco held up a big hand and with a stern look, shut them up. Nolan, who was watching from the shadows of the broken down front door, cocked an eyebrow in fascination.

Sol made a relatively brief statement regarding the incident of the day before and sticking solidly to the facts.

Then the questions started coming, tumbling one over the other. She listened carefully and chose a few to answer, including one inquiring why she thought the attack occurred.

Her answer was to the point that she had posted a critical article on the internet and made mention of the website and the repeated attempts to shut it down. She gave facts about the website and its content, naming people who have come under its scrutiny. She then left it to the media to connect the dots, she wasn't going to make the allegations.

Sol took a couple of more questions and then thanked everyone for coming. Any further inquiries could be made to her via her position at the Boise paper. The whole of the interview took a little more than fifteen minutes. She also thanked everyone for their prompt and courteous departure from the premises, quipping that the hospitality room was closed for the day.

The reporters continued to mill around, trying to catch someone to interview, but the tribal police were mum and the horses and squirrels weren't talking. After another fifteen minutes when the crews were obviously not packing up right away, Cisco came back onto the porch, and using a portable PA system from one of the police cars, asked everyone to vacate the premises within twenty minutes, that this was private property and if they had not left by that time, they would be subject to arrest for trespassing. Then he thanked them again for attending.

After Sol came back inside, Toddy emerged from the den and gave her a huge hug. "You done good, girl. That was fantastic," he added with a big grin.

"How would you know? You were hiding out in here."

"Saw it all on TV. You three were the epitome of tall, proud Americans, protecting life and liberty." He held up his arm mimicking the Statue of Liberty. "It was great."

"Yeah? Good, because I'm exhausted again. Those folks are leeches."

"You oughtta know," he said jokingly to which, she jabbed him in the gut with her elbow.

"Ow!"

"You deserved that."

"Probably. Anyway, Kasili is going to have real trouble climbing out of this hole. Even if he isn't behind it directly, someone in his camp is. It's too obvious for even the press to ignore, which, believe me, they will try," said Toddy.

"Oh, you think so, do you? Since when did you become such an expert on the media?"

"Since I started rooming with a member of the club."

She just rolled her eyes at him. "Well, maybe we'll have the chance to get off this mountain for a respite," she spoke hopefully.

"Not yet," Nolan butted in. "Unless you want to be mobbed. You two can't be seen together for awhile either, or they may start conjecturing as to he is," and he gave Toddy a meaningful look.

"All right, all right. We'll keep playing along. For now," she said, giving Nolan a mischievous look.

Gold Baron

Chapter 47

Things were heating up in the presidential polls but no one was making any gains and it was continuing as a dead heat. Knowing that the incident on the mountain could be of some benefit to keep the pressure on Kasili, Sol conferred with Anthea about what could be done to keep the event in the news. Anthea suggested trying to schedule an interview with a national television news magazine and when Sol agreed, despite the fact that she was uncomfortable with the TV gig, Anthea started contacting the networks.

To no one's surprise, the only national outlet willing to talk to Sol was Fox. None of the other networks would touch her because of the possibility of tainting the 'chosen one,' Kasili, with what they were calling smears and unsubstantiated allegations.

"Like I gave those guys riot gear and sent them up in a helicopter to shoot up my family's home just to get a little attention," she sneered. "I am so disgusted with people who even attempt to call themselves journalists anymore, I'm apt to be sick." The only person in the room was Toddy who was helping her gather her things to go meet the one anchor of a news opinion show who had the chutzpah to interview her. At this point, she wasn't even sure that she trusted this pundit not to try to blame her for being attacked in her home. However, she, Anthea and Toddy had decided that she needed to make an effort even if they skinned her alive on national television.

"You have the poise and bearing of a princess," said Toddy before she got in the rig to head to the Spokane studios where the anchor was flying in to shoot the meeting. "This man will treat you with the respect you deserve, or you can bet I'll flay him." He hugged her tightly before allowing her to climb in the back seat and buckle up.

Russ Tarlington was behind the wheel and Cisco rode shotgun as they took off for town and, what they hoped would be, solid and fair news coverage. Cisco was recruited for added protection and to help keep the focus on the minority issue. Toddy and Nolan were relegated to sit it out on the hill and watch the interview as it was broadcast. Nolan still thought it a good idea to keep Toddy under wraps supposing that Sol was safe enough with all the national attention she had received over the last couple of days.

When Fox touted the upcoming interview for the two days previous to the event, the Kasili machine at first thought to ignore it, but after pressure from other media corners, they issued a statement. It wasn't much of one, but then, in Sol's view he never said much of anything that could ever be pinned down. The official statement consisted of a couple of lines about how unfortunate the incident was, but that it could have nothing to do with the Kasili campaign in that he had always supported the rights of Native Americans and all minorities.

"Uh huh," said Sol as they heard the quote over the radio news once they reached town. "The right to do what? Be part of his silent partnership? Because that's all anyone is once they climb on his bandwagon. Put up and shut up."

Cisco just grinned out the windshield as he listened to his auntie grump in the backseat.

Before driving up the grade they stopped for gas. Sol and Cisco got out briefly and were waylaid by distant family and ended up talking a little longer than expected. She was the celebrity du jour and as soon as a cousin saw her they wanted to catch up on the latest news.

Russ filled the tank and was trying to keep an eye on the other two while he was at it, but the station was a very busy one and it was difficult to notice everything around them.

It ended up taking more than ten minutes to get gas and talk to family before they could get back on the road, but it wasn't enough of a delay to make them late for their appointment in Spokane. Finally they loaded up again, Sol having purchased espresso for everyone.

✳✳✳

The drive was uneventful until they stopped at the one rest area on the way to the city.

Parking the Excursion in front of the one building, Sol went inside to wash up. The coffee had been a fine idea until she spilled some on her pants. She'd brought extra clothes for the television appearance, but she didn't want to arrive looking sloppy either. As she exited the rig, another car drove in and parked facing the other direction rather than pulling in next to the facility.

Russ was standing outside the car with his arm on the open door when he saw that the other driver wasn't getting out of his vehicle. No big deal. He just assumed that the guy had pulled in on the other side of the lot to take a nap without being disturbed by all the activity at the building.

When Sol pushed open the door of the rest room and started toward their truck, the driver's side door of the parked car flew open and a man dropped to his knee and started shooting in her direction. If the last few weeks had implanted anything on Sol's subconscious, it was the innate need to be wary and above all, quick to respond.

Upon hearing the first shot, she jumped back and caught the bathroom door before it closed, practically falling over herself to get back inside. The building was constructed of cinder blocks, which offered fairly good protection from ordinary bullets, so she assumed that she might be safe. Her worry was that Cisco and Russ were out in the open and she hadn't even had time to notice whether or not there were any other cars, which would mean bystanders could be caught in the line of fire.

She cursed herself for having left her purse in the car and her gun inside it. All she could do was sit down with her back against the wall, calmly breathe and pray that the boys would be safe.

She heard only a few more shots before everything seemed to fall unnaturally silent. She found herself holding her breath until she heard the door being carefully opened a little at a time and then hearing Cisco call in a low voice, "Auntie? Are you okay?"

She let the air out of her lungs all at once and practically hiccupped when trying to catch a new one.

"Yes," she gasped. "I'm fine. What about you? Russ?"

"We're just dandy, but the perp... hmmm he doesn't look so good," she could hear the amusement in his voice.

"Oh hell," she said exasperated as she hauled herself off the grungy floor and out of the building to take in the result of her bodyguards' handiwork.

When she came back out to the Excursion, she saw Russ on the phone talking to the police, she assumed. The man who had shot at her was sitting against a post, his good arm handcuffed in a most uncomfortable position to a length of chain that dangled from an eye that was welded to the top of the post.

She looked at Cisco who had moved back to check on the shooter, whose other arm had taken a bullet and was lying uselessly next to his side. He was barely awake as Cisco bent down to tie a strip of some fabric he had grabbed from the back of the truck, around the guy's wound.

When he came back, Sol simply said, "Handcuffs?"

He grinned and replied, "Don't leave home without 'em."

It wasn't long before the area patrol officer with the Washington State Police arrived to apprehend the shooter, call an ambulance and take a report.

"Here," said Tarlington, handing Sol the cell phone. "You'd better call the studio because we won't be leaving here for a couple of hours." Ticked off at yet another attempt on her life and a delay in getting on with it, she plucked the phone unceremoniously out of Russ' hands and went to her purse to dig out the number and make the call.

While she was on the phone, another unit drove up and cordoned off the rest area.

"This is just grand," she muttered, not intending for anyone to hear, however, the producer on the other end caught it and asked what she meant.

"Well, as I just told your operator, we are stuck at the rest area north of Colfax. It's cordoned off because some idiot just tried to shoot me, again."

"You're kidding!" he practically yelled with glee.

"Unfortunately, no, I'm not kidding. In any case, we are going nowhere fast. The police are here and since the shooter was himself shot, we will be here for hours yet to go through the whole rigmarole." She sighed in frustration.

"But, that's great!" she heard the producer exclaim.

"What? No it's not *great*. We were assaulted again and I can't make the interview. You'll have to give the host my apologies."

"No way. I'm calling in a helicopter right now and he will be down there in a half hour to interview you at the site." She could hear him put his hand over the phone and call out to someone about getting the 'Mister' on the chopper ASAP.

"You're a journalist. This will be great TV!"

She was in shock as he finished. "Look, I know you've just been through a hair-raising experience..."

"That's an understatement."

"... But you wanted coverage, right? This will be picked up nationwide. No one's going to turn down stuff like this. We'll be there before you can get your lipstick on." And he hung up.

The producer was right. She hadn't even reapplied her lipstick before the Fox News chopper hove into sight. The WSP officers looked up with disdain as it came to a landing outside of the roped off rest area.

The lieutenant in charge pointed his thumb over his shoulder at the group disgorging from the fuselage, the national news personality and the camera crew who came up to the yellow police tape and stopped to set up the equipment for an on the spot interview.

The pundit was trying to look grave as he approached the tape, an officer walking over to talk to him, but his eyes gave away his elation at the thought that he had just stumbled into one of the best stories of the campaign. If he weren't already a respected television host, this would have put him over the top.

The onsite interview was relatively brief, ten minutes was all that Sol was able to do before Cisco stepped in, seeing how his aunt was visibly upset even though she seemed to be holding her own.

The anchor knew that showing a side of compassion would get him more than if he were a hard-nosed reporter, wound down the interview with some words about the police being on the spot and doing an excellent job, yada, yada, yada, before signing off and promising more follow-up as soon as possible.

Closing the live broadcast, he posited a suggestion that instead of her coming into the studio to finish the interview, if it would be possible to do the rest at her house, the site of the first assault.

Partially numbed by the events of the last few days, she looked to Cisco and Russ for support. Both were no longer engaged with the cops as they had finished their report and checking with one another for answers, they nodded that it seemed a good idea.

Russ stepped forward as the senior member of the security detail and instructed the news crew with directions, giving them sanction to arrive tomorrow morning at eleven a.m.

Thanking Sol, Cisco and Russ for their time, the TV man tried to get a few words from the lead officer on the spot before packing up and heading back to the studio.

The next morning, the tribal police set-up a road block at the bottom of the hill allowing only local traffic and authorized vehicles through. Because of the shooting incident at the rest area, reporters from all over had descended on the valley and were trying to gain access to the Greyfisher farm. The police were adamant in following their instructions and only the Fox crew was ushered through the line. They showed up at ten a.m. to set-up for the shoot and Cisco, who had gone home for the night after they brought Sol back early, drove back up the hill with Gary Mathers, his neighbor, at about the same time.

Wanting to give Sol as much opportunity as he could to prepare for yet another television invasion, Nolan volunteered Cisco to walk the TV man around the grounds and explain what had occurred during the shootout almost a week prior. Always reticent to give too much information, Cisco was succinct in his answers to the newsman's questions and didn't elaborate. The pundit tried to pry more information out of him about the shooting the day before as well, particularly since the assailant was being held under maximum security and was apparently not talking to anyone. In fact, rumor was that the guy hadn't opened his mouth once and there was all kinds of speculation as to who he was and who had sent him or if he was operating as a lone gunman.

Early in the morning, Toddy had been spirited out the door and up and over the mountain instead of down and into town, before Sol had even gotten out of bed. He felt all kinds of guilty at not being allowed to stay and offer support, but Nolan, and then Zeke who called to give his opinion, were inflexible about keeping his identity a closely held secret.

"This is no game," Zeke had told him resolutely. "You can't be seen at this point because they are not giving up easily. So, get your ass off that mountain and let Sol do her thing. She can handle it."

"That doesn't make running away right," answered Toddy unhappy to follow directions.

"No, but do it anyway."

Finally at eleven o'clock Sol exited the house and sat down in one of the two chairs that had been prepared for the interview. She was jumpy but tried to keep her uneasiness under control, knowing that what she said was going to find it's way hacked into unflattering soundbites on all the major stations. At this point she had to trust the man sitting before her to give her a fair shake and, so far, from what she'd seen on his network, he'd done so.

When the TV man asked her what she thought of Kasili's response to the incident at her home a week ago, she blew it off as being unworthy of comment. Instead she countered with reiterating the perspective she had delivered in the article that had been posted on the changingwind.org website that seemed to have triggered the whole string of events. "Whether or not he is personally involved in what occurred here, it doesn't change the fact that his supposed support of minority empowerment is nothing more than rhetoric crafted to sweep them behind his cause, which actually contradicts his agenda.

"Look, he's made it no secret as to where he stands on redistribution of wealth, environmental control of economic growth and expansion of government programs and entitlements. None of these things promote independent minority advancement. In fact, it promotes the exact opposite. People need to do their homework instead of being persuaded by pretty words. This country was founded on the premise of hard work to achieve goals and even though my people have suffered at the hands of that same government in the past, the opportunities today are the same for everyone *if* they'll take advantage of them. No one has to be without a voice."

The newsman didn't have a response to her words that wouldn't bury him so, he used it as a closing remark and thanked Sol for joining him after having been through such difficult circumstances over the previous week. He looked at the camera and praised the honor and courage of women such as Sol in today's tough world.

Later that evening, when Russ finally brought Toddy back up the mountain, he found Sol alone in the den, playing with her grandmother's yarn collection and petting one of the dogs who had taken to sitting at her feet. He came in and settled himself next to her, pulling her into his arms as she just collapsed under the strain of having to put on such a fearless front that she didn't at all feel.

Although she wanted to just let the tears slide down her face in abandon, she tried to keep her composure until he pulled her even closer and kissing her brow, she allowed just one to slip from her eyes and trickle off her chin. They sat there for hours, saying nothing and just holding one another, answering a deep need to console the loneliness that both had been experiencing even as they had been keeping such close company. Finally, they left the realm of friendship into something deeper.

Chapter 48

The Seattle financial leader had finally taken some time for a brief vacation, not that he really knew the meaning of the word, at his estate on St. John in the U.S. Virgin Islands. Even there, amid the tropical paradise that was mostly national park except for a few private holdings, he had been keeping abreast of the news in the mainland states. The story about the assault on the Indian journalist on a reservation, no less, had caught his attention. He had been apprised of the probable connection between the changingwind website and the Native American woman, who now had admitted to writing the article that had been posted there, before the incident had occurred.

Although he had been mulling over how best to take the sting out of the blog, this last rash of events went beyond the pale, in his opinion. He hadn't authorized anything so stupid but he had an idea who had.

Moving over to his desk in the front upstairs room that consisted of a full wall of glass that overlooked a different sea than his Puget Sound office, this one the color of rich turquoise, he pulled open a drawer and extracted a satellite phone.

Knowing that the line was well protected, he dialed the one of two numbers that were logged in the address book. He didn't care what time it was where he was calling, this was a call that couldn't be avoided.

He heard the ringing on the other end and when the other party answered, he asked him what he thought he was doing.

The man in the hotel suite on the campaign trail in Cincinnati, sounded abashed at the insinuation. His deep resonant voice was awash with denial of having anything to do with the Northwest incident on the reservation.

The man in St John maintained his silence. He hadn't even mentioned why he was calling. The other man had jumped to a conclusion that only solidified his suspicions. How could he have trusted a man who could be so foolish?

Finally he spoke, telling the man in Ohio to keep his nose clean, continue to deny everything and that it could have been any radical group reacting to the incendiary blog.

He didn't give the other man a chance to respond before hanging up.

Still gazing out at the rippling waters of the Caribbean, he made one more call.

When the phone was answered he gave the listener directions to set-up a scapegoat organization, one that was not associated with the Kasili campaign but had perhaps supplied verbal support. Maybe a terrorist cell that hadn't approved of what was being said on the website about Arab states being blamed as accomplices in the growing economic woes of the United States, that they were deeply involved in hedge funds that were devaluing the dollar. Something along the lines that they took such strong offense that they had bankrolled the assault. Then, he told his connection, make certain that anyone with knowledge of who masterminded the attack on the Indian is dealt with permanently.

Chapter 49

A public relations event sponsored by buildingbridges.org was pulled together using Kasili as the master of ceremonies to announce a new endowment fund for both the Northern Tier Indian College in Eastern Washington and the Diné University in New Mexico. It seemed more than obvious to Sol and Toddy that the Scirras-Kasili bond had undertaken the diversion of giving money to redirect attention away from the fiasco of the 'reservation assault,' as the incident had become known.

The television in the den was tuned into the event and Kasili sauntered up to the podium looking smug and considerate at once as he settled himself behind the microphone. Focusing on the teleprompter he adjusted the microphone.

"We need to show our support for our first Americans. Buildingbridges.org and the Free State Foundation has provided a 7.5 million dollar endowment fund for environmental studies programs at these Native American colleges. Building for the nation's future by giving back to this continent's first shepherds of our resources is a worthy goal of any institution, and ah, ah, it is our duty to support every opportunity for all Americans to reach their full potential."

"Just turn it off. I can't take any more of his self-serving platitudes," said Sol. "I mean, this is just another way of infiltrating even more institutions of higher learning with their agenda. And, forgive me, but the nerve of someone who is doing his damnedest to restrain access to resources on the reservations is going to fund programs to teach Indians how to care for the earth's gifts?" She was fuming at the television, even though it was muted. "Excuse me if I don't get how a lawyer who hasn't worked or lived in the real world thinks he has a clue about how the earth manages her resources, let alone believes that he can preach to people who have been working in harmony with her for generations." She sat down, exhausted and exasperated at some people's arrogance believing that any human could control the earth and her future in any fashion. "I just need to write," and she pulled over her laptop and started in on another scathing article.

Since the events on the mountain in North Idaho, interest in changingwind.org had exploded. Whether or not they believed that they had anything to do with it, and frankly they didn't believe it, Toddy and Sol could see that some of the information being disseminated was cutting into Kasili's poll numbers.

As a result Eddinger and Cristóbal's percentages were rising among the previously waffling fence sitters. Once Eddinger started speaking as a full-fledged capitalist, taking on the issues of shrinking government spending, promoting resource development and backing off the ultra-left environmental agenda, the two parties were exchanging leads in the polls. No one was arguing how to get there anymore. The republican ticket was talking turkey.

Chapter 50

The election was just weeks away and the numbers were reversing no matter what Kasili had tried to pull out of his bag of tricks. The allure was fading for Prince Charming and the mastermind behind bringing him up from obscurity was beginning to think that he'd created a monster, someone who was so taken with himself that he no longer took advice from his handlers or his financial backers. He'd turned off his implant weeks ago.

Back in his Seattle abode and finding that the money giveaway had garnered the ticket very little, the finance man was contemplating his options. Actually, the stunt had been seen as pandering even though the mainstream press pushed the issue as a broad gesture of compassion for the underserved Native community.

He was thinking seriously about giving Governor Castor a salutatory call. They'd had conversations before and it was evident that were anything to happen to Kasili, she'd be the heir apparent, judging by the split in primary vote numbers. If anyone could reinvigorate the democratic vote, it was probably her since her true followers hadn't been disposed to jump on the bandwagon with his candidate. He was fairly certain that he could control her. She liked money and although her eye was on the seat of power, he was pretty sure that she would look askance at an agenda as long as it complimented hers and she got what she wanted.

With the puppet trying to pull the strings, he decided to make the covert contact.

Just as he thought. The response was excellent.

Dean Castor had never been good at keeping anything under his hat.

Although people joked about the Castors not sharing the same bedroom at night, it was evident that they conferred with each other. The Dean was making allusions to his wife's becoming more active in the campaign, making more appearances in favor of the democratic ticket, that she was finally coming out of her snit and seeing the light that her party needed her in order to gain the top office.

What he wasn't saying was whether she had any real regard for Kasili personally. He still avoided the issue of whether or not Kasili had the experience to lead the country. He was working the crowd but more for his wife than for the candidate. Some people thought that was curious but wrote it off to his personality and loyalty.

That was until Kasili's plane fell out of the sky.

That wonderful Boeing 737 with the purple special 'K' painted on the tail. It turned out that one of the engines hadn't been properly maintained and, of all things, the fan came loose and simply flew on its own out of the housing, shearing through the wing, which led to the plane plummeting to the earth. Everyone aboard was lost, including Kasili's wife who had joined him on the campaign trail.

✸✸✸

The ensuing grief from the media at large was dramatic in its scope. Both campaigns were suspended as the democratic party scrambled to reposition itself in the midst of such a huge loss. The golden prophet of change was lost to the world and the bereaving press was inconsolable. No one was happy about the turn of events, even Kasili's opponents. They were beating him fair and square.

Only the Dean had trouble concealing his emotions and they weren't exactly in accord with the common thread of sorrow.

Chapter 51

Shock at the news literally knocked Solana on her butt. She fell back onto her chair from a position of half standing up as she'd been rising to fetch some papers she'd just run off the printer. Looking a little foolish with her mouth hanging partially open, Toddy swung into the room with a sandwich in one hand and the other on the doorjamb.

"I don't believe it," he said as he slipped around the open door and dropped onto the couch, the sandwich missing a bite and almost forgotten in his grip.

"What, that the hero of the left is gone? Or that it was an accident at all?" She spoke from a place of utter astonishment. That she could even think what she had just said aloud was possible, astounded her.

"Both, I guess. But think about it. If the man who was driving Kasili had had enough of this guy's shenanigans, don't you think he'd take him out?" Remembering his lunch in his hand, he decided that he was no longer hungry and laid the sandwich on the sofa table. "I'd like to invoke Bill Cosby and his bit on his dad and how he said 'I brought you into this world and I can take you out.'"

She looked at him cockeyed. "I'll be damned if you might not be right. Maybe it was no accident."

"One odd thought, and don't get angry with me for saying this because it's really insensitive… we are probably free to travel the country again."

The meaning of what he just said took a little time to saturate her mind, but when it did, her jaw practically dropped. "Oh, my Lord," she said, stunned. "You're right. If he was the one behind the tracking and all…" She couldn't finish the thought without cringing. "Do you think that his 'boss' would be interested in continuing the persecution?"

"I doubt it. The fact that the man is gone, God rest his soul, probably also puts to rest a lot of what we were writing about. The

Scirras-Kasili connection. Unless," and he got a devilish glint in his eye, "we write something about his willingness to dispose of his candidate smack in the middle of a campaign because he could no longer control him."

Sol slumped back in the chair and smacked her forehead with the palm of her hand. "I guess you don't believe in leaving well enough alone," she slid her eyes at him sideways, hoping that maybe he would do just that.

Toddy opened his palms to her as he leaned over the back of the sofa, in supplication of her understanding. "If he did take out his man, then he has to have someone waiting in the wings and we're still in danger of losing this country. Don't I have to continue the battle?"

She gave in with a sigh. "We may as well move in here permanently. Just pack off Grandma and P'lahka to some retirement resort. Oh, they'd love that," she said sarcastically.

"It won't come to that. Kasili was a fool for trying to lock down some small blog with no clout. In the end, he gave us the voice we wanted by paying attention to us. Scirras isn't so dumb."

"Go ahead. Have it your way," she gave in, defeated at his logic. "You'd do it anyway."

"Yes, I would," and he got up to give her a kiss before picking up his half-eaten sandwich and polishing it off on his way back to the kitchen.

❁ ❁ ❁

The finance guru was feeling quite satisfied about how well everything seemed to be falling into place. As much as he hadn't wanted to take any drastic measures, things were too far gone to be corrected before the election, and all his years of planning were evaporating under the ill-timed emergence of one man's ego.

He'd been left no other choice than to eliminate the threat to the overall strategy. One simply doesn't throw away decades of methodical design in favor of a single person's hubris. Particularly that of someone who had not earned the right to such overbearing pride.

Now, he could relax as the support for his replacement nominee was only a step away from being ushered in to take the helm in this time of distress. He had seen the wringing of hands of the DNC hierarchy as they met with Castor and the vice presidential candidate. He had made some well placed calls to garner support for his preference, promising the continued support of his 527's unlimited funding, something that was going to be essential at this late date.

So now, he could sit back and observe the machinations that he had put into action and deal with a few small projects that had been on the back burner for a while.

That crusty pain in the backside, changingwind.org had been urging people to sell twenty percent of their gold holdings for some time, to little point. The blogger had been pushing the issue that Scirras had been withholding gold production and manipulating the market to force the price up to outlandish levels for the past few years. All in order to get so many people so steeply invested that when he was ready to short sell the commodity, he would make a killing, they would lose most of their savings and become even more dependent on the government to bail them out of their financial crises. This very tactic of undercutting the stability of the financial system, throwing the dollar into a tailspin, would catapult the new candidate of his choice into office and the government under his thumb.

A bit simplistic in describing the scenario, even to himself, but essentially the concept worked. People were so predictable. And power was so easily to hand.

He found it ironic that it was his beloved gold that he would use to subjugate the one people who were so complacent that they had no suspicion they were on the verge of losing their precious freedom.

This evening, before heading downstairs to a pleasant dinner with his wife, who had accompanied him from the islands for a respite before flying back to their British residence, he was taking a moment to himself.

Comfortably situated in his favorite chair, he admired the magnificent solar map that had come into his hands just months before. The symbolic rings of orbit traveling around a dying sun with the rising Jupiter taking the place of honor within the changing system of power illustrated how he viewed the state of affairs he had engineered.

He contemplated how he would be able to pull the strings of a new puppet and salvage the campaign. There will be the sympathy vote, after all. He chuckled under his breath a little. *Sympathy for whom?*

Sipping at the precious liquid in his snifter and marveling at the craftsmanship of the golden threads in the panel that hinted at the gold he would use to maneuver his new candidate to the presidency, his thoughts went blank. The glass dropped to the ground and he fell back in his chair, mouth slack in death.

Perhaps it was only appropriate that he met his end through the employ of the favorite weapon of centuries of political intrigue – poison. Just as the kings of old had been, the successor was removed by his rivals. This was the manner in which power was reserved to the brokers who had hovered in the background for hundreds of years, carefully handing down rule from generation to generation.

Interlopers were not to be tolerated.

The shadows shifted as a figure emerged from concealment to silently gather up the spoils of this quiet battle. He slipped the priceless panel of golden suns and jeweled moons into a felted sleeve and disappeared into the darkness.

Chapter 52

There was just one surprise after another in this convoluted race to the White House. When everyone was so sure that Governor Castor would be the heir apparent as the democratic nominee, the tables were turned and Cameron Van Schaal, the vice presidential pick, was ushered up the steps to take the place on the ticket as the new presidential candidate.

Castor and all her following were staggered by the decision and furious at being thwarted from her birthright, again.

Her devotees were rocked at her exclusion from the selection process and utterly indignant at the outcome. The DNC had gone back and forth over the decision, knowing full well that whichever way they went, they would be dealing with toxic fallout from the Kasili accident.

The committee's greatest hurdle was the perception by Kasili supporters that Castor may have been privy to possible plans to derail the Kasili campaign by pure means or foul. Unfortunately, her reputation hadn't been completely unsullied in the past and rumors of her having even peripheral knowledge of her adversary's untimely demise were running rampant amongst both parties.

The decision to elevate the veep candidate to the prime position had been laborious but deemed necessary in the end. Unfortunately for her, Castor was bypassed for the vice presidential slot for the same reason.

As unhappy as the world at large knew that she obviously was, she had been approached by the committee and fully understood how her role in the election would have to play out. The frustration level of her lost campaign was tremendous and the Dean was furious, but the hearty suggestion to set aside her feelings and throw everything she had behind the new nominee was acknowledged and accepted. There would be no further grumblings.

With the new face leading the pack for the democratic party, the presidential race took on a whole new atmosphere. The mantra of 'change' was not replaced but was augmented with a feeling of familiarity rather than the overwhelming emotion of a messianic emblem. Van Schaal was a staid Washington plutocrat who had been groomed to this nomination in the political backrooms for years. His ties to the Wall Street power brokers and magnates who had engineered the disappearance of one of their own financial tycoons was long standing and built on a comfortable and sympathetic understanding.

Politics as usual.

Epilogue

The baby came just two weeks before election day.

With all the excitement that had led up to the event, Cisco had been glad to be able to spend the last weeks of his wife's pregnancy at home with her, preparing for the newborn's arrival.

The protection operation closed up right after Van Schaal was awarded the lead spot on the democratic ticket. The goodbyes turned out to be more difficult than anyone had anticipated since the crew had been together almost six weeks. Zeke had flown out to conclude affairs and make sure everyone was prepared to move on. Oddly enough, after spending so much time in one another's company, Nolan, Tarlington, Cisco, Seth, Mathers and Toddy and Solana had practically become family.

In folding the venture, Nolan finally made the decision to call it quits and retire, much to the relief of his family. His wife had stayed with him throughout the years of government work, but this last assignment and enforced separation for such an extended period had played a major role in his choice to leave the job. Zeke wasn't thrilled about losing his top man, but having Tarlington as his new assistant director was consolation enough. News that his first book was going to be published by Christmas was enough to settle any question Nolan had about taking the leap.

As everyone parted ways, Solana and Toddy were able to finally vacate the Greyfisher's by the end of September after Toddy had overseen all of the repairs and even mended Millie's rocking chair with a professional finesse himself. He packed up and went back south while Solana moved back into town, got back to work and waited until Lainie went into labor.

Sol was up to her ears in straightening out the workings of the tribal paper. Not that Drury had done anything wrong, he just wasn't a newsman, though being left pretty much on his own, he had come a long way in learning how to run a weekly. It actually didn't take more than a couple of weeks to reorganize a few things to get them running a little better so that Drury would be able to undertake everything without problem should anything ever arise again.

Toddy kept the blog going as the campaign weeks dwindled and the race heated up. He was blasting the leftist policies Van Schaal was promoting and pushed hard at Eddinger to keep up the capitalist cause. Due to all the exposure the website had received the previous month, there was a steady stream of visitors and he was even quoted fairly often by talk radio and columnists, though still nobody had any idea who he was.

He followed the gold situation, which leveled out after a while. Apparently, production in many of the previously closed mines had resumed and there was more product available, keeping the market from skyrocketing at the speed it had been predicted earlier in the summer.

Toddy still advocated that gold buyers keep themselves from becoming too heavily vested in the market as international traders holding major quantities could divest themselves at any time, under-cutting the gains of people who bought in late. The result was a drop in gold value but the extreme dive never materialized, allowing average gold owners to show a healthy overall gain as it didn't fall below the doubled value of where the commodity had been three years prior.

Cisco ran to the back door of the big house to inform Anthea that he was taking Lainie to the hospital as his wife was climbing, awkwardly and with just a little difficulty, into his father's pick-up.

Anthea immediately called Toddy to tell him the good news while Lainie was on the phone with Sol, urging her to meet them at admitting. Sol then called her sister, Neta, and mother while hopping in her new car to meet them at the hospital. By the time she called Toddy, she only reached his answering machine.

Sol tried calling Toddy again and again to no avail, the machine kept picking up with the mechanical voice telling her to leave a message. She was really disappointed that he was nowhere to be found. Even on his cell phone she kept getting his voicemail.

The wait had become interminable. The beleaguered Lainie was in labor for twenty-one hours with the doctor starting to pester her to let him go in for a Caesarian halfway through the vigil. She was adamant that her daughter, for she was sure that it was a girl, would make her entrance in her own time and unless there was a true health emergency, she would have none of the knife.

Lainie got her way, and the little girl poked her head out a full day after her mother had been admitted to the natal ward. The family was there by then, Neta and Mama Ciel had driven over from Montana, Cisco's parents and Lester and Millie Greyfisher had also arrived.

Solana was feeling a little let down because she still hadn't been able to get a hold of Toddy. After leaving the rest of the family to take over in the room to coo and fuss over the newborn, she went to sit down in the waiting room. Exhausted from staying the night to soothe the frazzled nerves of the father-to-be, who was busy pacing and worrying through the wee hours when Lainie had kicked him out of the room, Sol put her feet up on the coffee table and sank into the lumpy couch. She had just closed her eyes when she felt warm fingers trace down the side of her neck and start massaging the corded muscles. Assuming it was her sister, she just let out an audible sigh.

"Now that's what I'd call a welcome greeting," a far deeper voice than that belonging to any female relative whispered next to her ear. Sol's eyes popped open and she turned to be caught with a kiss from the bewhiskered face of Toddy.

"You're here," she said huskily. "I couldn't reach you and thought you'd forgotten about us."

He came around to sit next to her on the couch and encircle her with his arms. "Hardly. Anthea called as soon as she heard the baby was on the way and I drove to catch the next flight out of Las Cruces. It took forever to get here. There is, evidently, no such thing as a non-stop or even a five-stop flight from anywhere in New Mexico to this podunk town."

"I'm just glad you made it. Lainie will be pleased that you're here and, frankly, I think that Cisco would come kick your ass if you hadn't shown up. I believe they're going to ask us to be the baby's godparents."

"Really?" The smile of pure pleasure widened to include every feature of his face with a light she hadn't expected.

Well, no. Maybe she had.

-30-

ABOUT THE AUTHOR

Former newspaper publisher and editor, A. Dru Kristenev has more than three decades of experience in periodicals. Kristenev grew up in the publishing industry working every angle of a paper, from ad sales and production to writing and overseeing editorial content. The author carries a Bachelor of Arts degree, a Master of Science and a California Community Colleges Lifetime Teaching Credential and taught at the foremost colleges and universities in the Inland Northwest.

Since 2010, Kristenev has been on the road as an independent Christian missionary, crossing the United States more than ten times. She has also been a columnist for CanadaFreePress.com since 2014.

THE BARON SERIES

Four books in the series of stand-alone novels based on current, factual occurrences, the relationship of characters leads from one story to the next, weaving an ongoing tale of journalists running across criminally tainted philanthropy and politics. Caught by their own curiosity to uncover the truth, they are pulled deeper and deeper into the investigations, unexpectedly putting their lives at risk…

Land Barons- the first book in the Baron Series of romantic suspense novels that rely on solid research of environmentalist influence on American lifestyles, touching on the long reach of government regulation and media/corporate power. Anthea Keller is seeking a peaceful place to ply her trade as a PR agent. Instead, she finds herself in the center of a land scam, drawn in by Gary Mathers, an ex-cop who just can't reconcile the deadly misfortunes of local property owners forced to sell off assets. And who is waiting in the wings to snap up the firesale deals?

Gold Baron- the second work in the series. Fact meets fiction in the election process of the 2008 presidential campaign season, drawing on the reality driving the candidacies - who's influencing who and to what end with global markets and politics as the backdrop. Solana Greyfisher returns home to Idaho only to be snagged by a fascinating story that leads her to Toddy Littman, researcher extraordinaire. Together they dig through the morass of campaign funding paper trails only to attract the murderous ire of power brokers working the system to their own benefit.

Energy Barons - the third novel, whirls around political manipulation of the environmental movement causing economic upheaval in the West and endangering lives of the innocent. Ambitious Allie Maitland is caught by surprise while investigating what appears to be anything but an accident at the new power plant. Sawyer Aleman, former marine, wheedles his way into the FBI inquiry, under Allie's skin and into the role of guardian. Before they know it, the story rolls from Wyoming to Alaska and everyone involved is walking a perilous tightrope of greed, murder and mayhem.

BLOOD BARONS - the fourth novel in the Baron Series brings the tale full circle.

NYC: a metropolis of 8 million people; 500 disappear each year. Of those, three dead end case files lie open on Special Agent Roy Esteban's desk. Who are they? Why doesn't anyone know they're gone and why does no one care?

Lack of leads and an ASAC that wants the cases closed drives the FBI agent to take on an unorthodox partner in Researcher Debra Chorister. Together they track an unwholesome alliance between corporate science and government healthcare. And those three lone individuals? They're not the only ones who can't be found.

UNKNOWN PREDATOR

Hands tied by regulations, what does a rancher do to forestall the concocted destruction of a traditional way of life by officials cowering behind an "unknown predator?" Not what you'd think.

When neighboring landowners take action, dropping them into the middle of a legal quagmire, individuals obsessed with their own righteous cause threaten the ranchers' livelihood... and their lives.

A. Dru Kristenev
ChangingWind Ministries
changingwind@earthlink.net

Scripture Led Politics:
Mutual Exclusivity Be Damned

Wonder how Scripture relates to the political atmosphere in which we live?

Numerous legislative, judicial and regulatory decrees have altered life in America to a degree that our parents' generation would find it unrecognizable. To what end? Who benefits from the draconian coding that now cages the free thinker, particularly the faithful?

As government draws each new line in the sand, Author A. Dru Kristenev has taken a scriptural view of the cascading legal enactments, noting how they are fundamentally changing the American Dream. These commentaries open a deep discussion of how believers must tap their intellect and view the shifting political landscape in the historical light of the Bible, contemplating its significant lessons and their application.

···········

Read all of A.Dru Kristenev's books available on Amazon.com...

THE BARON SERIES Political Suspense novels:

Land Barons

Gold Baron

Energy Barons

BLOOD BARONS

UNKNOWN PREDATOR

Non-fiction Books:

Scripture Led Politics: Mutual Exclusivity Be Damned

Pay Attention!! ...your life, family and nation depend on it

www.ingramcontent.com/pod-product-compliance
Lightning Source LLC
Chambersburg PA
CBHW071246250626
47163CB00002B/343